Late for
the Wedding

By the same author

Dangerous
Deception
Desire
Mischief
Mistress
Mystique
Ravished
Reckless
Rendezvous
Scandal
Seduction
Surrender
Affair
With This Ring
I Thee Wed
Wicked Widow
Slightly Shady
Don't Look Back

Late for the Wedding

AMANDA QUICK

ROBERT HALE · LONDON

First published in Great Britain 2003

ISBN 0 7090 7468 9

Robert Hale Limited
Clerkenwell House
Clerkenwell Green
London EC1R 0HT

2 4 6 8 10 9 7 5 3 1

Typeset in 10/13 New Century Schoolbook by
Derek Doyle & Associates, in Liverpool.
Printed in Great Britain by
St Edmundsbury Press, Bury St Edmunds, Suffolk.
Bound by Woolnough Bookbinding Limited.

For Frank,
with all my love

Acknowledgments

It is the small details that add atmosphere and immediacy to a story, just as they do in real life. For the important bits involving a diadem, a certain lamp, and a Cleopatra wig, I am indebted to Donald Bailey, formerly of the Department of Greek and Roman Antiquities, British Museum. I also wish to thank him for his patient instructions in the art of making a proper gin and tonic. Any errors in either the text or the G&T are strictly my own.

Late for the Wedding

One

The first indication he got that his carefully laid plans for the night were doomed came when he opened his bedchamber door and found Cleopatra standing in the hallway.

'Bloody hell,' he said very softly. 'I was expecting Minerva.'

His long-anticipated vision of a night of passion spent in a comfortable bed with his lover and occasional business partner, Lavinia Lake, faded into a hazy mist.

His past had come back to haunt him at a most inconvenient moment.

'Hello, Tobias.' The woman in the hall lowered the green and gilt mask attached to the little gold post in her hand. The cobra diadem that graced her long, elaborately braided black wig gleamed in the light of a nearby wall sconce. Wry amusement lit her dark eyes. 'It has been a long time, has it not? May I come in?'

It had, in fact, been three years since he had last seen Aspasia Gray, but she had changed very little. She was still a stunningly beautiful woman with a classical profile that was well-suited to her guise as the queen of Egypt. He knew that her real hair was a deep, rich brown. Her tall, elegantly proportioned figure was displayed to advantage in a pale green gown trimmed with gold embroidery.

The last thing he wanted to do tonight was renew old acquaintances, Tobias March thought. But the sight of Aspasia Gray had definitely shattered the mood. Memories from that very dark time three years ago crashed over him with the force of storm-driven waves.

He collected his wits with an effort and quickly surveyed the darkened hallway behind Aspasia. There was no sign of Lavinia.

Maybe, if he acted swiftly, he would be able to rid himself of his unwelcome visitor before his evening was entirely ruined.

'I suppose you'd better come in.' Reluctantly, he stepped back.

'You have not changed, sir,' she murmured. 'Still as gracious as ever, I see.'

She entered the firelit room with a soft rustle of silken skirts and a whisper of exotic perfume. He closed the door and turned to face her.

He had not noticed any Cleopatras at the costume ball earlier in the evening, but that was not surprising. Beaumont Castle was a huge, sprawling monstrosity of a house, and tonight it was crammed with people. He had been interested in only one particular guest.

The invitation to the house party had come through the auspices of Lord Vale. Tobias's first, automatic inclination had been to decline the offer. He had little interest in such affairs. House parties, in particular, struck him as tedious at best, albeit his experience of them was limited.

But then Vale had reminded him of the one singular attraction of a properly organized country-house party.

Yes, there are the lengthy, boring breakfasts and the frivolous conversations and the silly games, but bear in mind this vastly important, highly relevant point: you and Mrs Lake will each be provided with a private bedchamber. Furthermore, no one will pay the least attention to which of those bedchambers you decide to occupy at night. Indeed, the true objective of a well-planned house party is to provide ample opportunities of that sort.

The reminder of the true nature of a large house party had struck Tobias with the force of a lightning bolt. When Vale, who had no intention of attending the Beaumont affair, graciously offered the use of one of his private carriages for the journey, Tobias had felt himself inspired.

He had been surprised, not to say greatly relieved, when Lavinia agreed to the plan with very little fuss. He suspected that her enthusiasm was generated in large part because she viewed the house party as an excellent opportunity to fish for new business. But he refused to allow that fact to depress his spirits. For the first time in their acquaintance, they would enjoy the luxury of being able to spend the better portion of not one but two entire nights in the cozy warmth and privacy of a real bed.

The prospect had been dazzling. For once there would be no need to sneak about in remote sections of the park or make do with the desk in Lavinia's little study. For three glorious days he would not be obliged to rely on the benevolent graces of Lavinia's housekeeper, who could sometimes be persuaded to take herself off to shop for currants when he came to call.

He certainly savored the all-too-brief encounters alone with Lavinia in town, but those occasions – stimulating though they were – tended to be rushed and occasionally nerve-racking. The weather had a nasty habit of delivering rain on afternoons when he chose the park for a tryst, and one never knew when Lavinia's niece, Emeline, might select an inopportune moment to return home.

There was also the unpredictable nature of the business in which he and Lavinia were engaged. When one offered one's services to persons who wished to commission private inquiries and investigations, one never knew when a client might knock on the door.

He looked at Aspasia. 'What the devil are you doing here? I thought you were in Paris.'

'I am well aware that you have a tendency to be blunt to the point of rudeness on occasion, Tobias. But surely I deserve a warmer welcome from you. It is not as though I am only a casual acquaintance, after all.'

She was right, he thought. The two of them were forever linked by the events of the past and by a dead man named Zachary Elland.

'My apologies,' he said quietly, 'but the truth is, you have caught me very much by surprise. I did not see you this afternoon when the other guests descended on the castle, nor did I notice you at the costume ball tonight.'

'I arrived quite late, after the evening festivities had commenced. I saw you at the ball, but you were preoccupied with your little redheaded friend.' Aspasia stripped off her gloves with languid grace and held her hands out to the fire. 'Who on earth is she, Tobias? I would not have said that she was your type.'

'Her name is Mrs Lake.' He did not bother to conceal the edge to his words.

'Ah, I see.' She looked down into the flames. 'You are lovers.' It was a statement, not a question.

'We are also business partners,' he said evenly. 'On occasion.'

Aspasia glanced at him, fine brows lifted in a faintly quizzical expression. 'I do not understand. Do you refer to some financial dealings in which the two of you are engaged?'

'In a manner of speaking. Mrs Lake and I both make our livings in the same fashion. She takes commissions for private inquiries, just as I do. We investigate certain cases together.'

She smiled fleetingly. 'I suppose the private-inquiry business is a step up from being a spy, but surely it is not nearly as respectable as your previous career as a man of business.'

'I find it suits my temperament.'

'I will not ask how your *partner* made her living before she went into this odd profession.'

Enough was enough, he thought. There were limits to one's obligations to old acquaintances. 'Aspasia, tell me why you are here. I have plans for the remainder of the night.'

'Plans that no doubt include Mrs Lake.' Aspasia sounded genuinely apologetic. 'I truly am sorry, Tobias. Please believe me when I tell you that I would not have come to your bedchamber at this hour had it not been extremely urgent.'

'Can this matter wait until morning?'

'I'm afraid not.' She turned away from the fire and walked slowly toward him.

Aspasia was a woman of the world. He knew that she was well-schooled in the fine social art of concealing her private sentiments and feelings. But now he glimpsed a disturbing shift in the shadows beneath her cool veneer. He had seen that same emotion often enough in others to recognize it instantly. Aspasia Gray was afraid.

'What is wrong?' he asked, somewhat more gently this time.

She sighed. 'I did not come here to spend a few days rusticating in the country. As of last night, I had no intention whatsoever of accepting the invitation to Beaumont's house party. Indeed, I sent my regrets some weeks ago. But things changed. I am here now because I followed you, sir.'

He glanced at his pocket watch lying on the dressing table and saw that it was nearly one o'clock in the morning. The house had settled down for the night. In a few minutes Lavinia would knock on his door. He very much wanted to get rid of Aspasia before that happened.

'Why the devil did you chase all this way after me?' he asked. 'It's a six-hour drive from Town.'

'I had no choice. This morning I went straight to your address in Slate Street but you had already departed. Your man informed me that you had left for Beaumont Castle and would be gone for several days. Fortunately, I remembered that the invitation mentioned the costume ball. I managed to find this wig and a mask at the last minute.'

'You received an invitation to this affair?' he asked, curiosity stirring.

'Yes, of course.' Aspasia brushed that aside. 'Lady Beaumont sends invitations to everyone in Society. She delights in entertaining. It has been her passion for years, and Lord Beaumont is only too happy to indulge her.'

Everyone in Society certainly did not include Lavinia or himself, he reflected. They managed to hang around on the fringes of the polite world thanks to connections with some wealthy, powerful former clients such as Vale and Mrs Dove, but that association did not automatically qualify them to be placed on any hostess's regular guest list.

Aspasia's pedigree, on the other hand, was impeccable. She was the last of her line, and she controlled a substantial inheritance that she had received from her father. At seventeen she had been briefly married to a man some forty years her senior. His death six months after the nuptials had left her with an additional income. Tobias calculated that she was now twenty-eight. The combination of beauty, breeding, and money made her an extremely attractive addition to any guest list. It was not at all surprising that she had received an invitation to Beaumont Castle.

'I'm surprised the housekeeper was able to find a bedchamber for you on such short notice,' he said. 'I thought the castle was filled to the rafters.'

'It is quite crowded. But when I arrived and made it plain that there had been "a mistake with the invitations," the butler and housekeeper consulted together. They managed to find a very pleasant room for me just down the hall. I suspect that they arranged to move someone of lesser consequence to a less desirable location.'

'Tell me what this is about, Aspasia.'

She began to pace back and forth in front of the hearth. 'I'm not sure where to start. I returned from Paris last month and took a house in Town. Naturally I had intended to call upon you in due course after I was settled.'

He watched her face very closely and decided that he did not entirely believe that last statement. He was quite certain that, if she'd had a choice in the matter, she would have been content to avoid him indefinitely. He understood. She would always associate him with the tragic events of three years past.

'What changed your mind?' he asked.

Her expression did not alter, but her elegant bare shoulders stiffened with tension. It would, he reflected, take a great deal to rattle Aspasia's nerves.

'Something happened this morning,' she said, gazing into the fire. 'Something quite unsettling. I could not think of anything else to do but to consult with you immediately, Tobias.'

'I suggest you come straight to the point,' he said.

'Very well, but I fear you will not credit what I have to say if I do not show you what was left on my front step early this morning.'

She opened a tiny, beaded reticule and removed a small object wrapped in a linen handkerchief. She offered it to him on the palm of her hand.

He plucked the small parcel from her fingers and carried it across the room to examine it in the light of the candle. There he untied the handkerchief and let the cloth fall away.

He looked at the ring that had been revealed and felt the hair lift on the back of his neck.

'Hell's teeth,' he whispered.

Aspasia said nothing. She folded her arms beneath her breasts and waited, eyes shadowed.

He studied the ring more closely. The band was set with black stones. The darkly glittering gems framed a small gold coffin. He used the tip of one finger to raise the lid.

A tiny, exquisitely detailed white skull grinned up at him from inside the miniature sarcophagus.

He angled the ring to read the Latin inscription on the inside of the lid, translating the ancient warning silently to himself. *Death comes.*

He met Aspasia's eyes. 'It is an old memento-mori ring.'

'Yes.' She hugged herself more tightly.

'You said it was left on your doorstep?'

'My housekeeper found it. The ring was inside a small box covered in black velvet.'

'Was there a note? A message of some kind?'

'No. Just that damned ring.' She shuddered, no longer bothering to conceal her disquiet. 'You see now why I went to such lengths to find you tonight?'

'It is impossible,' he said flatly. 'Zachary Elland is dead, Aspasia. We both saw the body.'

She closed her eyes briefly in pain and then looked at him very steadily. 'You do not need to remind me.'

The old guilt slammed through him. 'Of course not. My apologies.'

'Afterward,' she said slowly, 'you told me you'd heard rumors of another man who once made a profession of murder, just as Zachary had done, a killer who used the same ghastly signature.'

'Calm yourself, Aspasia.'

'I recall you told me that he was never caught and that there was never any proof of murder in the first place because the deaths always appeared accidental or natural.'

'Aspasia—'

'Maybe he's still out there, Tobias. Maybe—'

'Listen closely,' he said in a tone that finally succeeded in silencing her. 'The original Memento-Mori Man, if he ever actually existed, would be quite elderly by now. Dead, most likely. Those rumors dated from decades back. Crackenburne and some of his companions heard them years ago when they themselves were young men.'

'Yes, I know.'

'They eventually concluded that the tale of a professional killer for hire was never anything other than just that, a grisly legend. It was fed by rumors among servants who gossiped in the taverns and told tall tales to their friends. Zachary no doubt took pleasure in invoking the old stories because it suited his sense of melodrama. You know how he thrived on excitement.'

'Yes, of course.' The room was warm, but she rubbed her arms as though she felt a chill. 'He craved thrills and drama the way some are addicted to opium.' She hesitated. 'He no doubt enjoyed re-creating the legend of the Memento-Mori Man. Now it would appear that someone else has the same taste for melodrama.'

'Perhaps.'

'Tobias, I do not mind telling you that I am quite frightened.'

'Obviously someone else knows about Zachary Elland and his connection to you.' He contemplated the miniature skull in the gold coffin. 'Are you sure there was no note?'

'I am positive.' She stared bleakly at the ring. 'He left that death's-head on my step to terrify me.'

'Why would he do that?'

'*I do not know.*' A visible shiver went through her. 'I've been thinking about that question all day. Indeed, I've thought of little else.' She paused. 'What if . . . what if whoever left that ring blames me for Zachary's death and seeks some sort of crazed revenge?'

'Zachary took his own life when he realized that I was about to have him brought up on charges of murder. You had nothing to do with his death.'

'Maybe whoever left that ring doesn't know that.'

'Indeed.' But that conclusion did not feel right, he thought. He raised the little skull to the light again. The death's-head stared back at him with its empty eye sockets, taunting him with its macabre grin. 'We must also consider the possibility that this was intended as an announcement of some sort.'

'What do you mean?'

He weighed the ring in the palm of his hand. 'You are one of the very small number of people who would comprehend the significance of this ring, because you are one of the few who knew that Zachary Elland styled himself the Memento-Mori Man and used such rings as his signature. I wonder if this is some new villain's way of telling us that he plans to take up Zachary's professional mantle.'

'You mean there might be another murderer out there who seeks to emulate the Memento-Mori Man? What a terrible thought.' She paused. 'But if that were true, it would have been far more logical for him to leave his calling card with you, not me. You were the one who hunted Zachary down.'

'For all I know there will be a ring waiting for me when I return to Town,' he said quietly. 'I set off very early this morning. Perhaps he delivered this ring to you first, and by the time he got to my house I was gone.'

She swung around and took a step toward him, anxiety clear in her eyes. 'Tobias, whoever left that ring has something dreadful in mind. If you are right and this is a calling card, we are dealing with a new Memento-Mori Man. You must find him before someone is murdered.'

Two

Lavinia heard a door open as she reached the bottom of the shadowed staircase. Midway along the stone corridor, a wedge of candlelight appeared. A gentleman moved stealthily out of the bedchamber and started toward her.

Yet more traffic. This was not the first time she had been obliged to pop into a closet or hurry around a corner in the past few minutes. The passageways of Beaumont Castle were as busy as a London street tonight. All the comings and goings between bedchambers would have been amusing if not for the fact that she herself was attempting to make her way to a clandestine rendezvous.

It was her own fault, she reminded herself. Tobias had suggested that he visit her in her bedchamber after the house quieted down for the night. It would have been an excellent plan, if she had been allowed to remain in the spacious, comfortable room that she had been given when she and Tobias arrived this afternoon. But earlier this evening, for reasons that remained quite unclear, she had been moved to a very small bedchamber.

She had taken one look at the cot in her new room and realized that it would be extremely uncomfortable for two people, especially when one of them was a man endowed with very fine shoulders. She had informed Tobias that she would come to his room instead, never imagining for a moment that the task would be so difficult to carry out without drawing attention to herself.

She was well aware that most of the guests were not unduly concerned with the prospect of being spotted navigating between bedchambers. It was understood that these sorts of goings-on were to be ignored by passersby. Such was the way of the world when one moved in elevated social circles, she reminded herself.

But she had a feeling that it would not be good for business for a lady who made her living conducting discreet, private inquiries to be seen behaving in a very indiscreet manner. One had to consider the possibility that some of the elegant people who had been invited to the Beaumont estate this week might prove to be future clients.

She was suddenly very glad that she'd had the foresight to bring along the silver half-mask, sword, and shield that she'd worn to the costume ball in her guise as Minerva.

Raising the mask to conceal her features, she stepped into the deep pool of darkness behind the stairs.

The gentleman with the candle never noticed her. He was too intent on reaching his destination. When he started up the stairs, she heard a solid thump followed by a muffled groan.

'Od's blood.'

The gentleman paused and bent down to feel gingerly about in the vicinity of his toes. Then, with a few more muttered oaths, he limped up the stairs.

She waited until she was certain he had disappeared, and then she made to move cautiously out from her hiding place.

At that moment another door opened a short distance down the hall.

'Damnation,' she whispered under her breath. At this rate she would never get to Tobias's bedchamber.

In the dim glow cast by a wall sconce, she saw two figures emerge from the chamber. The woman gave a deep, throaty chuckle.

'Come along with me, sir; ye won't be sorry, that I promise.'

One of the maids, Lavinia realized. Obviously the guests were not the only ones who took part in the late-night revelries of a country-house party. Suppressing her irritation with an effort, she raised the mask again and slipped back into the shadows behind the stairs.

'Don't see why we cannot have our sport in my bedchamber,' the man said. His words were slurred with drink. 'I've got a nicely warmed bed.'

'I'll soon have ye warmed good and proper, sir. No need to fret yerself about that.'

The man chuckled hoarsely. 'Let's get to it, then. Where's your bedchamber?'

'Oh, we cannot use my bedchamber, sir. There's three other maids sharing it with me tonight on account of the house is so full. We'll go out on the roof. It's a little cool, but I've got some cozy quilts up there waiting for us.'

'Hell's teeth, you mean to tell me I've got to climb all the way to the top of this bloody castle just to enjoy a romp?'

'It'll be worth it, sir. I've got some very special apparatus that is sure to amuse a man of the world such as yerself.'

'Apparatus, eh?' The gentleman's anticipation and excitement were clear even through the fog of drunkenness. 'What sort of equipment do you use, my girl? I'm partial to the whip, myself.'

The maid whispered something that Lavinia could not hear.

'Well, now.' The man's voice thickened even more with lust. 'That sounds interesting, indeed. I'll look forward to a demonstration.'

'Soon, sir.' The maid hurried him toward the staircase. 'Just as soon as we get to the roof.'

The pair continued toward the foot of the stairs. Lavinia caught a glimpse of a portly gentleman who appeared to be in his early sixties. He was garbed in a plum-colored velvet coat and old-fashioned breeches. He wore an elaborately tied cravat. His balding head gleamed in the light of the wall sconce.

The maid was dressed in the manner of the rest of the staff at Beaumont Castle. She wore a plain, dark gown and an apron. Her face was almost entirely hidden beneath the shadows of a large, floppy cap.

The gentleman put one foot on the bottom stair and stumbled awkwardly. The misstep made him chortle. 'A tribute to Beaumont's excellent brandy, eh? Let me try that again.'

'No, not this staircase, m'lord.' The maid tugged on his arm. 'We'll use the back stairs. It would cost me my post if the butler or the housekeeper saw me with you.'

'Oh, very well.' The bald man obligingly allowed himself to be led on down the hall.

The maid picked up her skirts, revealing sturdy, sensible shoes and stockings. She hurried her companion past the small pool of light cast by another wall sconce. Several thick golden-blond corkscrew curls bobbed beneath the edge of the large cap.

The inebriated gentleman allowed himself to be steered around a corner into another darkened hall.

Relieved to find herself alone again in the corridor, Lavinia moved briskly out from behind the staircase and hurried toward Tobias's bedchamber. At this rate she was going to need a glass of sherry to settle her nerves when she arrived at her destination.

There was a thin edge of light showing beneath Tobias's door. She raised her hand and then hesitated. The occupant of the neighboring bedchamber might hear the knock and grow curious.

Grasping her sword, shield, and mask in one hand, she tried the doorknob. It turned easily in her fingers. Casting one last glance down the passageway to make certain that she was not being observed, she opened the door.

The sight of the couple locked in a close embrace in front of the fire brought her up short. The man had his back to her. He had removed his jacket and cravat and unfastened his collar. There was something very familiar about the strong line of his shoulders. She could not see his face, because his head was bent intimately toward a woman with long black hair, who had her arms around his neck.

'I beg your pardon.' Mortified, Lavinia quickly averted her gaze and retreated back into the hallway. 'Wrong room. Dreadfully sorry to disturb you.'

'Lavinia?' Tobias's voice crackled across the short distance.

No wonder the set of those shoulders had looked familiar. She spun back around, aware that her mouth had fallen open in stunned shock.

'*Tobias*?'

'Bloody hell.' He disengaged himself from the woman's arms in a single swift motion. 'Come in and close the door behind you. I want you to meet someone.'

'Oh, dear.' The woman stepped away from Tobias and surveyed Lavinia with cool amusement. 'I do believe that we have shocked poor Minerva.'

Feeling as though she had just been caught in some dark magician's spell, Lavinia moved a short distance back into the room and shut the door very carefully.

Tobias, looking very grim and dangerous, crossed to a small, round table and picked up a cut-glass decanter. 'Lavinia, allow me to introduce you to Mrs Gray.' He poured himself some brandy. 'She came here tonight to see me in regard to a professional matter. Aspasia, this is my, uh, associate, Mrs Lake.'

Lavinia recognized the cold, uninflected tones. Something was very wrong in this room. She turned back to Aspasia. 'I assume that you are one of Tobias's clients, Mrs Gray?'

'I believe I have recently become one.' She gave Tobias an unreadable glance. 'But, please, you must call me Aspasia.'

Lavinia could see that she was very sure of herself and of her place in Tobias's life. These two had formed a connection long ago, she thought. There was a bond between them that excluded her.

'I see.' A chill went through her. She turned back to Tobias, fighting to keep her voice even. 'Will you be needing my assistance on this case?'

'No,' Tobias said. He took a swallow of the brandy. 'I will handle this matter by myself.'

That flattened her spirits as nothing else could have done. Perhaps she had presumed too much, she thought. After the successful completion of the affair of the mad mesmerist a few weeks ago, she had found herself slipping more and more often into the habit of thinking of herself as Tobias's full-time business partner. But that was not how things stood and she would do well not to forget that fact, she thought.

In truth, their business arrangements more or less mirrored their personal relationship. They sometimes worked together, just as they sometimes made love together. But they each maintained separate careers, just as they maintained separate households.

Nevertheless, Tobias had not hesitated to involve himself in her last two cases, and it came as a decidedly painful surprise to discover that he did not welcome her assistance in this one.

'Very well.' She pulled herself together, summoned up what she hoped was a polished, businesslike smile, and opened the door. 'In that case, I will bid you both good evening and allow the two of you to return to your private affairs.'

Tobias's jaw hardened in a telltale warning sign that she had come to recognize. He was not in a good mood. Fair enough, she thought. Her own mood at the moment was not what anyone would describe as sunny.

His powerful hand tightened around the neck of the brandy decanter. For an instant she thought he might change his mind and ask her to stay. But in the end he made no move to keep her from leaving. Anger replaced the hurt his words had caused. What was the matter with him? It was obvious to her that he needed her assistance.

'I will come to see you later,' Tobias said deliberately, 'after Aspasia and I have concluded our business.'

He had practically ordered her back to her bedchamber and told her to wait upon his convenience. Outrage leaped within her. Did he really believe that she would open her door to him tonight after he had ejected her from this room in such a summary fashion?

'Do not trouble yourself, sir.' She was pleased that her smile did not waver so much as a fraction of an inch. 'It is late, and as we had to endure that very tedious carriage ride as well as the various entertainments here at the castle earlier this evening, I'm sure you'll be quite exhausted after you and Mrs Gray finish your discussion. I would not dream of allowing you to go to the effort of climbing that extremely long flight of stairs. I will see you at breakfast.'

Anger burned in Tobias's ice-and-fog eyes.

Satisfied that she had made an impression, Lavinia stepped smoothly out into the hall and closed the door with a good deal more force than was necessary.

Halfway up the stairs she decided that she did not like Aspasia Gray.

Three

He missed his footing again on one of the high, cramped steps and likely would have fallen if the maid had not held his arm with such a firm grasp. The close call sent a small tingle of dread through him. It was a long way down to the bottom of the narrow staircase.

'Steady as ye go, m'lord,' the maid said bracingly. 'We don't want ye to have an accident before we get there, do we? Come along now.'

'What d'ya expect? It's bloody damned dark in here.' Perhaps he should have refused those last two glasses of brandy she had pressed on him before they left the bedchamber. His head was spinning and he was starting to worry about his stomach. 'Ought to have used the main staircase.'

'I told ye, sir, the master doesn't like staff to entertain guests alone in their bedchambers.'

'Beaumont always was a bit prim and proper when it came to that sort of thing.'

She was a strong wench, he thought; stronger than she looked. She was able to hold the candle in one hand and maintain her grip on his elbow with the other. But, then, good maids were required to be sturdy, he reminded himself. They not only had to be able to hoist heavily laden breakfast trays, full chamber pots, and huge stacks of linens all day long, they routinely carried their burdens up and down long flights of steep stairs like this one. In addition to the exercise, there was all that sweeping and scrubbing and washing. Bound to build stamina in a wench. But he liked 'em that way. That was the reason he preferred to take his evening sport with one of the hardworking girls in a household rather than with the professional whores in the brothels. The latter were inclined to be weak and listless from an excess of gin and the milk of the poppy.

He told himself that the long climb would prove worthwhile when they reached their goal. Doggedly, he plodded up another few steps.

'How much farther?' he muttered. His heart was beating so strongly he wondered that she did not hear it.

'We're almost there.'

The step in front of him seemed to waver in the flaring candlelight. He had to work hard to set his foot down on it, and even at that he nearly missed.

The maid tightened her grip on his arm and urged him upward. 'Come along now.'

When he reached the top of the cramped stairs, he was wheezing. The maid halted in front of a door. He was grateful for the pause, because he could no longer conceal his ragged breathing. He was sweating profusely too. *Should have left my coat and neckcloth in my bedchamber. Ah, well, I'll have them off soon enough.*

'Are you feeling all right, sir? You look a trifle feverish. Mayhap you had a bit too much to drink tonight, hmm? I trust you'll be able to last long enough to give me a nice romp before you fall asleep. I'd hate to think we climbed all this way for naught.'

There was something different about her now, he thought. Her speech no longer suited her station. It had taken on a more cultured, educated tone. She did not sound like a servant.

He wanted to ask her a question, but his tongue was thick in his mouth and no longer functioned properly. The dizziness was getting worse.

For some reason the sight of the night sky sent a jolt of terror through him.

'Don't worry, m'lord, brandy has this effect when you put a drop or two of laudanum in it.'

'What's this about laudanum?'

'Never mind, I know just what you need to restore your senses.' The maid opened the door. 'Some fresh night air.'

'N-no.' He shook his head when she tugged him through the opening. 'I'm not feeling well. I think I'd better go back to my bedchamber.'

'Nonsense, m'lord. You need the exercise. I hear you're engaged to marry a young lady in a few months. She's young and healthy and she'll expect a lusty husband on her wedding night.'

He peered blearily at her. 'How . . . how did you know that I'm engaged?'

'Gossip gets around, m'lord.'

The balmy night air did nothing to clear his head. The full moon began to move in a circle overhead. He closed his eyes, but that only made the spinning sensation worse.

'Almost time for you to have your little accident, m'lord,' the maid said cheerfully.

Sudden panic shot through him. He managed to get his eyes part-way open. 'My wh-wh-what?'

'Rest assured that there is nothing personal about this. Just a matter of business.'

Four

As exit lines went, the one she had just used to bid Tobias good night had not been particularly clever or original, Lavinia thought. While it had no doubt made her point, she was already regretting it by the time she reached her bedchamber a short time later.

This floor of Beaumont Castle had clearly been reserved for the less important guests such as herself, as well as a sprinkling of companions, valets, and ladies' maids. One extremely fashionable guest, Lady Oakes, had brought along her own personal hairdresser, who had been provided with a room halfway down the hall.

Lavinia let herself into the cramped little bedchamber and lit the candle on the dressing table. The light flickered in the cracked looking glass, casting a weak glow across the sparse furnishings.

She strongly suspected that this room had once been occupied by a maid or a very poor relation. The narrow bed took up most of the available space. There was a small wardrobe against one wall. The basin and pitcher on the washstand were badly chipped.

She went to the window and opened it. It was cool for a night in late June, but not cold. She would survive very well without a fireplace for warmth. Moonlight flooded the gardens and grounds below. The deep silence of the countryside was a stark contrast to the familiar clatter and din of London's nighttime streets. All this resounding quiet would no doubt make it difficult to get to sleep.

Lavinia folded her arms on the ledge and brooded on the tranquil scene. There was no getting around the fact that she had not handled things well in Tobias's bedchamber. What on earth had she been thinking when she had as much as told him not to come to her room tonight? Indeed, she'd had every right to lose her temper, but the unfortunate result was that she would not be able to discover what was going on between those two until breakfast. She was quite certain that her curiosity could not be contained that long.

She drummed her fingers on the stone and considered how to proceed.

There was no help for it. She would have to make the trek back downstairs to Tobias's bedchamber. He owed her some answers, and she knew she would not be able to rest if she did not get them tonight.

Furthermore, she did not at all care for the notion of Tobias spending a great deal of time down there alone with Aspasia Gray.

She tried to decide how long to wait before she returned to his room. Twenty minutes? She could only hope that she would not collide with any of the people she had managed to avoid on the first trip.

So much for the delightful diversions of a house party. She'd had her doubts from the start, but Joan Dove had assured her that she would enjoy herself immensely. *Yes, there are some boring games and conversations and you will have to put up with some obnoxious people, but, trust me, you will find it all worthwhile. The thing about a country-house party, Lavinia, is that no one cares what you do or where you go after the lights are turned down for the night.*

Obviously Joan had not anticipated a complication like Aspasia Gray.

A sudden thought sent a prickle of dread down Lavinia's spine. What would she do if she discovered that the woman was still in Tobias's bedchamber when she returned?

She was not jealous, she assured herself. She was *deeply concerned*. Tobias had been in exceptionally good spirits earlier this evening. Whatever had transpired between him and his new client was serious enough to plunge him into that ice-cold mood that she had learned never boded well. It was not the fact that he appeared quite menacing at such times that worried her. After all, he was no threat to her, only to those whose intentions were villainous. Rather, it was that he was inclined to take risks when he was in that frame of mind.

A soft knock startled her out of her reverie. She swung around, hurried back across the room, and yanked open the door.

Tobias stood in the shadows of the dimly lit hall, looking even more dangerous than he had a short time earlier. He had not bothered to put on his coat or neckcloth. He had not even refastened the collar of his white shirt. She could see some of the dark, curling hair that covered his broad chest.

'Well, this is a surprise, sir.'

He glanced down the corridor, apparently assuring himself that there was no one around, and then he stalked into the tiny room.

'Do me a favor,' he muttered, shutting the door behind himself. 'In the future, if I ever again suggest that we accept an invitation to a country-house party, kindly tell me to go stand out in the rain until the fit passes.'

'How odd that you should say that. I was having similar thoughts.' She went back to her post by the window. 'Who is she, Tobias?'

'I told you who she is,' he said quietly. 'Her name is Aspasia Gray. An old acquaintance.'

'I collect that the two of you were once quite close.'

'I said *acquaintance*, not *lover*.' He came to stand behind her. 'Bloody hell. Surely you don't think there was anything of significance in the fact that she had her arms around my neck when you walked into my bedchamber, do you?'

'Well, as a matter of fact—'

'I can explain that rather unfortunate scene. Aspasia was merely thanking me for agreeing to make some inquiries on her behalf. I did not want to be rude by shoving her away.'

'I see.'

'Damnation, Lavinia, she caught me off guard. I heard you open the door and the next thing I knew her arms were around my neck.'

'Mmm.'

'What is this?' He closed a hand over her shoulder and tugged her gently around to face him. 'Surely you do not think for one moment that I was engaged in a serious embrace with Aspasia? I love you. You know that. I thought we had agreed that we trusted each other.'

Some of her tension eased. She touched his face. 'Yes, I know. I love you and I trust you, Tobias.'

He exhaled deeply. 'Thank God. You had me worried for a moment.'

She raised her brows. 'I do not know Mrs Gray, however, and I have no particular reason to trust her.'

He shrugged. 'You need not concern yourself with the subject of Aspasia.'

'Yes, well, I *am* concerning myself with that subject. Furthermore, the fact that I trust you does not mean that I relish the sight of you standing in your shirtsleeves with another woman's arms draped around your neck.'

He smiled slowly. 'You make yourself quite clear, my dear.'

'You are not to make a regular practice of that sort of thing, sir. Is that understood?'

He raised one hand to trace the engraving of the goddess Minerva that decorated the silver pendant she wore at her throat. 'You are the only woman whose arms I want around my neck.'

She got almost no warning – just a brief glimpse of the candle flame reflected in his eyes – before he kissed her. The urgent, driving hunger in him thrilled her senses. But it also made her wonder again about the precise nature of his conversation with his new client.

She had experienced this incendiary desire flowing from him often enough in the past to recognize it. His dark passions had their source in a well of midnight buried deep within him. He kept the channel to that place closed and locked for the most part, but it had been opened tonight. She suspected that was Aspasia Gray's doing.

'Tobias.'

He locked her hard against him, one arm around her neck, the other anchoring her waist. 'When you told me not to bother coming here tonight, I felt as if you had plunged that spear you carried straight into my heart.'

'I did not mean it,' she whispered against his neck. 'Indeed, I was only biding my time up here until I went back downstairs to your bedchamber.'

'You had every right to be angry.' He kissed her mouth, her cheek, and then her throat. 'But there was no need, I swear it.'

'She did it deliberately, didn't she? She heard the door open and she put her arms around you at that instant so that I would see the two of you together.'

'No, I'm sure that she meant only to convey a token of her gratitude, because I had just agreed to make inquiries on her behalf. You happened to open the door at the wrong moment.'

'Rubbish.'

'Devil take it, forget that damned embrace. I do not care about Aspasia.' He lifted her off her feet and started across the small room. 'You are the only one I care about and this is the only embrace that matters.'

'Tobias, the bed—'

'I am getting us there as swiftly as possible.'

'But it is much too narrow for the two of us.'

'You and I are nothing if not resourceful, madam. We have, upon occasion, made do with the seat of a carriage. I feel certain we can manage a small bed.'

He spilled her carefully onto the cot and came down on top of her. She felt herself crushed into the bedding. The skirts of her expensive new gown, purchased especially for the jaunt to the country, were getting crushed, but in that moment she did not care a jot.

Tobias lowered her bodice and kissed her until her skin burned hot. She framed his face between her palms and responded with a passion that never failed to astonish her. Until she met Tobias, she had not dreamed that she was capable of such intensity of feeling. Even at times like this, when he was in the grip of his darker passions, she responded to him. No, it was more than that, she thought, she *needed* to respond to him, *especially* at such times.

On these rare occasions when he opened the path to that deep wellspring of midnight inside himself, she glimpsed an aspect of his true nature that he allowed no one else to know. She recognized the powerful, elemental force within him all too well because it called to an opposite but equally strong aspect of her own being.

In the past few weeks she had slowly begun to accept that she and Tobias were linked in some metaphysical fashion that she did not yet fully understand. Perhaps she would never entirely comprehend the nature of the connection between them, but she knew now that she could no longer deny it.

She had not dared to speak of these matters to Tobias. She knew that he had no use for metaphysics and would not welcome such a discussion.

But sometimes, when he was deep inside her, holding her as though he would never let her go, not even in death, she wondered if he, too, sensed the bond between them.

He pushed her skirts up with a rough, impatient motion of his hand and slid his fingers between her thighs. She was aware of the hunger pulsing through him. Her own need rose to meet his. She opened his shirt to his waist and flattened her palm on his chest, glorying in the feel of him.

He probed gently until he found the exquisitely sensitive bud. When he stroked slowly, she heard herself whisper the most shocking words, words she would never have used in polite company, words that, until she had met Tobias, she had not realized she knew.

He let his finger glide deeper.

'Tobias.' She tightened and moved against his palm.

He reached down to unfasten his trousers.

A blood-freezing scream sliced through the summer night, shattering the moment with the impact of a thunderclap. Lavinia flinched and opened her eyes just in time to see a dark shadow plummet past the open window.

'What the bloody hell?' Tobias rolled off the bed and onto his feet just as the dreadful cry ended with appalling finality.

'Dear heaven, what on earth was that?' Lavinia scrambled up off the bed. 'Some sort of night bird? A large bat?'

Tobias was already at the window, having covered the distance in two strides. He gripped the edge and stood looking down into the gardens.

'Merciful God,' he whispered.

Lavinia hurried toward the window. 'What has happened?'

Somewhere in the distance, another scream rent the night. A woman this time. Lavinia leaned out the window and glanced to the left, seeking the source of the second scream.

She saw the occupant of a neighboring bedchamber, clad in a dressing gown and nightcap, standing on a stone balcony. The woman stared, transfixed, into the garden.

Lavinia braced herself and looked down. A figure garbed in formal evening attire lay crumpled on the grass like a broken clockwork doll. Horror turned her stomach ice-cold. The shadow hurtling past the window a few seconds earlier had been a man.

'He must have fallen from the roof,' she whispered.

'I wonder what he was doing up there?' Tobias said. 'He is certainly not a member of the household staff.'

Lavinia looked down again and saw a bald pate gleaming in the moonlight. 'Oh, no. Surely not.'

She heard more windows thrown open. Shocked exclamations echoed in the night. Down below, a footman, lantern in hand, appeared and walked with great reluctance toward the dead man.

'I will go and see if there is anything to be done.' Tobias turned away from the window. 'Wait here.'

'No, I am coming with you.'

'There is no need,' he said gently. 'It will be extremely unpleasant.'

She swallowed. 'I cannot be certain until I get a closer look at him, but I fear that there may, indeed, be a reason for me to accompany you.'

He paused at the door and glanced back, frowning. 'What is that?'

'I may have been one of the last people to see him alive.' She adjusted the bodice of her gown and reached up to feel for her hairpins. 'Except for the maid, of course.'

'What the devil are you talking about?' Tobias opened the door and went out into the hall. 'Do you know that man?'

'Not exactly.' She followed him out into the dim corridor and paused to close the bedchamber door. 'We were never introduced, but I believe I saw him a short while ago, when I went to meet you in your bedchamber. To be more precise, I hid behind the staircase while he went by in the company of one of the maids.'

That got his attention. 'He was with one of the servants?'

'Yes. I got the impression that they were on their way up to the roof to engage in what the gentleman referred to as a bit of sport. The maid seemed quite cheerful about the prospect. He no doubt promised her money.' She paused. 'I wonder if Lady Beaumont knows that sort of thing is going on in her household.'

'I suspect there is a good deal of that sort of thing going on at this affair.'

They reached the top of the staircase and started down. Lavinia heard doors opening in the hall behind her. Bewildered and curious people began to emerge from their bedchambers to ask one another what had happened.

'I wonder how he came to fall from the roof,' Tobias said.

'It was no doubt an accident. He was quite drunk when I saw him.'

More doors opened on the floor below. People in various stages of dress and undress appeared. Some joined Tobias and Lavinia on the staircase. Most chose to remain in the hall, speculating on events with their neighbors.

When they reached the ground floor, Tobias led the way outside into the gardens. A small group had gathered around the body.

Lord Beaumont, short, round, and bald, rushed out of a side door. He was partially dressed, in trousers, slippers, and a silk dressing gown. He stopped abruptly when he saw Tobias. Then he altered course to intercept him.

'March. Thank you for coming down. Vale told me that you were an excellent man in a crisis.' Beaumont belatedly noticed Lavinia and bobbed his head. 'Mrs Lake. There is no need for you to put yourself through this ordeal. Please, you really must go back inside.'

She started to explain why she had come downstairs, but Tobias interrupted.

'Who is it?' he asked quietly.

Beaumont glanced uneasily at the crowd around the body. 'The footman who came to fetch me said it was Lord Fullerton.'

'Have you sent for the doctor?'

'What? No. Everything has happened so quickly. I hadn't even considered—' Beaumont broke off and made a visible attempt to gather his wits. 'Yes, of course. The doctor. He will know what is to be done with the body. Certainly cannot leave it here in the garden. Yes, yes, I shall summon him immediately. Excellent notion, March.'

Obviously relieved to have a specific goal, Beaumont turned and beckoned frantically to a footman.

'I want to take a closer look,' Tobias said softly to Lavinia. 'Are you certain you wish to do this?'

'Yes.'

They walked to where Fullerton lay on the damp grass. Lavinia was not in the least surprised when the cluster of people gathered around the body parted to make way for Tobias. He often had that effect on others.

A thin man was on his knees beside Fullerton. Hands clasped, he rocked back and forth, moaning.

'Disaster,' he muttered. 'Disaster. What am I to do? This is a disaster.'

Tobias glanced at Lavinia. 'Are you all right?'

'Yes.'

It was not the first time she had found herself in the proximity of violent death, but she knew that she would never grow accustomed to the sight. In this case there was no blood, but Fullerton's neck was twisted at an unnatural angle that caused her stomach to churn. For a few terrible seconds she was afraid she might be ill.

She forced herself to concentrate on details and immediately recognized the bald head, the plum-colored coat, and the elaborately tied cravat. This was, indeed, the man she had seen going down the hall with the blond maid a short time ago.

'Well?' Tobias prompted softly.

'Yes, that is the man I noticed earlier,' Lavinia said.

The thin man continued to rock and moan. 'Disaster. What will I do?'

'Odd.' Tobias studied the body. 'He is fully dressed.'

'I beg your pardon?'

'You said that he and the maid were evidently intent on a rooftop tryst, but he is still entirely clothed. His breeches and shirt are fastened and his neckcloth is knotted.'

'Oh, yes, I see what you mean.' She considered that for a few seconds. 'Perhaps they, uh, did not have time to pursue their plans before he fell.'

Tobias shook his head once, coldly certain now. 'He was up there for some time. Plenty of time to get his breeches open, at least.'

She looked up quickly. 'Are you implying what I think you are implying?'

'I'm not sure yet.' Tobias raised his voice and spoke to the keening man. 'Who are you?'

The thin man regarded him with a dazed expression. 'Burns, sir. His lordship's valet. That is to say, I *was* his valet. It was an excellent position. We had just finished placing an order for several new coats and a dressing gown. His lordship was to be wed, you see. He wanted to appear in the first stare of fashion for his new bride. I wonder what will become of all his fine clothes?'

'You will pack them up and return them to his family, of course,' Lavinia said.

'Oh, no, madam, I shall not do any such thing.' Burns scrambled to his feet and took a step back. 'There is no one to pay me now. I must find a new position.'

'When did you last see his lordship alive?' Tobias asked.

'This evening, when he went downstairs to the costume ball. He looked his best tonight, I saw to that. He was very pleased with the knot in his cravat. I invented it and named it for him, you know.'

'You did not see him after that?' Tobias pressed.

'No. He instructed me not to wait up for him.'

'Was that unusual?'

'No, sir. His lordship was fond of a bit of sport with a willing wench before he went to sleep. He did not like me to be in the way.'

'Come.' Tobias tightened his grasp on Lavinia's arm and steered her away from the scene.

'Where are we going?' she asked.

'I want to take a look at Fullerton's bedchamber.'

'Why? What do you expect to find?'

'I have no notion.'

Tobias stopped the partially dressed butler and asked him which room had been assigned to Lord Fullerton. The man gave him directions. Lord Beaumont, still quite agitated, trotted forward.

'What is it, March?' he asked. 'Has something else happened?'

'No, sir,' Tobias said. 'I merely wish to have a look around Fullerton's bedchamber. Perhaps it would be best if you accompanied us.'

It was a thinly veiled command, but Beaumont did not appear to be aware that he was being ordered about by a man who was his social inferior.

'Yes, of course,' Beaumont said. He turned quickly and led the way back toward the house.

When Tobias spoke in that deep, resonant, utterly sure voice, people tended to obey without question, Lavinia thought. He had an uncanny ability to assume command at times when others were dashing about mindlessly. She suspected that the subtle skill was more complex than he knew or would ever acknowledge.

In the course of their last major investigation, an incident had occurred that had convinced her that Tobias possessed the raw, untrained talent of a powerful mesmerist. She was certain that the source of his abilities lay deep in that pool of midnight inside him. She was equally certain that he would never acknowledge those abilities, not even to himself. For reasons she did not fully comprehend, he had chosen to bury that side of his nature beneath several layers of stubborn logic and an iron will. Until he met her, he had labeled all mesmerists charlatans and frauds who preyed on the weak and the gullible.

When he had discovered that she was trained in the art, his first reaction had been to dismiss her skills. Lately she had sensed his grudging acceptance of her abilities, but she was very well aware that he still preferred to ignore them as much as possible.

Inside the castle, she and Tobias followed their host up the main staircase. Beaumont was breathing heavily by the time they reached the landing. He paused to catch his breath.

A large number of guests milled about on this floor. One of them was a woman with lustrous brown hair bound up in a loose knot.

Lavinia did not recognize her until she turned around. Aspasia had removed the black wig and cobra diadem, and she had changed into a heavily embroidered green silk dressing gown.

She spotted Tobias and walked swiftly toward him.

'What is going on?' she demanded in a low voice. 'Everyone is saying that Fullerton fell from the roof and broke his neck.'

'That seems to be the case,' Tobias said.

Beaumont whipped out a handkerchief and wiped his brow. He surveyed the flock of guests. 'Terrible accident. Quite dreadful, actually. But I assure you that matters are in hand. The doctor is on his way. You may all return to your bedchambers.'

Aspasia's fine brows puckered in a small frown. Her lips parted on a question. Lavinia saw Tobias shake his head once in a small, silencing motion.

Aspasia obediently closed her mouth.

'You must excuse us,' Tobias said. 'We are in a hurry. Lord Beaumont is taking us to Fullerton's bedchamber.'

Aspasia appeared startled, and then Lavinia saw a flicker of comprehension in her dark eyes.

'Tobias?' Aspasia whispered in husky tones. 'Do you think—'

'I will speak with you later,' he said gently.

'Yes, of course.' Aspasia moved gracefully out of the way. Her gaze rested thoughtfully on Lavinia.

The moment of communication that had passed between Aspasia and Tobias was brief, Lavinia reflected as she accompanied the two men down the hall, but there was no mistaking the intimacy of it. Aspasia clearly felt that she had a claim of some sort on Tobias, and he, in turn, accepted some obligation toward her.

If there was one thing that she had learned about Tobias during the past few months, Lavinia thought, it was that he took his perceived responsibilities very seriously.

She glanced back just in time to see Aspasia disappear through a bedchamber door. It was a very *familiar* bedchamber door.

Well, that was certainly one mystery solved tonight, she thought. She now knew why she had been summarily shifted upstairs to that unpleasant little room at the end of the hall. The housekeeper and butler had conspired to give her comfortable chamber on this floor to Aspasia Gray.

Beaumont came to a halt in front of a door.

'This was Fullerton's bedchamber,' he announced.

Tobias entered first. He lit a candle and surveyed the space. Then he crossed to the window and drew aside the curtains.

Moonlight flooded into the chamber, adding to the weak illumination of the candle.

Lavinia stepped in and looked around. The bedchamber was as large as the one Tobias had been given. The wide, heavily draped bed had been turned down in preparation for sleep. It was obvious that no one had used it. The sheets and pillows were still neatly arranged. The handle of a warming pan projected from beneath the edge of the quilt.

'He asked her why they could not use his bed,' she murmured to Tobias. 'He told her that it had been nicely warmed.'

Tobias was busy opening and closing the drawers of the dressing table in a brisk, methodical fashion. He did not look up from his task. 'What else did he say?'

'He asked the maid why it was necessary to go all the way up to the roof.'

Beaumont scowled from the doorway. 'What's this about a maid?'

'When I saw Lord Fullerton earlier this evening,' Lavinia said, 'he was in the company of a tall, blond maid. I gained the clear impression that they were on the way to the roof for some dalliance.'

'Nonsense.' Beaumont's whiskers bristled in genuine indignation. 'Everyone in this household is aware that inappropriate intimacies between staff and guests are strictly forbidden. Lady Beaumont does not countenance that sort of thing.'

Lavinia stopped in front of the night table and studied the assortment of small items arrayed on the polished wooden surface. 'This maid seemed to be quite eager to oblige Fullerton. She was the one who suggested that they go upstairs to the roof rather than use his bedchamber.'

'Rest assured, I shall have my butler look into the matter.' Beaumont broke off with a quizzical expression. 'A tall, blond woman, you say? I don't recall anyone on my staff who fits that description. Probably one of the local village girls taken on for the week. With so many guests in the house, extra maids are required.'

'I see.' There was nothing unusual about the collection of items on the night table, Lavinia thought. She saw a candlestick, a pair of spectacles, and a ring.

She went to the wardrobe and opened it. Tobias came to stand behind her with the candle. Together they surveyed the array of expensively cut garments.

'I want to speak with the blond maid.' Tobias opened the drawers of the wardrobe, glancing briefly at carefully folded handkerchiefs and small clothes. 'Will you ask your butler to locate her, sir?'

'If you feel it is necessary.' Beaumont took a step back and then hesitated uncertainly. 'What is it that concerns you about this situation, March?'

'I would like to find out if Fullerton was still in the company of the maid when he fell to his death.' Tobias turned away from the wardrobe and went to the night table. He stood looking down at the objects on the surface. 'Perhaps she can describe precisely what occurred.'

'Very well, I shall go and have a word with Drum.' Beaumont swung around and disappeared down the hall, seemingly relieved to have another clear goal.

Lavinia opened a trunk and looked inside. It was empty. All of the items that had been packed in it were no doubt hanging in the wardrobe. She closed the lid and looked at Tobias, who was in the process of going down on one knee to peer beneath the bed.

She saw his jaw tighten when he shifted his weight to his left leg, but she resisted the urge to ask him if he was in pain. He did not welcome constant inquiries on the subject of the injury he had sustained in Italy a few months earlier. The wound had long since healed, but she knew it still bothered him on occasion.

'What on earth do you expect to find under there?' she asked instead.

'How the devil should I know?' He finished his perusal of the floorboards, grasped a bedpost, and hauled himself back to his feet. 'I believe we are finished here.' He massaged his left thigh impatiently. 'Now for the roof.'

'Tobias, what is this all about? You do not think that Lord Fullerton's death was an accident, do you?'

For a few seconds he looked as if he intended to evade the question. Then he shrugged. 'I think he was murdered.'

'I was afraid that you had concluded as much. But what leads you to believe that?'

'It is a long story.' He headed for the door, taking the candle with him on a small stand. 'One that I do not have time to go into just now.'

He was putting her off again, she thought. But this was not the moment to argue the point.

'Very well, but mark you, sir, I do intend to obtain a proper explanation from you at the earliest possible opportunity.'

She found herself speaking to thin air. Tobias was already outside in the hall, moving toward the staircase.

She was about to follow him, but something made her glance once more around the room they had just finished searching. Her eyes went to the night table. A pale wedge of moonlight illuminated the objects on the surface. It seemed to her that something had changed in the arrangement of the items.

In the next breath she realized what the difference was. The ring was gone.

An uneasy sensation fluttered across her nerves. Tobias was no thief. He had taken the ring for some very good reason, one that he had chosen not to confide to her or to Beaumont.

Her partner had been acting in an exceedingly odd manner since his conversation with Aspasia Gray.

'I really do not care for that woman,' she said aloud to the empty room.

Five

The servants' floor mirrored the same scene of confusion, curiosity, and excited dread that Lavinia had seen on the lower floors. Small groups of people hovered in the narrow, low-ceilinged corridor, talking in soft voices.

At the sight of Lavinia and Tobias, all conversation ended abruptly. Everyone turned to look at the intruders from the guest floors.

Tobias focused on the nearest person, a young maid in her nightclothes.

'Where are the stairs to the roof?' he demanded.

The girl gasped and went as still as a rabbit confronted by a wolf. She gaped at Tobias, eyes widening with fear. She made several attempts to speak but only managed a meaningless stammer.

'The roof, girl,' Tobias repeated, voice accented with faint echoes of impending doom. 'Where is the bloody staircase?'

Her companions retreated rapidly, leaving her to face Tobias alone.

'Puh-puh-please, sir—' The girl stopped altogether when Tobias loomed closer. She looked as if she was about to burst into tears.

Lavinia sighed. It was time to take charge.

'Enough, sir.' She stepped between Tobias and the maid, who was now trembling visibly. 'You are terrifying her. Allow me to deal with this.'

Tobias came to a halt, clearly annoyed at having been deprived of his prey. He did not take his icy gaze off the shivering girl.

'Very well,' he growled to Lavinia. 'But be quick about it. There is no time to waste.'

She did not blame the poor maid, Lavinia thought. Tobias was extremely intimidating at the moment. His attitude tonight put her in mind of the first time she had met him.

She recalled the occasion quite vividly. On that fateful night in Rome, he had swept into the small antiquities shop she and her niece, Emeline, had operated and proceeded to smash every statue in sight. She had thought at first that he was a madman, but then she had seen the chilling intelligence in his eyes and realized that he knew precisely what he was about. Somehow that had only made him seem all the more menacing.

'Calm yourself,' she said to the maid. She fingered the silver pendant at her throat and spoke in the low, soothing tones that she used when she wished to induce a light mesmeric trance. 'Look at me. There is no need to be afraid. All is well. No need to be afraid. There is nothing to fear.'

The girl blinked once or twice and tore her anxious gaze away from Tobias's implacable face. She stared at the pendant.

'What is your name?' Lavinia asked gently.

'Nell. My name is Nell, ma'am.'

'Very good, Nell. Now, where is the staircase that leads to the roof?'

'At the end of the hall, ma'am. But Drum has instructed the staff not to go up onto the roof. He's afraid someone might fall. The wall is very low, y'see.'

'I understand.' Out of the corner of her eye, Lavinia saw Tobias move off down the hall, heading toward the staircase. She was about to follow, but she paused for one last question. 'Do you know all of the members of the household staff, Nell?'

'Yes, ma'am. We all come from the village or one of the farms.'

The girl was talking freely now. There was no need to hold her attention with the pendant. Lavinia stopped manipulating the necklace.

The maid blinked again and raised her eyes to meet Lavinia's. 'Are you acquainted with a maid who is somewhat taller than yourself and perhaps a few years older? She has very bright blond hair. Lots of heavy corkscrew curls. This evening she wore a large cap trimmed with a blue ribbon. It looked new and it had a brim that was much wider than yours.'

'A new cap with a blue ribbon?' Nell seized on what was evidently the most important aspect of the description. 'No, ma'am. If one of us was lucky enough to get a new cap, we'd all know about it, I can tell ye that much.'

'Are any of your companions tall and blond?'

'Well, Annie's tall but her hair is dark. Betty's got yellow hair but she's shorter than me.' The girl's features knotted with concentration. 'I can't think of anyone quite like the girl you described.'

'I see. Thank you, Nell. You've been very helpful.'

'Yes, ma'am.' Nell gave a tiny curtsy and cast an uncertain glance down the hall at Tobias, who was opening a door. She swallowed uneasily. 'Will sir be wanting to ask more questions?'

'Don't be alarmed. If he wants to talk to you again, I will be sure to accompany him.'

Nell looked relieved. 'Thank ye, ma'am.'

Lavinia went swiftly down the corridor. By the time she got to the staircase door, Tobias had already disappeared.

Lacking a candle, she was obliged to feel her way up the narrow flight of steps. But when she reached the top, the door was open.

She stepped out into the moonlight and saw Tobias at the low wall. He was looking down into the gardens. She walked toward him.

'Is that the place where Fullerton fell?' she asked.

'Yes, I think so. There are marks in the dirt on the wall here. Do you see them?'

He raised the candle to angle the light across the barrier. There were several smears in the dust, soot, and grime that caked the stone. They certainly appeared to be traces left by a man grasping desperately to keep himself from plummeting to a certain death. A chill went through her.

'Yes,' she whispered. 'I see.'

'It would appear that the woman lured him up onto the roof.' Tobias paced deliberately along the wall. 'You said Fullerton was quite drunk. He would no doubt have been unsteady on his feet. It would not have required much strength to topple him over the edge, merely careful timing.'

'I know that for some reason you have yet to explain you are convinced this was murder,' she said quietly. 'But I have seen nothing yet that indicates it could not have been an accident.'

'What of the tall, blond maid?'

She hesitated. 'Nell could not think of anyone who matched my description,' she admitted.

He paused at that and looked at her. In the candlelight, his face had a decidedly sinister aspect. She could understand Nell's reaction. If one were not well acquainted with Tobias when he was on the hunt, she thought, one would be strongly inclined to run for one's life.

'One of the guests, perhaps,' he said slowly. 'Dressed in a costume that she wore to the ball earlier this evening?'

She summoned up the brief glimpse she'd had of Fullerton's female companion. 'I do not think it was a costume that any of Beaumont's guests would have worn to a ball. It was too ordinary, too realistic, if you see what I mean. The materials were not fine enough for any of the ladies here tonight. The gown was fashioned of a dull, sturdy fabric. The shoes, stockings, and apron looked very much like those worn by Beaumont's chambermaids.'

'Not a costume, then, but a true disguise,' he said slowly.

'Tobias, I think it is time you told me precisely what is going on.'

He said nothing for a moment, resuming his prowl of the rooftop instead. She knew that he was looking for other signs of what had taken place here a short time ago. She feared that he would attempt to avoid her question.

But when he reached the far corner he began to speak.

'I have told you that during the war I conducted several confidential inquiries for the Crown on behalf of my friend Lord Crackenburne.'

'Yes, yes, I know that you were a spy, sir. Pray get to the meat of the matter.'

'I prefer to avoid the term *spy* when discussing my former profession.' He leaned down to take a closer look at something he saw in the dust. 'It has such unsavory connotations.'

'I am well aware that the profession is not considered a proper career for a gentleman. But there is no need for either of us to mince words when we are alone like this. Indeed, you were a spy. I was obliged to engage in trade in order to survive in Rome. Neither of us possesses the sort of past one would wish to have made common knowledge in elevated social circles. But that is hardly important at the moment. Continue with your tale.'

He straightened and stood gazing out into the night. 'Bloody hell, Lavinia, I am not even sure where to start.'

'Why don't you begin by telling me why you took that ring from Fullerton's night table.'

'Ah, you noticed that, did you?' Tobias smiled a little. 'Very observant. You are making great progress in acquiring the skills of your new profession. Yes, I took the damned ring.'

'Why? You are no thief, sir.'

He reached into his pocket and took out the ring. For a moment he examined it in the light of the candle. 'Even if I were inclined toward thievery, I would not have willingly pinched this particular bit of jewelry. I took it because I am quite certain that it was left there for me to find.'

Ice melted slowly down her spine.

She walked to where he stood and looked at the ring on his palm. In the flickering candlelight she could make out a miniature gold coffin. Tobias opened the lid with the edge of one finger. A ghastly little death's-head stared up at her from a bed of crossed bones.

'A memento-mori ring,' she said, frowning slightly. 'They were quite popular in past eras, although why anyone would want to be constantly reminded of the inevitability of death is beyond me.'

'Three years ago, an aging countess, a wealthy widow, and two gentlemen of means died in a series of what appeared to be accidents and suicides. One afternoon I chanced to engage my friend Crackenburne in a discussion of the events. It occurred to me in the course of the conversation that, in each case, someone had gained substantially from the unexpected demise.'

'You refer to inheritances?'

'Yes. In all four cases. The end result was that several large fortunes, a couple of sizable estates, and a title or two changed hands.'

'What struck you as odd about that? Such things happen when wealthy, titled people die.'

'Indeed. But there were other aspects of the deaths that aroused my curiosity. The two suicides, for example, seemed unlikely to me. Crackenburne, who is always in the know when it comes to the affairs of the ton, was not aware that either of the two men who died in that manner suffered from melancholia or desperately ill health. Neither had sustained any recent financial losses.'

'And the accidents?'

'The aging countess went through the ice that covered a pond while out taking a walk on a cold winter afternoon. The wealthy widow fell down a flight of stairs while alone in her house one night. She broke her neck.'

There was a short silence. Reluctantly Lavinia looked toward the place where it seemed Fullerton had made a frantic attempt to avoid the fall that had killed him.

Tobias followed her gaze and nodded once. 'Indeed, her death was not unlike Fullerton's.'

'Continue, sir.'

Tobias resumed his slow pacing. 'Crackenburne urged me to look into the deaths. Discreetly, of course. No suggestion of murder had been implied, and none of the families in question would have welcomed one.'

'What did you discover?'

'In the course of making some inquiries into the demise of the widow, I learned that her housekeeper had found a very unpleasant item of jewelry near the body.'

Apprehension made her palms grow cold. 'A memento-mori ring?'

'Yes.' Tobias closed his hand tightly around the ring. 'The housekeeper had served her employer for many years and was positive that the ring was not part of the widow's collection of jewels. When I investigated the two suicides, I was told that similar odd rings had been found in the libraries of both men. Neither man's valet recognized the ring.'

She was suddenly keenly aware of the slight chill in the night air. 'I begin to perceive why you are so concerned about Fullerton's death.'

'A fortnight after I began my inquiries, there was a fifth death. An elderly peer had apparently taken an overdose of laudanum. But this time I learned of the suspicious suicide almost immediately, thanks to Crackenburne's connections. With his assistance, I was able to get into the house before the body was removed and study the bedchamber where the man had died. I found the ring on his desk. But that was not all I discovered.'

'What else did you learn?'

'There was also some mud on the windowsill. It looked as though someone had climbed into the bedchamber that night, perhaps to tamper with the laudanum. In the garden below the bedchamber, I discovered a scrap of fine black silk that had snagged on a tree branch. I eventually located the shop where it had been sold and got a description of the man who had purchased it.'

'Brilliant work, sir.'

'Other clues came to light.' Tobias paused. 'I will not bore you with the rest of the details. Suffice it to say that one thing led to another and eventually I identified the killer. But he realized that I was closing in on him.'

'Did he flee the country?'

Tobias put one foot on the low stone wall and braced his forearm on his thigh. He appeared to be lost in whatever he was looking at on the dark horizon.

'No,' he said eventually. 'He considered himself a gentleman who had challenged me to a lethal duel of sorts. When he perceived that he had lost, he chose to put a pistol to his head.'

'I see.'

'I found his collection of memento-mori rings together with his journal of accounts detailing the crimes stored in a hidden safe in his study.'

'Good heavens, he actually kept a journal of accounts?'

'Yes.'

'What of the rings? Why did he leave them at the scenes of his crimes?'

'I believe that the rings were his signature, his way of taking credit for the murders.'

She stared at him, appalled. 'You mean he signed his horrid deeds the way an artist signs a painting?'

'Yes. He took pride in his skills, you see. Obviously, he could not risk boasting openly in his club, so he settled for leaving a memento-mori ring among the victims' possessions.'

'Thank God you realized what he was about and put a stop to his career.'

'The entire affair was hushed up, of course. There was never any direct proof of murder, and none of the wealthy families involved wanted to invite the scandal of an investigation.' Tobias's voice hardened. 'I have often thought that if I had paid closer attention and acted more quickly, I might have saved some lives.'

'Rubbish.' She went to stand directly in front of him. 'That is quite enough of that sort of talk, Tobias. I will not have you blaming yourself because you did not solve the case immediately. It sounds as if no one even realized that people were being murdered until you put the pieces of the puzzle together. Obviously you identified an extremely clever killer who would no doubt have continued to murder indefinitely if you had not stopped him.'

Tobias clenched his hand very fiercely around the ring and said nothing.

'Did this man commit murder merely for the sport of it?' she asked. 'Or did he have some crazed motive?'

'There is no doubt but that he did it, in part, for the money,' Tobias said. 'He took fees for each of the deaths. The transactions were all neatly recorded in the journal of accounts, complete with the dates of the deeds and the amounts he had received. He was quite careful to protect his clients. Their names were not written down. Evidently they, in turn, never knew the identity of the man they had hired to do cold-blooded murder.'

'A professional murderer for hire,' she whispered. 'What a truly appalling way to make a living. You said this man was a gentleman?'

'Indeed. He possessed excellent manners, an eye for fashion, and a good deal of charm. He was well-liked by both men and women. He never lacked for invitations. Belonged to two or three clubs. In short, he moved freely in Society.' Tobias looked at the little death's-head. 'That was his hunting ground, you see.'

'*Hunting ground*. What an unpleasant turn of phrase.'

'He found his clients and his victims in the polite world. He had nothing but disdain for ordinary footpads, thieves, and murderers. He did not consider himself a common criminal.'

'Yes, well, as we have discovered, sir, there are any number of criminals born into respectable circles.' She paused, concerned more than ever by his haunted mood. The events of that case three years ago had obviously been very personal for him. Her intuition flared. 'Tobias, were you acquainted with this person before you learned that he murdered people for money? Did you consider him a friend?'

'There was a time when I would have trusted Zachary Elland with my life. In fact, there were occasions when I did precisely that.'

The stark admission told her everything she needed to know.

'I am so sorry.' She touched his shoulder. 'How terrible it must have been for you to discover the truth.'

'It was our bloody *friendship* that kept me from seeing the truth for so long.' The hand resting on his thigh tightened in a gesture of self-disgust. 'He counted on that connection. He used it in the vicious game he played with me. He even pretended to help me investigate the killings.'

'Tobias, you must not talk as if you failed. You solved the case.'

He paid no attention to her. Instead, he gazed out over the moonlit woods beyond the gardens. 'Crackenburne introduced us. He had been watching Zachary at the gaming tables because he knew that we needed someone skilled at cards for a particular investigation. He also sensed that Elland had the sort of temperament that would make him useful as a spy. Zachary enjoyed taking risks.'

'I see.' She kept her hand on his shoulder, trying to give him some wordless comfort. 'I still do not understand why all this concerns you so intimately, Tobias.'

'I regret to say that I may have been the one who was responsible for setting him on the path that led him to become a murderer for hire.'

'Sir, that is outrageous.' Shocked, she gripped his shoulder very tightly. 'You cannot possibly mean that you are to blame for the fact that your friend became a killer. That is utter nonsense.'

'I only wish that were true. But the fact of the matter is, the first entries in his journal were dated shortly after he and I began to work together.'

'Tell me what made you conclude that you had a hand in turning him into a killer.'

'I was his mentor. I taught him his craft as a spy. I was the one who gave him his assignments.' Tobias exhaled deeply. 'He certainly had an aptitude for the work.'

'Go on.'

'On his second assignment, there was an incident. I should have paid more heed.'

'Describe this incident,' she said crisply.

'I had set him to follow a man we suspected of having a direct link to a ring of traitors. According to Zachary, his quarry spotted him and pulled out a knife, intending to murder him. Zachary told me later that he was forced to defend himself. He killed the man and got rid of the body in the river. At the time there was no reason to question his version of events.'

'Pray continue.'

'Zachary acquitted himself well in that investigation and was eager for more of the same sort of work,' Tobias said. 'Crackenburne's highly placed friends in the government were extremely pleased. The death of the traitor certainly did not bother them. I was told to give Elland other tasks.'

'Were there more such deaths?'

'One more that I was aware of. Again, Crackenburne's friends in the government agreed that it was a clear case of self-defense, and since the man who died was a killer himself, no one shed any tears.

There may have been two other such incidents. I will never know for certain. Zachary did not admit to them, and no one wished to conduct an investigation.'

'Because the deaths were convenient for the government?'

'Not only that, they resulted in the acquisition of vital French military and shipping intelligence.' Tobias hesitated. 'I have often wondered if Zachary acquired a taste for the business of murder during that time when he served as a spy.'

'But what happened after Napoleon was defeated the first time?'

'Zachary went back to the gaming tables. He seemed to be doing rather well for himself. Our paths separated. We met on occasion in the clubs, but for the most part we saw little of each other.'

'Is that when you first heard rumors of mysterious deaths in the polite world?'

'Yes, I suppose so. But I must admit that the occasional demise of an elderly lord or a rich widow did not arouse curiosity or interest in me or anyone else. I was busy with my career as a man of business and raising Anthony. There was little time to spare for idle speculation. Then Napoleon escaped from Elba and we were once again at war.'

'And Crackenburne summoned you back to your other profession,' she said.

'He also summoned Zachary. But this time Crackenburne did not ask me to give Elland his instructions. Elland and I were colleagues of a sort and we exchanged information, but we did not work together.'

'When did you become suspicious of him?'

'In the months following the victory at Waterloo, the series of suicides and accidents I mentioned occurred in a fairly short span of time. At that point I was on my way to establishing my new career as a private-inquiry agent. I began to notice some of the similar details of the deaths, as I told you.'

'And you eventually tracked down Zachary Elland,' she concluded.

'Yes. In the course of the investigation I showed the death's-head rings to Crackenburne. He remembered old rumors of a professional murderer who had once used the same signature. They called him the Memento-Mori Man. It was said that no one who met him and learned his true identity ever lived to tell the tale. Elland obviously had heard the stories and decided to pattern himself on a legend.'

'Tobias, listen to me. Elland's decision to become a professional murderer had nothing whatsoever to do with the work he did for you.'

'There was a note in the safe where I discovered the rings and the journal. It was addressed to me. In it Zachary said that if I found the letter it meant that I had won. He congratulated me as though I were the victor in a chess match.'

'Such villainy is almost incomprehensible.'

'In the note he informed me that I was a worthy opponent. The last line of the letter read, *It is the thrill of the hunt that I will miss the most.*'

'He was truly a monster.'

'I must tell you,' Tobias said in a low voice, 'there are times when I can comprehend his passion for the hunt all too well.'

'*Tobias.*'

'There is a very intense sensation that comes over me when I know that I have picked up the scent of the quarry. There is no denying that there is a certain dark thrill attached to the business.' He looked at her across the candle. In the light of flaring flame, his eyes glowed like those of some great beast of the night. 'Elland once told me that he thought the two of us had a great deal in common. He may have been right.'

'Stop it at once, Tobias.' She squeezed his arm very fiercely. 'Do not dare to suggest that you and Elland were alike in any way. To take satisfaction in the hunt is one thing. It is your nature to seek answers and to see that justice is done. It is quite another matter altogether to take pleasure in death. We both know that you could never do that.'

'Sometimes late at night, I have wondered if the difference between Elland and myself is only a matter of degree.'

'Damnation, Tobias, I will not abide such foolish talk. Do you hear me, sir?'

He smiled humorlessly. 'Yes, Mrs Lake, I hear you.'

'I never met your old acquaintance, but I can assure you that you and Zachary Elland are as different as night and day.'

'Are you quite certain of that, madam?' he asked much too softly.

'I am absolutely positive of that fact. My intuition, as you well know, is extremely keen.' She wanted to shake him. 'You are no killer, Tobias March.'

Tobias did not say a word, but his gaze was disconcertingly

steady. Belatedly, she thought about their last case, the one she had privately titled the Affair of the Mad Mesmerist in her journal.

She cleared her throat. 'Yes, well, there may have been one or two unfortunate incidents along the way over the years, but they were accidents, as it were.'

'Accidents,' Tobias repeated neutrally.

'No, *not* accidents,' she corrected instantly. 'Desperate acts of great bravery required to save the lives of others such as myself. Most definitely not cold-blooded murder. There is a vast difference, Tobias.' She drew a breath. 'Now, then, enough of that subject. Tell me where Aspasia Gray fits into this affair.'

'Aspasia?' He frowned. 'Did I not explain?'

'No, sir, you did not.'

'She was Zachary's lover.'

'Elland's lover. I see. That explains a few things, I suppose.'

'They met in the spring before Waterloo. Aspasia conceived a great passion for Elland, and he appeared equally enthralled by her. They made plans to wed. When Zachary returned to his work as a spy that summer, he used Aspasia's entrée in Society to obtain access to certain wealthy people. We believe that in addition to using the introductions to gather intelligence, he also took advantage of those opportunities to acquire some of his private clients.'

'Dear heaven.'

'One evening Aspasia stumbled onto the truth about how Elland made his living. In her horror, she fled from him. I have often wondered if the real reason he put the pistol to his head that night was not because I was closing in on him but because he had lost the woman he loved.'

'I find it rather difficult to believe that a killer would have such a romantic sensibility,' she muttered.

'The odd thing is that, in his own way, Elland's nature was both dramatic and romantic. He reminded me of an artist or poet who lusts after any experience that will provide him with the highest peaks of emotion and sensation.'

'Without regard to the price he must pay?'

'Elland never counted the cost. He lived for the next thrill.'

'What did Aspasia do after she learned he had taken his own life?'

'She was utterly distraught. It is the only time I have ever seen her in such a state. Elland was the only man she had ever truly loved, and she was inconsolable. It was not just the fact that he had taken his own life that wounded her so deeply.'

'It was that she had loved him and not seen the truth of his nature?'

'Yes. Aspasia is a woman of the world, as I'm sure you have guessed. She considered herself too intelligent and too strong-minded to be deceived in matters of love. Zachary's deception shook her to the core.'

She told herself that she ought to feel some sympathy for Aspasia, but every time she thought about how she had discovered the other woman with her arms around Tobias's neck, she found it impossible to summon up much pity.

Nevertheless, she had to admit, learning that one's lover was a professional killer who took such a degree of satisfaction in his work that he marked it with his personal signature was enough to give any woman, even Cleopatra, a bad case of nerves.

'I collect that you feel a sense of obligation in all this,' she said. 'And Mrs Gray is no doubt playing on that sensibility. Does she blame you for starting Elland down the path that led to his personal destruction?'

'She did not say as much aloud, but, yes, I suspect she does.'

'Rubbish,' she said again, very harshly this time. 'Absolute rubbish.'

'I think she also feels a measure of guilt, because she was the one who helped him achieve the connections in Society that led to certain murders.'

Lavinia sighed. 'What a sad tale.'

He opened his hand once more so that the candlelight flared on the small skull and crossbones. 'And now it would seem that someone is determined to retell it.'

'Surely you do not believe that Zachary Elland has come back from the grave to resume his career?'

'No, of course not. I myself found Elland's body, and I saw him buried. But this new killer sent a ring such as this to Aspasia, and I am quite certain that he intended for me to find this one tonight.'

'An old acquaintance announcing that he is back in town?'

'So it would seem. The discovery of the ring on her doorstep this morning threw Aspasia into a panic. That is why she followed us here.'

'Hmm.'

Tobias frowned. 'What is it?'

'I must tell you, sir, that Aspasia did not appear to be in a *panic* tonight.'

His mouth twisted wryly. 'She is hardly the type to succumb to a fit of the vapors. But I know her better than you do, and you may believe me when I tell you that her nerves were in a very rattled state tonight.'

'If you say so. Personally, I believe that she is attempting to use guilt as a means of manipulating you.'

'She has no need to go to such lengths to acquire my assistance in this matter, and I'm certain she is well aware of that.' Tobias pocketed the ring. 'No one wants to find this new Memento-Mori Man more than I do. He has thrown down the gauntlet and there is no time to waste.'

'You must allow me to help you, Tobias.'

'I do not want you anywhere near this case.'

'You have said it is imperative that you resolve this matter as soon as possible. You need all the assistance you can obtain. Furthermore, it is not as though I am an amateur at this sort of thing.'

'Bloody hell, Lavinia—'

She raised her hand to silence him. 'I would remind you that I am the only witness you have at the moment. Granted, I cannot give you a good description of the maid who accompanied Fullerton up here tonight, but I noticed some details that may be helpful.' Out of the corner of her eye she glimpsed a bit of white cloth in the deep shadow of a chimney. 'Well, well, what have we here?'

She took the candle from his hand and hurried toward the chimney.

Tobias took his foot down off the stone wall and followed her across the roof. 'What is it?'

'I'm not sure. But if it is what I believe it to be, we have our first clue.' She bent down and scooped up the object. 'Her cap.'

'Are you certain?' Tobias took the large, floppy cap from her hand and examined it carefully by the light of the candle. 'It looks like any other woman's cap to me.'

'Not quite. It has an unusually large brim and a ribbon. That is most certainly the one the blond maid was wearing. I would not be surprised to find a few blond hairs inside when we take a closer look in a strong light. Tobias, this proves that the new killer is a woman.'

Tobias studied the cap for a long moment. 'Or a man who wore women's clothes to disguise himself.'

Six

Downstairs they found Beaumont waiting for them in the library together with his butler, Drum, and a nervous little man who was introduced as Dr Hughes.

Beaumont appeared even shorter and rounder seated behind his vast desk. Tobias noticed that he had a glass in one hand. Half of the contents had already been consumed.

The spirits had clearly had a medicinal effect upon his nerves. He no longer seemed anxious or uncertain. His lordship was once more firmly in command of his household.

In response to Lavinia's inquiry, Drum informed them that no one employed on the regular household staff matched her description of the blond maid.

Lavinia brandished the cap. 'What of this, may I ask?' They all stared at the cap.

'I do not doubt that you did, indeed, see Fullerton with a woman,' Beaumont said to Lavinia. 'One of the village girls, perhaps. In any event, it is obvious that Fullerton had too much to drink, went in search of a willing wench, and found his way to the roof for a bit of dalliance. What happened next was an extremely unfortunate accident.' He glowered at the doctor. 'Is that not correct, Dr Hughes?'

'Indeed.' Hughes cleared his throat and made an attempt to sit a little taller in his chair. 'I have examined the body,' he announced gravely. 'There is no doubt in my mind that Fullerton was the victim of an accident.'

Tobias swore silently to himself. It was clear that Beaumont had decided to close the door on the subject of Fullerton's accident as swiftly as possible. He would not welcome any suggestion of murder.

Lavinia's brows snapped together. 'Sir, Mr March and I suspect that this *willing wench*, whoever she is, deliberately lured Fullerton up to the roof. We must see if there is anyone who can identify her.'

Beaumont beetled his brows at Drum.

The butler assumed an impassive air. 'As his lordship has indicated, the maid was likely one of the village girls taken on temporarily. She no doubt panicked when Lord Fullerton suffered his unfortunate accident and fled the castle before she could be questioned. She certainly had every incentive to disappear. After all, if word spread locally that she had been caught entertaining a gentleman alone on the roof, she would have an extremely difficult task finding other employment in the neighborhood.'

'It is also possible that she is still right here in the castle,' Lavinia said forcefully. 'We must assemble the entire staff as well as the guests and question them.'

Beaumont turned red. His mouth opened and closed several times before he finally managed to speak. 'Question the guests? Are you mad, Mrs Lake? You will do no such thing. I forbid it.'

'Sir, we may be talking about a matter of murder.'

'*Fullerton was not murdered*. It was an accident.'

'We have every reason to think—'

'Think what you wish, Mrs Lake. But this is my house and I will not allow my guests to be inconvenienced any more than they have been already.'

This approach would gain them nothing, Tobias thought. He looked at Beaumont. 'You agree that Fullerton was with a woman shortly before he fell but you do not think she had anything to do with his death?'

'The man was in his cups.' Beaumont took a hefty swallow of his brandy and lowered the glass. 'He lost his balance. That is the end of the matter. A great tragedy, but certainly not a case of murder.'

It was a pity that Beaumont had recovered from his earlier confusion and had acquired allies in the shape of his butler and the local doctor, Tobias thought. The situation was back under control so far as his lordship was concerned and he had reasserted his authority. One could hardly blame him for not wanting to acknowledge the scandalous possibility of murder. That sort of gossip could hang around for a very long time.

'Sir,' Tobias said evenly, 'allow me to tell you that in my professional opinion there are a number of questions relating to this affair that should be answered. With your permission, I would like to continue my inquiries into the matter.'

'That is quite impossible, March.' Beaumont slapped his palms flat on the desk and surged to his feet. 'This has gone far enough. There has already been entirely too much disruption in the household. Lady Beaumont is extremely overset.'

Lavinia tapped one toe on the carpet. Tobias could see the fulminating expression in her eyes. He tried to signal her but she ignored his silent warning.

'Lady Beaumont's concerns are quite understandable, sir,' she said briskly, 'but as we have just explained, we may well be dealing with a matter of murder. Surely, under the circumstances, a few discreet questions are warranted. They will pose no great inconvenience to your guests.'

'For the last time, I have determined that this is not a matter of murder.' Beaumont bristled. 'And I will be the judge of what constitutes an inconvenience to my guests, madam.'

'Sir, I really must insist that you allow us to investigate,' Lavinia said. 'I assure you that we have had experience in this sort of thing and—'

Beaumont reacted very much as Tobias had anticipated. His lordship exploded.

'You insist?' Beaumont's round face turned an unsightly shade of purple. 'You *insist*, Mrs Lake? Who do you think you are, madam?'

Tobias exhaled deeply and prepared himself for the inevitable. And she had the nerve to accuse him of not being sufficiently diplomatic with clients, he thought.

'It is not your place to insist upon anything in this household,' Beaumont roared. 'Not to put too fine a point on it, madam, but neither you nor Mr March would even be here tonight were it not for the fact that I was induced to repay an old favor to Lord Vale.'

'I quite understand, sir,' Lavinia said hastily. 'Indeed, it was very kind of you to extend the invitation to your house party. I can assure you that Mr March and I have enjoyed ourselves immensely. Everything has been most elegant. Admittedly, my bedchamber is rather small and inadequately furnished, but I suspect that was merely an oversight.'

'What's this?' Beaumont's eyes bulged. 'Now you wish to complain of the size of your bedchamber?'

'Do not concern yourself, sir. I am certain that it was not your fault that I was removed from a perfectly satisfactory bedchamber on the second floor and sent upstairs to a room that is considerably less desirable.' She waved that aside. 'It will do for the short time we are here. Now, then, regarding our theories about events tonight—'

Beaumont gripped the edge of his desk with both pudgy hands and leaned forward in the manner of a bull preparing to charge. 'It occurs to me, madam, that as you and March appear to be obsessed with your bizarre theories of foul play, you will doubtless be unable to enjoy the remainder of your stay here.'

'It is kind of you to concern yourself with our pleasure, sir, but there is no need. We shall manage nicely, I'm sure.'

'I don't see how that will be possible,' Beaumont growled. 'Both of you no doubt wish to return to London as soon as possible.'

'No, really—'

'Drum will send a maid and a footman to each of your bedchambers first thing in the morning to assist you in your packing. Your carriage will be waiting for you at nine. On second thought, let's make that eight-thirty. It is a long trip back to Town. I'm sure you'll want to set out early.'

Lavinia stared at him for a few seconds, mute with shock. And then outrage leaped in her eyes. Her lips parted.

'Excellent suggestion, sir,' Tobias said before Lavinia could speak. He crossed to her side, clamped a hand around her arm, and drew her toward the door. 'Come, Mrs Lake. We had best go upstairs and see to our travel preparations.'

For a few seconds he thought that she would not follow his lead. He tightened his fingers around her arm in silent warning.

'Yes, of course.' She gave Beaumont a steely smile. 'Good night, sir. I do hope that there are no more *accidents* among your guests after we take our leave. Heavens, only consider the possible effects of another such incident. Why, you and your lady might find that your house parties were not quite so fashionable in the future if it got around that guests are inclined to suffer unexplained *accidents* while attending your affairs.'

Tobias winced, but it was too late. The damage had been done.

Beaumont's whiskers twitched in fury. 'How dare you, madam? If you are implying for one moment that I am deliberately attempting to conceal an act of murder—'

'That is certainly open to question, is it not?' Lavinia shot back much too smoothly.

'Enough,' Tobias said in her ear. He looked at Beaumont. 'You must make allowances for her, sir. I fear Fullerton's death has shattered her nerves. You are quite right. It is best that I take her home to London as soon as possible. Never fear, we will be on our way first thing in the morning.'

Beaumont was somewhat mollified. 'Mrs Lake is obviously quite overwrought. I'm sure she will feel much more herself when she is back in her own home.'

Tobias sensed Lavinia preparing a scathing response to that observation. Fortunately, he had got her as far as the door. He managed to haul her through it and out into the corridor before she could add any more fuel to the flames.

He could feel her vibrating with outrage on his arm. The air around her almost sizzled.

'Correct me if I am mistaken,' she said, 'but I believe that Beaumont just tossed us out of the castle.'

'Your observation concurs with my own. So much for our jolly little outing in the country. Perhaps you and I were not made for such fashionable entertainments, madam.'

Seven

They started up the main staircase in silence.

'I suppose you feel that it is my fault that we have been asked to leave,' Lavinia said on the first landing.

'Yes, but you need not concern yourself overmuch with the matter. As it happens, I had already concluded that it would be best to return to London.'

She glanced at him, astonished. 'But what of our investigation here at the scene of the crime?'

'I believe we have already learned as much as we can here. The killer has completed his work. I doubt he will hang around for long. I would not be surprised if he has already left the neighborhood.'

'Mmm. I take your point. He planned for Fullerton's death to take place here because he knew that you would be in the immediate vicinity, did he not? He wanted to make certain that you were aware of his handiwork.'

'I suspect that is the case,' Tobias said.

They emerged on Lavinia's floor and found a small gathering in the narrow hall. Two women of indeterminate years, garbed in chintz wrappers and voluminous nightcaps, stood talking animatedly to a man who appeared to be in his early twenties. It was obvious that Fullerton's death was the topic of conversation.

'Some of my neighbors on this floor,' Lavinia explained in low tones as they walked toward the group. 'Lady Oakes's hairdresser, Mr Pierce, and two ladies who are here as companions to two of Beaumont's guests.'

All three heads turned toward Lavinia and Tobias. Avid curiosity glittered in each pair of eyes, but there was something particularly penetrating about the gazes of the two women, Tobias noticed. They were staring at him with an oddly riveted, albeit slightly dazed expression.

Even if he had not been warned by Lavinia, he would have had no difficulty determining the role of these two, he thought. Both possessed the resigned, self-effacing, slightly faded quality one associated with impoverished ladies who have been obliged to undertake careers as professional companions.

Tobias suspected that the women had gone to bed early this evening. Their posts had likely excluded them from the evening's festivities. Companions generally found themselves in the same peculiar, uncomfortable, in-between world as governesses. They were not servants, but neither were they the social equals of those they served. The combination of gentle breeding and poverty had doomed them to a profession in which they were expected to keep silent and remain discreetly in the background.

It occurred to him that this late-night gossip about violent death was probably the most exciting thing that had happened to this pair in some time.

He had met only two companions in his entire life who did not fit the usual mold of the species, he reflected: Lavinia and her niece, Emeline. They had not remained in the profession for long, and with good reason. Neither of them possessed a temperament that was suited to such a career.

'Mrs Lake!' the hairdresser exclaimed. 'We were just speaking of you. We feared that perhaps you had been overcome by the ghastly sight down below in the garden. Are you all right? Do you need a vinaigrette?'

'I am fine, thank you, Mr Pierce.' Lavinia gave him a reassuring smile and then looked at the women. 'You must allow me to introduce you. Miss Richards, Miss Gilway, this is my friend, Mr March.'

Tobias inclined his head. 'My pleasure, ladies.'

They both blushed furiously.

'Mr March.' Miss Gilway beamed.

'Sir,' Miss Richards whispered.

'And this is Mr Pierce.' Lavinia swept her hand out in a gracefully dramatic gesture, as if heralding the arrival of a noted actor on stage. 'He is the one responsible for Lady Oakes's enchanting headdress this evening. Surely you recall it, sir?'

'Can't say that I do,' Tobias admitted.

'Tier after tier of the most intricately fashioned curls piled high in the front?' She held her hands above her forehead in a little pyramid shape to demonstrate. 'The chignon in back, braided and coiled with more curls across the top? I vow, Lady Oakes looked very impressive.'

'Uh, certainly.' He had no recollection at all of Lady Oakes's headdress this evening, but he nodded once at Pierce. 'Striking.'

'Thank you, sir.' Pierce made a deep bow and assumed a demeanor of artistic modesty. 'It came out rather well, I thought. The row of curls at the top of the chignon and the loop around the coil are my own inventions. I consider it my signature.'

'Mmm.'

Lavinia smiled. 'I was delayed returning to my bedchamber because Mr March and I felt the need to make a few inquiries into Lord Fullerton's accident.'

'I see.' Pierce regarded Tobias with a brief, considering look. 'Yes, I recall that you did mention that you and your associate occasionally engaged in a rather odd hobby. Something to do with taking commissions for private inquiries, I believe. But, really, you should not have subjected yourself to such a shocking scene, madam. That sort of thing can give a delicate lady such as yourself nightmares.'

The hairdresser's concern for Lavinia was irritating. It occurred to Tobias that Pierce was one of those men whom young ladies such as Emeline and her friend Priscilla described as so *terribly romantic looking*.

He was no expert on such matters, he conceded silently, but he was fairly certain that the seemingly negligent arrangement of the curls that tumbled so artlessly over Pierce's forehead was no random act of nature. Several of Anthony's acquaintances currently affected a very similar style. Anthony had explained that he had avoided it primarily because it required the use of a dangerously hot curling iron and extended periods of time in front of a mirror.

Pierce appeared to have been interrupted in the act of getting ready for bed. He wore a frilled white shirt and a pair of stylishly pleated trousers. A dashing black ribbon was knotted carelessly around his neck in the tradition set by Byron and the romantic poets. It did little to veil the expanse of bare skin that was exposed in the opening provided by the unfastened shirt.

'What sort of inquiries did you and Mr March make?' Miss Gilway asked without taking her eyes off Tobias.

'We tried to ascertain that there had been no foul play,' Lavinia said.

'*Foul play*.' Miss Richards shared a look of delighted horror with her friend. 'Never say it was *murder*?'

'Heavens.' The second woman fanned herself with her hand. 'How perfectly dreadful. Who would have thought it?'

'Murder.' Pierce stared at Lavinia. 'Are you quite serious, Mrs Lake?'

It dawned on Tobias that he had seen that same fascinated expression on Anthony's face. It was the reflection of a young man's enthusiasm for all matters macabre.

'According to Lord Beaumont and the local doctor, it could not possibly have been a case of murder,' Lavinia said neutrally.

'Oh.' Pierce's excitement evaporated.

The two companions appeared equally disappointed.

'Thank goodness,' Miss Gilway said politely.

'Such a relief,' Miss Richards added in a dutiful tone. 'One would hate to think that there was a murderer running about Beaumont Castle.'

They both returned to gazing fixedly at Tobias.

'Indeed,' Lavinia said. 'There is no great cause for concern. I'm sure you will all be quite safe in your beds tonight. Don't you agree, Tobias?'

'Yes.' He took her arm. 'Allow me to see you to your door. The hour grows late, and we must leave early in the morning.'

'You are going back to London tomorrow?' Miss Gilway asked quickly. 'Why so soon?'

'Personal business,' Lavinia said coolly. She smiled at the three. 'I will say my farewells now, as you will all no doubt be asleep when I depart.'

'I wish you a very pleasant journey, madam.' Pierce made another graceful little bow. 'And remember what I said earlier this evening when you went downstairs to the ball. I would be delighted to take you on as a client. I feel I could do wonders with your hair.'

'Thank you, Mr Pierce, I will bear that in mind.' She hooked her hand under Tobias's arm and then hesitated. 'By the by, speaking of the business of hairdressing, I have a question for you, sir.'

'I am at your service, madam,' Pierce said gallantly. 'Would this question by any chance be in regard to the events of this evening?'

'Just a minor point,' she assured him. 'In your career you are required to have a great expertise with wigs and false hair and the like, are you not?'

'Every fashionable young lady simply must possess a false chignon or two at the very least,' he said in a voice that rang with absolute conviction. 'After a certain age it is imperative that a woman invest in a variety of full wigs. There is simply no alternative available if she wishes to remain in style.'

'You watched the guests go downstairs to the costume ball tonight. Did you by any chance spot any ladies wearing blond wigs?'

'Blond?' Pierce gave a shudder. 'Good God, no, madam, I did not. Indeed, I should have been positively horrified if I had seen such a sight.'

Tobias scowled. 'Why the devil would you have been shocked? You just said no fashionable woman should be without a couple of wigs.'

'Yes, but not *blond* ones.' Pierce raised his eyes to the heavens, evidently seeking to be delivered from such stupid inquiries. 'Really, sir, it is obvious that you know nothing of style. Allow me to inform you that when it comes to wigs, switches, puffs, and the like, blond hair is very nearly as unfashionable as red.'

There was a short, heavy silence. Everyone looked at Lavinia. Her very red hair gleamed in the light of the wall sconce.

It occurred to Tobias that the hairdresser had just insulted her. He fixed Pierce with a hard look.

'I happen to think that Mrs Lake's hair suits her perfectly,' he said quietly.

Although he had not raised his voice, Miss Richards and Miss Gilway both flinched. Each took a step back. They were still staring at him, but not with the same peculiar interest they had been displaying. Now they looked as though he had turned into a ravening beast before their eyes.

'Tobias,' Lavinia hissed in a low voice, 'stop this at once.'

He was in no mood to stop. He was annoyed. It had been a long, extremely difficult evening.

Pierce seemed oblivious to the fact that he was in some danger. His attention was concentrated on Lavinia.

'Madam, you really must allow me to pay you a visit after we all return to London,' he urged with what appeared to be genuine concern. 'There is so much I could do with you. I vow, you would look splendid in a dark brown wig. Such a dramatic contrast with your green eyes.'

Lavinia frowned and raised a hand to touch her hair. 'Do you really think so?'

'There is no doubt about it.' Pierce folded one arm across his chest, propped his elbow on it, and stroked his chin in a thoughtful manner. He contemplated Lavinia in the manner of a sculptor studying a half-completed statue. 'I can envision the results, and they would be astounding, I assure you. I believe I would use some puffs and a bit of frizzing to add height, of course. You lack the stature required for true elegance.'

'Bloody hell,' Tobias growled. 'Mrs Lake is just the right size, as far as I am concerned.'

Pierce spared him only a fleeting look that somehow managed to sum up every aspect of his appearance and dismiss him out of hand.

The *Cut Direct*, Tobias thought, grimly amused. From a hairdresser, no less.

'Indeed, sir,' Pierce murmured, 'you are hardly an authority on fashion, so you are in no position to judge Mrs Lake's potential.'

Tobias contemplated the pleasure of ripping Pierce's head off his shoulders, but he reluctantly abandoned the prospect when he felt Lavinia's fingers clench very tightly around his elbow. She was right, he thought. It would be a messy project, and the hour grew late.

'You are so kind to give me your professional opinion, Mr Pierce.' Lavinia smiled her brightest, most polished smile. 'I shall consider your offer.'

'Allow me to give you my card.' Pierce whipped one out of the pocket of his trousers and presented it to her with a flourish. 'Please feel free to send word to that address when you are ready to move to a higher plane of elegance and style. I shall be delighted to fit you into my schedule.'

'Thank you.' Lavinia took the card and inclined her head in farewell to Miss Richards and Miss Gilway. 'Good night. I trust you will all have a safe journey home.'

There was a small chorus of farewells. Pierce retreated to his bedchamber. Miss Gilway and Miss Richards retired to the room they shared.

Tobias and Lavinia continued down the hall.

'Why are you glowering so, sir?' Lavinia opened the door of her bedchamber, stepped into the room, and turned to face him. 'I vow, you put me in mind of an oncoming storm.'

Tobias glanced back along the now vacant hall, thinking about the conversation that had just transpired. 'Your question to Pierce concerning a blond wig was very astute. It raised some interesting possibilities.'

'Thank you.' She did not trouble to hide her pleasure in the small compliment. 'Of course, if blond wigs are so very unfashionable, it stands to reason that the killer would not have purchased one that would stand out in the memory of possible witnesses. Therefore, perhaps it is safe to assume that the murderer is, indeed, a woman who possesses very vivid blond hair.'

'On the contrary, I think we can conclude precisely the opposite.'

'I beg your pardon?'

'Consider it closely, Lavinia. The killer's yellow hair seems to have been his most striking feature. That and the very large cap are the two things that made the strongest impression upon you when you saw the maid in the hall, correct?'

'Yes, but—' She broke off, eyes widening in comprehension. 'I understand. You believe the murderer intended those two features to be the most memorable in the event that he was seen by a witness?'

He nodded. 'The Memento-Mori Man's stock-in-trade was a gift for misdirection. If this new killer has patterned himself on such a master, he will favor the same strategy. Therefore, I think we can assume that the blond hair was false. And I am also certain that the female attire was meant to conceal a man.'

She hesitated. 'I do not feel that we can assume the murderer is a man. But I do agree that there is a strong likelihood the blond hair was a wig.'

'It is a starting point, at least.' He wrapped one hand around the door frame and considered. 'If blond wigs are so unfashionable, they will be uncommon in the shops. There cannot be that many wig-makers in London. We should be able to discover which ones sold yellow false hair in recent months.'

'Do not be so sure of that. It is true that any wig-maker who took a commission for a wig in such an unfashionable shade would no doubt remember his client well. But I fear that we cannot depend upon locating the shop. The wig may have been commissioned somewhere other than London. A great many fashionable ladies and gentlemen obtain their wigs in Paris. There is also the possibility that the false hair was stolen from a theater or taken from an actor's trunk. A search for the particular wig-maker who created the killer's false hair could well prove to be a complete waste of time.'

'Nevertheless, the blond wig is a clue, and at the moment it is one of the few in our possession.'

She did not quarrel with that conclusion, but her brows knitted in thought. 'Tobias, is it merely the fact that the killer may have worn false hair that makes you believe we are dealing with a man? Because I really do not think we should depend too heavily upon that. We might overlook valuable evidence if we ignore the possibility that it was a woman I saw with Fullerton tonight.'

He gripped the door frame tightly. 'There is more to it than the business with the wig.'

'Is it so difficult for you to imagine a woman as a professional murderess?'

'Not entirely. It is the matter of the memento-mori ring that convinces me we are hunting a man,' he said quietly. 'The signature is far too deliberately reminiscent of Zachary Elland's work.'

'What of it? A woman might wish to emulate him.'

He shook his head, uncertain how to shore up with logic what he intuitively felt had to be true. 'It seems more likely that a man would seek to compare himself to another man.'

'Ah, yes,' she said with a wise air. 'I have noticed that men are inclined to be intensely competitive. They do love their horse races and boxing matches and wagers, do they not?'

He raised a brow at that. 'Pray do not try to tell me that women lack the competitive instinct. I have seen the gentle warfare that is conducted in the ballrooms of the polite world during the Season. It is no secret that a matchmaking mama is capable of a degree of plotting and strategy that would incite awe and admiration in Wellington himself.'

To his surprise she did not smile. Instead, she inclined her head in somber acknowledgment of that observation.

'The business of marriage warrants extreme attention and sober planning. After all, a woman's entire future as well as the future of whatever children she may bear is at stake.'

'Huh. I suppose I had not thought of it in quite such dramatic terms.'

'In my experience, men rarely do contemplate marriage in such *dramatic* terms.'

He frowned, aware from her tone that he might have missed

something, but before he could demand further explanations, Lavinia raised a hand to pat a tiny yawn.

'I really do not think that I can give this case the serious contemplation it requires tonight,' she said. 'I suggest we save this discussion for the morrow. It is a long drive back to town. We will have a great deal of time to talk.'

'Do not remind me.' He gazed thoughtfully down the long hall.

'Good night, Tobias.'

'One question before I leave.'

'Yes?'

'Is it the fashion among hairdressers to wear their shirts half unfastened in front of respectable ladies?'

Lavinia chuckled. 'Hairdressers are artists, sir. They are entitled to set their own fashion.'

'Huh.'

She stepped back and started to ease the door closed. Her eyes gleamed with amusement in the shadows. 'You need not concern yourself with the delicate sensibilities of either Miss Richards or Miss Gilway. Although the vision of Mr Pierce in dishabille was no doubt one of the most stimulating sights they have seen in years, I must point out that you yourself gave them a great deal to admire as well.'

He realized she was gazing pointedly at his chest.

'What the devil?'

He glanced down and was startled to see that his shirt was unfastened several inches. It had no doubt come undone in the course of the few minutes he and Lavinia spent together before Fullerton so dramatically interrupted their tryst. He now comprehended all too well the curious, veiled looks Miss Richards and Miss Gilway had cast in his direction.

'Hell's teeth,' he muttered.

'I do believe that together, you and Mr Pierce have provided Miss Richards and Miss Gilway with enough inspiration for conversation and speculation to last them for months,' Lavinia said.

She chuckled and closed the door very gently in his face.

He released his grip on the door frame and walked back toward the staircase, brooding on the disaster that the country-house party had become. It had all seemed like such a brilliant notion back at the start, he reflected. But just about everything that could go wrong had gone wrong. Even his left leg, which had been behaving rather well for the past month thanks to the warm, sunny weather, ached a little now. Too much running up and down staircases this evening, no doubt.

He had not even managed the one event he'd planned for with such optimism and enthusiasm: an uninterrupted night in a comfortable bed with Lavinia.

In point of fact, he could not even retire to his own bed yet. There was something else he had to do first.

He made his way downstairs and found that all was once again quiet on this floor. The guests had returned to their bedchambers and the house was settling once more for what remained of the night.

A pair of wall sconces lit the path to Aspasia's door. In front of her room he stopped, hesitating for a second or two. Then he rapped softly.

She opened the door at once, as though she had been waiting for him. Her green satin wrapper swirled around her ankles. Ill-concealed anxiety shadowed her eyes. Tension tightened her full mouth.

'Well?' she whispered.

He looked at her, a part of him realizing that she was probably the most beautiful woman he had ever met, and he was suddenly very tired. He also understood that this was a weariness that was too deep to be cured by a few hours of sleep. It would haunt him until this brush with the past was finished.

Absently, he rubbed the back of his neck. 'Your conclusions are correct. Someone has, indeed, reinvented himself as the Memento-Mori Man. Whoever he is, he was here tonight.'

She clutched the edges of her satin robe at her throat. 'Fullerton?'

'Yes. I found a ring in the bedchamber.'

She squeezed her eyes shut briefly. When she opened them, he could see the fear that even she, with all her worldly skills and experience, could not hide.

'He staged this murder deliberately for your benefit, didn't he?' she asked. 'He knew that you would be here tonight. He wanted to make certain that you understood he was back.'

Irritation sparked through him. 'Do not say that. Elland is not back from the dead.'

'Of course. I know that.' She sighed. 'I should not have spoken so carelessly. Forgive me. I have been possessed by chills and the most dreadful nervous sensations since my housekeeper brought me that little box with the ring in it this morning. I fear the combination has left me somewhat muddleheaded.'

He should not have snapped at her, he thought. She was an intelligent, strong-willed woman, but she had gone through a great deal because of Zachary Elland three years ago. Now it seemed she would have to go through it all again. So would he.

'Someone has made certain that we are aware there is now a new Memento-Mori Man,' he said quietly. 'Very well, the message has been received. I will hunt him down, just as I did Elland.'

She gave him a tremulous smile. 'Thank you, Tobias. I know I can depend upon you. I only wish I had realized that three years ago instead of allowing myself to be blinded by Zachary's charm.'

He did not want to hear any more of this conversation, he thought. He stepped back from the door. 'Get some rest, Aspasia. I must leave early in the morning, but I will meet you again in London.'

She frowned. 'Why are you departing so soon?'

There was no need to explain that Lavinia had managed to get them both ejected from the castle, he decided. He had to consider the professional image of Lake & March.

'I have done all I can here,' he said coolly. 'I must return to Town to continue my investigation. Time is of the essence.'

'Yes, of course.' She hesitated, making no move to close the door. 'Tobias, I meant what I said a moment ago. I truly wish that I had understood the great difference between you and Zachary three years ago. I assure you, I am a far wiser woman now. I have learned much in the time we have been apart. I know that you, too, must have some regrets about what happened in the past. Do you want to come in and talk for a while?'

The invitation could not have been more plain if she had had it engraved on fine paper, he thought. She was asking him to join her in her bed.

'I do not think that would be a good idea,' he said. 'The hour grows late and I must rise very early. Good night, Aspasia.'

She smiled somewhat wistfully. 'Yes, of course. I understand. I am happy that you have found someone you care about, Tobias.'

He walked away from her door. It closed softly in the shadows behind him.

At the foot of the staircase he paused. The sensible thing to do was to continue along the corridor to his own room. If he was unable to sleep, he could spend the time packing.

He stood there for a while longer. There was no one else about. He heard no footsteps on the stairs. Evidently the violent death earlier had squelched some of the guests' enthusiasm for night games.

After another few seconds of close contemplation, he changed his mind about the wisdom of returning to his bedchamber. He went up the stairs to Lavinia's floor and walked along the hall to her door. He would knock very, very softly, he decided. If she did not answer, he would assume that she had gone to sleep. He would do the gentlemanly thing and go back to his own room.

He rapped once, lightly.

The door opened a few inches. Lavinia smiled at him through the narrow opening. She had changed into a long, white cotton nightgown. A dainty froth of white lace framed her throat.

He felt his blood heat at the sight of her.

'It occurred to me,' he said, moving through the doorway, 'that the night need not be completely wasted.'

'An excellent thought.' She closed the door and turned to face him.

She had taken down her hair. In the glow of the candle, the loosened tresses were a fiery nimbus around her intelligent, intriguing face. Her eyes were pools of sensual mystery.

She smiled the slow, secret smile that never failed to make everything inside him clench as tight as a fist.

He pulled her into his arms. When her mouth met his, the fires leaped between them. He experienced the same sensation that always came over him when he held her like this. *She had been meant for him*. He did not have to restrain himself with her. He did not have to tread warily for fear of frightening her. Lavinia's passions were as strong and fierce as his own.

She was different from any other woman he had ever known. With her he could take the risk of allowing her to get close to that part of him that he had spent a lifetime concealing and controlling.

He picked her up and carried her to the small bed. He set her down on the quilts and paused only long enough to strip off his clothing.

When he was ready she smiled at him and raised her arms to welcome him.

His own personal mesmerist, he thought. The only one who could put him in a trance.

'Lavinia.'

He settled himself between her soft, warm thighs, caught her wrists in both of his hands and anchored them gently on either side of her head. The aching urgency pounded through him.

He bent his head and kissed her throat.

'Sometimes I want you so much it is a wonder I do not go up in flames,' he whispered.

'Oh, Tobias, do you not understand? When you burn, I burn too.'

The need flared within him.

He released one of her wrists and reached down to ease the night-gown out of his way. He drew his palm up the silken skin of her inner thigh. When he reached his goal, he found her warm and already damp. The scent of her body acted like a drug on his senses.

He touched her. She sucked in her breath and stirred sinuously beneath him. Her free hand clutched his bare shoulders, fingers digging into his skin. Impatiently she tried to get her other wrist loose, but he kept it pinned gently to the bed.

'Not yet,' he murmured against her breast. 'First tell me how you want me to touch you.'

'You are touching me precisely how I want you to touch me.' She caught her breath. 'Indeed, you always seem to know just how to do it.'

He drew his fingertips a little higher, pressing the little nubbin back into its tiny sheath. 'Perhaps it would be better if I did this.'

She moaned and raised her hips a little off the bed. 'Oh, yes. That is perfect.'

'What about this?' He slid a finger inside her and pushed upward.

'*Tobias*.'

'I collect that is better yet?'

'Yes.' She gasped and moved urgently against his hand. 'Better than perfect.'

He started to remove his finger. Tiny muscles clenched.

'No.' She sounded breathless now. 'No, I want you to touch me like that again.'

'Tell me exactly how you want it.'

She threaded her fingers through his hair and forced his head down to her breast. 'You know how I want it. You are the only one who knows. Touch me, Tobias.'

The command set fire to his blood.

'Anything to oblige a lady.' He took one nipple into his mouth and simultaneously eased his finger back inside. He pushed once more against the upper wall of her snug passage.

She mumbled thickly, twisting beneath him, and struggled once again to free her right wrist. She was strong, he thought. So much stronger than she appeared.

'Not yet,' he muttered. 'I want to feel you come apart in my hands.'

'*Tobias*.'

He probed deeper, harder. She cried out softly. Her eyes squeezed shut.

He stroked her until she was tight and desperate, and only then did he release her other wrist. She grabbed him to her, wrapping her legs around his waist.

He thrust himself into her hot passage.

She convulsed around him with another soft cry. The small pulses triggered his own climax. It swept through him like some invisible storm.

Together they fell into the whirlpool.

A long time later, he roused himself from the sweet, heavy lethargy that had stolen over him in the wake of passion. The cot was, indeed, too small for the two of them, but he was not inclined to complain.

The scent of their lovemaking hung in the air, ripe and potent. He knew that he would forever associate it with her.

She lay languidly on top of him, her head pillowed against his shoulder, her hair spilling across his chest. Her nightgown was bunched up around her waist. The candle had burned low, but there was enough light left to reveal the rounded contours of her bare hips and thighs.

He stroked the length of her spine with the flat of his palm all the way down to the soft curve of her buttocks.

'Asleep?' he asked softly.

'No,' she mumbled.

'I love you,' he whispered. 'Whatever else happens, do not ever forget that.'

She stirred, raised her head, and kissed him softly on his mouth. 'I love you also, Tobias. Whatever else happens, do not forget that.'

He threaded his fingers through her tumbled hair. 'I will not, my sweet.'

It was as though they had taken their own private vows, he thought.

He shifted, reluctant to leave the warm bed. 'I should return to my room.'

She smiled at him. The mysteries in her eyes deepened. She moved her hand deliberately down his stomach. Her fingers closed around him.

'Do you really want to spend what little is left of this night sleeping?' she asked.

He felt himself stir and harden.

'It occurs to me that it is a long drive back to Town,' he said against her throat. 'We will have plenty of time for a refreshing nap.'

Eight

The miniature volcano erupted with a high-pitched hiss of escaping vapor. There was a crackle from the interior of the little mountain, and sparks shot from the top.

The audience gasped in appreciation. The lecturer, a spindly gnome of a man named Horace Kirk, took a step forward and made a small bow. When he straightened, he beamed at the crowd that filled the hall.

'And thus ends my lecture on the nature of hot vapors,' he said. 'My talk next week will concern the principles of electricity.'

A burst of applause filled the room.

Emeline, seated in the second row between Anthony and Priscilla, clapped along with everyone else.

Priscilla could scarcely contain her enthusiasm. She regarded the gnome as though he were one of the dashing romantic poets.

'Was that not the most astonishing experiment you have ever witnessed?' she whispered to Emeline beneath the cover of applause. 'I vow, Mr Kirk's lectures have opened up a new world to me.'

'Very interesting,' Emeline agreed. Privately she conceded that she was far more intrigued by the subject of antiquities than she was by the wonders of electricity and chemistry, but she had to admit the demonstration that had just concluded was quite exciting. 'I must tell you that when you suggested we subscribe to Mr Kirk's series of science lectures, I feared they would prove somewhat dull. But that is certainly not the case. Don't you agree, Anthony?'

'I certainly do,' Anthony said with genuine appreciation. 'It was an excellent notion, Priscilla.' He glanced at the small journal on her lap. 'I see you managed to fill several more pages with notes again today.'

Priscilla clutched the journal to her bosom and gave Professor Kirk another enraptured glance. 'I have learned so much from these lectures. I only wish that I could convince Mama to allow me to purchase some instruments and equipment. I would give anything to be able to set up a proper laboratory where I could conduct experiments. But she refuses to even consider the notion.'

Emeline was not surprised by that news. She had no difficulty whatsoever imagining Lady Wortham's horrified reaction to the idea of Priscilla setting up a laboratory.

Lady Wortham took her responsibilities as a mother quite seriously. Her chief ambition in life was to see her daughter married to a respectable gentleman from a good family, preferably one who was in line to inherit a comfortable fortune. To that end she had a great deal to work with, Emeline thought, because Priscilla was a very attractive young woman.

True, her friend's hair was a shade of molten gold that was not considered to be in the first stare of fashion, but Emeline thought the color complemented her blue eyes quite effectively. She also knew that she was not alone in that opinion. Priscilla certainly never lacked for dancing partners at the balls and soirees they attended together. Regardless of the prevailing views of those who set the fashion, it was clear that any number of gentlemen were attracted to ladies with blond hair.

Not that her friend did not possess a number of other fine attributes. In addition to a kind, charming manner, Priscilla was endowed with pretty, delicate features and a gracefully full, rounded figure.

It was unfortunate, in Emeline's private opinion, that Lady Wortham insisted that her daughter dress only in pink. The color did not particularly suit her.

But as far as Emeline was concerned, her companion's best features were her intelligence, good humor, and common sense. Those were the factors that had allowed a genuine friendship to blossom between the two of them.

By rights they should have viewed each other as rivals, Emeline thought. Their acquaintance had been fostered and encouraged originally by Lady Wortham for less than altruistic reasons. Priscilla's matchmaking mama liked the notion of her daughter going about with Emeline because she believed that her offspring's looks were set off to advantage by the contrast between the two young women.

Emeline was well-aware that her chief claim to fashion was her thick, dark hair. In other respects, she knew very well that she did not meet the demands of true connoisseurs of style. She was too tall and too slender and her personality was much too forthright. The last was no accident. She had deliberately patterned herself after her aunt. Lavinia rarely bothered to veil her intelligence, nor did she hesitate to state her opinions.

'After all those explosive demonstrations, I believe I feel the need of some cooling ice cream,' Anthony announced, getting to his feet. 'Can I persuade the two of you to join me?'

'You will not have to ask me a second time,' Emeline assured him. 'It is very warm in this hall, is it not?'

'Ice cream sounds wonderful,' Priscilla said. 'It is rather hot in here. I had not noticed until this moment.'

Emeline laughed. 'That is because you were too occupied with the wonders of Professor Kirk's demonstrations.'

Anthony stood back to allow Emeline and Priscilla to go ahead of him down the aisle toward the front of the hall. The crowd thickened briefly as several people left their seats at the same time and made for the doors.

When the path cleared a moment later, Emeline caught sight of the man who lounged with negligent ease, one shoulder propped against the wall. A disturbing sensation went around her. This was not the first time Dominic Hood had materialized in the vicinity of herself and her companions in the past few days.

'Bloody hell,' Anthony muttered behind her. 'Hood is here.'

Priscilla was the only one who was unabashedly delighted to see him. 'I did not know that Mr Hood was interested in science.'

'What an astounding surprise,' Anthony growled.

'Calm yourself,' Emeline said in low tones. 'I do not know why it is that you and Mr Hood have taken such a dislike to each other, but I do not want any awkward scenes today. Is that understood?'

'What occurred yesterday at the museum was not my fault.'

'Mr Hood may have started things off on the wrong foot when he gave us his opinion of that statue of Hercules and the Hydra, but you, sir, made matters a good deal worse when you informed him that he knew nothing about art.'

'I merely spoke the truth,' Anthony said, icily virtuous. 'Hood has no eye for art or antiquities.'

'That may be true, but it was very poor manners to tell him so to his face.'

'He should have kept his remarks about the statue to himself. I wonder if he will prove to be as ignorant about science?'

'I am serious, Anthony. There will be no scenes. Do you understand?'

He smiled coldly in a way that was uncomfortably reminiscent of Mr March.

'I give you my word that I will not start a public quarrel,' he said.

There was no time to pin him down on the details of that too-precisely phrased promise, because they had almost reached the door. Emeline busied herself tying her bonnet strings. She used the moment to study Dominic Hood more closely, wondering again what it was that had created such immediate hostility between him and Anthony. In her opinion, they should have been instant friends, she thought. On the surface, they appeared to have a great deal in common. Dominic was the same age as Anthony, who had turned twenty-two last month. They were also of a similar height and both were endowed with lean, athletic frames.

They shared a sense of style too, she thought. The coat Dominic wore was remarkably similar to Anthony's, dark blue and cut to emphasize his shoulders. Their pleated trousers and patterned waistcoats were almost identical. They both had handsome fobs attached to their pocket watches and intricate knots tied in their snowy white cravats.

It was true that Dominic appeared to possess the sort of resources that enabled him to patronize a more expensive tailor, but the overall effect was nearly identical to the effect that Anthony's tailor achieved. Perhaps that was because neither man depended on his clothes for the impression he made, Emeline thought. Each of them radiated a certain forcefulness of personality that would have been obvious even if both dressed in rags.

At that moment Dominic straightened away from the wall and inclined his head to Priscilla and Emeline.

'Ladies,' he said, 'what a pleasure to see you here today. You are both in excellent looks.'

'Mr Hood.' Priscilla glowed. 'You did not mention that you would be attending Professor Kirk's lecture today.'

'Science is a hobby of mine,' he said laconically. His eyes met Anthony's. There was no mistaking the challenge in them. 'Do you claim the same expertise in chemistry and related matters as you do in art and antiquities, Sinclair?'

'No,' Anthony said brusquely. 'I have not made a close study of science.'

'I see,' Dominic drawled. 'Perhaps that is for the best. Comprehension of the principles of electricity, astronomy, and the like requires a mind that is trained in logic and reason. Science is quite different from art and antiquities in that it is not subject to the whims of fashion, taste, and emotion. It follows the laws of nature instead.'

Emeline felt Anthony stiffen angrily. She hastened to take charge of the conversation.

'I thought today's lecture was particularly enlightening,' she said quickly. 'Especially the last demonstration, with the model volcano.'

'Positively exhilarating,' Priscilla declared.

'It was entertaining.' Dominic shrugged. 'I will grant you that. But when you come right down to it, I'm afraid Professor Kirk is more showman than chemist.'

Priscilla frowned slightly. 'What do you mean, Mr Hood?'

Dominic switched his attention to her. 'I am currently working on a new formula for fireworks explosives that I assure you would produce effects far more spectacular than those Kirk created with his silly volcano.'

Priscilla's eyes widened. 'You have your own laboratory, sir?'

'Yes.'

'But that is wonderful,' Priscilla breathed. 'What instruments and apparatus do you own, if I may ask?'

Dominic hesitated, looking torn. Emeline got the distinct impression that he'd had another goal in mind when he had intercepted them at the door. She thought it best to keep pushing him in this other direction.

'Indeed, Mr Hood,' she said, 'this sounds very intriguing. Please tell us about your laboratory equipment.'

'I possess the usual assortment,' he allowed finally. 'A microscope, an electrical machine, telescope, a balance, some chemical apparatus.'

'Your very own electrical machine.' Priscilla was clearly dazzled. 'You are extremely fortunate, sir. I would give anything to possess a properly equipped laboratory.'

Emeline felt a small rush of curiosity. 'Can you create little balls of fire that fly about, the way Professor Kirk did today?'

'Certainly. Kirk's lightning show was no more than a simple

trick.' He paused, glanced at Priscilla, and then smiled very deliberately at Emeline. 'I can arrange some demonstrations that I think you would find even more exciting than those Kirk performed for you this afternoon.'

'I would love to see them,' Priscilla said quickly.

'It does sound intriguing,' Emeline agreed. 'I must admit, I have not taken a great interest in science until recently, but Mr Kirk's lectures have been quite stimulating.'

Anthony's jaw hardened. 'Out of the question. The two of you cannot possibly go to Hood's lodgings unaccompanied. You both know that very well.'

Priscilla looked crestfallen. 'I wonder if I could persuade Mama to accompany us.'

She did not sound hopeful, Emeline thought.

'I doubt that Lady Wortham would care to spend a morning viewing science demonstrations,' Anthony said flatly.

'I suppose you are right,' Priscilla said. She looked resigned. 'Mama is more concerned with fashion.'

Dominic's jaw tensed.

'Well, that is that.' Anthony checked his pocket watch. 'It is getting late, ladies. We had best be on our way if we are to stop for ice cream.'

Emeline could not abide the deep disappointment in Priscilla's eyes. 'I'm sure that I would have no difficulty persuading Aunt Lavinia to escort us to a demonstration at your laboratory, Mr Hood.'

Priscilla's expression warmed with gratitude. 'Do you really think Mrs Lake would be willing to do that?'

'I do not see why not,' Emeline said. 'When she returns from her visit to the country I will ask her.'

'Thank you.' Priscilla was buoyant. 'That is so kind of you, Emeline.'

Dominic shot Anthony a triumphant smile and then bowed politely to Emeline and Priscilla.

'I shall look forward to entertaining the two of you and Mrs Lake as well at your earliest convenience,' he said. 'My lodgings are in Stelling Street.'

He turned on the heel of one gleaming Hessian and walked out of the hall and down the steps without a backward glance.

Anthony said nothing, but Emeline could feel the anger simmering in him.

For the first time in their relationship, she was worried.

An hour and a half later, after escorting a still-exuberant Priscilla to her door, Emeline and Anthony walked back to Number 7 Claremont Lane.

It was a lovely day for a stroll, Emeline thought. Surely there was no finer place on earth than London on a summer afternoon. Sunlight warmed the lush green parks where children played with balls and small wagons. The flower sellers' carts brimmed with a profusion of colorful blossoms. Fruitmongers offered an array of juicy peaches and pears, sweet grapes, and an assortment of berries. Everyone seemed more cheerful and more brightly garbed than they did in winter.

Then again, maybe she felt that way because she was with the man she loved, she thought. What a pity Anthony was in such a foul mood.

'Do you know,' she said, aiming for a harmless topic, 'until she suggested that we subscribe to Mr Kirk's lectures, I had no notion that Priscilla had such a great interest in science. She told me that her mama warned her not to discuss the subject in polite company because she would be labeled a bore by her friends.'

'Lady Wortham is the bore in that family.'

'I suspect it would be more accurate to say that she is merely a devoted parent attempting to do her best to make an excellent match for Priscilla.'

'Huh,' Anthony said without a great deal of interest.

So much for attempting to lighten his mood. There were times, she reflected, when Anthony took after his brother-in-law. She was coming to understand why Lavinia occasionally lost her temper with Mr March.

'Out with it,' she said when they reached Number 7. 'You are annoyed with me because I agreed to ask Aunt Lavinia to accompany Priscilla and me to see Dominic's laboratory.'

'I'd rather not discuss the subject.'

'No, you would rather seethe in silence. Allow me to tell you, sir, that while such a mood is quite dramatic for a short time, it rapidly becomes annoying.'

She reached into her reticule for her key and opened the door. A gentle breeze wafted down the long hall that ran the length of the house. The back door stood open. She glanced toward the far end of the passageway and caught a glimpse of gray skirts moving about in the kitchen garden. Mrs Chilton was collecting vegetables and lettuces.

Emeline removed her bonnet and gloves. 'Why don't you tell me why you have taken such a dislike to Mr Hood?'

Anthony shut the front door and turned to face her. 'I dislike him because I know his intentions.'

'Indeed? What, in your opinion, are Mr Hood's intentions?'

'He has taken to hanging about wherever we happen to be because he wants to entice you away from me.'

Startled, she paused in the act of hanging her bonnet on a hook and stared at him. 'That is absolute rubbish.'

'On the contrary, it is the absolute truth.'

'Tony, I really do not think that is the case at all.'

'It bloody well is the case.'

'You're jealous,' she said, more than a little amazed.

'Do you blame me?'

'Yes, I do, sir. There is no need for you to worry about my association with Mr Hood. I think he is just somewhat lonely, that's all. He is obviously new in town and he evidently has no friends or social connections.'

'The lack of friends is perfectly understandable.' Anthony tossed his hat down onto a table. 'Hood does not possess what anyone would call a winning personality.'

She thought about the manner in which Dominic had held himself apart from the crowd in the lecture hall. 'He is rather aloof, is he not? And I will grant you that there is a certain intensity about him that no doubt makes it difficult for him to be at ease with people. I have the impression that he has not spent much time in Society.'

'I do not know about his experience in Society, but I can tell you that he must have some connections. He is a member of my club.'

'Is that where you were introduced?'

'Unfortunately, yes,' he muttered. 'He has become my shadow because he seeks to find a way to separate you and me.'

'Anthony, you are behaving in the most ridiculous fashion. I assure you there is absolutely no need—'

She broke off on a small gasp, because he abruptly took a long stride forward, gripped her forearms, and pinned her hard against him.

'He is not like the other gentlemen who flirt with you, Emeline,' Anthony said quietly. 'They are annoying but harmless. Hood is different. He is dangerous.'

Her irritation was suddenly transformed into anger. 'Surely you do not believe for one moment that I am attracted to him? How can you even imply such a thing? Do you really think that I am so fickle?'

'Of course not. I trust you completely, Emeline. Don't you understand? It is Hood's determination to destroy what you and I have found together that alarms me.'

She relaxed a little. 'I still do not believe that is his goal, but even if it were, I promise you he could not possibly tear me away from you.'

He shook his head once, as if she were the most naive creature in the world. 'You still do not comprehend my real fear. It is that he will do you some great harm.'

'What on earth are you talking about?'

'I would not put it past him to attempt to compromise you in some fashion.' He paused grimly. 'Perhaps worse.'

She searched his face and saw that he believed every word of what he had just said. 'You think he would . . . would . . .' She could not bring herself to say the word *rape*. 'But that makes no sense. Why would Mr Hood want to do something so utterly beyond the pale?'

'I wish to God I knew,' he said quietly.

'He cannot possibly hate me so much,' she whispered. 'He is barely acquainted with me.'

'You misunderstand, my love.' Anthony raised his hands to cup her face. 'I do not believe that he hates you.'

'Then why would he want to hurt me?'

'It is me he despises. I am the one he wants to hurt. And he has guessed quite correctly that nothing in the world would cause me more pain and grief than seeing you harmed.'

She gazed at him, shocked at the deep certainty in his words. 'But you have only just met him. What possible reason could he have for conceiving such a strong dislike of you?'

'I do not know. But I mean to find out. Meanwhile, I do not want you anywhere near him.'

'Even if I were to agree to keep my distance from Mr Hood, you know very well that you cannot prevent him from coming near me.

Not unless you intend to keep me locked up in this house, which I will never allow'

'Damn it, Emeline.'

She covered his mouth with her fingertips, silencing him gently. 'Listen to us. Once again we sound like Aunt Lavinia and Mr March when they are engaging in one of their heated discussions. It was our intention to go about things much differently, if you will recall.'

He narrowed his eyes. 'This is not about our personal relationship.'

'On the contrary, it goes to the very heart of it. Our association is supposed to be a harmonious metaphysical connection of two like-minded souls. We agreed that we would not quarrel and snap at each other as my aunt and your brother-in-law are so inclined to do. We vowed that we would not become as stubborn and set in our ways as they are, that we would not follow the same prickly path that they have chosen to travel.'

Anthony's mouth curved slightly. For the first time that day, she glimpsed a dash of genuine amusement in his eyes.

'I am starting to think that we are each just as strong-willed, opinionated, and stubborn as Mrs Lake and Tobias. I regret to say, Emeline, that we may indeed be headed down the same thorny path.'

'Nonsense. I'm certain that with a bit of effort we can avoid that fate.'

'There, you see? You have just proven my point. We cannot even refrain from arguing about whether or not we are doomed to argue.'

His mouth was very close to hers now, and she could feel the sparkling excitement uncurling within her. She tried to retain her concentration.

'We are not quarreling,' she insisted, a little breathless. 'We are having a serious-minded discussion.'

'Call it what you will.' He contemplated her mouth as though it were a rare and precious fruit that he planned to eat. 'At the moment I do not particularly care.'

'But we must settle this matter.'

'In my opinion, we cannot settle it satisfactorily, so we may as well do something else that is infinitely more satisfying.'

'Anthony, you are trying to change the subject.'

'How did you guess?'

Her kissed her, cutting off the remainder of her protests. She told herself they could finish the discussion later. It was exceedingly difficult to think clearly when he held her like this.

She slid her arms around his neck and abandoned herself to the exquisite delight of the moment. A heavy shudder of desire swept through him, leaving her in no doubt about the depth of his passion.

It had not escaped her notice that Anthony had begun to find an increasing number of opportunities to embrace her of late. Each kiss was more bold and more daring than the last. She had never allowed any other man such liberties, but, then, she had never loved any other man.

Society had rules about this sort of thing. She knew those rules. It was all very well for a widow such as Lavinia to indulge in a discreet affair. But a young lady who had never been wed was obliged to avoid any action that might possibly taint her reputation. Perception was all in the polite world.

But this was Anthony, and she loved him, and lately she found herself less and less concerned with being careful.

'Emeline,' he whispered against her throat. 'What are we to do? I love you. Even when we quarrel, I want you.'

'I love you too.' She tightened her arms around his neck. 'So very much.'

He raised his head slightly to look into her eyes. 'I am not yet in a position to ask you to marry me. You know that. The sad truth is that I cannot yet afford to keep you in proper style.'

'How many times must I tell you that I do not care about the state of your finances?'

'I most certainly care. I will not ask you to marry me until I am in a position to establish a household.'

'You are too proud.'

'That may be, but it does not matter, because I have made up my mind on the subject. In the meantime, my great fear is that you will lose patience waiting. Some other man may come along who is financially secure, one who can give you everything.'

'Never,' she vowed. 'I will wait forever, if need be. But I refuse to believe that two people as clever as you and I cannot find a way to be together sooner than that.'

He smiled slightly. 'I hope that you are right.' He hesitated. 'Sweetheart, there is something I want you to know. I was not going to tell you, because things may not work out as I wish. But the truth is, I took the fees that I earned assisting Tobias in his last case and

I purchased a share in one of Lord Crackenburne's shipping ventures. It will be several months before I will know whether or not I shall see a profit, however. There is always a risk in that sort of investment.'

She smiled. 'I, too, have a confession to make. Mrs Dove invited Aunt Lavinia and me to invest in one of her building projects. The houses are to be completed within the next six months. They will be sold or leased. If all goes well, I shall have some money of my own before the end of the year. If we combine our incomes I'm sure we shall manage.'

'Speaking of houses, that is another problem. Even if we marry, we must find a decent place to live.'

'We can move into your lodgings.'

'Absolutely not. My rooms do well enough for a single gentleman such as myself, but I would not dream of taking you out of this very comfortable little house and installing you in Jasper Street.'

'I would not mind,' she said quickly. 'Really, I wouldn't.'

'Well, I would most certainly mind.' He scowled. 'There is not even enough space for a housekeeper, always assuming we could afford one.' He groaned and folded her close. 'Any way you look at it, we must wait months before we can even announce our engagement.' He broke off abruptly, looking as though he had been struck by a sudden dazzling vision. 'Unless . . .'

She heard the sudden change of tone in his voice and recognized it immediately. Pulling back slightly, she looked up at him. 'I perceive that you have concocted a plan. What is it?'

'It is all a bit vague at the moment.' He spoke cautiously, clearly not wanting to raise her hopes at this early juncture. 'It would require a great deal of strategy. I shall have to proceed carefully, but there just may be a way to move matters along a bit faster.'

She was torn between excitement and frustration. 'You must tell me.'

'No. Not until I have some notion of whether or not it will work.'

'This is too much. You try my patience, sir.' She seized his lapels and attempted to give him a small shake. He did not move, but he did look amused.

His hand closed over hers. 'You are not the only one who is impatient, my love. There are nights when I wonder if I will go mad with the waiting.'

'I understand.' Reluctantly she released him and smoothed the lapels she had just crushed. 'It is very odd, is it not? One would think that a few kisses now and again would serve to release the frustration. But for some reason, the more often we embrace, the more I wish to do so.'

He smiled a wicked, sensual smile. 'Indeed, I have noticed the same strange effect.'

He bent his head to nibble on her ear.

She sighed. 'Perhaps it would be best if we refrained from this sort of thing.'

'No more kisses?' He raised his head quite suddenly. 'I would rather go mad, thank you very much.'

She started to laugh, but he found her mouth with his own and she moaned softly instead. He was right, she decided. Better to go mad than to deprive herself of his kisses.

His hand slipped to the back of her waist. He pressed her hips against his. She was intensely aware of the hard, bold contours of his aroused body. His kiss deepened.

A loud thud on the front step, followed immediately by the sound of a key in the lock, jolted her out of the sensual daze. Anthony stiffened and tried to step back. But the door opened wide before they could completely untangle themselves from each other's arms.

She stared in amazement at the sight of Lavinia sweeping into the small hall. Her aunt was closely followed by Tobias, who was assisting a coachman with a large trunk.

'Home at last.' Lavinia jerked off her yellow straw bonnet and sent it sailing toward the nearest table. 'Whoever said that life in the country was a soothing tonic for the nerves obviously did not have the faintest notion of what he was talking about.'

Nine

Mrs Chilton bustled back into the house just as Tobias sent the coach away. Her basket was overflowing with garden produce. She gazed in surprise at the small crowd in the front hall.

'What's this? Is something wrong? You weren't expected home until tomorrow, ma'am.'

'Plans changed, Mrs Chilton,' Lavinia said. 'It is a long story. Meanwhile, Mr March and I are famished. The food at the inn where we stopped for a meal was quite wretched. But, then, I suppose that is all of a piece with the entire, wretched trip.'

'Mrs Lake is right,' Tobias said. 'The food was, indeed, bad. I am feeling the pangs of hunger myself.'

Mrs Chilton snorted. 'I don't doubt that for a moment. Very well, I'll prepare a cold collation.'

'Thank you.' Tobias smiled deliberately at her. 'Would you happen to have any of those extraordinary currant tarts on hand, by any chance? I have been dreaming about them since we stopped at the inn.'

Mrs Chilton gave him a beady-eyed look of disapproval. 'I'm surprised you've got the energy left to eat any currant tarts, sir, what with that long, exhausting journey and all.'

'Vale's carriage was so nicely sprung I was able to get a bit of rest.'

Lavinia frowned at that blithely spoken untruth. Tobias had not slept a wink on the journey home. The two of them had spent most of the time plotting strategy and discussing the new case.

But Mrs Chilton made a clucking sound with her tongue and shook her head. 'I may have one or two tarts left over from the batch I made up for the basket you took with you on your trip to the country.'

'I am very much obliged, Mrs Chilton,' Tobias said, a little too humbly.

Lavinia watched the pair closely. This was not the first time she had cause to suspect that she was missing some secret joke shared by the two. Tobias and Mrs Chilton were not the only ones who appeared inexplicably amused. Anthony was examining the floor very intently, the corners of his mouth twitching. Emeline suddenly turned away to hang the yellow bonnet on a hook.

Lavinia had had enough. She planted her hands on her hips and narrowed her eyes at Tobias. 'More currant tarts? Allow me to tell you, sir, that you have become obsessive about currants in recent weeks. You are forever requesting that Mrs Chilton provide you with some delicacy made of currants. I vow, there have been enough currant jam, currant cakes, and currant tarts around here to feed an army.'

'I am obviously lacking something in my diet that can only be satisfied with currants,' Tobias said.

'I'll bring the tray into the library,' Mrs Chilton said quickly.

She hurried off down the hall toward the kitchen.

Lavinia reluctantly decided to abandon the subject of currants for the moment. There were other, more-pressing matters.

She led the way into her study. Tossing the notebook that she had removed from her reticule onto a little table, she went straight to the sherry cabinet.

'We shall tell you the whole story,' she assured Anthony and Emeline. 'But first, I believe that Tobias and I are both in need of a tonic.'

'I will not quarrel with that,' Tobias said. He lowered himself into the largest of the chairs and propped his left foot on a stool, making himself at home, as had become his habit of late.

Lavinia was still not certain how she felt about the ease with which he had begun to embed himself into her daily life. It had happened gradually over the past few months, she realized. Tobias owned a perfectly pleasant house of his own a few blocks away in Slate Street, but he seemed to be spending less and less time in it. Instead, he had got into the habit of showing up on her doorstep whenever the notion took him.

She grumbled frequently to Emeline and Mrs Chilton about how often he managed to arrive just as breakfast was served. He did not hesitate to take a seat at the table and help himself to coffee and eggs. He also had an uncanny knack for appearing when she was alone in the house. His timing on those occasions was really quite remarkable, she reflected. He seemed to know when Mrs Chilton and Emeline would be absent, and he frequently took advantage of the privacy to make passionate, if somewhat hurried, love to her.

She declared loudly to anyone who would listen that it was exasperating to have Tobias constantly underfoot, but the truth was, she was growing accustomed to his presence in the household.

The knowledge that, deep down, she rather liked having him about was unsettling.

A decade ago, when she had wed John, she had not experienced any of these qualms. She had been in love with her gentle poet of a husband, and marriage had seemed the logical culmination of that romantic attachment.

But the union had ended after only eighteen months, when John had succumbed to a fever of the lungs. For four years she had been obliged to make her own way in the world and then Emeline had come to live with her. She was well aware that the responsibility of taking care of herself and her niece had changed her in some ways. She was not the same woman she had been all those years ago.

Not only was she older and more worldly now, she thought, but she had come to value the freedom and independence that her status as a widow bestowed upon her. Unlike Emeline, she was no longer subject to the strict rules of decorum that governed younger, unwed ladies. She was free to indulge in the occasional passionate affair if she chose. All that was required of her these days was that she be reasonably discreet. Widows enjoyed the best of both worlds, she told herself. They could savor the pleasures of passion and still retain the control and independence allowed by their single state.

Somewhere along the line, she thought, she had reached the conclusion that she would remain unmarried for the rest of her life. She had been quite content with that prospect.

Until recently.

Matters were no longer so clear to her. In point of fact, she thought, her future appeared quite murky at the moment.

Falling in love with Tobias had caught her off guard and was also proving to be a decidedly disturbing experience. It had taken her some time to even comprehend what had happened. She had not immediately identified her feelings for Tobias as the bonds of love, because the emotions were so markedly different from the tender, innocent sentiments she had known in her marriage.

Granted, ten years had passed since John's death, but to the best of her recollection the two of them had never disagreed, let alone quarreled in the course of their marriage. Of course, she reflected in a sudden burst of insight, there had been very little to quarrel about. The truth was, John had been only too happy to turn over all of the decision-making to her.

John had been dedicated to his poetry. He had yearned for nothing more than to be freed from dealing with all the pesky details of daily life, including the necessity of making a living.

She had taken charge from the outset of the marriage. Not only had she managed their household but, because John's brilliance as a poet had gone unrecognized and he had therefore been unable to secure an income from his writing, she had supported them both with her skills in mesmerism.

The arrangement had actually worked quite well over the short course of the marriage. She had been content. She told herself that John had loved her and she was certain that was true. But looking back, she knew now that he had reserved his deepest passions for his writing.

Perhaps that was the real reason why they had never quarreled, she reflected. John simply had not cared enough about anything except his writing to be bothered to argue.

Her relationship with Tobias was altogether different. The emotions that flared so easily between them were far more intense than those she had experienced with John, but those heated discussions resulted more often than not in heated lovemaking.

She was obliged to admit to herself that she could not manage Tobias the way she had managed John. She was not certain how she felt about that.

An affair was the perfect solution, she assured herself. It was a familiar litany, one she repeated quite often late at night when she found herself lying awake and alone in her bed.

She pushed the disquieting thoughts aside and poured the sherry. When she turned around to hand one of the glasses to Tobias, she saw that he was absently massaging his left leg. She frowned.

'Is your wound bothering you?' she said.

'Do not concern yourself.' He took the glass from her. 'The long carriage ride stiffened my leg somewhat. A glass of sherry will soon fix the problem.' He swallowed half the contents of the glass and eyed the small amount that remained. 'On second thought make that two or three.'

She refilled his glass, sat down, and propped her heels on the hassock.

'I cannot tell you how good it is to be home,' she said to Emeline and Anthony.

Emeline took a chair near the globe. Her pretty face filled with concern. 'What happened at Beaumont Castle?'

'The entire affair was a complete disaster,' Lavinia announced.

Tobias drank more sherry and looked thoughtful. 'I would not say that. The house party had its moments.'

She saw the glint in his eyes and knew that he was recalling the passionate interlude they had shared late last night in her bedchamber. She gave him a quelling look, which he did not appear to notice.

'Out with it.' Anthony lounged on the corner of the desk, arms folded. 'Emeline and I cannot tolerate the suspense. What occurred to bring you both back to London in such a great hurry?'

'Where to start?' Tobias turned the nearly empty sherry glass between his palms. 'I suppose one could say that the murder of Lord Fullerton was something of a turning point.'

'*Murder*.' Emeline's lips parted in astonishment. Then her expression brightened with interest. 'Well, that certainly explains a few things.'

'It does, indeed.' Anthony's enthusiasm was plain. 'Can I conclude that we have a new case?'

'You may.' Lavinia flicked a quick glance at Tobias. 'Always assuming our new client can afford us? As I recall, there was no discussion of our fees.'

Tobias finished his sherry and lowered the glass. 'Mrs Gray can well afford us.'

'I suggest you start at the beginning and tell us all,' Emeline said.

Lavinia waved a hand at Tobias. 'You may do the honors, sir. I believe I require more sherry.'

Tobias held out his own glass for a refill. Then he launched into an account of events at the Beaumont estate.

She listened carefully while she splashed sherry into the two glasses and reseated herself. To her relief, Tobias left out a few particulars, such as why she had come to be sneaking about in the castle hallways so late at night.

When he finished, Anthony and Emeline were both bubbling with questions, comments, and suggestions.

'Time is plainly of the essence here,' Anthony said. 'You will need our help on this case.'

'Yes.' Tobias's hand tightened around his glass. 'We will, indeed, require some assistance.'

'We made some plans during the trip back to London,' Lavinia said. She picked up the small notebook she had put on the table a few minutes earlier and flipped it open. 'There are several lines of inquiry to be pursued. The memento-mori ring we found in Fullerton's bedchamber appears to be old. There is a possibility that the killer purchased it or stole it from one of the antiquities shops.'

Emeline absently spun the globe beneath one hand and looked thoughtful. 'It could also have been pawned and sold by a jeweler.'

Tobias nodded. 'Quite true, although it does not appear to be the sort of ring a jeweler would want to purchase.'

'There is not a lot of demand for memento-mori rings these days,' Lavinia put in. 'They are not nearly so fashionable as they once were.'

'It is a clue,' Tobias added. 'We cannot afford to ignore it.'

Anthony looked at him. 'Emeline and I are to interview shop-keepers and jewelers who might know something about the ring, I assume?'

'Yes,' Tobias said. 'There is also the matter of the wig.'

'A blond wig.' Emeline considered briefly. 'Not at all in the current mode.'

'We believe that may be precisely the point,' Lavinia said. 'The killer wanted to be certain that, if he was seen, the only thing anyone would recall clearly was a woman's blond hair. Oh, and one more point. Although Tobias is certain the killer is a man, I am reserving judgment.'

Anthony looked at Tobias, brows elevated inquiringly.

'My intuition tells me that we are dealing with a man,' Tobias said. 'But Lavinia has a point. We cannot rule out the possibility that this new Memento-Mori Man is actually a woman.'

'Very well.' Anthony straightened away from the desk. 'Emeline and I will see what we can learn on the subject of blond wigs and missing memento-mori rings.'

'The first step is to draw up a list of wig shops and antiquities dealers who specialize in old rings,' Emeline said.

Tobias frowned. 'Have a care when you ask your questions. We are dealing with a killer who has openly challenged me. I fear that he is playing a vicious chess game, just as Zachary Elland once did. I want to ensure that his attention remains focused on me. I do not want this villain to take an interest in either of you. Understood?'

'Do not concern yourself, sir,' Emeline said quickly. 'Anthony and I will be extremely discreet in our inquiries.' She smiled. 'It is the motto of our little agency, is it not? *Discretion assured*.'

'What do you and Mrs Lake plan to do while we are investigating the ring and the wig?' Anthony asked.

Tobias looked at Lavinia. 'Our first goal is to find out who benefited most from Fullerton's death.'

'Of course.' Emeline smiled. 'I expect that will be quite straightforward. Just look to the heir, as you are so fond of saying, Mr March.'

Lavinia tapped her notebook against the arm of the chair. 'Our second objective may be far more complicated. We wish to discover whether or not there have been any other similar deaths in recent months and, if so, who profited from them.'

'The Memento-Mori Man prided himself on his professional approach to his business.' Tobias leaned his head against the back of his chair and closed his eyes. 'Elland did not kill at random. With the exception of his work as a spy, each murder involved a financial transaction.'

Ten

Tobias and Anthony left an hour later, after having demolished an entire leek-and-potato pie, a large wedge of cheese, a goodly portion of pickled salmon, most of a loaf of bread, and a number of small tarts.

'Mr March and Mr Sinclair are certainly blessed with hearty appetites,' Mrs Chilton said with an air of satisfaction as she cleared away the empty dishes. 'A sign of a healthy constitution in a man, I always say.'

'I don't know how any household can afford to feed two such healthy constitutions day in and day out,' Lavinia muttered. 'I do hope they will not get into the habit of dropping by for dinner or supper. It is expensive enough as it is to feed Mr March his breakfast every morning, to say nothing of those days when he is accompanied by Anthony. I vow, if they both dined with us for every meal they would soon eat us out of house and home.'

'Rubbish.' Emeline picked up her teacup and wrinkled her nose. 'It is not that bad and well you know it. Really, Lavinia, you do tend to exaggerate whenever you are discussing Mr March's little eccentricities and small foibles.'

'You call that appetite a little eccentricity?' Lavinia swept out a hand to indicate the few crumbs that remained on the plates. 'For heaven's sake, I do believe that Tobias ate every single one of Mrs Chilton's currant tarts.'

Mrs Chilton shook her head and hoisted the tray. 'Expect he'll be asking me to go out for more currants this week. Mr March's taste for currants seems to know no bounds.'

'Yes, I've noticed that.' Lavinia removed her low half boots and slid her stocking-clad feet into a pair of comfortable slippers.

'Indeed, he consumes them as though he believes them to be some sort of invigorating tonic.'

Emeline abruptly sputtered and coughed. 'Sorry,' she mumbled into a napkin. 'Difficulty swallowing the tea.'

Mrs Chilton made an odd noise and hurried out the door.

One of these days, Lavinia thought, she would discover what it was about currants that created such an effect on everyone else in the household.

'I vow, I am exhausted,' she said. 'Vale's carriage had excellent springs and was quite comfortable; nevertheless, it was a very long trip back from Beaumont Castle. I believe I shall go to bed early tonight. Tomorrow will be an extremely busy day.'

Emeline watched her closely for a moment and then slowly put down her cup. 'Were you enjoying the house party before the dreadful events occurred?'

'Oh, yes. With the exception of a rather upsetting episode involving a change of rooms, it was all quite festive. I was looking forward to the rest of the activities. That is, until I discovered Cleopatra in Tobias's bedchamber.'

Emeline stared at her. 'I beg your pardon?'

'Our new client, Aspasia Gray, came dressed as Cleopatra for the evening.'

'I understand, but what was she doing in Mr March's bedchamber?'

'An excellent question – one I asked, myself.' Lavinia drummed her fingers on the arms of her chair. 'They are old friends, as Tobias told you a while ago.'

'The sort of old friends who meet in each other's bedchambers?' Emeline asked, voice rising.

'Tobias assures me that the two of them never had that sort of connection.'

'I see.' Emeline was troubled. 'Do you believe him?'

Lavinia glanced at her, surprised by the question. 'Yes, of course. Tobias has his little eccentricities and small foibles, as you just pointed out, but lying outright to my face about a matter such as this is not one of them.'

Emeline's brow cleared. She looked knowing. 'The two of you do seem to have established a certain degree of trust.'

'Mmm. It is quite true that Tobias will answer my questions honestly.' Lavinia exhaled deeply. 'The problem, I have discovered, is that I must first ask the *right* questions.'

'I suppose it is only to be expected that a man of Mr March's age and experience of the world would have some private matters in his past that he might wish to remain confidential.'

'It is also a fact that a man of Mr March's nature is strongly inclined to keep his secrets,' Lavinia muttered.

'You are rather worried about this new case, are you not?'

'With good cause. We are dealing with a killer.'

'Yes, of course, but I have the impression that the links to Mr March's past have compounded your concerns.'

Lavinia pursed her lips. 'There are several aspects of this situation that bother me. Our client is one of them.'

'What is it about Aspasia Gray that worries you?'

'Most likely it has something to do with the fact that the first time I met her, she had her arms around Tobias's neck.'

'Never say that Mr March was kissing her?' Emeline was appalled. 'But you just told me that you were not alarmed by the nature of their friendship.'

'According to Tobias, she was attempting to kiss him. A token of her gratitude or some such nonsense. He assures me he was not a willing participant in the act and, as I said, I believe him.'

Emeline relaxed slightly. 'I see. One can understand the kiss, I suppose. Mrs Gray behaved in an extremely forward fashion, presuming on their past acquaintance, and poor Mr March simply did not know how to deal with the situation in a gentlemanly fashion.'

'In all the months that I have known *poor Mr March*, I have not yet seen him in a situation that he could not handle,' Lavinia said. 'In a gentlemanly fashion or otherwise.'

'Yes, well, I quite agree that he never seems to be without resources and he is certainly very competent.'

Lavinia brooded on her slippers for a moment or two.

'I trust Tobias,' she said eventually. 'But I do not trust Aspasia Gray.'

'Well, it is one of Mr March's axioms that one can never entirely trust the client, is it not?'

'I am more than willing to apply that rule in this case.' She touched the tips of her slippers together. 'But I am afraid that Tobias may not be following his own advice when it comes to Aspasia.'

'Calm yourself, Lavinia. Mr March is nothing if not cautious about such things. I am certain that he will not allow his personal feelings for Mrs Gray to get in the way of sound judgment.'

Lavinia tapped her slippers together. 'We can only hope that will prove to be true. In any event, there is very little to be done about the problem at this juncture. There is no getting around the fact that Tobias cannot avoid this case, even if he were so inclined.'

Emeline nodded knowingly. 'And so long as he is involved in it, you must be also.'

'I cannot allow him to investigate this affair alone.'

'I understand.' Emeline started to raise her cup and then paused with the vessel in midair. She studied Lavinia with an uncertain expression for a few seconds, and then her resolve appeared to firm. 'As long as we are discussing matters of a somewhat personal nature involving Mr March, there is something I feel compelled to discuss with you.'

Lavinia braced herself. 'If this is about your connection with Mr Sinclair, could we wait until some other time? I know that you are in love with him. However, he appears to be a responsible and entirely honorable young man, and I very much doubt that he will ask for your hand until he feels himself to be comfortably situated. Given his rather precarious career as an assistant to Tobias, that may take some time. Until then, I really do feel that it would be best if you—'

'This is not about my relationship with Anthony,' Emeline interrupted with surprising forcefulness. 'It is about yours with Mr March.'

Lavinia stared at her. She blinked a couple of times and finally managed to recover herself. 'What on earth are you talking about?'

'Please, I am no longer a child. Furthermore, our sojourn in Rome as companions to that dreadful Mrs Underwood gave me an excellent education in worldly matters. I am well-aware that you and Mr March have formed a very intimate connection.'

'Ah. Yes. Well.' She felt the heat rise in her cheeks. This was ridiculous. She was a woman of the world, after all. She cleared her throat. 'The exact nature of my association with Tobias is an extremely personal matter, Emeline.'

'Yes, of course.' Emeline's gaze did not waver. 'The thing is, although it is certainly *personal*, it is not exactly a secret, if you take my point.'

'It would be somewhat difficult to miss your point. Where is this conversation headed?'

Emeline took another deep breath. 'It has not escaped my notice that you and Mr March are spending more and more time in each other's company of late.'

'Our professional partnership requires a close association at times.' Lavinia strove to achieve an off-putting, suitably repressive tone, in the faint hope that it might discourage Emeline. 'We must consult frequently on various inquiries. You know that very well.'

Emeline did not look put off or discouraged. Her fine dark brows formed a determined line. 'I feel that I must be frank. We both know that it was not your professional relationship that required the two of you to travel together to Beaumont Castle.'

'I am rather tired.' Lavinia rubbed her temples with her fingertips. 'Could you please tell me why you are suddenly so concerned about my association with Mr March? For heaven's sake, I thought you liked the man. Indeed, if memory serves, you thought a good deal more highly of him the first time we encountered him than I did.'

'I *do* like him. Very much.' Emeline put down her teacup. 'It is not my feelings for him that we are discussing.'

'Mmm.'

'Aunt Lavinia, tell me the truth. You are in love with Mr March, are you not?'

'Mmm.'

'And he appears to be in love with you.'

'Mmm.' Lavinia glanced toward the door, wondering if she could plead sudden illness and make a dash for the stairs.

'Everyone knows why two people who have formed an intimate connection would accept an invitation to a large house party.'

'Indeed.' Lavinia clutched the arms of her chair. 'Long walks in the fresh air. The chance to commune with nature. The opportunity to enjoy jolly rustic entertainments.'

'I am not that naive, Aunt Lavinia, and well you know it. It is common knowledge that house parties provide opportunities for ladies and gentlemen who are involved in romantic liaisons to be private with each other. Do not try to tell me that that is not precisely what you and Mr March planned to do at Beaumont Castle.'

'Whatever plans Mr March and I might have made in regard to

our personal entertainment were drastically altered by Lord Fullerton's demise, I assure you.'

'I understand. But the point is, you did have some plans.'

Embarrassment sparked into annoyance. 'Accepting the invitation to Beaumont Castle was Tobias's idea, not mine.'

'But you agreed to the journey,' Emeline insisted. 'You must have known what it would entail.'

'*Enough.*' Lavinia pushed herself up out of the chair and went to stand at the window. 'What is the aim of this exceedingly personal interrogation?'

'Forgive me, but I feel I must be blunt,' Emeline said quietly. 'I expected that when you returned from Beaumont's house party, you and Mr March would announce your intention to wed.'

Lavinia's mouth went dry. The floor suddenly seemed to shift under her feet. She reached out and grasped a fistful of drapery to steady herself.

'You expected *what*?' she finally managed.

'You heard me,' Emeline said. 'I assumed that Mr March would ask you to marry him in the course of your visit to the Beaumont estate.'

Lavinia whirled around. 'Whatever put that notion into your head?'

'I have lived with you for several years, and I feel I know you well enough to state without hesitation that this connection you have formed with Mr March is unique.' Emeline rose to her feet. 'I realize that you have had one or two minor flirtations over the years, but none of them amounted to much. Certainly none of those other gentlemen was even allowed to get into the habit of joining us for breakfast on a frequent basis. You never went off to house parties with any of them.'

'Emeline—'

'You have as much as admitted that you are in love with Mr March, and he appears to be quite fond of you. I had every right to assume that this connection would lead to marriage.'

'*Every right*?' Lavinia realized she was crumpling the drapery. Very carefully, she released the fabric and smoothed the folds. 'Yes, well, your assumption was incorrect.'

Emeline's expression became one of astonishment mingled with outrage. 'Do you mean to say that Mr March has not even mentioned the subject of marriage?'

'No, he has not.' Lavinia elevated her chin. 'Furthermore, there is no reason why he should do so. Indeed, I do not expect an offer of marriage from him.'

'You cannot mean that, Lavinia.'

'The thing is, Emeline, our current arrangement suits both Mr March and myself very well.'

Emeline spread her arms. 'But as it stands, your arrangement is little more than an unconventional liaison, an affair. It cannot go on forever.'

The note of censure in her tone was extremely irritating, Lavinia thought. 'I do not see why it cannot continue indefinitely. A great many ladies engage in long-standing affairs.'

'Not you, Lavinia.'

'Bloody hell, you need not look so scandalized.' Feeling the need for another medicinal glass of sherry, she stalked back to the cabinet and yanked the door open. 'You know very well that, although a lady of your years and status would be ruined by such an *unconventional liaison*, as a widow I may do as I please in such matters.'

'I am well-aware that Society has a different set of rules for each of us,' Emeline said stiffly. 'But that does not mean that it is proper for you to bestow your . . . your favors upon Mr March without some understanding concerning the future of your relationship.'

'Good lord, Emeline, you make me sound like a member of the demimonde.'

Emeline had the grace to blush. 'I did not mean to imply any such thing. But I must tell you that I assumed from the outset that Mr March's intentions were honorable.'

'Oh, for pity's sake.' She splashed sherry into the glass she had used earlier. 'They *are* honorable.'

'I fail to see how you can say that if he has not asked you to marry him.'

'I cannot believe that you are presuming to lecture me on the subject of proper decorum and behavior.'

'It distresses me greatly to say this, but I fear we must consider the possibility that Mr March may be deliberately taking advantage of you.'

That was too much.

'Advantage? Of me?' Lavinia swallowed the sherry and set the glass down hard. 'Does it occur to you that I may be the one taking advantage of Mr March?'

Emeline's lips parted in shock. 'Whatever do you mean?'

'Consider the matter from my point of view' Lavinia headed for the door. 'As things stand now, I have everything a woman in my situation could possibly want. I enjoy a close connection with a gentleman, but I do not need to make any of the sacrifices that are so often required of a married woman. I retain all of my rights, both legal and financial. I can come and go as I please. I operate my own business. I answer to no man. Frankly, Emeline, there is a lot to be said for this sort of arrangement.'

Shock bloomed in Emeline's eyes.

Lavinia did not wait for her to recover. She went out into the hall and swiftly climbed the stairs.

It was only when she was alone in the sanctuary of her bedchamber that she acknowledged to herself that she had lied through her teeth to Emeline.

Not that all of the things she had just said to her niece were not true and accurate as far as they went. There were indeed a great many excellent reasons why she was better off unwed.

But none of them was the real reason why she feared marriage to Tobias.

Eleven

'Evidently country life does not agree with you, March.' Lord Crackenburne's bristling gray brows bunched above the rims of his spectacles. 'Let me see if I have got it all straight. In the course of the single night you spent under Beaumont's roof, a mysterious death occurred, you found evidence that a new Memento-Mori Man is at work, and a lady from your past managed to involve you in an awkward situation in front of your good friend Mrs Lake.'

'Nor is that the end of the list of lively particulars.' Lord Vale's eyes glittered with sardonic amusement. 'Let us not forget that this memorable visit to the country culminated in you and Mrs Lake being summarily tossed out of the castle before breakfast.'

Tobias stretched out his left leg, which still ached from the long carriage ride the previous day, and sank deeper into his chair. It was one o'clock in the afternoon and the club's coffee room was only sparsely populated. He and Crackenburne and Vale had the place almost entirely to themselves. Hardly surprising, he reflected. It was a fine day, and the majority of those members who had remained in Town for the summer had found some interesting occupations to pursue outside in the warmth of the sun. The gentlemen would not drift back into their clubs until this evening, when whist and claret and gossip called them indoors once more.

At this time of year, the demands of the social world were considerably diminished. The Season, with its rigorous schedule of balls, soirees, and parties, had ended for all intents and purposes. Many of the most fashionable hostesses had already retreated to their estates for the summer.

Not all of the high flyers fled London in the summer. For a variety of reasons – including the long, uncomfortable journeys, the lack of a suitable residence, or a dread of the sheer boredom of country life – a goodly number of those who moved in the better circles chose to remain in Town.

A few, such as Crackenburne, did not even leave their clubs.

Following the death of his lady several years earlier, the Earl had virtually taken up residence here in the coffee room. Crackenburne was such a familiar fixture that the other members were inclined to overlook him as though he were a comfortable old sofa or a worn carpet. They gossiped freely in his presence, as though he were deaf. The result was that Crackenburne absorbed rumors and news the way a sponge took up water. He knew some of the deepest secrets of the ton.

'I cannot take all of the credit for being chucked out of Beaumont Castle,' Tobias said. 'Mrs Lake played the leading role in that little melodrama. Had she not taken it upon herself to insist to Beaumont that a murder had occurred under his roof – or, to be more precise, *upon* his roof – we might not have been asked to leave so unceremoniously.'

Crackenburne was amused. 'One can scarcely blame Beaumont for not wanting to acknowledge the manner of Fullerton's demise. That sort of gossip would no doubt discourage some of the less adventurous members of Society from accepting future invitations to his wife's parties. Lady Beaumont would have been furious if her reputation as a hostess had been ruined by talk of murder.'

'True.' Tobias sank deeper into his chair. 'And it is not as though we had any proof to offer.'

'But there is no doubt in your mind?' Vale asked.

Tobias was not surprised by the cold interest in the other man's eyes. Vale had listened to the recitation of events at the Beaumont house party with the degree of interest he usually reserved for his collection of antiquities.

Nearing fifty, Vale was tall and elegantly slender, with the long fingers of an artist. His receding hairline set off a strong profile and a high forehead that would not have looked amiss on one of the Roman busts in his collection.

Tobias was not yet certain what to make of Vale's newfound interest in the investigation business. His lordship was a scholar and an expert on Roman artifacts. He spent a great deal of time excavating various ancient sites around England. But he was also something of a mystery. The fact that he was intrigued with the notion of consulting for the firm of Lake & March made Tobias a little uneasy.

On the other hand, there was no doubt that Vale's rank and wealth, combined with his very close and presumably intimate connection to Lavinia's new friend Mrs Dove, had proved useful on the last case. There was every possibility that he could be helpful on this new investigation as well.

Tobias reminded himself that he needed all the assistance he could get.

He steepled his fingers and examined the carved marble of the mantel in the vain hope that it might offer up a clue. 'I am quite certain that Fullerton's fall from the roof was no accident. Mrs Lake found the cap that the killer wore to conceal his features. But the memento-mori ring I discovered on the night table was all the proof I really needed.'

'Now you wish to know who might have benefited from Fullerton's death,' Crackenburne said with a meditative air.

'It appears that this new killer seeks to emulate his predecessor,' Tobias said. 'One of the few things of which we can be certain about Zachary Elland is that he considered himself a professional. He not only took pride in the strategy he devised to carry out his kills, he always sought to turn a profit. He was a man of business, right down to his journal of accounts.'

'Therefore,' Vale concluded, looking more intrigued than ever, 'it is very likely that this new murderer had a client who paid him for Fullerton's death.'

'Indeed. If I can identify his client, I may be able to discover who was hired to commit the murder.' At the moment that was all that concerned him. He had a client of his own, and he was determined to protect Aspasia.

'A logical approach.' Crackenburne turned pensive. 'There is one possibility, but I'm inclined to dismiss it out of hand.'

Tobias waited.

'Fullerton was married years ago,' Crackenburne continued. 'But there was no offspring. After his wife died, he seemed content with his mistresses and his horses. It was assumed that his fortune and title would eventually go to his nephew. But at the end of the Season this year, he astonished everyone in the ton by announcing his engagement to the Panfield chit.'

Vale made a small sound of disgust. 'Fullerton was sixty if he was a day. The Panfield girl is barely out of the schoolroom. No more than seventeen, I'll wager.'

'I am told that she is very pretty and quite charming in that naive, innocent sort of way that some men who should know better find alluring,' Crackenburne said. 'For his part, Fullerton had a fortune and a title to offer. All in all, an excellent match from the point of view of any self-respecting parent who desires to elevate the family's social status.'

Tobias pondered that news. 'Obviously the Panfields had every reason to want Fullerton to live at least until his wedding night. So I am left with the nephew as a possible suspect. That suits me. It has been my experience that money is always an excellent motive.'

'It may not be in this instance,' Crackenburne warned. 'The nephew is already quite well off in his own right. Furthermore, he is engaged to marry the Dorlingate heiress.'

'She'll bring a fortune to the marriage,' Vale observed. 'You're right, sir, it would appear that the nephew has no great pressing financial concerns.'

Tobias scowled. 'What of the title?'

'The nephew is already in line for an earldom from his father,' Crackenburne said drily.

'Huh.' Fullerton had been a mere baron, Tobias thought. Not a title worth killing for when one was set to become an earl.

'In addition,' Crackenburne said, 'I have heard that the nephew is a generous, easygoing sort who is devoted to his estates. He does not appear to be the type who would hire a killer to get rid of his uncle.'

'Is there anyone else who might have had a reason to get rid of Fullerton?' Tobias pressed. 'A disgruntled financial partner? Someone with a personal grudge?'

'Not that I know of,' Crackenburne said.

Vale shook his head. 'No one comes to mind.'

'Doesn't mean we're not overlooking someone.' Tobias glanced at Crackenburne. 'Would you mind very much digging a little deeper in that direction?'

'Not at all.'

'Can either of you think of any other recent deaths that seem somewhat suspicious or quite unexpected?' Tobias asked. Crackenburne and Vale meditated on that for a while.

Eventually Crackenburne shifted a little in his chair. 'The only other recent death in Society that struck me as unexpected was that of Lady Rowland last month,' he said. 'Died in her sleep. The family has put out the word that her heart failed her. But the gossip is that when her maid found her, she also discovered a half-empty bottle of the tonic Lady Rowland used for sleep.'

'A suicide?' Vale asked.

'That is the rumor,' Crackenburne said. 'But I knew Lady Rowland for years. In my opinion, she was not the type to take her own life.'

'She was very wealthy,' Vale pointed out. 'What is more, she used her money to control everyone else in the family. In my experience, people generally resent that sort of high-handed manipulation.'

'Just what I needed,' Tobias muttered. 'An entire family of suspects.'

'Better than no suspects at all,' Vale said.

Lavinia walked through the little park and came to a halt beneath the leafy canopy of a tree. She was dismayed to see the gleaming carriage drawn up in front of Number 14 Hazelton Square. Joan Dove was apparently entertaining visitors this afternoon.

She should have sent word to her friend announcing her intention to call upon her today. But the warm sunshine had beckoned and it had seemed the perfect opportunity for a pleasant stroll to the elegant street of fine town houses where Joan lived. The odds had been very much against encountering another visitor at Number 14. Although Joan had emerged from her widowhood and was getting out more these days, she was a private woman who did not maintain a large circle of close friends and acquaintances.

Well, there was no help for it, Lavinia thought. The only thing she could do was leave her card with the bull of a butler who guarded the front door and come back some other time.

She opened her reticule and groped inside with one gloved hand, searching for her little packet of cards.

At that moment the door of Number 14 opened. Lavinia glanced up and saw Joan's daughter, Maryanne, emerge and start down the steps. The young woman was as lovely and elegant as her mother. Her wedding to the Colchester heir at the end of the Season had been a lavish affair. The alliance was an excellent one, both socially and financially. But Joan had confided to Lavinia that she was particularly pleased because Maryanne and young Lord Colchester were very much in love.

Maryanne appeared to be in a hurry today. She walked swiftly toward the waiting carriage. Lavinia caught a glimpse of her tense, unhappy features when a liveried footman leaped to open the door for her. She was no sooner settled inside the vehicle than the order was given to set off.

The carriage rolled past Lavinia. Through the uncovered window she saw Maryanne dab at her eyes with her handkerchief. The young woman was crying.

A little chill of disquiet went through Lavinia. Whatever had passed between Maryanne and Joan, it had not been pleasant. Perhaps she ought to delay her visit until tomorrow.

She deliberated a moment longer and then started across the street. This investigation was too important to be set aside, however briefly, unless there was no alternative.

She went up the steps of the colonnaded town house and banged the knocker. The door opened immediately.

'Mrs Lake.' The massive butler inclined his head in somber recognition. 'I shall inform Mrs Dove that you are here.'

'Thank you.'

Relieved not to have been barred from entrance on the grounds that Joan was not receiving visitors, she whisked into the black-and-white-marble-tiled hall and removed her bonnet. A glimpse of her reflection in the large, gilded mirrors revealed that the fichu she had tucked into the snug bodice of her violet gown was askew. Madam Francesca, her tyrannical dressmaker, would have been outraged.

She had just finished making the adjustments to her attire when the butler returned.

'Mrs Dove will see you in the drawing room.'

She followed him into the yellow, green, and gilt chamber. The thick velvet drapes were tied back with yellow cord to frame the pleasant vista of the park. Light streamed through the panes of glass, illuminating the thick, patterned carpet. Huge vases full of summer flowers brightened the corners.

Joan Dove stood at one of the tall windows, gazing pensively out into the street. It struck Lavinia that she made an excellent match for her new lover, Lord Vale. Joan was in her early forties, but she possessed the sort of striking profile and graceful height that would allow her to carry her beauty with her for many years.

It never ceased to amaze Lavinia that she had become friends with this woman. On the face of it, they had very little in common. Joan had come to her first as a client. At the time of her husband's death a little more than a year ago, she had inherited not only his fortune but, quite possibly, his position as the head of a mysterious underworld organization known as the Blue Chamber.

At the height of its power under Fielding Dove's guidance, the tentacles of the Blue Chamber had stretched throughout England and beyond, onto the Continent. According to Tobias, who, in his capacity as a spy, had had every reason to know, the Chamber had operated a variety of businesses. Some of those enterprises had been legitimate. Others had been decidedly less so. The links between the two had often been murky.

The Blue Chamber was believed to have disintegrated in the wake of Dove's death. Those few who were privy to the truth about his illicit activities assumed he had concealed his role as the lord of a criminal empire from his beloved wife and daughter. It was understood, after all, that gentlemen, even those engaged in legitimate investments, seldom troubled their ladies with the details of their business ventures.

Dove had been not only a gentleman by birth, he had also been extremely secretive. There was no reason to think that he had taken Joan into his confidence.

Lavinia and Tobias, however, were not so certain. There were rumors in certain quarters of the underworld that the clandestine operations of the Chamber were now under new management. And the only person around who appeared to be capable of running such an extensive enterprise was Joan.

Lavinia had no intention of asking Joan if the gossip was true. It was, she reflected, one of those questions one did not ask if one could avoid it.

On the other hand, it was difficult not to notice that, now that she had emerged from mourning, Joan exhibited a decided preference for a particular shade of blue. Her fashionable gowns and many of the gemstones she wore could best be described as *azure* in color.

Azure had been Fielding Dove's secret title during the years when he controlled the Blue Chamber.

'Mrs Lake, madam.' The butler glanced at the silver tea tray. 'Shall I fetch another cup?'

'That won't be necessary, thank you, Pugh,' Joan said quietly. 'Maryanne declined to take any while she was here. Mrs Lake can use her cup.'

'Yes, madam.' Pugh bowed himself out of the drawing room and closed the door.

'Please be seated, Lavinia.' Joan's smile was warm but tinged with a wan, unhappy quality. 'I am delighted to see you, but I must admit this visit comes as a surprise. What happened in the country?'

'There were some complications.' Lavinia sank down onto one of the chairs and studied Joan's drawn features with concern. 'Are you feeling ill? I do not want to impose. Perhaps it would be best if I came back later?'

'No, this is an excellent time.' Joan seated herself on the sofa and reached for the teapot on the heavily worked silver tray. 'I have just concluded a most unpleasant conversation with my daughter, and I am badly in need of a distraction.'

'I see.' Lavinia took the cup and saucer Joan handed to her. 'Well, as it happens, I have one for you.'

'Excellent.' Joan picked up her own cup and looked at Lavinia with a determined anticipation. 'May I assume that Lake and March has taken on a new case and that it is connected to the rather sudden death of Lord Fullerton?'

Lavinia smiled. 'I never cease to be astonished by the manner in which you are always conversant with the latest news.'

'I daresay that word of Fullerton's fall from Beaumont's roof reached London before you did. And the fact that Vale got his carriage back somewhat sooner than planned told us both that you and Mr March were likely involved in the matter.'

'Yes, of course.'

Joan gave her a sympathetic smile. 'I am so sorry that your visit to the country was cut short.' She paused delicately. 'I don't suppose that you and Mr March had much opportunity to, mmm, enjoy some private moments communing with nature before the disaster occurred?'

'Fullerton managed to plummet straight past my window in the course of one of the few private moments Mr March and I were able to share.' Lavinia shuddered at the memory and took a breath. 'He screamed, Joan.'

'I presume you do not refer to Mr March.'

'I cannot envision Tobias screaming at the sight of the gates of hell, let alone in surprise at a body falling past a window. No, it was Fullerton who shrieked, and it was a most bloodcurdling sound, I assure you.'

'I can well imagine.' Joan sipped her tea and lowered her cup. 'And you immediately suspected murder most foul.'

'It was impossible to avoid that conclusion. In any event, we found proof shortly thereafter.'

She gave Joan a quick summary of events. When she concluded her tale, Joan studied her with an expression of grave concern.

'This is not merely another case, is it?' she asked.

'No.' Lavinia set her cup down with great care. 'I will be honest with you. Tobias thinks that the business with the memento-mori ring implies that this new murderer has issued a challenge, that he or she is playing out some deadly game. But I fear that the villain's real goal may be revenge.'

'Against Mrs Gray or Mr March?'

Lavinia shrugged. 'Perhaps both. But in truth, I am most anxious about Tobias's safety.'

Joan raised her brows. 'I collect that you are not overly fond of your new client?'

'Mrs Gray is very beautiful. She is also a woman of the world. My intuition tells me that she would not scruple to use her wiles to manipulate a man if she thought the tactic would prove effective.'

Joan's mouth curved upward at the corners. 'I very much doubt that such a strategy would work with Mr March. It has been my observation that he and Vale have a great deal in common. One of the attributes they share is a remarkable degree of sound judgment. Neither would be easily deceived by a beautiful face or an alluring manner.'

'I am aware of that, but the thing is, Tobias feels some responsibility for what happened in the past. He blames himself for having set Zachary Elland on the path that eventually led to his undertaking a career as a professional murderer.'

'That is absurd.'

'Yes, of course it is.' Lavinia spread her hands, relieved to be able to confide her deepest fears about the case. 'I explained that to him in no uncertain terms.'

'Yes, I'm sure you did. You are seldom reluctant to give Mr March the benefit of your opinion. But in this matter, I collect that he was unwilling to accept your view?'

'Unfortunately, when it comes to taking responsibility for events in which he was involved, Tobias is inclined to err on the side of assuming that he should have been in complete control of matters.'

Joan nodded sagely. 'That is a fault that I have observed in Vale as well. In my experience, men of their sort frequently blame themselves when things go wrong, even if there was nothing they could have done to alter the course of events. Fielding had the same habit. I suspect that inclination is a character trait that goes hand in hand with great strength of will and purpose.'

'Tobias also blames himself for not realizing sooner that Elland had become a professional murderer.'

'It is often most difficult to see evil in those whom we believe we know well.'

'Very true,' Lavinia said. 'Well, that is the whole of the tale, or at least as much as we know at this point. As you can see, the only way out of this tangle is to find the killer.'

'And to that end, you seek to discover who benefited most from Fullerton's death.'

'I came to you for advice on the subject because you have excellent connections in Society.'

'Let me think a moment. There is no doubt that Fullerton's nephew will benefit directly. But as I recall, the young man is quite wealthy in his own right and about to marry an heiress. He will also acquire a more elevated title when his father dies. I see no strong motive in that quarter.'

'I agree.' Lavinia was reluctant to let go of that theory, but she had to admit it did not hold much promise. 'Can you think of anything else that will be significantly changed because of Fullerton's death?'

Joan tapped her fingertip against the side of her cup. 'Obviously Lord Fullerton will no longer be going through with his wedding plans, which means that the Panfield girl will be back on the marriage mart next Season. I can only imagine that her mama and papa are feeling quite downcast at the moment. It is common knowledge that Panfield is fishing for a title for his daughter.'

Lavinia contemplated that angle for a moment. 'What about the girl herself? Was she equally enthusiastic about the marriage to Fullerton?'

'I have no idea how she felt about the situation. She is quite young and of course had very little to say in the matter. But I cannot imagine that a fat, aging baron was the romantic hero of her dreams.'

'Hmm.'

Joan looked amused. 'I think you can forget the notion that the girl could have arranged such a drastic means of ridding herself of an unwelcome fiancé. I doubt very much that an innocent young lady just out of the schoolroom could have secured the services of a professional murderer, let alone found a way to pay him.'

'I take your point,' Lavinia said. 'Well, then, what about the true romantic hero of her dreams?'

'I beg your pardon?'

'Is there perhaps some young gentleman who is passionately in love with Miss Panfield and who might have concocted a scheme to get Fullerton out of his way?'

Joan considered for a moment. 'Not that I am aware of, but I admit that I have not paid much attention.'

They drank tea together in a companionable silence for a while.

'I wonder what sort of temperament is required to make a person contemplate hiring a murderer,' Lavinia said finally.

'Presumably one with a great capacity for overwhelming greed or ambition.'

'Or perhaps one that is capable of harboring a deep rage,' Lavinia said slowly. 'Can you think of anyone who would have had a reason to hate Fullerton so intensely?'

'Not offhand, although I suppose any man of his age might have acquired some enemies along the way.' Joan looked intrigued. 'Do you want me to make some inquiries in that direction?'

'I would be very grateful if you would do that. There is no time to waste and we must pursue every avenue. This entire affair is so extremely muddled. We do not even know if Fullerton is the killer's first victim.'

Joan's cup paused halfway to her lips. Her eyes narrowed faintly. 'Do you have reason to suspect that there may have been others?'

'It's possible. We simply do not know.' Restless and frustrated, Lavinia rose and went to examine the large golden chrysanthemums in the nearest vase. 'Can you think of any other recent unexpected or unexplained deaths in Society?'

Joan pursed her lips. 'Apsley's heart failed him in May, but given his ill health, no one was surprised. Lady Thornby was taken off by a fever last month, but she had been bedridden for nearly a year.'

She fell silent, thinking. Lavinia listened to the ticking of the tall clock.

'I confess that I did wonder a bit at the news of Lady Rowland's death last month,' Joan said eventually. 'The gossip is that she accidentally consumed too much of her bedtime tonic and died in her sleep. But those who were close to her said that she brewed the concoction herself and had taken it regularly for years without incident.'

Lavinia turned quickly. 'Suicide?'

'I am strongly inclined to doubt it.'

'How can you be so sure?'

'The woman was a tyrant,' Joan said flatly. 'She controlled the purse strings in the family, and she did not hesitate to use them to force the others to bend to her will. At the time of her death, she had an excellent reason to live.'

Lavinia felt her curiosity stir. 'Why do you say that?'

'From all accounts, Lady Rowland was looking forward to the announcement of her eldest granddaughter's engagement next month. She had agreed to settle a vast sum on the girl, provided her papa accepted an offer from Ferring's oldest son. It was no secret that Lady Rowland was obsessed with seeing the marriage take place.'

'Why was that?'

'The *on-dit* is that in her youth, Lady Rowland conceived a great passion for Ferring's father. Her parents forced her to marry Rowland instead, but the gossip is that she never got over her feelings for Ferring. Indeed, they are rumored to have had a long-standing affair after Ferring himself was married. He died a few years ago.'

'Do you believe that Lady Rowland was determined to live out her dreams through her eldest granddaughter?'

'That is what I was told. It is certainly no secret that after her own husband died, she used the Rowland fortune to buy the Ferring heir for her granddaughter.' Joan sipped tea and slowly lowered her cup, eyes faintly narrowed. 'But I believe that has all changed now'

'Why is that?'

'Maryanne mentioned just last week that she had heard there would be no engagement announcement after all. Something about the young lady's papa having refused Ferring's offer.'

Lavinia felt excitement leap. 'What happened to change his mind?'

'I cannot say. At the time the subject was not of particular interest.' Joan paused. 'But I could probably find out for you.'

'Yes, I think I would very much like to know the particulars.' Lavinia tapped the toe of her half boot on the thick carpet. 'Who controls Lady Rowland's fortune now?'

'Her son, the granddaughter's papa.'

'Well, now,' Lavinia said to herself.

Joan gave her an inquiring look. 'What are you thinking?'

'It occurs to me that in the wake of both Lord Fullerton's and Lady Rowland's deaths, wedding plans were drastically altered.'

Joan tilted her head slightly to the side, considering that conclusion. 'Do you know, now that I study the question in that light, there may be a third death that fits the formula, that of a gentleman of some forty years named Newbold. He was found dead at the foot of his own staircase one morning a few weeks ago. Everyone assumed that he had had too much to drink and lost his balance on the top step.'

'What marriage plans were altered by his death?'

'His own.' Joan gave a tiny shudder. 'He was quite a dreadful man who was known to seek out the brothels that would supply him with very young children.'

'Vile creature,' Lavinia whispered.

'Yes. But a very rich vile creature. As was the case with Fullerton, he had recently got engaged to a young lady. I wonder if the chit knows how very fortunate she is to have had her wedding date canceled.'

'Well,' Lavinia said again.

Joan frowned. 'The thing is, Lavinia, as with the other two instances, no one involved appeared to be opposed to Newbold's marriage plans. Indeed, all three of these proposed alliances were excellent matches in terms of money and social connections. In Society, those are the only things that matter. You know that as well as I do.'

'In most cases, perhaps, but not always. For example, I know that you were very concerned for Maryanne's happiness when the plans were made for her marriage.'

'Yes, that is true.' Joan looked at the portrait of Fielding Dove that hung above the mantel, her expression unreadable. 'Fielding was equally concerned. Our own marriage had been such a warm and happy alliance, you see.'

Lavinia realized that Joan was working hard to conceal some strong emotion. She did not know whether to ignore her friend's mood or try to offer comfort. She and Joan were still in the process of forging a friendship. There were some boundaries she did not want to cross unless she was invited to do so.

She walked back to the chair she had occupied earlier and stopped beside it.

'I know you loved Fielding Dove very much,' she said carefully.

That seemed sufficiently noncommittal, she thought. If Joan wanted to maintain her privacy, she could let the remark pass with a simple acknowledgment.

Joan nodded, never taking her eyes off the portrait.

For a moment Lavinia thought that would be the end of the conversation.

Joan got to her feet and went back to stand at the window. 'Shortly before you arrived, my daughter took great pains to remind me of that very fact.'

'I do not wish to pry,' Lavinia said. 'But I sense that you are unhappy. Is there anything I can do?'

Joan's elegant jaw tightened. She blinked several times, as though she had something in her eye. 'Maryanne called today to lecture me about the impropriety of my new friendship with Lord Vale.'

'Oh, dear.'

'She seems to feel that I am somehow being unfaithful to Fielding's memory.'

'I see.'

'It is rather unsettling to be lectured on such matters by one's daughter.'

Lavinia winced. 'If it is any consolation, I recently endured a similar talk from my niece. Emeline made it clear that in her opinion my connection with Mr March has gone on long enough without the formality of a marriage license.'

Joan cast her a quick, wryly sympathetic glance. 'Then you can perhaps understand some of my feelings in this matter. Tell me truthfully, do you think that my connection with Vale is evidence that I no longer treasure and respect Fielding's memory?'

'Joan, the nature of your friendship with Lord Vale is none of my concern. However, since you have asked for my opinion, I will give it to you. From what you have said of your marriage, I believe that Fielding Dove loved you very much. Therefore, I cannot imagine that he would have wanted you to deny yourself the opportunity to experience happiness and affection after he was gone.'

'That is what I have told myself.'

'If you doubt it, try reversing the situation in your mind. If you were the one who had been taken off first, would you have wanted Fielding to be alone for the rest of his life?'

'No,' Joan said quietly. 'Above all else, I would have wanted him to be happy.'

'I suspect that is precisely what he would have said about you if someone had asked him the question.'

'Thank you.' Joan sounded somewhat relieved. She turned around and smiled. 'It is very kind of you to reassure me. I confess, Maryanne's tears and accusations today rattled me. I began to wonder if I was, indeed, failing to honor Fielding in my heart.'

'I assure you, Emeline's little homily on the proprieties sent a few tremors through me also.'

'I must say, under any other circumstance, our predicament would almost be amusing. You and I have both spent many years and a great deal of effort instructing two young ladies in the rules of decorum and proper behavior, and now they see fit to turn the tables on us.'

'It does give one pause, does it not?' Lavinia frowned. 'I wonder if it is an indication that the younger generation may be developing a taste for prudery.'

Joan shuddered. 'What a ghastly thought. Discretion and decorum are all very well, but it would be a great pity, indeed, if this current crop of young ladies and gentlemen were to become a nation of narrow-minded, straitlaced prigs.'

Twelve

Tobias went up the steps of Number 7 with a sense of anticipation that he had been savoring since breakfast. The prospect of an afternoon tryst with Lavinia was the only bright spot in what had proven to be an extremely frustrating and unproductive day. He wanted nothing more than to sink down onto the bed in the bedchamber upstairs and lose himself in his lover's arms for a stolen hour or two.

His hopes crumbled when Mrs Chilton opened the door.

'Mrs Chilton, this is a surprise. I could have sworn that at breakfast this morning you mentioned that you would be going out to shop for currants this afternoon and that Mrs Lake would be here alone for a time.'

'There's no need to look at me like that, sir.' Mrs Chilton drew herself up, glowering. 'Plans changed. Not my fault. First, out of the blue, Mrs Lake announces she's off to pay a visit to Mrs Dove. Says she'll return by three.'

'It is just now three, Mrs Chilton.'

'Well, she isn't back yet and that's all there is to it. Wouldn't make much difference to your plans if she were here, and that's a fact.'

'And why is that?'

Mrs Chilton glanced over her shoulder in the direction of the closed parlor door and lowered her voice to a conspiratorial whisper. 'Because not ten minutes past a lady called. When I informed her that Mrs Lake was out, she demanded to know when she was expected. I told her around three o'clock, and the next thing I know the lady declares that she'll wait.'

'Damnation. She's still here?'

'Aye. I put her in the parlor and gave her some tea. Wasn't anything else I could do.' Mrs Chilton wiped her large, rough hands on her apron. 'Claims she's a client. Thought perhaps she'd come in response to the notice Mrs Lake put into the newspaper a while back. You know how enthusiastic Mrs Lake is about advertising her services in the papers. Says it's the modern way to go about running a successful business enterprise.'

'Kindly do not remind me of that bloody advertisement.' Tobias stalked into the hall and sent his hat sailing toward the small end table. 'You know my feelings on that subject.'

'Aye, sir. You've made 'em clear.' Mrs Chilton closed the door. 'But as there haven't been any serious clients until now, it didn't seem to be doing any harm. To tell you the truth, I think Mrs Lake was getting a bit depressed about the entire project.'

'Unfortunately, she was not sufficiently cast down to call off the scheme.'

Thus far his fears that Lavinia's attempt to advertise her private-inquiry services in the newspapers would draw an unsavory crowd of potential clients to her door had gone unrealized. To date, only three people had responded to the notice concerning an expert available for the purpose of conducting inquiries of a personal and private nature. To his secret relief, all three potential clients had immediately changed their minds when they discovered that the expert in question was a female.

'It's not my fault the lady in the parlor chose to call upon Mrs Lake this afternoon,' Mrs Chilton muttered.

'I do not suppose there is anything you could have done.' Tobias started toward the parlor door. 'But I believe I shall just have a word with this new client before Mrs Lake returns.'

'Hold on there, sir.' Mrs Chilton hurried after him, alarmed. 'I'm not sure Mrs Lake would want you to be speaking to her client without her being present.'

'What objection can she possibly make?' Tobias smiled his most innocent smile. 'We are partners, after all.'

'Only on some cases. And you know very well that if she finds out you've cost her a paying client, she'll be furious.'

'I just want to assure myself that this client is respectable and can afford Mrs Lake's fees.'

He opened the door before Mrs Chilton could do it for him and walked into the parlor.

The lady seated on the sofa turned to look at him.

Bloody hell, Tobias thought. She *was* a client. So much for his plan to get rid of her before Lavinia returned.

'What are you doing here, Aspasia?' he asked.

'Tobias.' She gave him her cool, knowing smile. 'What a coincidence. I came here to talk to Mrs Lake because I assumed you would be busy with your inquiries. I wanted to find out how the investigation was proceeding.'

If this was any other client, he would lie through his teeth and tell her that he had made substantial progress. He always said that sort of thing to whoever was paying the fee for his services. But this was Aspasia, and she was not a typical client.

He went to stand with his back to the window, automatically putting the light behind him, and looked at Aspasia.

'I cannot speak for Mrs Lake,' he said, 'because I have not yet had a chance to compare notes with her this afternoon. But as for myself, I have made damned little progress. I sent our assistants out to make inquiries regarding the rings and the blond wig, however, and I have hopes that they will come back with some useful information.' He glimpsed Lavinia out of the corner of his eye. She was on the front step. 'I see my associate has returned. Perhaps she will have news.'

Lavinia was a vision in deep violet. He found himself smiling a little even though his plans for the afternoon appeared to be in ruins. Something inside him always responded to the sight of her, he thought. He was aware of a sense of bone-deep satisfaction whenever he was in her presence.

He heard the muffled sound of the front door opening and closing. A moment later Lavinia breezed into the parlor. She had removed her bonnet in the front hall. Her face was warm and flushed from her recent exercise. The feminine vitality that she radiated made his insides tighten with a familiar hunger. Visions of the bed upstairs tormented him.

'Mrs Gray.' Lavinia inclined her head a bare half inch. 'Forgive me. I wasn't expecting you.'

Her smile was so polished and professional that only someone who knew her well would notice the acute lack of warmth, Tobias thought.

'I'm sorry, Mrs Lake,' Aspasia said. 'But I simply could not rest. I returned to London yesterday afternoon. I came here today because I had to find out if you and Tobias had discovered anything useful yet.'

'Yes, indeed.' Lavinia sat down on a chair near the tea tray and arranged her skirts with a flourish. Her smile never dimmed. If anything it actually brightened. 'We have made substantial progress.'

Unlike himself, Tobias thought, she had no compunction about lying to this particular client.

'Indeed?' Aspasia raised her brows. 'Tobias was just telling me that he had not been terribly successful. Isn't that right, Tobias?'

He clasped his hands behind his back. 'I certainly do not have much to offer yet.'

Lavinia gave him a repressive glare. 'How fortunate, then, that I do have some useful information.'

She was certainly determined to follow his rules for dealing with a client, even if he was not bothering to do so, he thought.

'Your professional abilities never cease to astound me, madam,' he said dryly. 'What did you learn from your *private informant*?'

He saw at once that she had caught the slight inflection he had given the last two words. He doubted that Lavinia had had any intention of dragging Mrs Dove's name into this affair, but it was best to be cautious.

She turned to Aspasia with a businesslike air. 'I have discovered that there may have been at least two other recent deaths in Society that are highly suspicious. Lady Rowland and a certain Mr Newbold. Both departed this earth quite unexpectedly.'

That got his attention. 'I heard the rumor concerning Lady Rowland. An overdose of the medicine she took to help her sleep. No one mentioned Newbold.'

Aspasia's brows puckered in a delicate frown. 'Newbold died in a drunken fall down his own staircase a month and a half ago, I believe. I heard something about it shortly after I returned to Town. I did not pay much attention.'

'Most people ignored his death.' Lavinia's mouth tightened in a manner that emphasized her disgust. 'Evidently Newbold was quite dreadful. He was known to patronize the brothels that cater to those creatures who enjoy debauching children. In my opinion the young lady to whom he had recently got engaged had a very close call. Only imagine the horror of being wed to such a man.'

'Indeed.' Aspasia drank tea and made no further comment.

'The thing is,' Lavinia continued, turning toward Tobias, 'I find the coincidence extremely intriguing, don't you, sir?'

'Three unanticipated deaths? Yes, I do.'

'Not the deaths,' she said impatiently, 'the cancellation of the wedding plans that followed in each instance.'

She was serious, he thought. He could not believe it. Neither could Aspasia, to judge by her expression.

'Lavinia,' he said carefully, 'are you implying that the motive behind each of these three murders was a desire to stop a wedding from taking place?'

Lavinia set down the pot. 'Have you got a better motive?'

'I'm working on one.' Her certainty irritated him. 'All three deaths resulted in the transfer of fortunes. That makes for a lot of suspects among the family members.'

Aspasia's expression altered from one of stunned disbelief to thoughtful consideration.

'I heard the rumors about Lady Rowland's obsessive desire to see her eldest granddaughter wed to her old lover's grandson,' she said slowly. 'The woman had a reputation for using her money to manipulate everyone in her family. But what would be the point of murdering her? She was going to endow the girl.'

'Only if she consented to wed Ferring,' Lavinia reminded her. 'But now her papa has taken control of the Rowland fortune, and evidently young Ferring's offer was not accepted. The granddaughter is free to marry someone else. In one way or another, the other two young ladies have also been delivered from the prospect of extremely unhappy marriages.'

'Surely you are not suggesting that these innocent young girls could have concocted a diabolical scheme to hire a professional killer?' Tobias growled. 'That defies credibility.'

Aspasia's mouth tightened. 'He's right, Mrs Lake. It is an interesting theory, but it is impossible to imagine that three extremely sheltered young ladies with no experience of the world could possibly reason out how to hire, let alone pay, a professional murderer.'

Lavinia set her shoulders in a manner that Tobias had learned to recognize. She was preparing to defend her position.

'I would remind you both,' she said, 'that when it comes to alliances at that level of Society, there are many people besides the young ladies involved who might have a strong interest in the marriage contracts.'

'Do you believe that others in the families resorted to murder in order to halt the weddings?' Tobias folded his arms. 'That is a crazed conclusion. We are talking about a killer who is attempting to imitate the Memento-Mori Man. It is impossible to imagine a professional murderer hiring himself out to some matchmaking mama.'

To his surprise, Aspasia spoke before Lavinia could respond.

'Marriage is a very serious matter, and young girls have very little say in the arrangements that are made for them.' Her mouth curved coldly. 'I can personally testify to that. My papa certainly did not worry overmuch about my happiness when he accepted the offer for my hand.'

The sharp, icy edge on that last statement caught Tobias by surprise. It occurred to him that he had never heard Aspasia discuss her brief marriage.

Lavinia watched her quietly, not speaking. Tobias sensed that she was suddenly keenly interested in what Aspasia had to say.

'Nevertheless,' Aspasia continued, 'when it comes to alliances in the polite world, there is nothing unusual about such arrangements. I have certainly never heard of anyone committing murder to halt a wedding.'

'As professional private-inquiry agents,' Lavinia said in her most authoritative manner, 'I can assure you that Mr March and I have seen cases where murder has been done for far less reason.' She beetled her brows at Tobias. 'Is that not true, sir?'

The last thing he wanted to do was get caught in the middle of this little skirmish, he decided. He sought a diplomatic way out.

'There are any number of motives for murder,' he said, keeping his tone as neutral as possible.

Neither woman looked satisfied.

Aspasia frowned at him. 'I trust you will not waste time pursuing false leads.'

He inclined his head. 'I try to avoid that sort of thing.'

'So do I,' Lavinia said shortly.

Aspasia rose and walked toward the door. 'I must be off. Please keep me informed.'

'Of course.' Tobias crossed the parlor to open the door for her. 'Good day, Aspasia.'

She hesitated before moving out into the hall. 'I fear we do not have any time to waste, Tobias. You must find this new Memento-Mori Man, and you must do it quickly. Who knows what he is planning next?'

He gripped the doorknob so tightly it was a wonder it did not come off in his hand. 'I am well aware of the urgency involved here.'

Mrs Chilton was hovering in the hall. She opened the front door for Aspasia, who went swiftly down the steps.

Tobias waited until she was gone. Then he took out his pocket watch and smiled pointedly at Mrs Chilton. 'I believe that you still have time to go out for currants.'

Mrs Chilton rolled her eyes. 'Very well, sir.' She darted a glance into the parlor behind him and lowered her voice. 'But you had best be quick about it. Miss Emeline is due back around five. It would not do for her to walk in at an awkward moment.'

'Thank you for the warning, Mrs Chilton. I assure you it is unnecessary.'

'Humph.'

He went back into the parlor. Lavinia had risen and gone to stand at the window. She stood with her back to him, her attention on the street.

He crossed the room and came to a halt behind her. Resting his hands on her shoulders, he followed her gaze. Together they watched Aspasia vanish around the corner. Lavinia did not turn around.

'You must make allowances for Aspasia,' he said quietly. 'She is frightened and very anxious.'

'Mmm.'

'She has every reason to be worried. Zachary Elland was a cold-blooded killer, and whoever seeks to take his place is obviously of the same temperament. And you must admit that she's right: This notion that there is a connection between three possible murders and three changes of marital plans is not a particularly substantial theory at the moment.'

'Mmm.'

'Lavinia, I can see that you are disturbed. Did you and Mrs Dove discuss some other matter that you have not yet mentioned?'

'Joan asked me if I thought that she was betraying her husband's memory by forming a liaison with Lord Vale. Evidently her daughter is quite distraught about the relationship.'

'I see.' Whatever it was he had been expecting to hear, this was not it. 'What did you tell her?'

'I reminded her that her husband had loved her very deeply. I told her that I was certain he would have wanted her to be happy again, just as she would have wanted him to find happiness if she had been taken first.'

'Indeed,' he said, for lack of anything more inspired. What the devil was this about? 'Well, I'm certain that you reassured her. Now, then, Mrs Chilton mentioned that she is going out to shop for some items that she needs for dinner. What do you say we—'

'Tobias?'

'What is it?' he asked, deeply cautious now.

'If anything were to happen to me and you were left alone, I would want you to find happiness.'

Of their own accord, his hands clamped fiercely around her elegantly curved shoulders. He felt himself turn to stone at the thought of her being snatched from him by death. A crimson haze filled his head. It occurred to him that he would likely go mad if he ever lost her.

'I would want you to find happiness,' she reiterated softly, apparently unaware of the impact her words were having on him. '*But not with Aspasia Gray*.'

For some reason those last words freed him from the terrible spell. He discovered that he could breathe again. He used his hands to turn her around to face him.

'I cannot imagine wanting any other woman the way I want you,' he said. His voice sounded raw and harsh, even to his own ears.

'Oh, Tobias.' She put her arms around him and pressed her head against his shoulder. 'I do love you so.'

'I am delighted to hear that.' He kissed her hair. Her scent filled his head, driving out the last remnants of the red haze. 'But, please, if you have any regard for me at all, never, ever talk about being taken from me. I cannot bear the thought.'

Her arms tightened around him. 'Just as I cannot bear the thought of losing you.'

He folded her close, letting the sunlight warm them both. After a while, he drew her out of the parlor and up the stairs.

Later he raised himself up on his elbow and glanced at his watch on the bedside table. A quarter past four. Time to get dressed. It was becoming harder and harder to leave her bed, he thought. Reluctantly, he sat up and swung his feet to the floor.

'Tobias?'

He turned to look at her. She was lying back against the pillows, her eyes very green in the afternoon light.

'I must go, my love. Emeline will be home in less than forty-five minutes. I am to meet with Anthony at five. With luck he will have some news of the rings.'

'I know' She folded her arms behind her head. The movement caused one neatly shaped breast to escape the sheet. 'Tobias, I gave Joan the right advice, did I not? Don't you think that Dove would have wanted her to find happiness with someone else after he was gone?'

He did not reply. Instead, he leaned down and kissed her bare breast. Her skin was soft and warm from his lovemaking. He caught a trace of his own scent on her and knew a rush of fierce, unbridled possessiveness. His woman.

She frowned. 'You do agree with me, don't you? About how Fielding Dove would have felt in this situation?'

He looked at her for a long time and then very deliberately he leaned over her, caging her between his arms. He bent his head and brushed his mouth across hers.

'I cannot speak for Fielding Dove,' he said. 'But I can promise you this, Lavinia. If you should ever find with another man what we have found together, I would come back from the grave to haunt you.'

Thirteen

At half past five that afternoon, Tobias was back in his study, feet propped on the corner of his desk. The hour in Lavinia's bedchamber had relieved some of the tension that had plagued him since the events at Beaumont Castle, but he could feel the sense of urgency returning as he listened to Anthony's report.

'There were no recent sales or thefts of memento-mori rings at any of the antiquities shops we've checked thus far.' Anthony examined his notes. 'We have several more dealers left to question, however. Do you want us to continue our interviews tomorrow?'

'Yes.' Tobias studied the list of dealers they had compiled. 'Those damned rings are among the few real leads we've got. The killer had to obtain them somewhere. What about the blond wigs?'

'Emeline and I had enough time to talk to only two wig-makers yesterday afternoon. One of them did take a commission for a blond wig in recent months.'

Tobias looked up swiftly. 'Did you get the name of the client?'

'Yes, but it won't do you any good. The wig-maker has known her for years. He described her as very elderly and quite eccentric. She lives in the country and only comes to Town twice a year to shop. I doubt that she's your professional murderer, Tobias.'

'Damnation.' Tobias went back to contemplating the list for a moment longer and then he deliberately tore off a section at the bottom. 'You and Miss Emeline will finish questioning the antiquities dealers. Mrs Lake and I will take the remainder of the wig-makers. With all four of us working on the project, we should be able to speak with every establishment on this list within the next two or three days.'

'Very well.' Anthony sat back in his chair. 'Whitby said you are planning to meet with Smiling Jack at the Gryphon tonight. Do you want me to accompany you? That is not the safest of neighborhoods at night.'

'No, that won't be necessary. I'll take a hackney and pay the driver to wait.'

Anthony gave him a curious look. 'Why seek Smiling Jack's assistance on this case? From what you've told me, the previous Memento-Mori Man had nothing to do with the sort of common criminal who comes out of the stews. Do you think this new killer is different?'

'No. But it struck me last night that we actually knew very little about Zachary Elland. He had no family, apparently. After his death, no one came forward to collect his personal effects. There was, in fact, no trace of him in Society. After he was gone it was as though he had never existed. I wondered if perhaps I was overlooking some aspect of his past that might give us a clue.'

'I see.' Anthony uncoiled from his chair and started across the room. 'Good luck to you.' He paused at the door and glanced back with a small frown. 'Tobias, I have a question to ask. It is of a, uh, somewhat personal nature.'

'What is it?'

'I realize that Fullerton's murder upset your plans, but before he fell off that roof, did you and Mrs Lake have an opportunity to discuss your private affairs?'

Tobias slowly lowered the severed sheet of paper. 'Our what?'

Anthony reddened a little, but he made no move to slip out the door. 'Emeline and I both naturally assumed that you invited Mrs Lake to accompany you to the country-house party because you wanted to take advantage of the opportunity to bring up the subject of your intentions.'

'What intentions would those be?' Tobias asked evenly.

Disapproval coalesced in Anthony's eyes. 'Never say that you did not even mention the matter.'

'What the devil are you talking about?'

'I'm talking about whether or not you asked Mrs Lake to marry you, of course.'

'Bloody hell,' Tobias said softly.

'What happened?' Anthony's frown turned to alarm. 'Good lord, man, never say that you lost your nerve?'

'The status of my intentions toward Mrs Lake is none of your affair.'

'The two of you have been seeing a great deal of each other privately for some months now.'

'What of it? We are partners.'

'Partners? What about the business of sending Mrs Chilton out for currants?'

Tobias could feel himself turning surly. 'Mrs Chilton's currant tarts are far and away the best I have ever tasted.'

'This has nothing to do with Mrs Chilton's currant tarts and well you know it.' Anthony planted his booted feet a little apart on the carpet. 'Mrs Lake is a respectable lady. It's obvious that the two of you have formed a great attachment for each other. Don't you think it's time you did the gentlemanly thing?'

'You know damned well that I am not yet in a position to ask Mrs Lake to marry me. I invested everything I've got in those shares in Crackenburne's shipping venture. Until that bloody vessel returns to port, I have nothing to offer her.'

Anthony assumed a sympathetic air. 'I know you're concerned about your finances. I am equally concerned about my own. But as it happens, I have been thinking about our situation and I believe I have come up with a solution that will solve all our problems.'

'What do you suggest we do?' Tobias tossed the list of wig-makers onto the desk. 'Find ourselves an alchemist who can transmute lead into gold?'

Anthony swept his arm out, vaguely indicating the study. 'The way I see it, the answer is this house.'

'There is nothing wrong with this house. I own it. It is, in point of fact, my most substantial asset.'

'Yes, I know,' Anthony said smoothly. 'While I, on the other hand, can barely manage the rent on my rooms in Jasper Street.'

'You cannot place the blame for your inadequate lodgings on me. It was your decision to move out. I believe you said something about wanting your own rooms. As I recall, there was a good deal of talk about needing private quarters where you could entertain your friends at all hours of the day or night.'

'The thing is, while my lodgings are adequate for a single gentleman, I could not possibly ask Emeline to set up housekeeping in such a small space. She is accustomed to that very nice little house in Claremont Lane.'

'On that we agree.'

'The way I see it, Tobias, there is one residence too many here.'

'I beg your pardon?'

'I have worked it out and it is really very simple. If you were to do the honorable thing and marry Mrs Lake, the pair of you could move into Number Seven Claremont Lane together. I could give up my lodgings on Jasper Street, marry Miss Emeline, and move into this house with her. You see how neat and tidy it would be for all of us?'

Tobias suddenly understood.

'My *house*.' He took his heels down off the desk and got to his feet very deliberately. 'You're trying to get your hands on my house so that you can ask Miss Emeline to marry you. That's what this is all about, isn't it?'

Anthony took a step back toward the door, palm up in a placating manner. 'Now, Tobias, there is no call to lose your temper. I thought it was a very sensible plan, one that would benefit all of us. In addition, it would enable me to stop paying rent. Also, we would not need a third housekeeper. You could take Whitby with you, and Mrs Chilton could come to live with Emeline and me.'

'If you think for one moment,' Tobias said very softly, 'that I am going to allow you to take possession of my only major asset, you are out of your mind. Now, I suggest that you get back to the business for which I am paying you a good deal more than you deserve before I decide to hire another assistant.'

'Tobias, please listen for a moment.'

'Go.' Tobias aimed a finger at the door. 'Find out who sold those damned memento-mori rings to a professional murderer. Do I make myself clear?'

'Perfectly.'

Anthony whipped open the door and went swiftly out into the hall.

Tobias waited until he heard the muffled sound of the front door closing before he slowly sat down.

Morosely, he contemplated the study. It was filled with the things he had acquired over the years – his books, globe, telescope, and brandy decanter.

This house was not only his greatest financial asset, it was his home. He had purchased it with the help of a loan from Crackenburne shortly before he met Ann and her younger brother, Anthony.

He and Ann had had five happy years in this house before he lost her and his stillborn son to childbed. He and Anthony had endured their shared grief together under this roof.

Anthony had been thirteen at the time of his beloved sister's death. Her passing left him bereft. He felt himself to be utterly alone in the world. His mother had expired when he was eight, not long after his wastrel father had been killed in a quarrel over a disputed hand of cards.

Anthony and Ann had gone to live with their only remaining relatives, a ghastly aunt and uncle. They had lived in that grim household for only a few months before the aunt arranged to rid herself of her unwanted burden by forcing Ann into a compromising position with Tobias. Her goal had been to marry off her niece and then place her nephew in an orphanage.

Tobias had taken one look at the desperate plight of Ann and her small brother and determined to rescue them both. He had not intended to marry Ann that day when he took her and Anthony away from their aunt's house, but he had soon changed his mind. Ann was not only very beautiful, she was gentle and kind, the sort of woman the poets described as ethereal.

The feelings that she had aroused in him had been tender and protective. He had always been careful to treat her with the care he would have given a delicate blossom. Looking back, he knew that he had kept his passions in check with her, ever conscious of the need for restraint. He recalled no quarrels between them. He had never lost his temper with her.

But in the end he had been unable to protect her. Perhaps, as Anthony had often observed, Ann had, indeed, been too good for this world.

She may well have gone to a better place, but Tobias and Anthony had been left to deal with the harsh realities of this world. Anthony initially fought his fears the only way he knew how: with anger. He had assumed the defiant air that only a thirteen-year-old boy could manage and demanded to know when he should pack his bags and leave.

You'll not be wanting me hanging around now that she's gone. It was Ann you loved. You only took me in because she would not be parted from me. I understand. I'm not your responsibility anymore. I can look after myself.

Tobias had worked hard to reassure the desperate, frightened boy, even as he himself dealt with what he now recognized as a form of melancholia. After Ann was buried he had been consumed with his feelings of guilt. He was all too aware that it was his passion – controlled and restrained as it had been – that had got her with child and in the end had brought about her death. There were days when he told himself that he should never have wed her. He'd had no right to expose her to the perils and risks of the marriage bed. She had never been intended for such earthy pursuits.

He and Anthony had blundered around for a long time in this house, two wounded creatures swimming together through a sunless sea of emotions. But life made its inexorable demands. Dragging Anthony with him, Tobias had set about meeting those demands. Together they had found a curious solace in daily routine.

Eventually, in a process that was so gradual that neither noticed it was taking place, he and Anthony had made their way into more tranquil waters. This house had seen them both through the long struggle.

But today, sitting here in his study, surrounded with his books, globe, telescope, and brandy decanter, he found himself thinking about how much he had come to look forward to stretching out his legs in front of Lavinia's cozy hearth.

At ten-thirty that evening, dressed as a rough-looking laborer, he sat in Smiling Jack's office, drinking his host's excellent smuggled brandy. The noise from the adjoining tavern was muffled by the heavy wall.

Jack had opened the Gryphon two years ago when he retired from his career as a smuggler. During the war, he had imported information on French shipping and military movements as well as illegal brandy. Tobias, in his role as a spy, had been a steady customer.

They came from very different worlds, but somehow a strong bond had been forged between them. It was based on mutual respect as well as mutual profit.

Their association had continued after each of them had gone on to new careers. Jack's tavern had proved to be an excellent collecting point for the streams of rumors and gossip that swirled out of London's criminal underworld. And, in his new line as a private-inquiry agent, Tobias frequently found himself in the market for information from that world.

'The Memento-Mori Man.' Smiling Jack lounged his great bulk in his massive chair. He absently scratched the grisly scar that curved from the corner of his mouth to a point just below his ear. 'Would that be the first one or the second one you're talking about?'

'I came here to talk about the second man, Zachary Elland, but I'll take any information I can get on the subject of either Memento-Mori Man.'

'I'm not sure I can help you.' Jack cradled his brandy glass in his big hands. 'There were rumors about a gentleman murderer when Elland was active but, as you well know, he operated in a better part of town and mingled with a more exclusive sort. As far as I know he never dipped into the stews for his clients, his victims, or his pleasures. In that way, at least, I reckon you could say that he was like the one who came before him.'

Tobias paused in the act of swallowing some of the brandy. Slowly he lowered the glass. 'You'd have been a small boy when the tales about the first Memento-Mori Man began to circulate. What do you remember?'

'They used to talk about him in hushed whispers. It was said he was so skillful that no one ever knew how many commissions he'd taken in the course of his career. The murders all looked like accidents or suicides or heart attacks. He was a legend.'

'Because he got away with murder?'

'No, because it was said that in his own way, he was a man of honor. He only took commissions for those he thought deserved to die. According to the tales we heard, he preferred to hunt the vicious and the vile in Society – the wealthy, powerful sort who would have otherwise got away with their crimes. He would kill for you, for a price, but only if he decided that it was a matter of rough justice.'

'He appointed himself magistrate and executioner, is that it?'

'Aye. So they said.'

'Crackenburne told me that the rumors about him faded away several years ago. He thinks the killer probably died.'

'Most likely.' Jack squinted a little. 'But a few years ago there was a tale going around that the gentleman killer had retired from his business and gone to live in a cottage by the seaside.'

'The Memento-Mori Man retired to a seaside cottage?' Tobias was almost amused. 'What a charming notion. Good legends never die, do they?'

'If he isn't dead, he'll be in his dotage by now. Hardly a threat to anyone.'

'He certainly isn't the murderer I'm looking for at the moment.

Mrs Lake got a brief glimpse of our new Memento-Mori Man at Beaumont Castle. He was disguised as a woman at the time, but she was quite sure that, male or female, the killer was not elderly. She said he moved the way a vigorous, athletic young man or woman moves.'

'Stands to reason that a man in that line of work would have to be fit and in his prime,' Jack said. 'Expect it's a demanding profession, what with all that climbing into upstairs windows and sneaking around other people's houses late at night. Not to mention the strength it takes to smother someone or hold them under water until they drown.'

'Elland was very good at that sort of thing.' Tobias got to his feet. 'Thanks for the brandy, Jack. I'd appreciate it if you'd put it about that I'll pay well for any useful information on the subject of Elland or this new Memento-Mori Man.'

'I'll send word if I find anyone who knows anything. But I warn you, my friend, the odds are not good. This killer comes from your world, not mine.'

Fourteen

Dominic angled the burning lens to catch and focus the rays of the morning sun. The day was perfect for this demonstration, he thought, cloudless and warm. The little heap of papers he had put into the iron pot should flare up nicely. It was a silly sort of project, but people always responded with exclamations of excitement when the contents of the pot burst into flames.

Following the tour of his laboratory and several suitably spectacular demonstrations with the electrical machine, he had chosen the small park near his lodgings to show the power of his burning lens.

His little audience gathered around him expectantly. Mrs Lake, Emeline, and Priscilla had made no secret of their interest in the earlier exhibits. Even Anthony, who had arrived stone-faced and barely civil, had eventually revealed a degree of reluctant curiosity in the equipment and apparatus.

At that instant, the papers in the pot caught fire under the intensely focused sunlight. Right on schedule, Dominic thought, satisfied.

'Good heavens.' Mrs Lake watched the flames leap. 'That is really quite amazing, Mr Hood.'

She had appeared distracted and a bit impatient when she arrived with Emeline and Priscilla an hour ago. Somewhat apologetically, Emeline had explained that, with the exception of Priscilla, they were all involved in a new investigation and could not spend much time viewing the experiments.

But as the demonstrations had become more complicated and elaborate, Mrs Lake had begun to take a lively interest.

'Clever enough, I suppose,' Anthony allowed offhandedly. 'But I fail to see any useful purpose for a burning lens.'

'It enables one to conduct experiments that require intense heat,' Priscilla said eagerly. She gazed at the instrument with an enraptured expression. 'I wish I had one. But Mama would never allow it.'

For some reason, her fascination with the burning lens irritated Dominic. He found himself wondering what it would be like to have her look at him with that same degree of admiration. He reminded himself that she was not important. Emeline was his target. He had hoped to gain her attention with the flashy experiments earlier, and he had succeeded in part.

But it was Priscilla who had responded most favorably to his painstakingly prepared explosions and exhibits. She was the one who had understood the deeper implications and foresaw variations and possibilities.

He had been startled by the depths of her knowledge. With her sun-bright hair and sky-blue eyes, she looked as though she would have nothing in her head but air and fluff. Instead, she quoted Newton and Boyle with a casual facility that unsettled him. Her questions had been persistent and endless. What's more, she had taken voluminous notes.

Emeline had not been nearly as enthralled.

'Well, that was really most educational,' Mrs Lake said when the small blaze burned itself out in the pot. 'Thank you, Mr Hood.' She checked the dainty watch she wore pinned to her walking dress and gave Dominic a warm smile. 'Unfortunately, we must be on our way. Come along, Emeline and Priscilla.'

'Yes, of course, Mrs Lake.' Priscilla was reluctant to leave, but she did her best to conceal her disappointment. 'I cannot thank you enough for taking the time to come with us this morning to see Mr Hood's laboratory. Knowing you would be here was the only reason Mama allowed me to come today.'

'My pleasure.' Mrs Lake paused to glance past Dominic's shoulder. 'Ah, here is Mr March. I told him that we would be finished by ten o'clock. He must have grown impatient and decided to seek us out.'

'He does not appear to be in a pleasant temper,' Emeline observed.

'He has not been in a good mood since Beaumont Castle,' Anthony muttered.

Dominic turned to follow their gazes. A small chill went

through him at the sight of the hard-faced man walking toward them.

March had cut across the small park to shorten the distance. Against the field of verdant greens and flowery pastels, he was a dark, resolute force of nature. There was a slight hitch in his long stride. Dominic wondered if he had been injured at some time in the past. The faint limp should have implied weakness, but instead it gave March the appearance of a battle-scarred soldier who would be far more dangerous than any young, untried recruit.

Dominic gripped the burning-lens stand tightly in one hand. He must be very, very careful around this man, he reminded himself.

'Mr March,' Mrs Lake said, 'have you met Mr Hood?'

March came to a halt and gave Dominic an assessing look. He inclined his head an inch. 'Hood.'

'Sir.'

'What a pity that you were not able to join us sooner, Mr March,' Priscilla said. 'Mr Hood has just finished conducting the most interesting experiments.'

'Some other time, perhaps.' He switched his attention to Mrs Lake. 'Madam, if you are quite finished here, I would remind you that we have pressing matters to attend to.' He looked at Anthony. 'As do you and Miss Emeline.'

'Yes, sir,' Anthony said, obviously eager to leave the park. 'Emeline and I will see Priscilla home and then we will continue our inquiries.'

'There is no need to be concerned, sir,' Mrs Lake said, adjusting her gloves. 'The wig shops and antiquities dealers have only just opened for the day. We have not lost any time.'

Dominic told himself he should remain silent, but his curiosity got the better of him. 'May I ask what your inquiries are about?'

'We are searching for a man who has made a profession of murder,' Mrs Lake explained. 'He takes commissions, if you can imagine. Mr March is quite rightly concerned that he will kill again soon if we do not find him and stop him.'

'You hunt a murderer?' Dominic glanced at Anthony and then quickly looked away. 'I would have thought that was a job for Bow Street.'

'This killer is far too clever for the Runners,' Anthony said. 'So clever, in fact, that he leaves no evidence of a crime.' He gave Emeline his arm. 'Let us be off.'

Emeline smiled at Dominic. 'Thank you again for a most instructive morning, Mr Hood.'

'It was all quite fascinating.' Priscilla gave him a brilliant smile.

'My pleasure,' Dominic said brusquely.

Anthony did not bother with a polite farewell. He escorted Emeline and Priscilla away across the park.

March put a hand on Mrs Lake's elbow. 'Good day to you, Hood.'

'The same to you, sir.' Dominic bowed to Mrs Lake. 'And to you, madam. Thank you for accompanying Miss Emeline and Miss Priscilla this morning. I am well-aware that the dictates of propriety would have made it impossible for them to enter my lodgings without you in attendance.'

'I enjoyed myself immensely,' she assured him. 'I trust we will meet up again, Mr Hood, perhaps when we have more time.'

Dominic stood alone and watched them all walk away from him. He hated to admit it, but he was envious of Anthony. Tracking a murderer sounded like exciting work. He reminded himself that he had his own important task to carry out.

He knew now that he would have to come up with another strategy to achieve his goal. The plan he had devised to lure Emeline away from Anthony was not working.

A faint breeze stirred the nearby foliage. He thought he heard his mother's whisper in it, reminding him that his course had been set and must not be altered. He was the only one who could avenge her, he thought. There was no one else left to do it.

The small group had reached the far side of the park. They separated – Mr March and Mrs Lake heading to the left, Anthony with his two companions turning right.

He waited, trying to keep his attention on Anthony until the very last moment. He must not lose his concentration, he told himself. He must not allow himself to be distracted. But for some reason it was Priscilla's bright blond ringlets peeking out from beneath the edge of her pink straw bonnet that held his gaze until they all vanished around a corner.

After a while he reached down to pick up the iron pot. He stared for a long time at the charred remains of the papers he had set afire.

Revenge was a harsh taskmaster. He was beginning to wonder if, in the end, all he would have to show for it would be a handful of ashes.

Fifteen

Two days later, toward the end of another long afternoon, Lavinia accompanied Tobias into one of the few remaining wig shops on their list. Thus far their inquiries had resulted in no clues, and she was fast losing hope that they would have any more luck today.

She glanced around the premises of Cork & Todd and experienced the now familiar flicker of unease.

The interior of the shop was similar to those of the other wigmakers she and Tobias had investigated. She had concluded that it was the sight of the rows of display busts topped with false hair that disturbed her. She told herself that it was not the proprietors' fault that the models reminded her of so many severed heads.

The majority of the wax busts in Cork & Todd were female, but there were also a goodly number of masculine heads fitted with wigs styled for gentlemen.

There was no one behind the counter, but a cheerful rustling sound came from the back room.

'I shall be with you in a moment.'

Tobias removed the torn sheet of paper from his pocket and checked it with grim attention. 'Only three more wig shops after this one and then we will be finished with the lot. For all the good it has done us. We have wasted nearly three days trying to find whoever sold that blond wig to the killer, and we have nothing to show for it.'

'Perhaps Anthony and Emeline are having better luck with the antiquities dealers,' Lavinia said. She wandered over to one of the counters to take a closer look at an elaborately styled wig. 'Do not forget the first wig-maker's shop we tried this morning, the one with the sign in the window saying that it was closed for the month. What do you propose to do about it?'

'I shall take care of that one tonight.'

She spun around. 'You're going to pick the lock, are you not?'

He shrugged and said nothing.

Enthusiasm bubbled up within her. 'I shall come with you.'

'Absolutely not.'

The words had been spoken firmly enough, she thought, but his tone had a certain practiced, automatic quality. A matter of form. Resigned, almost.

She could win this match.

'It will be an excellent opportunity for me to observe you at work. I was thinking just the other day that I must perfect my lock-picking skills, and you have been very lax about demonstrations.'

'Not lax. Cautious.'

'Rubbish. I will not allow you to prevent me from learning all of the secrets of our profession, sir. We are partners, if you will recall. You really must be more forthcoming—'

She broke off when the curtains that covered the doorway behind the counter parted. A plump, middle-aged man dressed in a flowered satin waistcoat, a maroon jacket, and an extravagantly tied cravat emerged. His hair was suspiciously dark for a man of his years, Lavinia thought. There was not a speck of gray in the mass of tightly crimped curls that sprang up all around his head.

'Ah, sir, madam.' He beamed at them through a pair of gold spectacles. 'Welcome, welcome, welcome to my shop. J. P. Cork, at your service.' He switched his attention to Lavinia, his eyes widening first in shock and then narrowing in pity. 'Madam, you have come to the right place, I assure you. I can rescue you from your sad plight.'

'Indeed,' Lavinia murmured. She ignored the annoyance that darkened Tobias's eyes.

This was not the first time she had been greeted with such enthusiasm in the past two days. Every wig-maker they had interviewed had been horrified by the sight of her red hair and had vowed to save her from what those in the profession evidently considered a fate worse than death.

'Do not fear, madam.' Cork bustled out from behind the counter and seized one of Lavinia's gloved hands in two pudgy palms. 'When you leave this shop today, you will be a new woman.'

'That would be an interesting experience, I'm sure,' she said. 'But I'm afraid that my companion and I did not come here to purchase a wig.'

The proprietor made a tut-tutting sound with his tongue and shook his head gravely. 'If your natural shade were brown or black, you would be able to make do with a toupee or a chignon, but given that unfortunate red, I'm afraid you will find that only a full wig will solve your problem. Nothing else will entirely conceal your own hair.'

Tobias moved slightly, just enough to draw the wig-maker's attention. 'Cork, my name is March. I would like to ask you a few questions about your wigs.'

'I see.' Cork studied Tobias's closely cut dark hair with a professionally troubled expression. 'Forgive me, I was so stunned by madam's dreadful plight, I failed to notice your own misfortune. But now that I look more closely, I can, indeed, see those telltale signs of silver at the temples.' He tut-tutted again. 'You are quite right to take action now, sir, before you turn entirely gray. I have just the thing.'

'Devil take it,' Tobias growled. 'I am not interested in a wig for myself.'

But Cork had already gone to one of the male busts and whipped off a brown wig. He held it up in triumph, rather like a hunter displaying a fresh kill. 'I guarantee that this will do the trick, sir. It will conceal the ravages of time and make you appear at least a decade younger.'

'I said, I am not here to purchase a wig.' Tobias eyed the brown hairpiece as though it were a dead rodent. 'Mrs Lake and I wish to ask you a few questions. Nothing more.'

'We will make it worth your while,' Lavinia put in quickly, trying hard not to smile. Tobias had made no secret of the fact that he found these interviews exceedingly trying. Persons engaged in the business of wig-making and hairdressing considered themselves to be artists, and Tobias did not have a great deal of patience with the artistic temperament.

'Humph.' Cork's smile lost its warmth. 'What sort of questions?'

'Just one or two small inquiries concerning sales of blond wigs,' she assured him.

'Blond?' Cork screwed his face into a disapproving glare. 'Haven't had a commission for a full blond wig in months. Very unfashionable color, you know. Has been for some time. The shade never really recovered its popularity after Madam Tallien declared black to be the most elegant hair color some twenty years ago.'

'Madam Tallien?' Lavinia repeated curiously. 'The wife of the French revolutionary?'

'Never mind her dreadful politics.' Cork brushed that issue aside with one pudgy hand. 'The important thing is that her salons were truly splendid affairs, and she reigned supreme in the world of French fashion. Owned a vast assortment of wigs. Legend has it that she switched them several times a day. Wore one color in the morning and another in the evening. All of the most exclusive sort here in England strove to follow in her brilliant footsteps. I don't mind telling you that those of us in the wig-making and hairdressing professions were exceedingly grateful to her.'

'I can imagine,' Lavinia said. She was well-aware that the war between England and France had done nothing to hinder French influence on English fashion. Some things transcended politics. 'But what we'd like to know is—'

'She came along at a most critical moment, you see.' Cork sniffed disdainfully. 'The Crown had just placed that perfectly absurd tax on wig powder, which caused the demand for powdered wigs to plummet. When they went out of fashion, so did the taste for the truly grand coiffeurs. It was a sad passing. Very nearly ruined Mr Todd and myself.'

Lavinia caught Tobias's eye and made another attempt to interrupt the wig-maker. 'Mr Cork, what we would like to know—'

'Ah, yes, those were the days,' Cork said reverently. 'I have a nasty suspicion that we shall never see another such golden era for wigs in my lifetime. Back then every great house possessed a special wig closet where the false hair could be curled and papered and powdered. The hairdressers had to be extremely skilled. And they rose to the occasion, I must say. Why, I knew some who could create headdresses of such enormous height and magnificence that the ladies who wore them could not travel in their carriages unless they knelt on the floor or stuck their heads out the windows.'

'Mr Cork.' Lavinia injected a bit more firmness into her tone. 'We want to know—'

The door of the shop opened at that moment. A dapper-looking man, of about Mr Cork's age but less than half his girth, entered. He carried a package under his arm.

'Mr Todd.' Cork greeted him with a familiarity that spoke of an old friendship. 'There you are. I was wondering what had become of you.'

'Lady Brockton changed her mind at least three times about whether or not her daughter should have braids or ringlets.' Todd snorted. 'It was obvious to me that what the chit really required was a great many curls in front to conceal her rather high forehead. But convincing Lady Brockton of that obvious fact required the most extreme diplomacy and a good deal of my time. Luckily I had no other appointments this afternoon.'

'I know you find Lady Brockton quite trying, but she is a regular client.'

'Yes, yes, I am well aware of that.' Todd peered at Lavinia and Tobias. 'I say, I did not mean to interrupt.'

'Charles Todd, allow me to introduce Mrs Lake and Mr March,' Cork said. 'They called to ask some questions. I was just telling them about the grand old days of our profession.' He turned back to Lavinia and Tobias. 'As I was about to say, there was no need to worry overmuch about the exact shade of the false hair in those days, because one knew that it would all be covered in powder and pomade.'

Todd put his package down on the counter. 'And what lovely stuff the powder was.' He put his palms together and closed his eyes against what was evidently an excess of strong emotion. 'The variety of the tints one could create was nothing short of inspiring. When I mixed them I knew myself to be a true artist.'

'Todd here had a master's touch with the powder,' Cork confided. 'I vow, he had recipes for the most delicate shades of pink and blue, yellow, lavender, and pale violet. And the exquisite intricacy of his chignons had to be seen to be believed. At night in the ballrooms one could always identify his work. His headdresses outshone those of every other hairdresser in London.'

'Those were the days,' Todd agreed.

'I was just telling Mrs Lake and Mr March how Madam Tallien saved us when she set a new fashion for natural-colored wigs,' Cork said. 'And now we do very nicely with chignons, puffs, and toupees and such. But the wig business has never been quite the same.'

'There was another bit of uncertainty a few years back when the ladies all insisted upon cutting their hair very short to suit the taste for Greek and Roman fashions. But the demand for skilled hairdressers rebounded once more when they all wanted long hair again,' Todd said, not without a good deal of satisfaction.

'Thank heaven for the ever-changing tastes of fashion,' Cork added. 'Mr Todd is, I am happy to say, one of the most distinguished hairdressers in town. He has a very elegant clientele. His designs are truly unique and original works of art. The trained eye can spot them immediately on the street or in the ballroom.'

'Is that so?' Tobias said with very little interest.

'Indeed. Many of his competitors have attempted to copy his chignons, but they have all failed. No one can imitate a true artist.'

'A hairdresser is only as good as his chignon, I always say,' Todd declared. 'It is the basis upon which the entire headdress must rest. It is what gives the creation its true distinguishing elegance. If the chignon is uninspired in design or poorly situated on the head, no amount of frizzing or curling will save it.'

Lavinia thought about the designs Mrs Dove's hairdresser had created for Emeline and herself for certain important balls during the recent Season. The chignons had, indeed, been works of art, she thought, almost architectural in design.

'It is not just the design of the chignon that is critical,' Todd continued. 'The ornaments that are used to decorate the finished work of art must be chosen and placed with an eye to the overall effect. I regret to say that many in my profession are inclined to overdo the pearls and flowers, to say nothing of the feathers. Restraint must be a hairdresser's motto in such matters, just as Lafoy says.'

'Who the devil is Lafoy?' Tobias asked, apparently having abandoned any hope of regaining control of the interview.

Todd and Cork looked at him as though he were a barbarian at the gate.

'You are not acquainted with Lafoy?' Charles opened the package on the counter with a flourish and produced a book. 'I refer to *the* Lafoy.'

'Never heard of him,' Tobias said.

'Lafoy is not only an artist in the world of hairdressing, he is a great poet.' Todd opened the book. 'He published this excellent volume on the art of the coiffeur last year. This is my second copy. I was obliged to purchase another because I had quite worn out my first.'

Cork winked. 'He fell asleep while reading it in the bath one evening last month. The book was ruined.'

'Just listen to these verses on the noble art of hairdressing,' Charles urged. 'The sensitivity and the intensity of the emotions quite overcome one. Why, Lafoy's ode to his comb alone brings the tears to my eyes every time I read it.'

He cleared his throat, preparing to read aloud.

'Another time, perhaps, Mr Todd.' Cork held up one hand to silence his associate. 'Mrs Lake and Mr March are here on business.'

'Yes, of course. Forgive me.' Todd closed the book and surveyed Lavinia with pursed lips. 'You were right to come to us, madam. There really is nothing one can do about red hair except conceal it. I have some dyes that will darken hair, but nothing that is strong enough to tint yours. Once you have made your selection of a wig, I would be delighted to dress it for you. I see you in black hair, don't you, Cork?'

'Yes, indeed.' Cork beamed. 'Madam would be stunning in black.'

Todd circled Lavinia, assessing her hair very closely. 'I believe I will use one of my chignons *à la Minerva*. It will add height. What do you say, Mr Cork?'

'As always, when it comes to such matters, you are correct, Mr Todd,' Cork said. 'But, sadly, madam has made it clear that she does not wish to make a purchase today.'

'A pity,' Charles murmured. 'There are possibilities, you see. If only—'

'About the matter of blond-wig sales in recent months,' Tobias said evenly.

'Yes, indeed.' Cork clasped his hands behind his back and rocked on his heels. 'I believe you said you would make it worth my while to discuss recent sales of yellow false hair?'

Tobias glanced at Lavinia, one brow elevated. 'My assistant will handle the negotiations.'

Lavinia cleared her throat and prepared to make the same bargain she had struck with the other helpful wig-makers. 'Like yourself, we cater to a very exclusive clientele, Mr Cork. Only the most elegant sort apply to Lake and March for private inquiries.'

'I see,' Cork murmured.

'As we both know,' Lavinia continued smoothly, 'every business establishment thrives on the right sort of advertising. I propose that, in exchange for whatever information you can provide us today, I shall make it a point to recommend your wig shop to my own clients.'

Cork did not bother to veil his skepticism. 'I really don't see much use in that.'

'I assure you, sir, we are talking about some very high flyers in the ton,' Lavinia stated. 'A word in the proper ears here and there is worth far more than a notice in the newspapers, as I'm sure you are well aware.'

'Humph.' Cork rocked some more on his heels and then he nodded once. 'Very well, I was asked to create one or two blond toupees and a couple of puffs this past Season, but that was the lot. As I said, the color is simply not fashionable. I don't even bother to stock the excellent German yellow anymore. The majority of the demand is for French brown and black.'

'Thank you for the information,' Tobias said grimly. 'It is very much appreciated. Rest assured, Mrs Lake will mention the name of your establishment to her clients whenever the opportunity arises.'

He seized Lavinia's arm and propelled her toward the door.

'Well, that was a complete waste of time,' he said when they were safely outside on the street. 'I vow, I have learned far more about the arts of wig-making and hairdressing in the past two days than I ever wanted to know.'

'Nevertheless, you were correct when you said that we must pursue that line of inquiry. We could not afford to overlook such an important clue.'

'We will finish the last three shops now, and tonight I will have a look around the one that was closed and that will be the end of the matter. Hell's teeth, Lavinia, I must find another angle on this case.'

She smoothed the fingers of her left glove. 'I really feel that I should accompany you tonight, Tobias. You need me.'

'Indeed?' He sounded distracted, as though he was only half listening to her argument. 'Why is that?'

'Because in spite of our interviews yesterday and today, you simply do not possess an adequate knowledge of fashion to know what to look for inside a wig-maker's shop. You might well ignore a critical bit of evidence.'

He mulled that over for a few seconds and then, to her secret astonishment, he merely shrugged.

'Perhaps you are right,' he said at last. 'I suppose there is no great risk in tonight's venture. After all, the proprietor, Mr Swaine, is out of town.'

'Excellent.' She gave him an approving smile. 'I shall look forward to the expedition. When we get home you may lend me one of your picks so that I can practice a bit before we go out this evening.'

'Very well,' he said somewhat absently.

A sense of satisfaction welled up inside. Tobias was, indeed, starting to treat her like a true partner, she told herself.

But by the time they reached the end of the street and turned the corner, much of her triumph had faded. The little battle had been almost too easy, she thought. Tobias either did not have his heart in it or else he was too preoccupied with other matters relating to the case to bother to argue.

'Out with it, sir,' she said briskly. 'You are not yourself today. What are you brooding on so intently?'

'The evidence of the ravages of time that has begun to appear in my hair, I suppose.'

Her jaw dropped.

'The ravages of time? Of all the ridiculous concerns.' She came to an abrupt halt, turned to face him, and surveyed the silver at his temples. It went very nicely with the interesting crinkles at the corners of his mesmeric eyes, she thought. 'I cannot believe that you took Cork's comments seriously. For heaven's sake, he is a shopkeeper who was attempting to make a sale.'

'But he was right. I'm not getting any younger, Lavinia.'

'No, you are not,' she said crisply. 'I certainly agree that you are no callow youth. You are a man in the prime of his life. Furthermore, I must tell you that I find the evidence of the ravages of time in your hair immensely attractive.'

His mouth quirked at one corner. 'Immensely?'

'Yes.' She caught her breath at the interesting gleam in his seductive eyes. 'Immensely.'

'That is fortunate, indeed.' He took her chin on the edge of his hand and raised it slightly. 'Because I am inordinately fond of your hair too.'

The familiar little rush of heat and pleasure whispered through her. 'Even though the color is extremely unfashionable?'

'I will have you know, madam, that I have never been a slave to fashion.'

She started to laugh at that outrageously accurate remark. But he kissed her, right there on the street, heedless of passersby glaring with disapproval and curiosity.

She stopped laughing.

Sixteen

Anthony was in a good mood for the first time since Hood's demonstrations two days ago. He followed Emeline through the door of Mrs Lake's study with a sense of keen anticipation.

The first person he saw was Tobias, who was sprawled comfortably in his favorite chair, legs stretched out in front of him, a glass of sherry in his hand.

'Mr March.' Emeline smiled warmly. 'Mrs Chilton said you were here.' She looked around the small room. 'What have you done with my aunt?'

'Started her down the road to a career of crime, I regret to say.' Tobias took a swallow of sherry. 'But I must admit she does have an aptitude for the profession.'

'I'm right here.' Lavinia's head popped up from behind her desk. She waved a lock pick in the air. 'Practicing my trade. Mr March and I are going to break into a wig-maker's shop tonight.'

It struck Anthony that he had never seen a lady sitting on the floor.

'How exciting,' Emeline said. She hurried around to the other side of the desk to watch. 'May I come with you?'

'No, you may not,' Tobias said decisively. 'One overeager apprentice is all I can manage to supervise at a time.' He eyed Anthony over the rim of the sherry glass. 'You look pleased with yourself. Did you learn something useful today?'

This was a perfect opportunity to affect the same air of cool competence that Tobias always exhibited on this sort of occasion, Anthony reminded himself.

He lounged very deliberately against the side of the desk and folded his arms. 'I think we may have found the source of the memento-mori rings.'

Lavinia's head shot up again, her eyes bright with admiration. 'Did you, indeed? Why, that is excellent news.'

'Very good work,' Tobias said quietly.

Anthony felt the facade of coolness slip a little, allowing some of his pride and satisfaction to show. Praise from Tobias always had this effect on him, he thought. This was the man he admired most in the world, his model and pattern for all things masculine – except for matters sartorial, he reminded himself with affectionate amusement. His mentor's insistence that his coats be cut for ease of movement rather than style and his lack of interest in intricate neckcloth knots would forever keep Tobias from becoming a paragon of fashion.

'Emeline deserves most of the credit,' he said, nodding in her direction. 'She charmed the owner of the museum into admitting the loss of the rings.'

'But it was Anthony who suggested that we make some inquiries at that odd little museum after we had no luck with the antiquities dealers,' Emeline said quickly. 'It was a stroke of genius.'

Anthony grimaced. 'More like a stroke of desperation.'

'What's this about a museum?' Lavinia asked.

'We were getting nowhere with the dealers,' Anthony explained. 'But one of them mentioned that there was a large collection of memento-mori rings at a certain little museum in Peg Street. I thought we had little to lose, so we decided to make inquiries there.'

'The proprietor insisted that we purchase a ticket before he would talk to us,' Emeline said. 'And when we told him that we were especially interested in the rings, he became quite agitated.'

'But Emeline soothed him with a few smiles and gentle words,' Anthony said. 'And eventually he confided that his collection had been stolen.'

Tobias did not move in his chair. 'When?'

Anthony recognized the lethally sharp edge on the single word.

It was a very fortunate thing, indeed, he thought, that his brother-in-law was obsessed with justice and the righting of wrongs. Such skills in a man who was not bound by such a strict private code of honor would have been terrifying.

'The museum proprietor said that he noticed the rings had gone missing some two months back.' Anthony pulled out his notebook and flipped it open. 'I asked him if he could recall anyone expressing a special interest in them shortly before the theft.'

'Excellent question,' Tobias said. 'And the answer?'

Anthony glanced at Emeline and inclined his head.

She could scarcely contain herself. 'A day or two before the rings vanished, the proprietor noticed a woman with yellow hair examining them quite closely.'

Lavinia scrambled to her feet. 'A blond woman? Really?'

'Yes.' Anthony snapped the notebook shut. 'Unfortunately, the proprietor did not get a good look at her features because she wore a large hat with a heavy veil.'

'Age?' Tobias demanded in that same edgy tone. 'Physical size?'

'Unfortunately, he was very vague on such details,' Anthony said. 'It has been over two months, after all. The only thing that seems to have stood out clearly in his memory was the woman's yellow hair.'

Tobias raised his brows. 'He recalled that detail, did he?'

'Quite vividly,' Anthony said.

'A lady in disguise?' Emeline asked.

'More likely a man dressed as a woman,' Tobias said.

Anthony snorted. 'I must tell you, your theory that we are chasing a man who wears women's clothes to conceal his identity strikes me as extremely bizarre.'

Tobias cocked a brow. 'It is not as uncommon as one might think.'

Anthony chuckled. 'You jest, sir.'

'Why should it be so startling?' Lavinia said. 'Ladies' fashions have often imitated those of gentlemen. One need only recall all those stylish little hats and jackets that resembled military uniforms a few years ago, for example. I vow, every fashionable lady owned one or two such garments.'

'Yes, but they were designed to be worn with gowns,' Anthony said. 'Not trousers.'

'You know, I have often thought that there are occasions when it would be very convenient to wear trousers rather than skirts,' Lavinia mused.

'Yes, indeed,' Emeline said enthusiastically. 'So much more comfortable and practical.'

Anthony stared at her, too shocked to speak.

'Take tonight, for example,' Lavinia continued. 'If I were to wear trousers when we break into the wig-maker's shop, I could move far more freely.'

'When you consider the matter,' Emeline said, 'our profession is of such a nature that there will no doubt be many occasions when trousers would be the perfect attire. I wonder if we could persuade Madam Francesca to design some for us?'

Lavinia looked at her. 'What a positively brilliant notion.'

Anthony finally found his voice. He glared at Emeline. 'What the devil are you saying? You know perfectly well that you cannot go about in trousers.'

She smiled very sweetly. 'Whyever not, sir?'

'Uh.' The simple question brought him to a grinding halt. He looked at Tobias for assistance.

'Bloody hell.' Tobias downed the last of his sherry, got to his feet, and went toward the door. 'Come along, Tony. We had best make our escape while we can. I do not believe that it would be wise for either of us to hang about for the rest of this conversation.'

Anthony took one last look at Emeline's determined expression and concluded that Tobias was right. He was not prepared to fight this particular battle.

He quickly made his farewells and followed his brother-in-law into the front hall.

'You do not think they are serious, do you?' he asked as they went down the steps to the street. 'About the trousers, I mean?'

'When it comes to Mrs Lake I have learned to take everything she says quite seriously. I suspect you had best do the same with Miss Emeline. The alternative is to risk being taken by surprise. Never a wise position for one in our profession.'

'They were no doubt teasing us.'

'I would not depend upon that assumption, if I were you.'

Anthony hesitated and then elected to abandon the topic. 'Speaking of our profession, there is a question I wish to ask. It has to do with technique.'

'What is it?'

'How does one set about making inquiries into a gentleman's background?'

Tobias gave him a hard, searching look. 'With extreme caution. Why do you ask?'

'I am concerned about Hood.'

'You mean that you are jealous of him, do you not?' Tobias asked in a low tone. 'I assure you, there is no need.'

Anthony set his jaw. 'I do not like the way he watches Emeline.'

'Calm yourself, Tony. Miss Emeline has eyes for no man but you. Take my advice and do not go prying into Hood's affairs. Gentlemen, as a rule, do not take kindly to invasions of privacy. Some would view such inquiries as extreme insults. One misstep and you could find yourself invited to a dawn appointment.'

'I just want to be assured that he is no threat to Miss Emeline.'

Tobias was quiet for a moment. 'I'll ask Crackenburne to see what he can find out about Hood,' he said finally. 'He is in a position to make discreet inquiries without arousing interest or suspicion.'

'Thank you.'

'Meanwhile, I want your word that you will not do anything foolish in that direction,' Tobias said. 'I am very serious about this, Tony. Men have died in duels for lesser cause.'

'Yes, I know' He adjusted the tilt of his hat with unnecessary care, angling the brim just enough to keep the afternoon sun out of his eyes. 'My father, for example.'

Tobias shielded the small flame of the candle with his hand and watched Lavinia work on the lock of the back door of the wigmaker's shop. She crouched on the step, the folds of her dark cloak draped around her, and bent industriously to her task.

There was a near-full moon tonight and no clouds. The silvery light illuminated the entire city in an otherworldly glow. The beams seeped into even the narrowest alleys and lanes, making their task simpler in some ways and more dangerous in others: the same moon that made it easier for them to see also made it easier for others to see them.

There was a soft click.

'I've got it,' she whispered, sounding thrilled with herself.

'Hush.' He glanced over his shoulder, checking once again for shadows or signs of movement.

Nothing shifted in the night. A lamp shone faintly in a room above a shop at the far end of the street, but all of the neighboring establishments were shrouded in darkness. He listened to the silence for a few seconds and was satisfied.

'All right,' he said quietly. 'Let's go inside.'

Lavinia rose and twisted the knob cautiously. The door opened with a rusty squeak.

Stale, fetid air wafted out of the interior of the shop. It was laced with an underlying stench that was all too familiar.

'Dear God.' Lavinia gasped and tugged the edge of her cloak across her nose and mouth. She looked at Tobias, her eyes widening in appalled comprehension.

He realized that she, too, understood what the dreadful smell implied. This was not the first time they had engaged in a midnight encounter with the dead.

'I'll go first,' he said. Lavinia did not object.

He raised the candle and surveyed the small back room of the wig shop. It was tightly packed with the articles of the proprietor's trade.

Bald display busts were heaped in a large basket. In the flickering light the heads resembled nothing so much as the ghastly fruits of the guillotine.

Several wigs of various shades and shapes were spread out across a table. To Tobias, they looked like the skins of dead animals. Implements including scissors and combs were neatly arranged beside a stack of toupees. A small loom designed for weaving false hair occupied a nearby bench. The half-finished length of a dark brown hairpiece hung from it.

He raised the candle higher and saw a narrow flight of stairs that led to the rooms above the shop. The steps extended upward into thick gloom.

The foot of the staircase was concealed behind a crate, but he could make out a bit of crumpled white cloth and a stocking-clad foot.

'I think we have just found Swaine.' He went toward the bottom of the stairs.

Lavinia trailed after him.

Tobias came to a halt and raised the candle to examine the scene. The body was that of a balding elderly man dressed in a nightshirt. The victim sprawled facedown in a dreadfully tangled, most unnatural manner. There was a vast amount of dried blood on the floor beneath his head.

Lavinia stopped a short distance away and pulled her cloak more tightly around her. She gazed sadly at the body.

'Do you think he got up in the middle of the night and perhaps tripped and fell on the stairs?' she whispered without much hope.

'No.' Tobias bent down to examine the head wound. 'I suspect he was struck from behind with some heavy object and then pushed down these stairs so the deed would appear to be an accident. I would say that the murder was done fairly recently. Sometime within the past day or two, I believe.'

'Perhaps he surprised a burglar.'

He straightened and looked up into the darkness at the top of the stairs. 'Perhaps.' But his instincts told him that whoever had murdered the shopkeeper had been no ordinary burglar. 'I will go upstairs and look around.'

Lavinia turned on her heel, spotted a candlestick with an unlit taper, and picked it up. She lit the candle from his flame.

'I'll search the front room of the shop,' she said.

He stepped cautiously over the body and started up the steps. 'Look for business records and recent receipts.' He paused briefly. 'And a ring.'

She looked up at him. 'You think this is the work of the Memento-Mori Man?'

'You know how I feel about coincidences.'

At the top of the staircase he found a cozy room furnished with a desk, chair, table, and a small carpet. The quality of the objects gave evidence of quiet prosperity but not great wealth. A doorway led to a tiny bedchamber.

One of the fireplace pokers lay on the cold hearth. He picked it up and examined it in the light of the candle. There were tiny bits of gore and gray hair stuck to it. The wig-maker had certainly not fallen accidentally to his death.

He searched the adjoining room, rummaging methodically through the small wardrobe and the drawers of the washstand. A variety of wigs hung from pegs on the wall. Evidently the late Mr Swaine had worn some of his own creations.

When he was finished, he went back into the front room and started to search the desk. Downstairs he heard muffled noises that told him Lavinia was going through some cupboards.

He opened each of the desk drawers in turn and discovered the usual assortment of objects – a penknife, bottles of ink, various papers, and some journals of accounts.

He took out the journals and paged through them swiftly, hoping that luck would favor him.

He saw immediately that Swaine had, indeed, maintained meticulous business records. Each transaction was detailed and dated quite precisely. He selected the most recent one and tucked it under his arm.

Perhaps his luck had finally changed.

Raising the candle on high, he prowled once more through both rooms, pausing to look closely at the top of the night table and the washstand. He crouched on one knee to check beneath the bed.

There was no ring.

He stood in the middle of the dead man's sitting room for a while, thinking. When he experienced no inspiring flashes of insight or logic, he made his way back downstairs, stepping carefully over the body a second time.

Lavinia waited for him in the back room. 'What are we to do with the shopkeeper's body? We cannot just leave him here. There is no saying when someone will finally realize that something is wrong.'

'I will send word to the proper authorities. Matters will be handled quietly. I do not want it widely known that you and I were in here tonight.'

'Why not?'

'The less the killer knows of our progress in this case, the better.' He blew out the candle and led the way to the rear door. 'Not that we have made much. Unless you found something helpful?'

'No. But I agree that this was not the work of a burglar. There was no sign that anyone went through the cupboards searching for valuables.' She followed him outside and closed the door. 'What is that under your arm?'

'The wig-maker's journal of accounts for the past six months.'

'Do you think this was the shop where the Memento-Mori Man acquired the blond wig?'

'I think that is a distinct possibility, yes. But Swaine was killed quite recently. I suspect the murderer discovered that we were making inquiries at the wig shops and decided that it would be a good idea to silence the one wig-maker who might be able to describe him.'

'Dear God. Tobias, that means that we are—'

'In part responsible for Swaine's death.' He gripped the journal tightly. 'Yes, I'm afraid that is one way of looking at the situation.'

'I feel ill,' she whispered.

'We must find him, Lavinia. That is the only way to stop him.'

'Do you think there will be some clue in that journal?'

'I don't know. I can only hope that is the case.' He walked with her toward the end of the alley. 'I found no ring either.'

She glanced at him, her expression invisible in the shadow of the cloak hood. 'What do you think that means?'

'I believe it means that the killer did not consider this murder to be a matter of professional pride. This was not a commissioned kill, but rather a matter of expediency.' He looked back over his shoulder at the door of the dead wig-maker's shop. 'Just part of the cost of doing business.'

Seventeen

The new commission was an extremely lucrative one. The Memento-Mori Man was quite pleased with it. True, Sir Rupert did not meet all of the specifications set down by the one who had trained him, but he had concluded that those requirements were too stringent.

It was all very well for his mentor to carry on about the noble objectives of the firm, the Memento-Mori Man thought, but the reality of the matter was that the commission for Sir Rupert would earn him twice as much money as he had been paid for any of the last three projects.

In addition, it was a simple, straightforward operation. Sir Rupert was elderly and bedridden. True, his only crime was that, in the eyes of one of his very greedy heirs, he had lived a little too long, but that was not a great concern.

A farsighted man of business could not allow outdated notions of honor to stand in the way of profits.

The details of the new commission would be handled in the usual anonymous manner. The client was to leave the full payment at the appointed place in the small lane behind Bond Street. The Memento-Mori Man would retrieve his fee later, when there was no possibility that anyone would notice.

Business was picking up nicely. Word of mouth was, indeed, the best sort of advertising. In addition, the dangerous chess match with March added a euphoric excitement that no drug could equal.

He was well on his way to proving that he was as skilled and clever as Zachary had been. When he had surpassed Zachary's record of successfully completed commissions and made certain that March knew of that accomplishment, there would be time enough to take his revenge.

Eighteen

The following morning, Tobias dropped heavily into the chair across from Crackenburne. It was early in the day and the club room was nearly empty.

Crackenburne lowered his newspaper and peered at Tobias through his spectacles. 'You do not look to be in a good temper. This new investigation is not going well, I take it?'

'Nothing but dead ends and dangling threads thus far.' Tobias sat forward, resting his elbows on his thighs and gazing at the unlit hearth. It was too warm to warrant a fire today, he reflected. 'This case is like some damned Gordian knot. No matter how I approach it I cannot seem to find the key to untying it.'

'No luck at the wig-maker's last night, I take it?'

'I believe the Memento-Mori Man got there ahead of me and murdered the poor man.'

'That must have been the shop where he acquired the wig,' Crackenburne said quietly.

'It is the only explanation that makes sense. But I spent most of the night going through that damned journal, and there was no record of a sale of a blond wig in the entire six months preceding the events at Beaumont Castle. There was, in fact, only one purchase of yellow false hair recorded, and that took place two days *after* Fullerton fell off that roof.'

'You must not blame yourself for the wig-maker's death.'

Tobias said nothing.

'But of course you do. It is your nature.' Crackenburne exhaled deeply and fell silent for a moment. 'What is your next step?' he said eventually.

'Lavinia and Mrs Dove are pursuing their notion that the murders have all been commissioned by people who wish to stop a marriage from taking place. I must admit their theory is as good as any I've managed to concoct. Meanwhile, I'm hoping for word from Smiling Jack.'

'What makes you think that he will be able to assist you?'

'The fact that Zachary Elland seemed to have come out of nowhere has been nagging at me. Perhaps he was not born a gentleman, after all. Perhaps he invented himself as one.'

'He certainly would not have been the first to do so.' Crackenburne frowned. 'But I confess, I had not considered that possibility. He moved so easily in Society. All polish and charm and wit. There was no reason not to believe his claim that he was an orphan who was raised by a distant relative who had died.'

'I should have probed more deeply into his past after his death.'

'Do not torture yourself with recriminations,' Crackenburne ordered sternly. 'We all assumed that the affair of the Memento-Mori Man had ended with Elland's suicide. It was a very logical conclusion.'

'It certainly seemed logical at the time,' Tobias muttered.

Crackenburne peered at him. 'You look like you aren't getting enough sleep.'

'The last thing I can afford to do is waste time sleeping. The Memento-Mori Man is not the only problem I have at the moment. Do you know anything about a young man named Dominic Hood? He is about Anthony's age. Has a keen interest in science. Lodgings over on Stelling Street. Enough money to patronize an expensive tailor.'

'The name is unfamiliar to me. What is your interest in this young man?'

'Anthony has taken a strong dislike to him.'

Crackenburne's brows bunched in surprise. 'Thought Anthony got along well with most people.'

'Indeed. But he seems to feel that Hood is a rival for Miss Emeline's affections. Although I must say that I saw no sign Miss Emeline was interested in Hood. Nevertheless, I am worried that Tony will do something reckless in that direction.'

'I understand. Young men are hot-blooded creatures, inclined to do foolish things, especially when there is a lady in the middle.' Crackenburne folded his newspaper and set it aside.

'Does this Mr Hood belong to a club?'

'Yes. Anthony's, as a matter of fact.'

'In that case, I can no doubt make some discreet inquiries for you.'

'Thank you, sir. I am grateful.'

The porter, a hunched man of indeterminate years, came to stand near Tobias's chair.

'I beg your pardon, sir, but there is a rather dirty little boy outside. He claims he has a message for you. Most insistent.'

'I will deal with it.' Tobias gripped the arms of his chair and pushed himself to his feet. He nodded at Crackenburne. 'Good day, sir.'

'Tobias.'

That gave him pause. Crackenburne rarely called him by his given name.

'I am as concerned about this new Memento-Mori Man as you are,' Crackenburne said quietly. 'But I am equally concerned about the way in which it is affecting you. Remember, you have no reason to blame yourself because of what happened three years ago. It was not your fault that Zachary Elland became a killer.'

'That is what Lavinia tells me, but I cannot escape the notion that had I not taught him the work of a spy, he would never have developed a taste for dark excitement.'

'That is not true. Elland would have gone to hell one way or another. You must trust me on this matter. I have lived long enough to know that no man becomes a cold-blooded murderer because of some passing twist of fate. The malignancy must be there in him from the very start of his life, either born or bred early in the bone.'

Tobias nodded again, politely, and walked to the door. For all he knew Crackenburne and Lavinia were right. But deep down he feared that he bore some responsibility for what Elland had become. He was well-aware that Aspasia Gray agreed with that view.

The sun shone warmly enough overhead, but it seemed to Lavinia that very little of its heat and light reached into the shadows of the graveyard. The shade cast by the leafy trees fell across the headstones and sepulchral monuments like a dark, transparent shroud.

There was a sad, shabby, unkempt air about the cemetery. The heavy iron gates sagged on their rusted hinges. The high stone wall that surrounded the graves blocked out the sights and sounds of the street. The tiny stone church loomed forlornly. The doors at the top of the steps were closed.

All in all, Lavinia thought, it was a singularly depressing scene. This was the sort of cemetery that was frequented by the so-called Resurrection Men, who supplied fresh bodies to the medical schools. She would not be at all surprised to discover that a good many of these graves had been emptied of their contents long ago.

Not that progress in the field of medical science was not a worthy goal, she reflected. One just hoped that, when the time came, one's own mortal remains did not end up on a dissecting table at the mercy of a bunch of eager students.

Then again, the vision of being locked up inside a coffin and buried in the ground or walled up in one of these stone crypts was hardly more pleasant. Something deep inside her became quite frantic whenever she pictured herself confined inside a very small, closed space. Even now, just looking at the dark entrance of one of the nearby vaults caused the tiny little insects of panic to nibble at the edges of her mind.

Enough. Stop these silly imaginings. What on earth are you thinking to let this place affect you so strongly? It is just a graveyard, for heaven's sake.

Perhaps it was her nerves, she thought. They had been in an edgy state all morning. It was easy to blame it on the fact that she had been unable to sleep last night after she and Tobias discovered Swaine's body. But the truth was, this jumpy, overstimulated sensation had become noticeably worse when she left the house a short time ago. She had hoped that a brisk walk in the warm sunshine would clear her head and calm her. But the reverse had proved true.

Stop thinking about your nerves. There is work to be done.

She drew a deep breath and called upon her mesmeric training to push aside the disturbing thoughts.

She walked along a weedy gravel path and stopped beside Aspasia Gray.

'I got your message,' she said.

'Thank you for meeting me,' Aspasia said in a subdued voice. 'I realize that this is not the most cheerful location for a conversation. Indeed, I hope you will not conclude that I am generally inclined toward melodrama. But I wanted to impress upon you something that I feel you have not fully comprehended.'

'What is that?'

'I know you believe that I have designs on Tobias, but that is not the case.' Aspasia looked down at the gravestone. 'There is only one man whom I have ever loved or ever will love, and he lies here.'

Lavinia glanced at the simple inscription on the gray stone. *Zachary Elland. Died 1815.* A draft of cold wind seemed to whisper in the dead leaves that covered the grave.

'I see,' she said neutrally.

'We did not know the date of his birth, so we decided to leave it off the stone.' Aspasia gazed fixedly at the granite. 'We discovered too late that there was a great deal we did not know about Zachary.'

'We?'

'Tobias and I. We handled the arrangements together. There was no one else, you see.' Aspasia paused. 'We were the only ones who bothered to attend the funeral.'

'I understand.'

'Tobias and I shared much together because of Zachary. But we were never intimate. I want you to know that.'

'I am already aware of that fact. Tobias told me.'

Aspasia smiled slightly, knowingly. 'And you believe him because you love him and trust him.'

'Yes.'

'That is how I felt about Zachary, you know'

'I assumed as much. I am very sorry, Aspasia.'

Aspasia returned her attention to the gravestone. 'When I first met Zachary, I had no plans to fall in love, let alone commit myself to marriage. I learned my lessons early on, you see.'

'What do you mean?'

'My father was an exceedingly cruel man. He made my mother's life a hell on earth. Eventually she took an overdose of laudanum to escape. But there was no way out for me. I was forced to suffer his rages and, worse, his unnatural advances until I was sixteen. At that time he contracted a marriage for me. I did not object, even though my husband was many years older. I thought I had been rescued, you see.'

Lavinia said nothing, but it seemed to her that the dead leaves on top of the grave whispered more loudly. She sensed that Aspasia was speaking the truth.

'Instead, I found myself in another kind of hell. My husband was as vicious and cold as my father. It was my great good fortune that he was shot dead by a highwayman one night as he rode home from

London. My father died of a fever a short time later.'

'There is no need to talk about these things to me, Aspasia. I know they must be very painful to you.'

'Yes. So exceedingly painful that I have never spoken of them with anyone other than Zachary. I never even told Tobias. But I want you to understand. At seventeen I found myself alone in the world and in command of a substantial fortune. I made up my mind that I would never again allow any man to control my destiny.'

'I know how you must have felt,' Lavinia said quietly.

'I was twenty-five when I met Zachary. I had become a woman of the world. I had taken lovers, but I had never loved. I certainly never imagined for one moment that I could be fooled by a man. But all of my fine plans and convictions flew out the window when I lost my heart to Zachary.'

The dead leaves skittered as though stirred by skeletal fingers.

'I can only imagine what it must have been like for you when you realized that you were engaged to a man who made a career of murder,' Lavinia said. 'What caused you to realize his true nature?'

'It was not one single thing that aroused my suspicion. Rather, it was several tiny little events that eventually wove themselves into a pattern I could no longer ignore.'

'What sort of events?'

'There was his obsessive interest in Tobias's inquiries into the mysterious murders, for one thing. And his comings and goings at odd hours. Zachary always had an excellent, entirely reasonable explanation for his occasional disappearances. But one day, quite by accident, I learned that he had lied to me about where he had been the previous evening. As it happened, it was a night when the Memento-Mori Man had struck.'

'Was that when you realized he might be the killer?'

'No.' Aspasia linked her fingers. 'To be honest, I prepared myself for the possibility that Zachary had betrayed me with another woman. I thought my heart would shatter. I had to know the truth.'

'What did you do?'

'He had a safe. I reasoned that if he had any secrets they would be hidden inside. He always kept the key on his person. But one night after we had made love, he fell asleep. I seized the opportunity to make a wax copy of the key. A few evenings later I found an opportunity to go into his study. I opened the safe.' Aspasia grimaced. 'I'm sure you can imagine my relief when the first thing I saw was a journal of accounts.'

'What made you realize that the journal was no ordinary record of business transactions?'

'I grew curious when I realized that it was not a journal of household expenses such as many gentlemen keep. Rather, it was a list of dates and fees. It looked like a tradesman's book of accounts. But that made no sense.'

'Because Zachary Elland was a gentleman?'

'Precisely. He did not operate a business. I told myself that it was a record of his wins at the gaming tables. But I soon realized that the dates of the so-called transactions matched some of the information concerning the deaths that Tobias was investigating.'

'You knew about the details of his inquiries?'

'Of course.' Aspasia sighed. 'Tobias sat up many a night discussing the murders with Zachary. I was with them on several of those occasions. I even offered my own opinions. Tobias is one of those rare men who actually listens when a woman has something to say, as I'm sure you know. Zachary shared that trait. It was one of the many things that I . . . loved about him.'

'What happened after you found the journal?'

'I discovered the small casket of memento-mori rings at the back of the safe.' Aspasia's voice dropped to a tortured whisper. 'I could not believe my own eyes. I went straight to Tobias with the journal. I wanted him to tell me that I had got it all wrong. But I think I knew, deep in my heart, that all was lost. When Zachary found the open safe with the journal gone, he realized that his secrets had been stolen.'

'He put a pistol to his head.'

Aspasia's mouth twisted. 'They say it is a gentleman's way out. I suppose that it is, indeed, a better end than the gallows.'

It was all so dreadfully tragic, Lavinia thought. After years of shielding herself from the pain men had caused her, Aspasia had fallen for a cold-blooded murderer.

'My condolences on your loss,' Lavinia said eventually.

'Forgive me.' Aspasia blinked away the moisture that glittered in her eyes. 'I just wanted you to know that Tobias is quite safe from me. Even if I did think to seduce him, it would not be possible. It is obvious that he loves you. As for me, I will never take the risk of giving my heart to any man again.'

Lavinia could think of nothing to say to that, so she held her tongue.

'Good day, Lavinia. I wish you joy with Tobias. He is a fine man. I envy you, but not even for him would I trade places with you.'

Aspasia turned and walked swiftly away along the path. Lavinia watched her go out through the iron gates that guarded the entrance to the cemetery.

She stood alone at Zachary Elland's grave for a time and thought about the twists and turns of fate.

'You certainly did a great deal of damage while you were walking around up here,' she whispered. 'Who could possibly have admired you so much that he would wish to emulate you?'

The dead leaves danced a ghostly waltz across the grass.

Nineteen

Smiling Jack waited for him in the alley behind the Gryphon, his massive bulk silhouetted in the rear entrance of the tavern. He was barking orders at two men who were in the process of unloading several large shipping casks from a cart.

'Have a care with that French brandy,' Jack snapped at one of the men. 'Cost me a bloody fortune.'

Tobias walked down the alley and came to a halt beside Jack. He studied the casks.

'Brandy, Jack? Isn't that a bit elegant for the Gryphon? I was under the impression that your clientele prefers ale and gin.'

Jack chuckled, drawing the ghastly scar that ran from his mouth to his ear into a death's-head grin. 'Aye. This is for my own personal use.'

Tobias studied the large casks. 'That's a great deal of brandy for one man to drink.'

'I have a lot of guests.' Jack clapped him on the back. 'Take yourself, for instance. I like to be able to entertain gentlemen such as yourself in the manner to which you have become accustomed.'

'Speaking for myself, I appreciate that sentiment,' Tobias said.

He rarely came to the Gryphon during the day. He preferred the cover of night for his visits with Jack. But the boy's message had sounded urgent, so he had taken extra precautions to conceal his identity. Before making his way to this part of town he had taken the time to put on the work-worn clothes and heavy boots of a dockside laborer. In spite of the warmth of the day, he had added a voluminous, high-collared coat and an oversize wide-brimmed hat that was angled to conceal his features. In addition, he had used the alley entrance deliberately so as to avoid the front room of the tavern.

'I got your message,' he said, keeping his voice very soft so that his educated accents would not be overheard by the workers unloading the cart. 'What news do you have for me?'

'It's only a rumor.' Jack, too, pitched his voice to a low tone. 'No way to confirm it yet. But it was as nasty a bit of gossip as I've heard in a while, and I thought you'd better know about it as soon as possible.'

'Go on.'

'There's word going around that a young footpad who goes by the name of Sweet Ned has taken a commission.'

'What sort of commission?'

'Can't say.' Jack watched him with grim eyes. 'My source did not know exactly why Sweet Ned was employed. Something to do with following a particular person about, he believes. I doubt that he'll be offering to assist the lady across the street.'

Tobias went still. 'What lady would that be?'

'Yours.'

After a while Lavinia turned away from Elland's grave and went back along the path to the iron gates.

The narrow lane that bordered the graveyard was quiet and empty of traffic and passersby. The only person about was a young man who looked like a laborer or a stable lad. He was garbed in a worn, ill-fitting mud-colored coat and battered boots. His cap was pulled down low over his eyes.

There was something feral and hungry-looking about him. He made her think of the cats that survived by preying on rats and mice in alleys and warehouses. He was propped in the heavily shadowed doorway of a shuttered building at the open end of the lane.

The cap and the slouch were disturbingly familiar, she thought. Her stomach knotted with sudden tension. This was not the first time that she had seen the man today. She was almost certain that she had caught a glimpse of him earlier when she left Claremont Lane. She could have sworn that he had been loitering in the little park at the end of the street.

The fine hairs on the nape of her neck lifted. Her palms went icy cold.

She glanced toward the opposite end of the lane, thinking to leave by that route. But that was impossible. The narrow passage ended at a stone wall.

The man in the cap noticed her hovering between the gates. He straightened indolently and reached into his pocket. Slowly, tauntingly, he withdrew his hand.

Light glittered on the blade of the knife.

The only thing she could do was retreat back into the graveyard, but the surrounding walls and locked church door made it a trap.

The man in the cap started toward her, sauntering as though he had all the time in the world.

She took a step back into the graveyard.

He smiled, evidently pleased by her small show of anxiety.

She had no choice. She whirled and fled back into the cemetery.

Mrs Chilton wiped her hands on her apron. 'Mrs Lake said something about going out to a little cemetery in Benbow Lane. Said it was just off Wintergrove Street near a park. Mrs Gray sent a message asking her to meet there.'

'How long ago did she leave?' Tobias asked.

Mrs Chilton glanced at the clock. 'Going on an hour, I believe.' She frowned. 'Is something wrong, sir?'

'Yes.'

Tobias went back down the steps. He did not bother to hunt for a hackney. He knew the cemetery well. It was not far away, but it was surrounded by a maze of tiny lanes and narrow streets. He would make better time on foot.

Twenty

Sweet Ned took a deep breath and sauntered toward the gates of the graveyard. He wanted to handle this business in a professional manner.

Business. He liked the sound of that. He'd taken a real *commission* from a real *client*. He was no longer an ordinary street lad who picked pockets and snatched the odd valuable. As of last night, he was a professional with his own business.

When he'd struck the bargain with the woman, it was as though a magic door had opened, allowing him a tantalizing vision of a new future. It was a truly dazzling scene in which he was the master of his own destiny, successful and prosperous. Respected.

There would be no more dealing with the damned receivers who never gave fair value for the goods he risked his neck to steal. No more skulking about in alleys waiting to rob drunken gentlemen when they stumbled out of the hells and brothels in the wee hours of the morning. No more dodging the Runners. From now on he would only accept *commissions* from *clients* who were willing to pay well to have their dirty work done by an *expert*.

He'd have to consider how best to advertise his services, he thought as he strolled through the iron gates. Unfortunately, he could not put a notice in the papers. He would have to depend on word of mouth. But that should not be a problem after the news of how well he had carried out his first commission circulated. The woman would likely tell her friends and they would tell others, and in no time at all he would be swamped with commissions.

Too bad his pa had drunk himself to death before he'd had an opportunity to see his son move up in the world.

At the thought of his father lying dead in the stinking alley, a half-empty bottle of gin in one hand, the old rage came back, nearly blinding him. Memories of the beatings made him clench his hand around the handle of the knife. They had grown more frequent and more savage after his ma died. In the end he'd had no choice but to take to the streets.

There were times when the urge to hit someone or something nearly overpowered him. Sometimes he wanted to strike blow after blow until this rush of raw fury evaporated.

But he refused to give in to the fierce anger. He had vowed to himself a long time ago that he would not follow in his father's drunken footsteps. After today everything would be different. After today word would go out that he was a reliable professional and he would be launched on his new career.

But first he had to fulfill this commission.

He stopped just inside the cemetery gates, trying to ignore the little finger of dread that touched him at the back of his neck. He did not like graveyards. One of his friends, who was doing very nicely for himself robbing graves and selling bodies to the medical schools, had tried to convince him to join his gang of Resurrection Men. He had made some excuse about having bigger plans, but the truth was, he knew he'd never be a success in that line of work. The thought of digging up graves and opening coffins filled him with horror.

He looked quickly around the graveyard, searching for his quarry. Panic surged in his vitals when he realized that she was nowhere in sight.

Impossible. She had to be here somewhere. He knew this old boneyard. She could not have climbed the high stone walls, and the gates behind him were the only way out. The small church had been closed up for nearly a year, the door kept locked and barred.

The burial vaults, he thought. She must be hiding in one of them. Yes, that was it. She had realized that he was a threat, and the poor little fool had sought refuge in one of the large crypts. As if he'd let her slip away so easily.

He studied the array of stone vaults sprinkled around the cemetery. Some of them were enormous, built to house several generations of a family's dead. A small scrap of cloth fluttered on the ground in front of the door of a large crypt on his right.

It looked like a lady's handkerchief.

She was no doubt shivering in terror inside that dark chamber, alone with all those walled-up skeletons, he thought. He felt a pang of sympathy. He wouldn't want to be in her shoes. But if she was already trembling with fear, that would make his work all the easier.

At the door of the monument he stooped down to pick up the little bit of embroidered cloth. Just as he'd thought. A fine linen handkerchief. When this was finished he would give it to Jenny.

He opened the door of the crypt and peered into the gloom. A shudder went through him. This would not have been his choice of a hiding place.

'You in there,' he called. 'Come on out now. I've got a message for ye.'

His voice echoed on the stone walls, but nothing stirred inside the crypt. He wondered if she'd fainted dead away from fright.

'Bloody female. You had to go and make this difficult, didn't you?'

There was no help for it; he'd have to go in and haul her out. He wished he had a candle or a lantern. It was as dark as the Pit in there.

Reluctantly, he moved into the burial vault. The passageway at the entrance opened onto a cramped chamber, lined floor to ceiling with stones engraved with the names of the dead. There was just enough light to make out the edges of two massive, heavily carved coffins in the center of the room. She was no doubt crouched down behind one of them.

He eased deeper into the chamber. Decades of dust stirred at his feet.

Dust.

Belatedly, he glanced down. There was enough light slanting through the open door to see that there were no footprints in the thick dust other than his own.

'Bloody hell.'

He whirled and raced back toward the door. He got there just in time to catch a glimpse of the woman's green skirts flying out through the cemetery gates.

She'd tricked him. She had dropped her handkerchief in front of this monument and hidden behind one of the others.

He rushed toward the gates. He could outrun her, he promised himself, a sense of desperation pouring through him. He could outrun any fine lady.

He *had* to outrun her. His future depended on it.

Lavinia fled toward the entrance of the tiny lane, her skirts clutched in both hands. She could hear the man pounding across the graveyard. He would be through the gates in another few seconds. He was young and strong and fast, and she knew that she could not outrun him for long. Her only hope was to reach the street first and pray that there would be other people around to aid her.

This was, she reflected, one of those times when it would have been extremely helpful to be dressed in trousers instead of a gown. If she escaped the man with the knife, she would definitely make an appointment with Madam Francesca to discuss the matter.

The thud of boots on stone drew closer. She sensed the man reaching for her. She did not dare look back. The place where the lane met the street was not far now.

Dear God, two more strides and she would be safe. Perhaps.

She burst out of the tiny mouth of the lane.

And stumbled straight into the arms of a solidly built man in a large, dark coat and a low-crowned hat. Her first thought was that the villain with the knife had a companion. A fresh wave of fear crashed through her.

She struggled to break free, opening her mouth to scream.

'Lavinia.' Tobias's strong hands closed around her forearms like steel manacles. 'Are you all right? Answer me, Lavinia. Are you hurt?'

'*Tobias*.' Relief left her limp and breathless. 'Thank God. Yes, yes, I'm all right. But there's a man. With a knife.'

She swung around and saw that her pursuer had stopped just inside the entrance to the lane. He stared at Tobias.

'There he is,' Lavinia said. 'I think he followed me here. He waited for Aspasia to leave and then he came toward me with a knife and I—'

'Stay here.' He set her aside and started toward the young man with the blade.

She realized that he was going to try to capture her would-be assailant.

'Tobias, no. Wait. He's got a knife.'

'He will not have it for long,' Tobias said very softly. He kept moving, swiftly narrowing the distance between himself and the man in the lane.

Lavinia saw panic cross the young man's face. Whatever he saw in Tobias's expression had struck terror in him. He was trapped and he knew it.

Alarm swept through her. Cornered creatures were exceedingly dangerous.

Tobias did not seem to notice the knife in the young man's hand. He closed in on him with the long, prowling stride of a wolf moving in for the kill.

The man lost his nerve. Blade extended as though it were a talisman that could ward off a demon, he broke into a mad run, slashing wildly at the air. It was clear that he intended to try to rush past Tobias to the freedom of the street.

Tobias sidestepped the knife and grabbed the arm that held it as the villain went flying past him. Using the man's own momentum, he swung him in an arc that ended abruptly against the nearest stone wall.

The assailant squealed in fear and rage and pain. He crumpled to the pavement. The knife clattered on the stones.

Tobias scooped up the blade. 'Sweet Ned, I presume.'

The young man shuddered as if he'd been struck.

Lavinia hurried toward the pair. 'How do you come to know his name?'

'I'll explain later.' Tobias kept his attention focused entirely on Sweet Ned. 'Look at me, Ned. I want to see your face.'

Lavinia stiffened at the deadly edge on Tobias's softly spoken order. Uncertain of his temper, she shot another quick, searching glance at him. Beneath the brim of his hat, his features were as hard and unyielding as the face of one of the stone angels in the graveyard.

Another tremor went through Sweet Ned, and Lavinia knew that he, too, had heard the promise of doom in Tobias's voice. But as though compelled by instructions received from a powerful mesmerist, he slowly rolled onto his back. He stared up at Tobias.

For the first time Lavinia got a close look at his face.

'He's so young,' she whispered. 'He's not even as old as Anthony or Dominic. Seventeen or eighteen at most.'

'And given his choice of profession, he'll likely hang before he's another year older.' Tobias stood just out of Ned's reach and watched his victim with no sign of sympathy. 'What did you intend here today, Ned?'

Ned jerked a little at the question. It was as though he had received a shock from the words.

'I never meant to hurt the lady,' he gasped. 'I swear it on my mother's grave. I was only going to put a scare into her, that's all.'

'What sort of scare?' Tobias asked, lowering his voice a bit more.

Ned was clearly terrified now. 'I . . . I was to tell her to stop asking questions, that's all.'

'Questions?' The information shook Lavinia. Until that moment she had assumed that Ned was no more than a common footpad who had singled her out as a woman alone and therefore an easy victim.

Tobias, however, did not appear surprised by the answer.

'What sort of questions was the lady not supposed to ask?' he said to Ned.

'I don't know what sort. I took a commission, ye see. The lady paid me, half before, the rest to follow'

'Lady?' Lavinia moved a little closer.

'Describe this woman who hired you,' Tobias said evenly. 'If you value your life, you will give me every single detail that you can recall.'

'I don't . . . I don't . . . I can't think . . .' Ned's features tightened in terror. He was clearly struggling hard to remember, but his fear of Tobias had tangled his tongue.

This approach would gain them nothing, Lavinia thought. She reached up and unclasped the silver medallion she wore around her throat.

'I suggest that you allow me to question him, sir,' she said quietly to Tobias.

Tobias glanced at the medallion, hesitated, and then gave a small shrug. 'Very well. I want to know everything there is to know about the person who hired him to frighten you.'

'Sweet Ned, look at me,' she said gently.

But Ned appeared unable to drag his gaze away from Tobias. He was riveted by whatever it was he saw in the other man's eyes.

'Look away from him, Tobias,' Lavinia said quietly. 'He is transfixed by you. You must release him before I can deal with him.'

'I'm watching him.' Tobias did not take his eyes off Ned. 'I don't want any surprises.'

'For heaven's sake, you've got him in a sort of trance,' she muttered. 'You must break it. He can't. Look away for a few seconds. I think that will do it.'

'What the devil are you talking about? He's not in a trance. He's terrified, that's all.' Tobias smiled coldly at Ned. 'And with very good reason.'

Ned did not move. He did not even blink. He lay there on the ground staring at Tobias.

'Tobias, please,' Lavinia said, a little desperate now.

'Very well.' Tobias took his attention off Ned and looked at her instead. 'But if this does not work, I'll take charge. Is that understood?'

She glanced quickly at him, saw what Ned must have seen, and stopped breathing. Tobias's eyes were fathomless seas of a roiling silvery-gray mist. The world around her began to dissolve. She lost her balance and started to fall headfirst into a bottomless, dark whirlpool.

'Lavinia.' Tobias's voice cracked like lightning. 'What's wrong? You look as if you're going to faint.'

She snapped out of the trance and found her balance with an act of will. 'Rubbish.' She drew a deep breath. 'I'll have you know I have never fainted in my entire life.'

Hastily, she turned back toward Ned, who was propped on his elbows, shaking his head as though trying to clear it. At least he was no longer helplessly transfixed by Tobias.

She summoned her wits and pulled herself together. 'Ned. Look at my necklace.' She held the silver pendant so that it caught the sunlight. 'See how it sparkles.'

Ned's gaze snagged on the dangling medallion. She let it swing gently.

'Watch the pattern of the dancing light, Ned,' she said in the firm, compelling voice she employed to induce a mesmeric trance. 'It will calm your mind and steady your nerves. Your fears will be soothed. Concentrate on the dancing light. Feel the heaviness in your limbs. Listen to my voice. Listen only to my voice. Let everything else fade into the distance, where it cannot make you anxious.'

Ned's expression relaxed. He no longer seemed aware of Tobias or his surroundings.

'Describe the woman who hired you to follow me today, Ned,' she said when she sensed that he was in a deep trance. 'Picture her in your mind as though she were standing here in front of you. Is there enough light to see her clearly?'

'The moon is nearly full and she brought a lantern. I can tell that she is tall. Almost as tall as me.' The words were flat and completely lacking in emotion.

'What is she wearing?'

'She has a small hat with a veil. I can see her eyes glitter now and again, but that's all.'

'What does her gown look like?'

The question seemed to perplex Ned. 'It's just an ordinary dress. Dark.'

Frustrated, she tried again. 'Does it look like the sort of gown an elegant lady might wear? Is it made of fine cloth?'

'No.' He sounded very sure this time. 'It's plain. Brown or gray, I think. It looks like the gown my friend Jenny wears to work at the tavern.'

'Is she wearing any jewelry?'

'No.'

'What about her shoes? Can you see them?'

'Yes. She has set the lantern down at her feet. There is plenty of light near the ground, and she has her skirts hiked up a little to keep them out of the dirt. I can see her low kid boots.'

'Can you see the woman's hair?'

'Some of it.'

'What color is her hair?'

'It looks very pale in the moonlight. Yellow or white, I think. I can't tell which.'

'How does she wear it?'

Again, Ned seemed rather baffled. 'She has pinned it in a knot at her neck.'

'What does the lady want you to do for her?'

'She wants me to go to Number Seven Claremont Lane and watch for the woman with the red hair who lives there. When she leaves her house I am to follow her until I can get her alone. I am to threaten her with the knife. I must tell her that if she does not stop asking questions I'll come back and slit her throat from ear to ear.'

Tobias glided a step closer. Lavinia shook her head, silently warning him to remain quiet.

'Would you do that, Sweet Ned?' she asked gently. 'Would you try to cut the lady's throat if she doesn't stop asking her questions?'

'No.' In spite of the deep trance, Ned suddenly became extremely agitated. 'I'm no murderer. But I can't let the woman know that. She's my first client and I don't want to lose her. I tell her I'll do the job if it comes down to it. She believes me. I can see that she does.'

'Calm yourself, Ned.' Lavinia spoke quickly. 'Watch the glittering light dance on the silver pendant and let yourself grow heavy.'

Ned relaxed visibly and fell back into the depths of the trance.

'How did the woman who gave you the commission find you?' Lavinia asked.

'She said she'd asked around. Someone told her I was the man she wanted for the job.'

'If you had been successful today, how would you contact her to collect the rest of your pay?' Lavinia asked.

'She said she'd find me just like she did the first time.'

Lavinia glanced at Tobias. He shook his head once to tell her that he had no other questions for Ned.

'Bring him out of the trance,' he said.

She turned back to Ned. 'You will wake up when I snap my fingers, but you will not remember this conversation.'

She snapped her fingers.

Ned blinked owlishly and came back to full awareness of his surroundings. The anxiety returned to his eyes. He promptly dismissed Lavinia and switched his attention back to Tobias.

'If ye let me go, sir,' he said very earnestly to Tobias, continuing a conversation he did not realize had been interrupted, 'I swear I won't go anywhere near this lady again. On me honor as a professional.'

'A professional what?' Tobias asked mildly. 'Professional intimidator of ladies?'

'I swear I won't touch a hair on her head.'

'You're right on that account,' Tobias agreed. 'Turn over, Ned.'

Ned gave a violent start. 'What are you going to do with me? I promise that if ye'll let me go, I won't take any more commissions for this sort of work ever again.'

Tobias took a long, narrow strip of leather out of one of the deep pockets of the old trousers he wore. 'I said, turn over and put your hands behind your back.'

Ned looked as though he might cry. But he surrendered to the inevitable and reluctantly complied.

Tobias secured his wrists with a few deft twists. 'On your feet.'

Ned struggled slowly upright, face twisted in despair. 'Are ye going to hand me over to the Runners? Ye might as well stick a knife in me vitals now and be done with it. I'll hang for sure.'

Tobias grasped his arm. 'We're not going to Bow Street.' He looked at Lavinia. 'The three of us will walk to the corner. I'm going to put you in a hack and send you back to Claremont Lane. Wait for me there.'

She hesitated. 'What about Ned?'

'Leave him to me.'

She did not like the sound of that any more than Ned did. Tobias's mood was unreadable.

'He's just a boy, Tobias,' she said quietly.

'He is no boy. He is a young man well on his way to becoming a hardened villain. The next time he agrees to accept a commission, he might decide that murder is not beyond the pale.'

'No, never,' Ned said quickly. 'I'm no cutthroat. I'm a thief, but I'm not a murderer.'

'Tobias, I really don't think he meant to do more than frighten me,' Lavinia said.

'I will deal with him.' Tobias hauled Ned toward the entrance to the lane. 'Let us be off. I have several other matters to attend to this afternoon. I have no more time to waste.'

He would not do any great harm to young Ned, she assured herself. Tobias was in a dangerous mood but he was in full control, as always.

Sometimes one had to trust one's partner.

Twenty-One

Vale watched Joan walk slowly through his collection of ancient vases and stone sarcophagi. She stopped in front of a glass case that contained several necklaces set with various colored gemstones. Sunlight from a nearby window burnished her fashionably styled hair, turning it a color that was nearly identical to the ancient Roman gold in the jewelry case.

Her classical profile would have done justice to a statue of a Greek goddess, he thought. But it was not her looks that drew him to her. There were, after all, a host of younger women who could surpass her in that aspect, although to his eye, they lacked the elegance and confidence that came with maturity.

No, it was the invisible power of her personality that pulled him so fiercely, he thought. There was a strength in her that called to everything that was male in him.

He marveled at the intensity of his desire. He could not remember when he had begun to fall in love with this woman. He only knew now that the emotion consumed him. Indeed, it had become so powerful that it had overtaken his passion for his other great love, the antiquities the Romans had left behind in England.

He had never allowed himself to think of Joan in intimate terms while her husband was alive. Fielding Dove had been one of his very few close friends. He had honored that friendship and valued it too highly to allow himself to lust after Dove's beautiful wife. Not that it would have done him any good, he thought wryly. Joan would never have looked at another man while her beloved Fielding was on this earth.

But Fielding had been gone for over a year now, and Joan had finally emerged from the cocoon of mourning. He had waged a careful and very deliberate campaign of seduction, wooing her with his collection of antiquities and conversations concerning their many mutual interests. The passion had blazed between them easily enough, but somewhere along the line he had discovered that he wanted more from her.

He wanted her to love him as much as he loved her.

For a time he had begun to hope that his feelings were reciprocated. But in the past few days Joan had seemed to retreat from him. He sensed that he was in great danger of losing her, and the knowledge filled him with quiet desperation. But he was at a loss to know what had gone wrong.

'Has Mr March asked you to consult on this business of the memento-mori-ring murderer?' Joan asked. She did not look up from her examination of an onyx cameo. 'I know that he and Mrs Lake are extremely concerned about their new case.'

'March mentioned the matter, but I was unable to offer much assistance. He and Crackenburne are attempting to learn who might have profited from the commissioned deaths.'

'They are searching for a person who gained financially from the murders. But Mrs Lake and I find it interesting that these recent deaths have all resulted in a change of wedding plans for some young lady in Society.'

'You think there is a connection? That seems a bit far-fetched.'

'Do not be so certain of that.' Joan left the jewelry case and wandered over to a cabinet filled with pottery. 'At first glance it may be difficult to imagine that anyone would commission a murder merely to halt one marriage or promote another.'

'You must admit it sounds quite extraordinary.'

She trailed a gloved fingertip along the carved edge of a stone altar. 'Not if one considers how much is at stake in a marriage, especially one made in Society.'

Vale thought about the huge amounts of money that often changed hands in the form of marriage settlements. To say nothing of the estates and titles that were often affected.

'You may be right,' he admitted. 'Perhaps it is not at all improbable that a person might kill to change the fate of a particularly lucrative marriage contract. As March has frequently pointed out, money is always an excellent motive for murder. But I collect that these deaths did not result in any obviously substantial change in the fortunes of those who stood to benefit most.'

'There are other things at stake in a marriage.' Joan turned to look at him down the length of the gallery. 'In fact, given the enormous risk a woman assumes when she weds, it is really rather remarkable that there are not a great many more murders committed for the purpose of altering a young lady's future.'

He frowned. 'I beg your pardon?'

Joan moved to study a portion of a column he had removed in the course of an excavation of a Roman temple near Bath.

'For a woman there are a great many risks involved in marriage,' she said quietly. 'Not all of them have to do with financial considerations.'

'I'm afraid I do not follow your logic, my dear.'

'For a young lady, there is the grave risk of childbirth, not to mention the fact that she will lose all legal control of her finances.'

He nodded. 'It is the way of the world.'

She gave him a sharp, annoyed glare that caused him to wish he had kept that bit of conventional wisdom to himself.

'There is also the risk of finding oneself tied to a vicious man capable of doing physical harm to his wife or his own offspring,' she continued grimly. 'Or the threat of marrying a wastrel who might throw away the children's inheritance in a single night at the gaming tables. There is the possibility of finding oneself involved in a cold, loveless, desperately lonely business arrangement.'

'Joan—' He stopped, not certain what to say. The conversation had suddenly veered off in a direction he had not foreseen.

She turned slowly around to face him again, her eyes shadowed. 'And for a woman there is no escape from any of these risks once the vows have been spoken and the contracts signed.'

Was this how all women viewed marriage, he wondered, as an enormous risk, not only for themselves, but for their children? He had never contemplated it from that point of view.

Few alliances in the ton were love matches. More often than not, couples went their own ways after the birth of an heir. It was customary for both husband and wife to conduct discreet affairs in so-called polite circles.

But there were limits to the freedoms that were permitted, he reflected. And divorce was almost impossible. Joan was right, there was no escape once the bargain had been struck. He had to admit that, until this moment, he had not given much thought to the very real physical, emotional, and financial risks involved for a woman in marriage.

'I understand.' He lounged against the edge of a Roman sarcophagus and folded his arms. 'Very well, I concede that there are other matters involved besides money and estates. But where does that leave us in this case? From all accounts, the families seemed quite pleased with the marriage arrangements. I suppose it is possible the young ladies might have had some doubts, but do you really believe that they had the knowledge and means to hire themselves a professional killer?'

'No. Mrs Lake and I feel that the people who commissioned the deaths are likely older and, more to the point, financially independent. They are persons who each have a strong interest in the outcome of the marriage. I think it is entirely possible that the three who hired the killer may know each other quite well.'

He was intrigued. 'Why do you say that?'

'Partly because of the strong similarity in the reasons for these three murders. It seems likely that a professional killer catering to those who move in Society would, of necessity, be forced to rely on word of mouth to advertise his or her services.'

'Ah, yes, the problem of advertising.' He smiled slightly. 'I had not thought of that.'

'Thus far I have collected the names of older women in each of the three families affected who would have had very strong feelings about the outcome of each marriage. Each possesses a will of iron. And each controls a significant fortune.'

'These are high-ranking ladies of the ton?'

'Yes.'

He spread his hands. 'How would a lady who spends her time in Society's drawing rooms and ballrooms go about finding a professional killer whom she could trust with such a dangerous business? I will be the first to agree that the women who move in Society often have their quirks and eccentricities, but they do not generally consort with members of the criminal class.'

'I shall let Mr March and Mrs Lake work that one out. In the meantime, before I speak to them about these three names, I would very much like to find a link between them. I have established that two are lifelong friends who play cards together every Saturday and go about together frequently. But the third does not reside in London. I do not know if she is even acquainted with the other two.'

'Who are these three women you suspect might have hired the murderer?'

'Lady Huxford and Lady Ferring are the two who are constant companions. But the third is Mrs Stockard. She is not fond of life in London and she spends very little time here. She lives on one of her son's estates.'

'Well, well, well,' he said softly.

She turned away from her examination of some ancient Roman coins and peered intently at him. 'What is it, Vale?'

'I do not know if it means anything, but for what it's worth, I saw Mrs Stockard together with Lady Huxford and Lady Ferring in Bath last summer while I was conducting my researches on the mosaic floors of a Roman villa.'

Joan came toward him, her expression brightening with anticipation. 'You saw them together? Did they seem to be good friends?'

'You know me, my dear, I have little patience with Society and those who move in it. But Bath is such a small place that it is impossible not to be aware of members of the ton who happen to be in town.'

She smiled knowingly. 'And furthermore, it is your nature to be observant, sir. Tell me, what did you learn about those three ladies?'

'Not a great deal. I encountered them on the street on several occasions and once or twice in the bookshops.' He hesitated. 'But I got the impression from some things that were said that all three ladies were in the habit of meeting in Bath quite regularly to take the waters. I believe they have done so for many years.'

Tobias strolled into the study shortly after five o'clock, just as Lavinia was considering a second glass of medicinal sherry. She rose quickly, relieved to see him.

'There you are,' she said. 'I have been very worried. Do sit down, Tobias. I will pour you a glass of sherry.'

'Never mind the sherry.' He showed her the cloth-wrapped package that he carried under his arm. 'I have concluded that when we are involved in a case together, I require a somewhat stronger restorative.'

She frowned at the package. 'What is that?'

'French brandy.' He set the package on her desk and removed the cloth to reveal a dark bottle. 'Smiling Jack was kind enough to allow me to purchase some from his new shipment.'

She watched with interest as he opened the bottle and poured a large amount of brandy into a glass. 'Is it smuggled, do you think?'

He raised a brow. 'Given Jack's strong aversion to paying customs duties, I think we can be certain of it.' He downed a swallow of the brandy and looked at her. 'Frankly, I did not bother to inquire into its origins. Would you care for some?'

'No, thank you, I believe I will stay with my sherry.' She went to the cabinet, picked up the decanter, and poured out a judicious amount. She studied the level of spirits in the glass for a few seconds and added some more. It had been a trying day, she reflected.

Tobias took his favorite armchair and propped his left ankle on a footstool. She settled back into her own chair.

'Very well,' she said. 'Out with it. What did you do with Sweet Ned?'

'I turned him over to Jack.'

Startled, she lowered her glass. 'Why on earth would you do that?'

'The boy needs to learn a more reliable trade.'

'Well, yes, but what on earth will Jack do? Teach him the art of tavern-keeping?'

'No. At least, not straightaway. As it happens, thanks to the connections he made in the course of his old profession, Jack is well-acquainted with a number of ships' captains. They are always in the market for new crew members. As we speak, Sweet Ned is on his way to a glorious new career at sea.'

'From what you've told me of your friend Jack, poor Ned has no doubt become a member of a smuggler's crew.'

'Look on the bright side. If all goes well, the lad will earn enough to allow him to retire in a few years. You and I, my dear, can only hope to do the same.'

'And if things do not go well?'

'Do not concern yourself on that account. Jack will make certain that our Ned sails with an experienced captain who knows his business.'

She tilted her head against the back of the chair. 'He is so young, Tobias. Just a boy, really. Probably alone in the world.'

'Do not waste any sentiment on Ned. He thought nothing of taking money to threaten you with a knife. In another year or two, he might have been willing to stick that same blade between your ribs for a similar fee.'

'Oh, I really don't think—'

'Trust me on this, Lavinia. Sweet Ned has all the makings of a professional villain.'

'Perhaps. But when one considers that he no doubt grew up in the stews with no prospects for the future, one can only feel pity.'

'I assure you, pity was most definitely not the emotion I experienced when I found him with you in that lane this afternoon.'

She smiled. 'Do not tell me that you had no soft sentiments whatsoever. You could have taken him to Bow Street, where he would no doubt have been clapped in irons and later hung. Instead, you turned him over to Smiling Jack.'

'For all the good it will do.' Tobias looked down into the brandy. 'The lad is still likely to end his life dancing on the end of a rope.'

'If he does,' she said gently, 'it will not be because you sent him there.'

He took another swallow of brandy and said nothing. But some of the grimness eased from his expression.

They sat together in silence for a time. After a while Tobias shifted slightly in his chair.

'What was it Aspasia wanted to discuss with you today?'

Lavinia swirled the sherry in her glass and took a quick sip. 'She wanted to assure me that she has no designs on you.'

'I could have told you that.' He scowled. 'In fact, if memory serves, I did tell you that. In no uncertain terms.'

'Not exactly. What you told me was that you had no romantic interest in her.'

He shrugged. 'It amounts to the same thing.'

'Not quite,' she said coolly. 'But be that as it may, I got the impression that she was ill-treated by both her father and her husband. She had vowed never to give her heart or to marry. And then she met Zachary Elland. You were right – she did, indeed, believe that they were true soul mates. She was stunned when she discovered the truth about him.'

'I am glad that the two of you have reached a degree of mutual understanding. I just wish she hadn't dragged you off to that damned graveyard for that particular conversation.'

'It was not her fault. Sweet Ned followed me from the moment I left the house today. He was merely waiting for an opportunity to get me alone. If it had not been that lane outside the cemetery, it would have been somewhere else. An alley or a park, no doubt.'

'Do not remind me.' He drank more brandy and then he set the glass down on the arm of the chair. 'We must talk about why the killer would hire someone like Sweet Ned to warn you off the case.'

'Have you a theory?'

'I think it is likely that this new Memento-Mori Man sees you as a complication,' Tobias said. 'His goal is to challenge me and to frighten Aspasia, but he has no use for you.'

'So he wants me to simply go away?'

'He probably believes that I will not allow you to continue to assist me on this case if I think that your life is in danger.' Tobias met her eyes. 'He may be right.'

'Do not even think about it,' she warned. 'You cannot order me to stop my inquiries. I am too deeply involved now.' She broke off at the sound of a knock on the study door. 'Yes, Mrs Chilton?'

The door opened. 'Mrs Dove and Lord Vale to see you, madam,' Mrs Chilton said in the resonant tones she reserved for announcing distinguished guests.

'Good heavens. *Both* of them?' Lavinia leaped from her chair. She had grown almost blasé about entertaining Joan, but the knowledge that Vale was here was another matter altogether. 'Kindly show them into the parlor, Mrs Chilton. And bring a tray of tea, if you would. Use the new oolong. Tell them that Mr March and I will join them immediately.'

'Yes, madam.' Mrs Chilton retreated, closing the door behind her.

'I can't believe that Lord Vale is here in my house.' Lavinia shook out the folds of her gown and went to the mirror to check her hair. 'Do you think tea is sufficient for refreshments, Tobias? Perhaps I should offer him some sherry.'

Tobias got to his feet with a leisurely air. 'Something tells me that Vale would much prefer a glass of my new French brandy.'

She turned away from the mirror. 'Excellent notion. We'll need glasses. You go on into the parlor and I'll have a word with Mrs Chilton.'

Tobias was amused. 'You were not nearly this rattled this afternoon when I found you running out of that damned graveyard with a villain in pursuit.'

'This is *Lord Vale* we are talking about. There are hostesses in this town who would kill to have him in their ballrooms, and he is sitting right there in my little parlor.' She made shooing motions with both hands. 'Hurry. I certainly do not want him to feel that he is obliged to cool his heels when he comes to call. I'll tell Mrs

Chilton to get the extra glasses.'

'Ask her to put a couple of those little currant cakes on the tray, will you?' Tobias collected his brandy bottle and went leisurely toward the door. 'I believe she mentioned that she had a few left over.'

'Oh, very well. Off with you.'

He went down the hall toward the parlor. She turned left and rushed into the kitchen.

'Brandy glasses for the gentlemen, Mrs Chilton,' she said. 'And Mr March requested some currant cakes.'

Mrs Chilton hoisted the kettle. 'Aye, madam. I'll be right in with the tray. You go tend to your guests.'

'Yes, of course.'

She took a deep breath, composed herself, and went back down the hall. The door of the parlor was open. She swept into the room with what she hoped was a degree of aplomb.

Vale stood at the window with Tobias. Joan was ensconced on the sofa, every fold of her fine azure-blue gown arranged with perfect precision and grace.

'Ah, there you are, Mrs Lake.' Vale inclined his head. 'I must say you look quite well for a lady who spent the afternoon playing cat-and-mouse with a villain in a graveyard.'

'I see Tobias has already brought you up to date.' She made her curtsy.

'You were not hurt?' Joan asked with an anxious look.

'I am fine, thank you.' She sat down on one of the chairs, hoping that her skirts would fall as elegantly as Joan's. 'Tobias and I were just discussing the villain's motives. He believes that the killer has decided that I am a complication and wants to frighten me into abandoning my inquiries.'

'Your particular inquiries are what bring me here this afternoon.' Joan slanted a quick glance at Vale. 'I have some information that may be helpful. Indeed, I think I have almost managed to convince his lordship that these murders are all connected to the canceled weddings.'

Tobias gave Vale a considering look. 'Is that true?'

'I still have some difficulty with the notion,' Vale said. 'But I must allow that Joan has come up with the names of three elderly ladies who do, indeed, have undeniable motives for murder. And there is no doubt but that all three of them could afford to pay a killer, if they so chose.'

Elation soared through Lavinia. She looked at Joan. 'Three elderly ladies? Tell me about them.'

'The first is Lady Huxford. I believe she might have had good reason to commission the death of Lord Fullerton at Beaumont Castle. You will recall that he had recently got engaged to Panfield's daughter.'

'Yes, go on,' Lavinia said.

'Lady Huxford is the girl's maternal grandmother. She is in her sixties, about the same age as Fullerton. According to a very reliable source, he seduced her years ago when she was in her first Season. But he broke off the affair to contract a more advantageous marriage. Her father was wealthy enough to be able to find her another suitor before it was generally known that she had been ruined. But she was heartbroken and never forgave Fullerton.'

'Then, one day, years later, she learns that the man who took advantage of her has made an offer for her *granddaughter*.' Lavinia was struck by the horror of it all. 'Lady Huxford must have been beside herself with rage.'

'But there was nothing she could say or do to stop the wedding from going forward. Everyone else in the family thought it an excellent match. She could hardly tell them the truth about her own past, and it might not have done any good if she had.'

Mrs Chilton entered with the tea tray. Tobias poured brandy into a glass and handed it to Vale.

'Who is the second suspect on your list of possible clients?' he asked.

'The Dowager Lady Ferring,' Joan said. 'I believe she may have hired the killer to get rid of Lady Rowland, the woman who supposedly took an overdose of her own sleeping medicine. You will recall that Lady Rowland's death resulted in the cancellation of her granddaughter's engagement to Lady Ferring's grandson.'

Lavinia nodded. 'You told me that Lady Rowland was obsessed with seeing her eldest daughter married into the Ferring family because she had once conceived a great passion for the young man's grandfather.'

'Yes, well, it seems that Lord Ferring's wife, Lady Ferring, was well-aware of the affair and was insanely jealous of Lady Rowland, who was a great beauty in her younger days. Indeed, I am told that the two ladies engaged in some spectacularly outrageous scenes that shocked Society. Those quarrels occurred some thirty years ago, but rumor has it that the animosity between the two women has never abated.'

'Then one day the Dowager Lady Ferring awakens to the news that her old nemesis, Lady Rowland, is plotting to link the two families by marrying her granddaughter off to young Ferring,' Lavinia whispered. 'I'll wager she was enraged.'

'I do not understand,' Tobias said. 'Why would the wedding plans have been canceled after Lady Rowland's death?'

'Because she was the only one in the family who was determined to marry the chit off to Ferring,' Joan said. 'Once he got his hands on his mother's fortune, the young lady's papa made other plans for the money. It transpires that he has not one but seven daughters to see settled. He intends to divide up the inheritance equally among all of the girls. The eldest will not receive such a huge portion as Lady Rowland had intended and she is thus no longer considered a great prize. Young Ferring will be looking elsewhere for a bride.'

'Who do you believe commissioned the third murder?' Tobias asked, looking thoroughly intrigued now.

'The third death was that of Mr Newbold,' Joan said. 'In some ways it is the simplest to explain. Newbold was exceedingly wealthy, but he was a truly dreadful man. When he made his offer for young Miss Wilson, everyone in the family was willing to overlook his ghastly reputation in favor of his finances. Everyone, that is, except the young woman's maternal grandmother, Mrs Stockard. She herself had been married to just such a lecherous rakehell in her youth, and she was not about to see her granddaughter suffer the same fate.'

'This is excellent work, Joan.' Intense satisfaction swept through Lavinia. She turned to Tobias. 'There you have it, sir, strong motives and the financial means to accomplish their objectives.'

Tobias exchanged a look with Vale.

'There is a certain logic to the conclusion,' Vale said.

Joan cleared her throat. 'There is also one more rather significant link. These three women appear to share a long-standing friendship, one that goes back for many years. I can vouch for the fact that two of them, Lady Huxford and Lady Ferring, are almost inseparable.'

'Now, that is interesting,' Tobias said quietly. 'A close personal connection might explain how they all managed to happen upon the same helpful murderer. One discovered him and told her companions.'

Lavinia tapped her fingers on the arm of the sofa and concentrated on how to proceed. 'I would very much like to have an opportunity to question some of these ladies.'

No one said a word. She realized they were all watching her quite intently.

'With great subtlety, of course,' she added smoothly.

'Of course,' Tobias growled into his brandy. 'You are so extremely skilled in the art.'

'Now, Tobias—'

'As I recall, the last time you attempted great subtlety, you managed to get us chucked out of Beaumont Castle. Without breakfast.'

'Really, sir, do you intend to throw that tiny little incident in my face every time you see an opportunity?'

'Yes,' Tobias said.

Joan smiled. 'I had a feeling you might want to question the ladies, Lavinia. There is not much I can do about Mrs Stockard, as she does not reside in Town. But I might be able to arrange for you to meet Lady Huxford and Lady Ferring.'

'That would be most helpful,' Lavinia said. 'How do we go about it?'

According to my friend who told me the old gossip, both ladies are very fond of attending the summer concerts at Vauxhall on the evenings when a fireworks display is scheduled. In fact, they rarely miss such entertainments. There is such an event scheduled for tomorrow night. I thought you and I might go together. I can arrange for a casual introduction. Will that do?'

'Perfectly.' Lavinia felt anticipation swirl through her. 'This is great news. I have a feeling that we are very near the end of this case.'

Tobias looked out the window. 'Then why do I have the sense that we are missing some vitally important clue?'

'No doubt because it is your nature to view every occurrence from the most depressing vantage point,' Lavinia said crisply. 'You ought to cultivate a more positive, optimistic outlook, sir. It would do wonders for your spirits.'

Somewhat to Tobias's surprise, Vale elected to join him when he left

Number 7 to walk back to his club. One did not think of a man of Vale's notoriously secretive and reclusive nature as given to going about Town on foot, Tobias thought. On the other hand, the man did spend a great deal of his time in the country digging up his Roman ruins, so he evidently was not opposed to physical exertion on principle.

The long light of the fading summer day bathed the streets and parks in that clear, soft radiance that was peculiar to the time of year. There was a depth and definition about the street scenes that drew the eye. Each window and doorway was picked out with a crisp precision that would have been far beyond the skill of any human artist. Yet the clarity and warmth of the sunlit spaces only served to heighten the intensity of the shadows in the narrow lanes and alleys.

'It would seem that your partner's intuition concerning the motives for the murders may have been correct after all,' Vale said.

'I must admit that Lavinia and Joan have come up with a link between the three women and motives that I cannot afford to overlook any longer.' Tobias shook his head. 'Although the notion of three elderly ladies of the ton resorting to murder to cancel some marriage contracts is more than a little unsettling.'

'I will admit to you that when Joan first told me of the conclusion she and Lavinia had reached, a great shudder of dread went through me.'

Tobias almost smiled. 'All too often we are inclined to underestimate the fairer sex.'

'Indeed.' Vale glanced at a group of young boys flying kites in the park. 'Today I learned a rather disturbing lesson in that regard myself. I had a conversation with Joan that was nothing short of illuminating. Did you ever pause to consider precisely how little marriage has to offer an intelligent, mature woman of independent means?'

Tobias watched one of the kites soar high above the treetops. 'If you are about to inform me that the institution does not have a great deal to offer such a female, you may save your breath. I have had occasion to give the subject a good deal of thought myself lately.'

'I see.'

Tobias looked at him. 'Can I assume that you have also been thinking along similar lines?'

Vale inclined his head very slightly in the smallest of gestures. 'I had not planned to marry again after my wife died. Until recently, I saw no need. I have two sons, both of whom have set up their own nurseries, so the titles and the estates are secure. My researches into the ruins left by the Romans keep me occupied and provide me with much satisfaction. As for the particular comforts and pleasures one can obtain only from a woman, well, they are not so difficult to come by, as we both are well-aware.'

Especially when one was a wealthy, titled member of the nobility who could afford to keep any number of mistresses if it suited him, Tobias thought. But he did not offer that observation aloud. It was not entirely fair, in any event. Although Vale had no doubt conducted his share of discreet liaisons over the years, he was not one to flaunt expensive courtesans or consort with flashy members of the demi-monde.

'I had not been aware of a sense of loneliness until I began to spend more time with Joan,' Vale said. 'It is almost as though I discovered an elixir I did not know I craved until I took a taste of it.'

'And having had the craving awakened, you are now consumed by a dark dread of the possibility that you may not be able to fully assuage your thirst.'

Vale slanted him a wryly amused look. 'I see that you, too, have acquired a taste for a certain tonic.'

'I suppose there is one positive aspect to our predicament, Vale.'

'Indeed? What is that?'

'We may tell ourselves that men in our situations who do manage to convince our ladies to marry us at least have the satisfaction of knowing that they come to us in love and trust.'

'Rather than because of financial or social considerations?' Vale's smile lacked all trace of real humor. 'What the devil will we do if they turn us down?'

'I suspect it is that pressing concern that prevents us from asking for their hands in the first place.'

'Yes.' Vale exhaled deeply. 'Well, there is no purpose to be served by further discussion of that subject. It will only depress us both. Tell me, did you mean what you said a few minutes ago in Mrs Lake's parlor? Do you truly believe that you are missing some important clue in this murder case?'

'I'm sure of it.' Tobias watched one of the kites pitch steeply and fall, spinning wildly out of control toward the ground. 'My partner is not the only one who possesses a degree of intuition. I have learned to my cost not to ignore my own instincts in these matters.'

Twenty-Two

Crackenburne lowered his newspaper with more alacrity than usual and peered at Tobias. 'There you are. Where the devil have you been?'

'Detecting clues.' Tobias lowered himself into the vacant chair in front of the club's hearth. 'That's how I earn my living, if you will recall. Not all of us are so fortunate as to be able to spend our entire lives in our clubs as you do, sir.'

Crackenburne snapped the paper closed and tossed it onto the small table beside his chair. 'You're in a bloody bad temper this evening. I assume this means the detecting business is not going well.'

'On the contrary, I've got more clues than I can handle, and none of them is giving me any useful answer.' Tobias rested his elbows on the arms of the chair and stretched out his left leg. 'Tell me, sir, has it ever occurred to you that a mature lady might commission a murder to ensure that her granddaughter marries well?'

Crackenburne blinked a couple of times. Then he scowled. 'Hadn't actually considered the question, but there's no getting around the fact that marriage is damned important business in the ton. Where there are fortunes and titles involved, who is to say what a strong-minded person with no scruples might do? I've known parents to conspire to compromise their own daughters with young gentlemen to force an offer. Every Season some ladies and gentlemen as good as sell their offspring into a miserable alliance in order to secure an inheritance. Why not commit a murder if it would achieve one's ends?'

'Indeed. Well, it appears that our new Memento-Mori Man may have noted that unique demand in the marketplace and seized the opportunity. Mrs Lake and Mrs Dove are convinced that Lady

Huxford, the Dowager Lady Ferring, and a certain Mrs Stockard may have been among his clients.'

He explained Lavinia's theory.

'How very odd.' Crackenburne frowned. 'But now that I consider the deaths from that perspective, I must admit such a conclusion is not beyond probability. I remember some of those scenes Lady Ferring and Lady Rowland conducted. Quite entertaining. And those old rumors about Lady Huxford and Fullerton. Well, we did wonder at the time. I am not well-acquainted with Mrs Stockard, but it is not difficult to see why an intelligent person would object to an alliance with Newbold.'

'Mrs Lake and Mrs Dove are going to attempt to discreetly question Lady Huxford and Lady Ferring tomorrow night at Vauxhall. Meanwhile, I will continue to flounder about in my own rather ineffectual fashion in hopes of finding some clue to the identity of the person who sent a villain to try to frighten my partner.'

'Have you any notions in that direction?'

'A few. To hire someone like Sweet Ned, one must make inquiries in the underworld. In my experience, that sphere is a mirror image of Society, governed by the same immutable laws of nature.'

'In other words, the rivers of gossip flow just as freely.'

'Precisely.'

'It certainly did not take long for the rumors concerning the employment of Sweet Ned to reach your friend Jack at the Gryphon.'

'Jack is continuing to fish in that pond on my behalf. With any luck, he will pull up something useful.'

'Has he turned up anything regarding Elland?'

'Not yet.'

Crackenburne's brows knit above the rims of his spectacles. 'Do you know, your observations concerning Elland's deliberate avoidance of the stews and the poorer neighborhoods struck me as quite interesting. I have been giving them a great deal of consideration. You are correct. He fancied himself as an elegant sort of murderer, did he not? He took professional pride in the fact that he moved in Society, not in that mirror-image world you describe.'

'I recall that on several occasions when I asked him to assist me in gathering intelligence at some dockside tavern or brothel, he always refused. He claimed that he had no knowledge of those environments and that he would be unable to be effective in them. But looking back, I believe that he had more than just a disdain of those whom he considered his social inferiors. I think there was an element of fear in his attitude.'

Crackenburne looked thoughtful. 'He certainly would not have been the first to employ outward scorn to mask such an emotion.'

'I am hoping that in Elland's case he had good reason to be wary of the stews.'

Crackenburne frowned. 'What is that?'

'If he came from that world, it would make sense that he would not have wanted to take the risk of going back into it.'

'For fear of being recognized, do you think?'

'Or triggering someone's memory. Who knows? But whatever the answer in Elland's case, evidently our new Memento-Mori Man does not share the same inhibitions. He was willing to go into a notoriously bad neighborhood to find Sweet Ned.'

'Perhaps he was simply desperate.'

'Regardless, I can hope that in seeking assistance in that quarter, he will have left some traces.'

'I wish you the best of luck in your hunt.' Crackenburne cleared his throat. 'By the way, I have a bit of news for you on another subject.'

Tobias stilled. 'Dominic Hood?'

Crackenburne leaned back in his chair. 'I do not know if you will find it helpful, but it may provide you with a place to start looking.'

Tobias slipped the lock pick back into its leather sheath and studied the heavily shadowed laboratory. He recognized some of the apparatus and equipment. Rows of glass beakers glinted on a nearby shelf. A large electrical machine loomed in the corner. He saw a handsome telescope on a bench. Next to it was a microscope.

There were several other items that he could not identify, but all looked expensive and all spoke of a passion for science. He had already searched the bedchamber and the small parlor. The laboratory had been locked, so he had saved it for last. Now, standing amid the treasures Dominic Hood clearly valued most, he knew that if the young man had secrets to conceal, they would be hidden here.

It was just after nine o'clock. He had watched Dominic leave his lodgings a short while earlier. The young man had been dressed for an evening at his club or the gaming tables. He would not be back for several hours. His manservant had left shortly afterward, looking as though he were headed for a nearby coffeehouse.

Tobias went about the search swiftly but methodically. He was aided by the orderly precision of the laboratory. He found what he was looking for in a small, locked drawer in the desk near the window.

The diary was bound in leather. The handwriting was feminine. The dates of the entries began twenty-two years earlier.

. . . My heart beats so rapidly when he touches my hand that it is a wonder I do not faint. I cannot begin to describe the intensity of this great emotion that his presence creates within me. Just knowing that he is near fills me with delight. He has warned me that I must not tell Mama or Papa or any of my friends, but how can I keep this astonishing secret to myself?

Tobias flipped forward several pages and paused at a sprinkling of other entries.

. . . I cannot believe that he has abandoned me. He swore that his passion for me was as great as mine for him. Surely he will come for me as he promised. We will run away together. . . .

* * *

. . . Mama says that I am ruined. She has spent the entire day crying in her bedchamber. Papa went into his study this morning and locked the door. He has not come out all day. Phillips says that he is getting drunk on claret and brandy. I am very frightened. I sent a message to my love but he has not responded. Dear God, what will I do if he does not come for me? I cannot bear to contemplate my life without him. . . .

* * *

. . . Papa has just informed me that my love is married to another. Mama claims that he not only possesses a wife, but that there is a small daughter and another babe due in the summer. This is not possible. Surely he would not have lied to me. . . .

* * *

. . . We are to leave for the country in the morning. Papa says that he has no choice but to accept Mr Hood's offer for my hand. I must be wed immediately or I am doomed. Phillips took another message to my love this afternoon, but again there was no response. Dear God, my heart is broken. I do not care if I live another day. Mr Hood is an old man. . . .

Anthony shot to his feet. 'He's my *brother*?'

'Half-brother, to be precise.' Tobias sank down on the edge of his desk. 'It was all there in the diary. Helen Clifton named your father as the man who seduced her when she was brought to London for her first Season.'

'It's impossible.' Anthony stalked tensely across the study to the window. He scowled at the night-darkened garden. 'Surely I would know if I had a brother.'

'Not necessarily. It would have been a dark family secret as far as the Cliftons were concerned, and Hood was only too pleased to acknowledge Dominic as his son. Crackenburne tells me that the man was twenty years older than Helen. He had been widowed twice and had no offspring. He was desperate for an heir.'

'So when his young wife informed him that she was with child, he was only too willing to believe that the babe was his?'

'He was no doubt told that the babe was born before its time. It is a common enough story. In any event, the last entry in the diary was made some three months after Dominic was born. In it, she states that she loves the babe and for his sake she will keep her secret until he is old enough to understand and forgive her. I suspect that she may not have told him the truth until she was on her deathbed. Perhaps she did not tell him at all.'

'Do you think Dominic found the diary after she was gone?'

'I cannot say. Either way, it must have come as a great blow.'

Anthony gripped the windowsill very tightly. 'What a terrible way to discover the secrets of your own life.'

'Crackenburne informed me that Hood died about five years ago. Dominic's mother was taken off last year.'

'A fever?'

'No. Apparently she suffered from spells of melancholia. According to Crackenburne's sources, those who knew her believe she deliberately took too much laudanum one evening. By the time they found her, she was gone. Dominic inherited a considerable amount of property and a comfortable income from both sides of his family.'

'That certainly explains his fine boots and the excellent cut of his coats,' Anthony muttered. 'As well as all that expensive laboratory equipment.'

'He may be comfortably situated, but he is alone now in the world.' Tobias paused a beat. 'Except for you.'

'It is difficult to grasp the notion that I might have a brother.' Anthony turned around, revealing the confusion and uncertainty in his eyes. 'But if what you say is true and Dominic has both a respectable name and a substantial income, why does he hate me so much?'

'I suggest that you ask him,' Tobias said.

Twenty-Three

The following evening, Lavinia sat with Joan in a colonnaded supper box and gazed with unabashed delight at the booths, rotundas, and fanciful pavilions that surrounded them.

Vauxhall was ablaze with lights tonight. Countless lamps and lanterns concealed in the trees illuminated the grounds, while the thrilling music of Handel drifted over the scene. Mysterious grottos, historical tableaux, and galleries hung with paintings drew large crowds. A short distance away, the pleasure garden's notorious tree-lined walks, many of them dark and secluded, lured amorous couples into the shadows for a bit of mildly scandalous dalliance.

If it were not for the fact that she and Joan were here on very serious business, Lavinia thought, she would have enjoyed herself immensely.

'I have not been here in years,' Joan said, examining the selection of cold meats on her plate with dry amusement. 'But I vow nothing has changed. The ham is still sliced so thinly that one could read a newspaper through it.'

'My parents and I visited Vauxhall on a few occasions when I was young,' Lavinia said. 'They purchased ice cream for me. I remember a balloon ascent and some acrobats and, of course, the fireworks.'

Memories floated up from the past, bringing images of another time when she had lived sheltered and secure in the warm bosom of her small family. The world then had been a very different place, she thought. Or, more likely, she was the one who had been different. In those days she had still been innocent and naïve.

But one had to grow up eventually. She had done just that a decade ago when, in the course of eighteen months, she had been married and widowed and lost her beloved parents at sea. In what had seemed a single, shattering moment, she found herself alone in the world, forced to survive on her wits and her skills at mesmerism.

Joan's life had taken some equally difficult twists and turns, she reflected. Perhaps that was the basis of the bond of friendship that had grown between them.

'You appear to be lost in thought.' Joan forked up a dainty bite of the very thin ham. 'Are you contemplating how to go about questioning Lady Huxford and Lady Ferring?'

'No.' Lavinia smiled slightly. 'You may find this odd, but I was pondering how you and I come to be sitting here tonight, eating this vastly overpriced meal and wearing gowns created by one of the most fashionable dressmakers in London.'

Joan was briefly startled. Then, without warning, she gave one of her rare chuckles. Her eyes danced with laughter and shared knowledge.

'When but for the hand of fate we could so easily have come to another, far less pleasant end? Quite right.' Joan picked up her glass of wine. 'Let us drink to the fact that neither of us ended up as an impoverished governess or some man's discarded mistress.'

'Indeed.' Lavinia touched her glass to Joan's. 'But I do not think that we should give fate all the credit for helping us avoid either of those dreadful professions.'

'I agree.' Joan took a sip of wine and put down her glass. 'Neither of us was afraid to grasp our opportunities when they appeared, were we? We have both taken some risks along the way that I fear would cause others to shudder.'

'Perhaps.' Lavinia shrugged. 'But we survived.'

Joan's expression turned thoughtful. 'I do not think that either of us could have contemplated doing anything else, at least not for long. Our temperaments are such that we must take command of the course of our own lives and fortunes. Fielding always said that one of the things he admired most in me was my willingness to turn a corner and go forth into the future.'

Lavinia smiled. 'May I take that comment to mean that you have decided that your new connection to Lord Vale does not dishonor your old love for your husband?'

'You may.' Joan cut another slice of ham with a resolute motion of her hand. 'I gave your comments on the subject a great deal of close thought and I am certain of my heart. I have told Maryanne as much. It may take her some time to accept the situation, but I hope that eventually she will come to understand that I cannot live shrouded in the past. Nor would Fielding have wanted me to do so.'

'She will come around in time. She is still very young.'

'Yes, I know.' Joan chewed delicately and swallowed. 'Do you think that we were ever so young and innocent? I cannot remember—' She stopped, eyes narrowing faintly. 'Ah, here they come at last. I was beginning to fear that they had changed their plans for the evening.'

'Lady Huxford and Lady Ferring?'

'Yes. This is perfect. They are being shown to the table directly behind you, just as I requested.'

The request had been honored, Lavinia thought, because Joan had tipped handsomely to ensure that outcome. She resisted the urge to turn around in her seat.

'Lady Huxford has noticed me,' Joan murmured. She smiled coolly at a point just past Lavinia's right shoulder and raised her voice slightly. 'Lady Huxford, Lady Ferring. How lovely to see you here this evening.'

'Mrs Dove.' The first voice was brittle and sharp.

'Mrs Dove.' The second voice was raspy and rather hoarse.

'Allow me to introduce my very good friend, Mrs Lake,' Joan said.

Lavinia forced herself to take her time. She turned slowly in her seat and, following Joan's lead, inclined her head ever so slightly.

Her first thought was that she had made a terrible mistake. Remorse swept through her. Surely neither of these two women teetering on canes was capable of commissioning a cold-blooded murder.

Lady Huxford was frail and nearly as thin as the slice of ham on Joan's plate. Lady Ferring appeared sturdier, but it was clear that in her younger days she had probably been several inches taller. Her shoulders were now bent and rounded.

Lavinia's pang of guilt faded when she found herself meeting two pairs of eyes that glinted with the undimmed fires of strong, forceful personalities. The chilly arrogance in those gazes spoke of long lives spent manipulating events and people to obtain their own ends. Their bodies might have succumbed to the weight of the years, but there was nothing wrong with either Lady Huxford's or Lady Ferring's mental faculties, Lavinia thought.

Or with their sense of style either, she noticed. Lady Huxford's bronze gown was trimmed with yellow ribbons. Lady Ferring was garbed in an expensively cut dress of heavy rose silk. Both wore high, stiffly pleated lace ruffs, no doubt designed to conceal wrinkles and loose skin at the throat.

Each wore a fetching little hat too. The charming confections were perched jauntily atop great quantities of silver-gray hair piled and curled into elaborate coiffeurs. Wigs, Lavinia thought. The false hair was fashionably arranged with a great deal of frizzing on top to add height. She could not see the back of the ladies' heads from this angle, but she had a hunch the chignons were equally elaborate.

'Lady Huxford,' Lavinia said very casually, 'please allow me to extend my condolences on your recent loss.'

Lady Huxford raised her lorgnette and squinted at Lavinia. 'What loss? I haven't lost anyone of note since his lordship died fourteen years ago.'

'I refer to the untimely death of your granddaughter's fiancé, Lord Fullerton,' Lavinia said. 'I'm certain her parents must be devastated. Such an excellent match.'

'They will soon make another one that is far more advantageous.' Lady Huxford lowered the eyeglass.

Lavinia turned to Lady Huxford's companion. 'Speaking of canceled engagements, I collect that your grandson no longer intends to make an offer for the hand of Lady Rowland's eldest granddaughter. What a pity. It seemed like such a fine alliance. Everyone thought that your grandson's title went quite nicely with the girl's inheritance.'

Lady Ferring's expression closed like a heavy door swinging shut.

'But I suppose the financial aspects of the situation changed when Lady Rowland died so unexpectedly,' Lavinia continued smoothly. 'The timing of her death was most unfortunate, was it not? The *on-dit* is that she succumbed before she got around to changing her will to endow the eldest girl. Her papa controls the money now, and they say he intends to divide the inheritance among all seven of his daughters.'

'Fate works in mysterious ways,' Lady Ferring observed.

'Indeed, it does,' Lavinia said. She turned back to Lady Huxford. 'Why, as fate would have it, I was at Beaumont Castle the night Lord Fullerton fell to his death.'

She could have sworn that Lady Huxford flinched a little at that news. But the woman recovered quickly.

'Any number of people were there that night, according to what I heard,' she said in her shards-of-glass voice. 'Beaumont's country-house parties are always absolute crushes.'

'Yes, there certainly were a great many people present,' Lavinia agreed. 'But I was evidently one of the last to see Lord Fullerton alive. Can you believe it? He passed me in the hall shortly before his fall.'

Lady Huxford regarded her in stony silence.

'I've no doubt but that he was in his cups,' Lady Ferring rasped. 'The man drank like a fish.'

'He did, indeed, appear intoxicated.' Lavinia made a tut-tutting sound. 'I regret to say that when I saw him, he was in the company of a young maid.'

'Men will be men.' Lady Huxford's eyes glittered with disdain. 'It is hardly a matter to be discussed in polite company.'

'Well, in this case, it is an important observation,' Lavinia said just as coldly. 'You see, my associate, Mr March, and I have been asked to look into the matter of Lord Fullerton's death. It is our opinion that he was murdered and that the maid was actually the killer in disguise.'

Lady Huxford's jaw dropped quite visibly. '*Murder.* What are you talking about? There has been no hint of murder.'

'On the contrary,' Lavinia murmured. 'There has been more than a hint of foul play. In fact, it is safe to say that the villain made some mistakes this time.'

'This time?' Lady Ferring bridled. 'Are you implying that there have been other murders?'

'Oh, yes, indeed. We are quite suspicious about Lady Rowland's demise, as a matter of fact.'

'Heard it was an overdose of sleeping tonic,' Lady Ferring gritted. 'No one said anything about murder.'

Lady Huxford's face tightened with outrage. 'I cannot understand why anyone would ask you to look into the matter.'

'Don't you know?' Joan said with an air of surprise. 'Mrs Lake and her associate, Mr March, are in the private-inquiry profession. They take commissions from persons who wish them to discover the true facts of certain suspicious matters such as these recent deaths.'

'Private inquiries?' Lady Ferring glowered at Lavinia. 'What an absurd notion. Hardly a fitting career for a lady.'

Lady Huxford's eyes glittered with near-feverish intensity. 'Who gave you this ridiculous commission to investigate Fullerton's death? Never heard that anyone in the family was concerned.'

'Oh, I could not possibly divulge the name of our client,' Lavinia said. 'I'm sure you can understand. Mr March and I work only for the most exclusive sort of clientele, and persons of quality demand great discretion. But I can assure you that my associate and I are making excellent progress in our investigations. When we identify the killer, I'm sure we will also discover who employed him.'

'Outrageous,' Lady Huxford muttered. 'Absolutely outrageous. Private-inquiry agents. Never heard of such a thing.'

'As it happens, you may be able to assist me in my investigation, madam,' Lavinia said. 'You were no doubt acquainted with Fullerton. He was approximately the same age as yourself. You must have known him since the days when you were first brought out. Can you think of anyone who might have had a reason to kill him?'

Lady Huxford stared at her in stunned shock.

'You are quite mad,' she whispered hoarsely.

Lavinia turned to Lady Ferring. 'You know, madam, when one considers the matter, one sees a marked similarity in the deaths of both Fullerton and Lady Rowland, don't you agree? I must make a note to discover what they had in common. I wonder if the motives for the murder were the same in both instances. Something to do with altering plans for a wedding, perhaps.'

Lady Ferring's eyes widened. 'I have no notion of what you are talking about. This is the most ridiculous chatter I have ever heard. Lady Huxford is right – you are, indeed, a candidate for Bedlam, Mrs Lake.'

'I have had quite enough of this lunatic, Sally.' Lady Huxford was on her feet, crumpling her napkin with one gloved hand. She seized her cane with the other. 'I do not intend to eat in such company. Let us be off.'

'I quite agree.' Lady Ferring gripped an ebony walking stick with both hands and levered herself to her feet. She glared about with a ferocious expression. 'Daniels? Where are you? We're leaving.'

'Aye, madam.' A harried-looking footman hurried forward to take her arm.

Another man in different livery followed quickly. He took hold of Lady Huxford's elbow. 'Sorry, madam. Didn't realize that you wanted to leave so soon.'

'The quality of the company is not what it should be,' Lady Huxford declared. 'Quite intolerable.'

The two footmen prepared to escort their employers back through the maze of supper boxes.

Joan watched the slow progress with a mix of amusement and dismay.

'I thought you intended to question them with great subtlety,' she murmured.

'Bah, I saw immediately that subtlety would achieve nothing with those two.' Lavinia looked at her across the table. 'I decided to rattle their nerves instead. Tobias assures me that making suspects anxious sometimes results in them giving themselves away.'

Joan eyed the departing ladies. 'I cannot say if they are rattled, but they do seem to be quite annoyed.'

'Either way, perhaps they will grow careless and make some move that will provide us with a clue.'

'Assuming they are guilty.'

'Now that I have met them, I am certain they are both quite capable of hiring a killer if they thought it would achieve their ends.'

'It is certainly true that it would be extremely unwise to get between those two and whatever they happened to covet,' Joan agreed.

'I do not doubt that for a moment.' Lavinia turned around to glance at Lady Huxford and Lady Ferring.

The progress of the two women was quite slow, almost stately. They had not gone far.

Lavinia stared at the backs of the voluminous silver-gray wigs.

'Oh, my God,' she whispered.

'What is it?' Joan followed her gaze, frowning. 'Is something amiss?'

'Their chignons.'

Joan peered at the two elegantly styled hairpieces. 'They are certainly quite elaborate, are they not? What about them?'

'They're identical in design. Do you see the little rows of curls at the top of the upper portion and the manner in which the lower section is twisted around a braided coil?'

'Yes, but what of it?'

At that moment the music swelled, the lights in the trees dimmed as though by magic, and a series of crackles and explosions announced the start of the fireworks display.

Sparkling showers of fire filled the night sky. The crowds oohed and aahed. A roar of applause went up.

'The hairdresser,' Lavinia said.

'What?' Joan raised her voice to be heard above the din. 'I cannot hear you.'

'The same hairdresser did both wigs,' Lavinia shouted back.

'That is hardly a surprise. It is obvious that the same dressmaker designed both of their gowns. I told you, Lady Huxford and Lady Ferring have been close friends for years. Why would they not share a dressmaker and a hairdresser?'

'You don't understand,' Lavinia yelled above the uproar. 'The hairdresser who did those two wigs was the same one who accompanied Mrs Oakes to Beaumont Castle. He styled her false hair in precisely the same manner for the costume ball. He told me that the row of curls at the top of the chignon and the loop around the coil are his signature.'

'What are you implying?'

'Don't you see? The hairdresser is the Memento-Mori Man.'

Tobias came down the steps of his town house in two long strides. The great sweep of the high-collared coat he wore over his dark shirt and trousers gave him the appearance of a thoroughly menacing highwayman.

One of Joan's liveried footmen hastened to open the door of the maroon carriage. In spite of his bad leg, Tobias did not wait for the step to be lowered. He grabbed the handhold on the side of the opening and hauled himself up into the softly lit interior of the cab. He sat down beside Lavinia and looked first at her and then at Joan.

'What the devil is this about?' he asked. 'I was just about to leave to visit Jack at the Gryphon. He thinks he may have found someone who knows something about Zachary Elland.'

'Lavinia is convinced that she has just identified the Memento-Mori Man,' Joan said.

Tobias turned his highwayman's gaze on Lavinia. 'You mean to say that you actually learned something useful at Vauxhall tonight?'

'You need not sound so astounded, sir.' She drew herself up in the seat. 'I told you that it would pay for me to question Lady Huxford and Lady Ferring, and I was right. I believe that the hairdresser who traveled to Beaumont Castle with Lady Oakes may be the murderer-for-hire whom we are seeking.'

To his credit, Tobias did not immediately reject the possibility. Then again, she reflected, he was desperate for clues.

'Are you referring to that fool who told you red hair was unfashionable?' he asked warily.

'He is one of many who have pointed that out to me recently, but, yes, I am talking about Mr Pierce. You will recall that he dressed Lady Oakes's wig with an extremely elaborate chignon.' Lavinia touched the back of her head. 'Lots of little curls and a braided coil?' She used her finger to trace the design in the air. 'It was a very unusual creation.'

'I have no recollection whatsoever of Lady Oakes's headdress.'

'The thing is, Tobias, I got a close look at Lady Huxford's and Lady Ferring's chignons this evening when they left the supper box. Both were wearing wigs and both of their headdresses were identical to the one Lady Oakes wore at Beaumont Castle.'

'What of it?'

'Really, sir, were you not paying attention when we interviewed the wig-maker, Mr Cork, and his associate, Mr Todd? They made it quite clear that a fashionable hairdresser takes great pride in creating his own unique designs. Mr Todd emphasized that he considered his chignons his signature.'

Tobias looked at Joan as though seeking assistance. She moved one shoulder in an elegant little shrug.

'I tried to tell her that it could, indeed, be a coincidence,' Joan said. 'But the more I consider the matter, the less I am inclined to believe that myself. It is, indeed, quite odd that the hairdresser who created coiffeurs for the two women we believe hired the killer was also at Beaumont Castle the night of Fullerton's death.'

Lavinia watched Tobias's face closely. She could see that he was not entirely convinced but he was considering the possibilities closely. 'It would explain a great deal about this case,' she said persuasively.

He frowned. 'You refer to the blond wig?'

'Yes. A hairdresser would be well aware of just how memorable such a shade would be in the event that he was spotted in the course of his crime. If Mr Pierce is the killer, it would also explain the unusual height of the maid. The hairdresser's stature was not particularly remarkable for a man – indeed, he was slightly on the short side – but dressed in women's attire, he would have appeared rather tall.'

Joan adjusted her glove. 'It would also explain how three high-ranking ladies of the ton came to meet a professional murderer. A hairdresser, after all, is invited directly into the house. Indeed, he often practices his art in a lady's dressing room or her bedchamber.'

Tobias narrowed his eyes. 'If you are correct, it would imply that all three of these wealthy ladies discussed the most personal and confidential matters with their hairdresser.'

'Well, yes,' Lavinia said. 'What of it?'

'Do you really expect me to believe that a lady would confide secrets to her hairdresser that she would not discuss with anyone other than her closest friends?'

Lavinia exchanged a glance with Joan.

'You had best tell the poor man the truth,' Joan murmured.

'What truth is that?' Tobias demanded.

'I know this will likely come as a shock to your nerves,' Lavinia said gently, 'but I must tell you that ladies routinely confide secrets to their hairdressers that they would not think of telling anyone else. There is a certain intimacy about the process of having one's hair dressed, you see. There you are, alone in your bedchamber with a man who is concerned only with combing and curling your hair. It is really quite pleasant.'

'*Pleasant*?'

'Alone with a man who is only too happy to discuss matters of fashion and style,' Joan added. 'A man who brings with him the latest gossip. A man who listens to every word you say. Yes, I think it is entirely possible that a woman might plot murder with just such a man.'

'Hell's teeth,' Tobias muttered. 'What an unnerving thought.'

Lavinia met Joan's eyes again in silent, mutual understanding. How did one explain the intimacy between hairdresser and client to a man?

'Who in her right mind would trust a hairdresser to know how to carry out a murder without getting caught?' Tobias asked. 'What if he betrayed her and accused her of commissioning the crime?'

'I very much doubt that anyone in a position of authority would take a hairdresser's word over that of a high-ranking member of the ton,' Lavinia said. 'Also, as you have so frequently pointed out, who would believe that an elderly lady of the ton who has spent her entire life in the most exclusive drawing rooms would know how to go about finding and hiring a professional killer?'

'The clients probably did not realize that they were hiring the hairdresser,' Joan said, sounding thoughtful. 'I suspect that they believed he was simply a sort of go-between. I'm sure it was all done with a wink and a nod. Mr Pierce may have told them that he knew someone who knew someone who could arrange for this sort of thing to be done, as it were. I doubt very much that he billed himself as a murderer-for-hire.'

'What of his fees?' Tobias asked.

Joan moved one hand slightly. 'Anonymous payments are easy enough to arrange.'

Lavinia looked at Tobias and knew that he was thinking the same thing she was. As the widow of a man who had run a vast criminal organization, Joan undoubtedly knew a great deal about how such matters were handled.

'Very well,' Tobias said eventually. 'I cannot deny that there is a coincidence here, and you know how I feel about coincidences. So let us say for the sake of argument that Mr Pierce is involved in this affair. I wonder how he persuaded Lady Oakes to take him to Beaumont Castle. Do you think she might have known what he was about that night?'

'Personally, I'm inclined to believe that Lady Oakes had nothing to do with the plot to kill Fullerton,' Joan said firmly. 'She is very sweet-natured but she is not known for her sharp intellect, to put it kindly. I do not think it would have been at all difficult for Pierce to convince her that she needed her hairdresser with her the night of the costume ball.'

Silence welled up in the interior of the carriage.

Tobias sat back in the seat and studied the front door of his house. Absently, he massaged his left thigh. 'As astonishing as it is, I cannot deny that the hairdresser is a link between the suspects and the death of at least one of the victims. Tomorrow I will see if I can discover some connections between him and the other two murders.'

Lavinia felt both relieved and vindicated. 'I knew you would see reason eventually, sir. It was just a matter of time.'

'Your faith in my powers of logic is deeply gratifying,' he said grimly.

'What happens next?' Joan asked with great interest.

Tobias glanced at Lavinia. 'Do you still have Pierce's card? The one he gave you that night at the castle?'

'Yes. His lodgings are in Piper Street.'

'I am not entirely convinced that the hairdresser is the Memento-

Mori Man,' Tobias said. 'But until we can sort through the chaos of this affair, I think it would be wise to keep an eye on him.'

Twenty-Four

The gaming room of the club was thick with the invisible miasma of frenzied excitement that radiated from the players. For the most part, the fierce passions that accompanied each roll of the dice or new wager at the card tables were concealed behind the requisite masks of ennui and jaded amusement. Good form demanded that each of the elegantly dressed gentlemen vie to outdo his companions in expressing a supreme lack of concern for the outcome of the play.

But nothing could conceal the smell of sweat and anxiety that mingled with the smoky haze, Anthony thought. It was a stench that permeated the entire room.

This was the hellish atmosphere of feverish desperation that his father had chosen to breathe. In the end it had lured Edward Sinclair to his death.

He stood in the doorway for a time, listening to the click of the dice and the clink of bottles and glasses on the card tables. It likely made no difference how much one drank while playing hazard. The result of a toss of the dice was in the hands of the fates, unless the management had secretly weighted the small cubes. But it made no sense at all to drink oneself into a stupor while attempting to employ some logic to a hand of whist, he thought. Yet drinking deeply was precisely what almost all of the players chose to do.

With the exception of Dominic Hood.

Dominic played whist in the same style as the others, with a bottle of claret at hand. But Anthony noticed that he did not sip from his half-filled glass. There was a small pile of papers on the table. Vouchers from those who had lost to him.

Anthony studied him closely, searching for the evidence of their shared blood. There were, indeed, some similarities between them, he concluded. Their father had left his stamp on the shape of their noses and the angle of their shoulders. *And on the color of our eyes,* he thought. Why had he not noticed until now that Dominic's eyes were the same shade of golden brown as those he saw in his shaving mirror every morning?

The hand of whist came to an end at Dominic's table. In spite of his caution with the claret, this time he was the one who was obliged to scrawl his promise to make good on his wager on a small slip of paper. Sobriety might increase one's odds of winning at cards, Anthony thought, but it certainly did not guarantee the outcome of the game. No amount of astute and logical play could make up for a bad hand.

With an easy smile and a bored nod to his companions, Dominic left the table and turned to walk toward the door. When he saw Anthony, he hesitated ever so slightly. Then his jaw clenched. He continued forward.

'I'm surprised to see you here this evening,' he said as he made to move past Anthony. 'I got the impression that you avoided the gaming tables.' He smiled with faint derision. 'Something to do with a fear of losing, no doubt.'

The insult sliced to the bone, but Anthony was proud that he was able to manage a thin, cold smile in return. 'Something to do with a strong desire to avoid ending up dead because of a foolish dispute over a hand of cards.' He paused deliberately. 'As our father did.'

A flicker of dark emotion came and went in Dominic's eyes. He swiftly veiled the expression. 'So you finally reasoned it out, did you? It certainly took you long enough. Perhaps you would do well to reconsider your choice of profession. One would expect a private-inquiry agent to be somewhat more astute, don't you agree?'

'I believe that I shall stick with my career. Unlike you, I do not have the option of amusing myself with science experiments all day and card-playing all night. That sort of pleasant idleness is only for those who were so fortunate as to inherit property and an income.'

Dominic nodded. 'I retract what I said about you not being observant, Sinclair. You are quite right. I never knew my father, but I do, indeed, have an inheritance. Which means that I have a good deal more to offer to a lady such as Miss Emeline than you do.'

He turned on his heel and walked off without waiting for a response.

Anger flashed through Anthony. 'Bloody hell,' he whispered.

He pursued Dominic across the coffee room and out into the front hall, where an uneasy porter quickly handed both of them their hats and hastened to open the door.

'Stay away from Emeline,' Anthony said fiercely from the top of the steps.

Dominic came to a halt and spun around. In the harsh glare of the gas lamps, his face was a mask of barely contained rage. 'Now, why should I deprive myself of the pleasure of her company, *brother*?'

'You do not love her.' Anthony went slowly down the steps, hat clenched in his fist. 'You seek to use her in order to exact your revenge against me. Admit it, Hood.'

'I do not intend to discuss my interest in Miss Emeline with you.'

'Hell's teeth, man, this has nothing to do with Emeline. I am the one you want to destroy. Would you hide behind a woman's skirts to gain your vengeance?'

'Damn you, I could call you out for that insult.'

'Be my guest,' Anthony said. 'But at least have the courage to admit why you are challenging me. I ask you again, sir, why do you hate me? Is it because your mother allowed herself to be seduced by our father? You cannot blame me for that. You cannot blame her either. The only one you can fault is Edward Sinclair, and he's been dead and buried for some fourteen years.'

'Damn you to hell, Sinclair.' Dominic hurled his hat aside and launched himself forward. 'Do not dare to mention my mother. Your father ruined her.'

Anthony employed the sliding maneuver that Tobias had taught him and managed to duck his brother's wildly swinging fist.

Although Dominic's blow did not strike its target, Anthony was unable to avoid him altogether. The impact of the collision spun him around and carried both of them to the pavement. They rolled together across the hard stones. He found himself struggling to ward off a series of erratically aimed punches while he tried to fight back.

In the heat of the first real fight in which he had ever participated, his brain ceased to function logically. Tobias had warned him that it would be like this. It was impossible to think clearly, impossible to recall the nuances of the art and science of the various pugilistic techniques they had practiced together. Anthony fell back on what seemed blind instinct, not even feeling the pain of Dominic's blows.

But the lessons Tobias had taught him must have taken root somewhere deep inside, because he succeeded in landing a number of solid-sounding punches to Dominic's ribs and one to his jaw. Each time he felt a shudder go through his opponent's body, a fierce satisfaction roared through his veins.

He never heard the rattle of carriage wheels and horses' hooves. The first indication he had that he and Dominic were no longer alone on the street was when he felt himself seized by the collar and hauled forcibly off his brother. He was then dropped rather carelessly onto the pavement beside Dominic.

He opened his eyes, blinked away the blood that blurred his vision, and found himself looking up at Tobias.

A familiar maroon carriage stood a short distance away. Mrs Lake and Joan Dove peered anxiously from the windows. His first rational thought was that he was in luck. Emeline was not with them.

He sat up cautiously, raising his sleeve to mop the blood he could feel trickling down his face.

'Tobias? What the devil are you doing here?' he muttered.

Beside him, Dominic got to his knees, one hand on his ribs. He watched Tobias warily.

'I apologize for interrupting your entertainment this evening, gentlemen.' Tobias contemplated both of them with cold eyes. 'But I happen to be in great need of some able-bodied assistants. There may well be a life hanging in the balance. I would take it as a great favor if you would both agree to continue this wholesome exercise at some other time.'

'What is going on?' Anthony staggered to his feet, grabbing the iron step railing to steady himself. Then the reason for Mrs Lake's and Mrs Dove's presence in front of a gentleman's club at this hour finally registered. Excitement flashed through him, temporarily overriding his anger. 'Have you found the killer?'

'Mrs Lake believes we may have identified him,' Tobias said. 'But I am not so certain. Nevertheless, we cannot afford to take chances.' Tobias switched his attention to Dominic. 'I propose to mount a clandestine watch on our suspect. I think it would be best to use two men rather than one, in case action is required. Are you interested?'

'Action?' Dominic got to his feet, wincing again. 'I don't understand.'

'If my associate is right, the man is a cold-blooded murderer.

There is every reason to believe that he plans to kill again. If someone tries to interfere or if he feels cornered, he will likely become desperate and quite dangerous. Better to have two men on hand to stop him in that event.'

'Why do you need me?' Dominic scowled and gingerly touched his jaw. 'You've got Sinclair and yourself, sir.'

'I cannot spare the time from my inquiries to watch one possible suspect. What about it, Hood? Would you be willing to aid me in this endeavor? As I said, a life may be hanging in the balance.'

Dominic gave Anthony a quick, unreadable glance and then slowly lowered his hand from his jaw. 'You think this man will kill again?'

'It is only a matter of time. I will consider myself very much in your debt if you could see your way clear to help me keep this villain under surveillance tonight.'

'I suppose I could afford to spend some time keeping an eye on this suspect for you,' Dominic said carefully.

'Thank you,' Tobias said. 'All the murders thus far have occurred at night, so I think we can assume that our killer prefers to act under cover of darkness. Therefore, for the rest of this evening, I want you two to watch his lodgings. You must not let him see you. Follow him if he leaves his residence, but do not interfere with him unless he looks as though he is about to commit another act of violence. Is that clear?'

'Who is this person?' Anthony asked, his blood heating again, not with anger but with anticipation of the hunt.

'I was afraid you would ask that question,' Tobias said.

'We're to keep watch on a bloody *hairdresser*?' Dominic lounged deep in the shadows of the narrow alley and gazed glumly at the door of Mr Pierce's lodgings. 'I don't believe it. How do you suppose he goes about the job of murdering his victims? Do you think he smothers them in wigs?'

'It was your decision to agree to assist Tobias in this matter,' Anthony growled from the other side of the alley. 'No one forced you to volunteer.'

'March said there was a life at stake. But I must tell you that it is extremely difficult to envision a hairdresser as a cold-blooded murderer-for-hire.'

'Perhaps that is why he has been successful thus far,' Anthony offered dryly. 'No one suspects him.'

'Huh.' Dominic sounded struck by that possibility. 'Hadn't thought of it that way.'

'I think Tobias has a few doubts about this theory too,' Anthony said. 'But he has learned not to discount Mrs Lake's intuition.'

Conversation lapsed. They went back to watching the front door of Pierce's lodgings in silence. Moonlight and a sprinkling of weakly glowing gas lamps lit the narrow, night-shrouded street. The occasional hackney or nightman's wagon rumbled past now and again, but otherwise it was quiet.

Anthony was aware of tenderness and swelling in the vicinity of his eye, and his ribs ached in numerous places. He suspected that he would have some bruises by morning. He consoled himself with the knowledge that Dominic was almost certainly nursing similar mementos of their skirmish.

'Mrs Lake is an exceedingly strong-minded lady,' Dominic said after a while.

Anthony almost laughed at that comment. But he stopped, wincing, when he felt the cut on his lip open and dampen with blood. 'Tobias frequently makes a similar observation. But not usually in such restrained terms.'

He raised the cloth soaked in clear, strong spirits that Mrs Lake had given him and dabbed at the corner of his mouth. Dominic had a similar spirit-drenched cloth. Mrs Lake had insisted upon ordering one for each of them from the harried club porter before she had allowed them to be driven here to take up their posts.

After a moment he heard Dominic unwrap the packet of meat pies that Mrs Lake had also commissioned from the porter.

'She may be somewhat forceful in her temperament,' Dominic said, 'but I'm glad she thought about the pies.' He paused. 'Do you want one?'

Anthony realized that he was famished. 'Yes.'

Dominic handed him a pie and took one for himself. They ate without speaking for a few minutes.

Dominic brushed crumbs from his hands. 'What was he like?'

Anthony knew whom he meant. 'I do not remember a great deal about him. He got himself killed shortly after I turned eight. Mother died later that same year. Ann and I went to live with relatives for a few months.'

'You must recall something about him.' Dominic sounded angry again. 'You had him for over seven years.'

'Father wasn't around much.' Anthony shrugged. 'We lived in the country. He spent most of his time in London. He preferred the hells to family life.' He paused. 'Ann had a miniature of him that she left to me.'

'Describe him.'

'I'll show you the portrait tomorrow. He looked a lot like—'

'Like who?'

'Like us. Same eyes. Same physique. Same nose.'

'Was he ill-tempered? Quick to laugh? Clever?'

'Not clever enough to avoid a stupid argument over a hand of cards, apparently,' Anthony said. 'As for the rest, I believe women found him quite charming.'

There was a heavy sigh from Dominic. 'Yes, I suppose that must have been the case.'

'What I recall is that he made my mother cry often and that he lost everything, including our house, in that last game of cards.'

'That's the lot? That is all you can remember?'

Anthony felt his temper start to slip again. 'You want to know what I remember most vividly? I remember the man who raised me to manhood. I remember that it was Tobias who taught me how to play chess. It was Tobias who hired a tutor for me so I did not have to go away to school after Ann died. It was Tobias who gave me my first razor and showed me how to use it. It was Tobias who talked to me about what was expected of a man and the importance of honor. It was Tobias who—'

'Enough.' Dominic raised a hand in the shadows. 'I take your point.'

Anthony picked up another meat pie and took a large bite. 'What was he like? The man who raised you as his son.'

Dominic looked out into the dark street. 'He seemed more like a grandfather than a father at times. He was plagued with gout. I remember that he used to keep one foot propped on a little stool a great deal of the time.'

'That is all you recall?'

Dominic hesitated. 'No. I remember that he gave me my first telescope and showed me how to view the moon. He instructed me in mathematics. He took me to my first science lecture and later bought me some equipment so that I could perform simple chemistry experiments.'

'He treated you as a son.'

'Yes. And I loved him and respected him. He died when I was seventeen. I did not discover the truth about my real father until I found my mother's diary after her death. If Bartholomew Hood ever knew that I was not his real son, he never gave any indication to me.'

'When you consider the matter closely,' Anthony said, 'it appears that we were both rather fortunate in the men who reared us. We could have done a good deal worse.'

Dominic made an odd sound, part groan, part ironic laugh. 'You mean we could have been raised by someone like our real father? I had not thought of it in that light. You may be right.'

Lavinia poured herself a small glass of sherry and sat down in the chair next to the one Tobias occupied. She propped her feet on the little hassock and contemplated the small blaze on the hearth.

It was nearly two o'clock in the morning and the house was quiet. Mrs Chilton and Emeline had both retired to their beds before she and Tobias had returned. Tobias had refused Joan's offer of the use of the carriage, saying that he would make his own way home after he discussed the next move in the case with Lavinia.

She wished now that she had argued against the dismissal of the comfortable vehicle. Although he hid it well, she sensed the weariness in Tobias tonight. It had been plain in the way he lowered himself into the large chair and the manner in which he absently massaged his left leg. She could see it in the lines of tension at the corners of his eyes and his mouth.

She was well-aware that he had not slept much since they had returned from Beaumont Castle. This case was taking its toll on him. She did not care to think about him having to walk back to his own house later tonight. But she also knew him well enough to know that he would not welcome her fussing.

'Do you think it was wise to leave Anthony and Dominic alone together to watch Pierce?' she asked. 'What if they decide to engage in another bout of boxing?'

'I do not think that will happen so long as they are both committed to the task of spying on Pierce.' Tobias took a swallow of his brandy. 'With any luck, the time spent sharing the acute boredom of keeping a long night watch will encourage them to work out their differences.'

'Ah, yes, I comprehend the full scope of your crafty scheme now.' She leaned her head against the back of the chair and smiled slightly. 'Force the pair of them to spend several hours together and hope that they start talking to each other. Very clever of you, sir.'

He gazed into the fire. 'We shall see.'

'How did you know that Dominic would agree to assist you by keeping watch with Anthony?'

'Young men of that age yearn for a quest that is important and fraught with meaning. I was almost certain that, unless he was a complete scoundrel, the possibility of saving a life and helping to trap a murderer would override his need to avenge his mother. At least for a while.'

She examined the sherry in the firelight. 'Do you believe that is the source of Dominic's resentment toward Anthony? He feels that he owes something to his mother's memory because of what happened all those years ago?'

'I suspect it is a bit more complicated than that. He is also no doubt having problems dealing with the knowledge that he was not told the truth about his past. He is angry, and Anthony is the only one left on whom he can vent his pain and frustration.'

'But vengeance is not possible in this instance. Anthony's father is long dead. There is no way that Dominic can achieve any sort of justice at this late date.'

Tobias sipped his brandy and lowered the glass. 'Young men are rarely inclined to take a practical view of life. They are far more apt to let fanciful ideals, a too-refined sense of honor, and a passionate notion of what constitutes right and wrong interfere with logic and common sense.'

'Perhaps.'

'There is no *perhaps* about it.' Tobias tilted his head against the back of the chair and closed his eyes. 'I have seen the same tendencies in Anthony often enough to recognize them on sight. I shall have to find a way to ensure that both he and Dominic learn they do not carry the burdens of old sins on their shoulders.'

She smiled, lowered her glass, and got to her feet. Tobias opened his eyes halfway and watched her come toward him.

She sank slowly down onto her knees on the carpet in front of his chair and rested one arm on his right thigh. The skirts of her lavender-blue gown crumpled around her legs.

'I do not think that Anthony and Dominic are the only ones who sometimes fail to take a perfectly practical view of the world.' She could feel the heat of him through the fabric of his trousers. 'You are a fine man, Tobias, a man of ideals and honor with a passionate, deeply rooted sense of right and wrong. Do not rail too harshly against such attributes. They are among the many reasons that I love you with all my heart.'

Surprise and then dark passion stirred in his partially shuttered eyes.

'Lavinia.'

With a soft, urgent groan, he reached for her, drawing her up into his arms so that she lay cradled against his chest. His mouth closed over hers, compelling and fierce and heavy with desire. She spread her fingers across his shoulder and returned the kiss with all of the intense emotion that he inspired in her heart.

She had judged him near to exhaustion, but when his arms closed around her and his palm covered her breast, she concluded that she had been wrong. It was as though he had drunk some reviving tonic rather than brandy. His arousal was swift and complete in a matter of seconds.

She felt his fingers on the back of her gown, and a moment later he lowered the bodice to her waist. His thumb glided across her bare nipple. Her breath caught in her throat. This was certainly not the first time that he had touched her like this, she thought, but he never failed to achieve the same effect. He somehow managed to steal her breath on each occasion.

The rough costume he had chosen to wear tonight did not include a cravat. She edged her hand beneath his shirt and savored the play of muscle beneath skin. Gliding her fingertips lower, she found the fastenings of his trousers. When she freed him, he thrust his member against her palm. She encircled him with her fingers and stroked him until he made a hoarse sound. Hastily, he covered her hand with his own, stilling her fingers.

He made to ease her off his lap. She knew that he intended to put her down on the floor in front of the hearth and make love to her.

'No,' she whispered against his throat. 'Let me do this for you tonight.'

'Lavinia—'

She silenced him with another little kiss. Then she slid back to her knees on the carpet between his thighs and took him into her mouth.

The air left his lungs in a low, heavy groan and his hands locked in her hair.

Within a very short time she felt the muscles of his thigh tighten into steel bands. Once again he made to halt her lovemaking.

'I cannot wait any longer,' he muttered.

She released him briefly, her fingers cupping him. 'I do not want you to wait.'

She took him between her lips again. His hands fell away from her hair. He gripped the arms of his chair. His entire body went rigid. His head tipped back.

She felt his climax pulse through him in a series of surging waves. He made almost no sound. It was as though he abandoned himself so completely to the release that he had no energy left to whisper or even groan.

After a while he went limp and still. Slowly, she looked up and saw that his eyes were closed, his head resting against the wing of the chair.

She rose slowly and reached down to take hold of his right leg. Tobias did not stir when she propped one booted foot alongside the other on the hassock.

She opened a cupboard, took out the blanket stored inside, and arranged it around him. When she was satisfied that he was covered, she checked the fire, picked up the candle, and went to the door of the study.

She let herself into the hall, closed the door softly behind her, and climbed the stairs.

A few minutes later she lay in her bed, alone in the darkness, looking up at the shadowed ceiling. She thought about Tobias sleeping downstairs in her study for a long time before she finally turned onto her side and closed her eyes.

Twenty-Five

The muffled clatter of pots and pans awakened Tobias the next morning. His first thought was that Whitby was making a good deal more noise downstairs in the kitchen than usual. His second thought was that he felt rested and refreshed. This was the first good night's sleep he'd had since Beaumont Castle, and he'd needed it. He was no longer Anthony's age and able to stay awake until dawn night after night without suffering the consequences, he reflected.

Those damned ravages of time.

Then he opened his eyes and saw the books of poetry on the shelves next to the hearth.

Lavinia's study.

He glanced toward the window, where the cheerful light of a summer dawn was streaming into the cozy little room. The clang and bang was coming from Mrs Chilton's kitchen, not Whitby's domain.

Images from his final waking moments last night came back to him in a warm, pleasant rush. The memory of Lavinia on her knees between his legs caused his cock to harden again.

He raised his eyes to the ceiling and contemplated a mental picture of his business partner upstairs in her bed. She would be snuggled beneath the quilts, flushed with sleep, her red hair tucked up beneath a pretty little lace cap.

Another telling crash of metal disrupted his reverie. Mrs Chilton was apparently trying to send him a message. Light footsteps sounded overhead.

It finally occurred to him that Lavinia and her housekeeper were not the only ones in residence. Miss Emeline was a sensible young lady, but she would no doubt be shocked to the core if she were to discover that he had spent the night in Lavinia's study. Young people these days seemed to have developed rather rigid notions of propriety. One could only hope that they would eventually outgrow them.

He tossed aside the blanket and got to his feet, stretching his arms toward the ceiling. He rolled his shoulders a little to work out the tightness created by a night spent in a chair.

He contemplated making use of the small water closet tucked away behind the staircase but reluctantly decided against it. There was every possibility that Emeline might appear just as he was emerging from the facility.

He could wait until he happened upon a private spot in a park on the way home.

With a few quick, efficient moves, he put himself to rights, shoving his shirttails into the waistband of his trousers and raking his fingers through his hair.

When he was ready, he went to the door of the study and opened it cautiously.

Mrs Chilton stood in the hall, a steaming mug of tea in hand. Her expression was unreadable.

'Thought you might like to drink this on the way home,' she said brusquely. 'Here's a hot currant muffin for you to eat with it. You can bring the cup back when you return for breakfast.'

'Mrs Chilton, you are an angel.' He took the mug and muffin from her and headed for the front door. 'I shall see you in a couple of hours.'

'Aye, I've no doubt of that.' She followed him down the hall and reached around him to open the door. Casting a meaningful glance over her shoulder at the staircase that led to the floor above, she narrowed her eyes.

'This sort of thing cannot continue, sir,' she said in a low voice. 'There is a young, unmarried lady in the house. It simply won't do.'

'I'm well aware of that, Mrs Chilton.' He went outside onto the step. 'Lovely day, isn't it?'

'Won't last,' she said. 'There's a summer storm on the way. I can feel it coming.'

She closed the door very quietly but very deliberately in his face.

He blew the steam from his tea, took a large bite of the warm muffin, and went down the steps.

A trickle of awareness between his shoulders made him glance back at the windows of the upper floor of Number 7. Lavinia looked down at him from her bedchamber. She wore a flower-spattered wrapper. He could make out the little white lace cap that crowned her tousled red hair.

She raised a hand, smiled at him, and blew a little kiss. Mrs Chilton was wrong about the storm, he thought. Birds were singing and the sun was out. There were only a few puffy clouds in the summer sky. It was going to be a fine day.

The sun was still shining two hours later when Mrs Chilton cleared away the last of the breakfast dishes.

'I still say there's a storm brewing,' she muttered as she swept past Tobias's chair.

Lavinia looked up from her newspaper and saw a peculiar steely glint in Mrs Chilton's eyes.

'It won't do any harm if there is. A little rain will wash out the alleys.' Tobias helped himself to some more currant jam. 'Getting low on the jam, Mrs Chilton.'

'Not at all, sir.' Mrs Chilton prepared to back through the doorway into the kitchen, a loaded tray in her hands. 'I've got three more pots on hand. Expect that will do us for a few days.'

'I doubt it.' Tobias spread jam on a slice of toast. 'I can go through three pots in no time, Mrs Chilton.'

'If I were you, sir, I'd make those three pots last,' Mrs Chilton said in a very pointed manner. 'There's no telling when I'll have time to make up another batch.'

She bustled through the door and disappeared into the kitchen.

Tobias ate a bite of his toast.

Lavinia rattled her newspaper a little and glared at him. 'Did you say or do something to annoy Mrs Chilton when you arrived for breakfast this morning? She is in a rather sharp mood today.'

'Yes, I noticed that as well.' Emeline poured coffee into her cup. 'Quite prickly, isn't she?'

'I won't have you upsetting my housekeeper, Tobias,' Lavinia warned him.

He gave her an expression of injured innocence. 'I don't have any notion what you are talking about. I assure you, I said nothing untoward to Mrs Chilton. Wouldn't think of doing such a thing. Indeed, I am enormously fond of her. You know that.'

'Humph.' Unsatisfied but not quite sure what to do about the matter, Lavinia retreated to her paper.

She did not know what to make of the odd relationship that had developed between Tobias and the housekeeper. She had gained the impression that the pair had come to an understanding in recent weeks. Indeed, Mrs Chilton had seemed to take a decidedly indulgent attitude toward Tobias, who, for his part, was inclined to alternately tease her and praise her cooking, especially any delicacy made with currants.

But things had changed since the return from Beaumont Castle. Mrs Chilton was no longer quite so good-natured and approving toward Tobias. It was as if she was in a state of expectation, anticipating that he would say or do something. But thus far he had disappointed her.

A pang of alarm shot through her. She lowered the newspaper again with a decided snap. 'Tobias, I trust you are not plotting to steal Mrs Chilton away from this household.'

He looked genuinely surprised by the accusation. 'Wouldn't think of it,' he mumbled around a mouthful of jam-smeared muffin. 'Whitby would never forgive me if I brought a housekeeper into his domain.'

Emeline chuckled. 'Do not concern yourself, Lavinia. I'm sure Mrs Chilton would never dream of allowing herself to be lured away from your employ.'

'Mmm.' Lavinia lowered her gaze to her newspaper again. She had more misgivings than ever now. Something was wrong.

Mrs Chilton might be in an unfortunate mood this morning, she thought, but Tobias was certainly in fine spirits for a man with an unsolved murder case on his hands. When he had reappeared on her doorstep an hour ago, he was bathed and freshly shaven. Renewed determination gleamed in his eyes. Evidently a good night's sleep was just what he had needed.

'Do you know, I am not the least surprised to hear that Mr Hood is Anthony's half-brother,' Emeline said, returning to the conversation in which they had all been engaged before the small skirmish between Tobias and Mrs Chilton. 'It certainly explains a few of the similarities I had noted in both gentlemen.'

'Yes, it does,' Tobias said.

'Will you be needing my assistance on this case today, sir?' she asked hopefully.

'I don't think so, thank you.' He raised a brow when Emeline looked ruefully disappointed. 'Why?'

'Nothing. It is just that Priscilla sent a note around this morning practically begging me to call upon her this afternoon. I interpret that to mean that her mama has made some dreadfully boring appointnent for her with a dressmaker and she does not want to suffer alone.'

Lavinia tut-tutted. 'More pink, I suppose?'

'No doubt. Priscilla says that the only really good reason she can come up with for getting married is that her mama would no longer be able to force her to wear pink.'

Lavinia looked at Tobias. 'What of your plans, sir?'

'I must find some evidence of Pierce's involvement in this affair. I'm going to search his lodgings this afternoon when he goes off to pay his calls on his clients.' Tobias's face tightened. 'Assuming he actually does do some legitimate hairdressing.'

'I'm sure he does,' Lavinia said. 'He is quite skilled in that profession, as I have told you. He must have any number of regular clients.'

The muffled thud of the front door knocker reverberated throughout the house. Mrs Chilton's solid footsteps sounded in the hall.

Emeline put down her napkin. 'I wonder who that can be at this early hour. Perhaps a new client, Lavinia.'

'More likely an old client,' Lavinia muttered. 'Come to demand to know how the investigation progresses.'

Tobias looked amused. 'Clients do like to be kept informed.'

The murmur of voices drifted down the hall. A moment later the door of the breakfast room opened.

'Mrs Gray to see you and Mr March, madam,' Mrs Chilton announced.

'I knew it,' Lavinia said. 'Well, at least we have some news at last to give her.'

'Indeed.' Tobias took one last swallow of his coffee and got to his feet. 'Now all we need is a bit of evidence to go with it.'

At two o'clock that afternoon, Lavinia stood with Tobias in the sitting room of Mr Pierce's lodgings. Fortunately, Mrs Chilton's predictions of rain had failed to materialize, so they were not obliged to deal with dripping garments and wet shoes when they made their clandestine entrance. The curtains were drawn across the windows, blocking the afternoon sun. Long shadows cloaked the small, neat space.

A short while earlier, the young street urchin Tobias had paid to watch Mr Pierce during the day arrived, breathless, at the small park where Tobias and Lavinia waited. He told them that he had just seen the hairdresser leave, a large satchel in his hand, and that a maid at one of the houses across the street had told him Pierce went out every afternoon at this time. He was not expected back until five o'clock.

'Why is she so aware of Pierce's comings and goings?' Tobias asked, digging into his pocket for some silver to pay the small spy.

'I think she's sweet on him, sir.' The boy pocketed his coins. 'Don't worry, I'll watch at the corner. If I see him coming back sooner than expected, I'll toss a couple of stones against the window.'

Lavinia was intensely aware of the fizzing excitement in her stomach and the rapid beat of her pulse. She wondered if professional inquiry agents ever became accustomed to the thrill that came with knowing one was close to finding the answers.

She sensed the subdued, controlled anticipation that emanated from Tobias and knew he was feeling similar emotions. Perhaps heady anticipation was an addictive elixir for those in their line.

'Shall I take the bedchamber?' she asked.

'Yes. Do not forget the wardrobe.' Tobias opened a cupboard. 'And be quick about it. I do not like doing this kind of thing during the day.'

'Yes, I am well-aware of your preferences.' She walked into the small room and started to open drawers in the bedside table. 'I suppose it would be too much to hope that we will come across a blond wig and some women's clothing.'

'Who knows? He has to hide that damned wig and the clothing somewhere. It is certainly about time that we had some luck in this case.'

'Very true.' She closed the last drawer and got down on her knees to peer beneath the bed. 'Aspasia seemed quite stunned by our conclusions this morning, did she not? I vow, if you had not been there to reassure her, she would have dismissed me on the spot.'

Aspasia had been incredulous when they told her that they believed Mr. Pierce to be the killer. In the end Lavinia knew that she had allowed herself to be persuaded only because Tobias had assured her he was convinced of the hairdresser's guilt.

'She has every right to be astonished,' Tobias said from the other room. 'I am still amazed myself. I have encountered a great many villains in my time, but this is the first hairdresser I have suspected of murder.'

Lavinia rose and went to the wardrobe. She opened the door and surveyed the array of shirts and crisply ironed cravats. 'It really is the perfect cover for a professional murderer who wishes to move in Society, is it not? A hairdresser is invited into the most exclusive houses, and no one thinks twice about his entering a lady's bedchamber or dressing room.'

'It occurs to me that a bloody hairdresser is able to get into your bedchamber far more easily than I can,' Tobias grumbled. 'I am obliged to plot and plan and wait about until Emeline decides to call upon Priscilla and Mrs Chilton has set off on a shopping expedition.'

'It is hardly the same thing, Tobias.'

'It is damned unfair, that's what it is, not to mention extremely inconvenient. I have been meaning to discuss the matter with you.'

Her fingers froze on the knob of the wardrobe door. She waited, forgetting to breathe.

There was a short pause from the other room.

'Well, well, well,' Tobias murmured.

She took a deep breath. Her fingers relaxed around the knob. She could not say just what it was she experienced in those few seconds. Relief? Disappointment?

What had she expected? she wondered. Tobias was highly unlikely to raise the subject of marriage in the middle of the search of a murderer's residence.

She went to the doorway and saw that he had gone down on his good knee and raised a section of a carpet. He studied the floorboards with great attention.

'Find something?' she called softly.

'Perhaps.'

He took one of the lock picks out of its leather sheath and slipped it into the long crack where two boards met.

'I think there may be an opening here in the floor.' He probed gently with the pick. 'Wouldn't surprise me. Elland hid his safe in the boards beneath the carpet in his study. That was where Aspasia found his journal and the rings. Perhaps this new Memento-Mori Man seeks to imitate him in every particular.'

'Tobias, how can he possibly know so many things about Elland?

The rings, the style of the murders. Even the same type of hiding place? It is uncanny. He must have been well acquainted with him.'

'That is certainly the theory I am working on.' He pried more forcefully. 'Jack has arranged for me to meet tonight with someone who might be able to tell me something about Elland's past.'

She heard a faint squeak, and then a section of flooring swung upward.

'Good heavens.' She rushed forward and crouched down.

Together they gazed into the small space that had been revealed.

'Empty.' Tobias did not bother to hide his disgust. He let the hinged square of flooring drop back into place, rose, and kicked the carpet back over the boards. He turned slowly on his heel, examining the room, a hawk searching for prey. 'It has to be here somewhere.'

'What has to be here?'

'His financial records. I told you, Elland had a head for business. He kept an extremely detailed journal of accounts.'

'Tobias,' she said quietly, 'bear in mind that, although they may have been acquainted, this is not Zachary Elland we are dealing with here. There is no reason to think that he conducts his business in precisely the same manner as the other Memento-Mori Man.'

'I disagree. The more I try to untangle this Gordian knot of a case, the more I am convinced that the most striking clue is the great similarity in the methods and practices used by both Elland and this new killer. It is as if they studied their craft together.'

'Or perhaps one taught the other?' she suggested uneasily.

'Precisely.'

Tobias glanced down into the small space between the desk and the wall. His irritated expression told her that there was nothing hidden there. He went to a small table in the corner and opened the little drawer.

'I knew it,' he whispered with exquisite satisfaction. He reached into the drawer and removed a leather-bound volume.

'What did you find?' She went to stand beside him and watched him open the journal. Names, dates, and times were written down in an orderly fashion. 'It looks like an appointment book, not a journal of accounts.'

'You're right.' He flipped through the pages. 'It is merely a record of his daily activities and clients. But perhaps those who commission the murders are in here as well.'

'Somehow I do not think that Pierce would be so careless. He is, after all, a professional.'

'You need not remind me.' Tobias removed a sheet of paper and a pen from his pocket and started to jot down the names of recent clients. 'Nevertheless, this is better than nothing. At the very least it will give us some notion of his schedule for the next few days. That may be helpful.'

Lavinia studied the names. One popped off the page. 'Lady Huxford. Look, there was an appointment with her on the third. That would be a fortnight before the house party at Beaumont Castle.'

'It establishes a connection between Lady Huxford and Pierce, but we were already aware of it, thanks to your observations at Vauxhall. I wonder if we—' Tobias turned the page and went very still. His eyes were riveted on one of the entries. 'Bloody hell.'

'What's wrong?'

He put a finger on a name. 'His client this afternoon.'

She looked down and felt her blood chill. 'Oh, my God. He went to Lady Wortham's house. He is doing Priscilla's hair. That was the boring appointment that Priscilla did not want to endure alone.'

'I think we had better assume the worst. This is no coincidence. Pierce evidently knows of Priscilla's association with Emeline and therefore of Emeline's connection to you. He no doubt arranged this appointment with the goal of interrogating your niece's best friend in hopes of discovering what progress we have made on this case.'

Twenty-Six

'My dear Miss Priscilla, we cannot escape the reality of nature.' Mr Pierce drew his comb through the long, golden length of Priscilla's hair and met his client's eyes in the mirror. 'You are most certainly blond.'

Priscilla's cheeks burned. 'I am aware that it is not the most fashionable color.'

Emeline sat tensely in a chair a short distance away from the dressing table, feeling as though she were acting out a part in some strange, nightmarish play. To her enormous relief and never-ending admiration, Priscilla had stepped into the leading role without any sign of nerves whatsoever.

They'd had less than ten minutes to prepare.

Emeline was stunned when she had arrived at the Wortham residence and was told that Lady Wortham had scheduled a hairdresser for the afternoon. She had hoped that it was some amazing coincidence, but her work as an assistant to the firm of Lake & March had taught her not to trust such events. She had quickly briefed Priscilla, who had in turn made it clear that her mother was to remain innocent and oblivious. She feared her parent would fly into a panic if she discovered she had hired a murderer to dress her daughter's hair.

When Mr Pierce arrived at the door with his leather satchel filled with combs, curling irons, papers, scissors, and false hairpieces, Priscilla had risen to the occasion with great aplomb.

She had sat down in front of her dressing-table mirror, her shoulders draped in a pristine white cloth, and abandoned herself to the ministrations of the murderous hairdresser as though it was the most normal thing in the world.

She was, in fact, behaving so naturally and with so much enthusiasm that Emeline had begun to wonder if she was actually enjoying herself. Perhaps the fact that Mr Pierce was quite handsome – even dashing, with that black ribbon at his throat and those carelessly tousled curls – made things easier for her.

Emeline had to admit that it was difficult to imagine Pierce as a murderer-for-hire.

Lady Wortham was ensconced in a chair on the other side of the dressing table, blithely unaware that the man who was wielding a large pair of scissors in the vicinity of her daughter's throat had likely killed three people in the past few months.

'Do you think we should consider dyeing Priscilla's hair a darker shade, Mr Pierce?' Lady Wortham asked anxiously.

'Dye this hair? Perish the thought.' Pierce seized a length of Priscilla's mane and held it aloft with a flourish worthy of a magician. 'This is pure spun gold. It would be a crime against nature to alter it with elderberry or Grecian waters.' He rapped the comb against the edge of the dressing table and glared at Priscilla in the mirror. 'And I absolutely forbid you to even contemplate the use of henna. Is that quite clear?'

'Yes, Mr Pierce,' she murmured dutifully.

Lady Wortham fanned herself agitatedly. 'But if you say her hair must not be dyed, what do you suggest? A wig, perhaps?'

'Out of the question for one of her tender years. Also, it would be a shame to set false hair against such clear, fresh skin and classical profile.' Mr Pierce swept Lady Wortham a low bow. 'Both of which I can see that she inherited from you, madam.'

Lady Wortham stared at him, open-mouthed, for a few seconds. Emeline was astonished to see a dark blush rise in her cheeks.

'Why, thank you, Mr Pierce.' She fanned herself with even more energy. 'I don't mind saying that in my youth I never lacked for partners in the ballrooms. Priscilla does take after me.' She cleared her throat. 'Except for her hair, of course. That is a legacy from her papa, I'm sorry to say.'

'Indeed. Well, as I was saying, I try not to put any of my young ladies into wigs unless there is no alternative.' Mr Pierce paused for emphasis. 'And in this case there is an alternative. A glorious one at that.'

There was a breathless silence. Emeline realized that, in spite of the almost intolerable tension she and Priscilla were under, they were both as curious to hear what Pierce had to offer as Lady Wortham was.

'Yes, Mr Pierce?' Lady Wortham urged. 'What is the alternative?'

Pierce half-closed his eyes, as though sighting down the barrel of a pistol. 'As we cannot make it possible for your daughter to follow the fashion, madam, we have no choice but to transform her into a paragon of style who *sets* the fashion.'

'Oh, my.' Lady Wortham looked as though she might faint. 'Oh, my gracious. A paragon of style.'

'Leave it to me, madam. I studied my art in Paris. I know what I am about.' Mr Pierce reached into his satchel and took out some hairpins and curling papers. 'But before I proceed, I must have your word that my creation will never again be framed in pink.'

Lady Wortham stiffened, mouth agape, eyes wide. She was speechless.

Pierce picked up his scissors and fixed her with a stern gaze. 'Miss Priscilla does have some other colors in her wardrobe, I presume? Surely she does not always go about in this ridiculous color?'

Priscilla made a tiny choking sound and seized the cup of tea that sat on the dressing table. Emeline met her eyes in the mirror. Neither of them dared to speak.

Lady Wortham cleared her throat. 'I thought pink very suitable for her age and looks.'

Pierce sighed and went to work with the scissors. 'Allow me to tell you, madam, that pink, when added to pale gold hair, creates the impression of a cream cake topped with a great deal of overly sweet icing. A gentleman looks at such a cake and thinks, Well, now, that is a tasty-looking little treat. If it is available, I shall help myself to a bite or two and discard the rest.'

Lady Wortham went red with shock and outrage. 'A pink-and-white cream cake? My daughter? How dare you, sir.'

'There is no sense of substance or style to an iced cream cake, you see. It leaves no lasting impression on the tongue.' Pierce continued to work, paying no attention to Lady Wortham's scandalized expression. 'But when one puts a lady with Miss Priscilla's hair and excellent profile into a darker, jewel-toned gown – an emerald green, perhaps, or a deep sapphire blue – one no longer sees a cream cake.'

'What does one see?' Lady Wortham demanded warily.

'A goddess.'

Lady Wortham blinked. 'A goddess? My Priscilla?'

Pierce looked at Priscilla in the mirror. 'Do you have any such gowns in your wardrobe, madam? If not, you must make an appointment with your dressmaker immediately.'

'Well,' Priscilla murmured, 'there is the new walking gown that Aunt Beatrice ordered for me for my birthday.'

'I really don't think that it is at all suited to her,' Lady Wortham said, uncertain now. 'Beatrice ordered it without consulting with me.'

'Let me see it,' Pierce commanded.

'I'll fetch it.' Emeline leaped out of her chair. 'I think that it is quite striking.'

She went to the wardrobe and took out the new gown.

They all looked at the turquoise walking dress, awaiting Pierce's verdict.

'Perfect.' Pierce bowed deeply toward Priscilla. 'Absolutely perfect.' He turned to Lady Wortham. 'Rest assured, madam. Gentlemen will fall to their knees to worship at her altar.'

A short time later, Lady Wortham gazed, transfixed, at Priscilla. 'Incredible. She is spectacular. I would never have believed that such a simple style could look so elegant.'

Pierce smoothed Priscilla's sleekly arranged hair with professional pride. 'Simplicity is at the heart of all true elegance, madam.'

Emeline was almost as astonished as Lady Wortham. Pierce had defied the current fashion for intricately braided coils and a profusion of curls at the forehead and temples. Instead, he had brushed Priscilla's hair straight back from her face and, with the aid of only a few pins, had created a graceful twist high on the back of her head. The design emphasized the long, delicate line of her neck and her fine profile. Only a few wispy ringlets danced in front of her ears.

Priscilla had always been lovely, Emeline thought, but now her friend appeared more self-confident and assured. There was a touch of feminine mystery about her that had not been there before.

'Priscilla, you are magnificent,' Emeline whispered.

Priscilla blushed furiously, but she could not seem to take her eyes off the image of herself in the mirror. 'Do you really like it?'

'Oh, yes. I cannot wait to see you in your new gown.'

'I am delighted that you are all pleased.' Mr Pierce smiled at Emeline. 'As it happens, I am free for another hour or so. Would you care to have your hair dressed, Miss Emeline? I believe I can improve upon your present arrangement. Not that your style is unattractive – quite the opposite. But it is a bit too much in the current mode, if you know what I mean. You require a more original look.'

'Oh, I could not possibly presume on your time and Lady Wortham's hospitality,' Emeline said hastily, and not without a twinge of regret. Pierce might be a murderer, but there was no denying that he was an artist when it came to hair. It would have been so much fun to find out just how he would have transformed her.

'Of course you must let him dress your hair, Emeline.' Priscilla got up from the dressing table. 'Mama will not mind in the least.'

'Not at all,' Lady Wortham said magnanimously. 'Indeed, it is quite exciting to watch Mr Pierce at work. One feels oneself to be in the vicinity of a great talent.'

Reluctantly, Emeline sat down at the dressing table. 'Thank you.'

Pierce shook out the white cloth and arranged it around her shoulders. He picked up his comb and met her eyes in the mirror.

'Yes, I know just what to do here,' he said. 'It is such a pleasure to work on young ladies who are concerned with the latest fashions. Most of my clients are older women who insist upon the more elaborate coiffeurs of the past, the sort that were designed for those towering powdered wigs they wore in their youth.'

'I must admit, I remember those wigs all too well,' Lady Wortham said. 'They looked quite elegant on the dance floor, but they were ever so hot and heavy.'

Mr Pierce removed the pins that anchored Emeline's hair with a few quick motions. 'As I was saying, I generally cater to an older clientele. But it is so much more entertaining to work on the heads of young ladies. Tell me, Miss Emeline, did your aunt happen to mention that I made her acquaintance at Beaumont Castle?'

Emeline went cold inside. Out of the corner of her eye, she saw Priscilla tense. Lady Wortham, still blithely oblivious, poured some tea.

Emeline steadied herself. 'She mentioned that she had met a hairdresser who told her that red hair was not a fashionable shade. But she did not recall his name.'

Pierce was clearly offended. 'I did give her my card.'

'She must have lost it,' Emeline said smoothly.

'I see. Understandable, I suppose. I know that she and her friend

Mr March were rather preoccupied at the time. They were convinced that Lord Fullerton's death was not an accident. I believe they were attempting to prove it.'

'Not an accident?' Lady Wortham looked surprised. 'I had not heard any mention of foul play in connection with Fullerton's death.'

'That is because Mr March and my aunt were not able to find any evidence of murder,' Emeline explained. 'Furthermore, Lord Beaumont made it clear that he did not want an investigation taking place under his roof.'

'So, all in all, their inquiries came to naught?' Priscilla asked in a casual, innocent tone.

'I'm afraid so,' Emeline murmured. 'It is difficult to investigate a case of murder if no one believes that one has occurred.'

'Fascinating.' Pierce paused in the act of combing out her hair and looked at her with great interest. 'Have they made any progress here in Town?'

'None. Mr March is quite frustrated, I'm afraid. My aunt feels that they are wasting their time. She is attempting to persuade him to abandon his inquiries.'

She was rather proud of that last bit, she thought.

'I see.' Pierce's expression did not change. 'Do you think that she will be successful?'

'Oh, yes,' Emeline said. She lowered her tone to a confidential level and prepared to lie outright. 'Fullerton's family does not want any inquiries made, nor does anyone else. My aunt is very concerned with the collection of fees, and, as there is no client in this case, she feels that she and Mr March must turn their attentions to other matters.'

'No offense, my dear,' Lady Wortham said in tones that dripped with disapproval, 'but I must tell you that Mrs Lake's little hobby strikes me as quite odd.'

Emeline wondered what Lavinia would say if she were to tell her that Lady Wortham considered her career a mere hobby.

'I imagine that an intelligent lady such as Mrs Lake no doubt finds such work an interesting challenge,' Pierce murmured.

Emeline could feel the fine hairs stirring on the nape of her neck. She prayed that Pierce could not see them.

Twenty-Seven

Emeline and Priscilla walked together to the entrance of the park where they had arranged to meet Anthony and Dominic. Their parasols were raised against the late sun. After a short discussion they had elected to forgo their bonnets so as not to conceal the full glory of their new hair arrangements.

'Dear heaven, I can still feel my pulse,' Emeline said. 'I wonder if my heart will ever slow to a normal rate.'

'I am shaky myself.' Priscilla made a face. 'Every time I looked in the mirror, the only thing I could see were those scissors in his hand. I kept thinking about all the people he has likely killed.'

'I, for one, will never look at another hairdresser in quite the same way again.'

'Neither will I. It is really most unfortunate that Mr Pierce is a murderer, though,' Priscilla said wryly. 'I will be forever in his debt. In the course of one afternoon, he has changed my entire life by convincing Mama that I do not appear at my best in pink.'

Emeline surveyed the new turquoise walking dress. 'He was quite right. You do look excellent in stronger colors.'

'Thank you.' Priscilla spun her parasol. 'It turned into a rather exciting day, after all, did it not? I believe we dealt with Mr Pierce quite cleverly. Do you think that we were born for the stage?'

'Never suggest such a scandalous career to your mama. She would faint dead away. But, yes, I do think we rose to meet the crisis rather nicely. You were especially brilliant.'

'You did quite well yourself. Pierce may not believe that Mr March and Mrs Lake will entirely abandon their inquiries because of a lack of a client, but I am certain that he left with the impression that they have made very little progress in their investigations.'

A tiny shudder went through Emeline. 'I trust that is the case. Wait until I tell them what happened at Lady Wortham's today. They will not believe that we found ourselves confronted with their suspect.'

'He obviously set up the appointment with Mama in hopes of learning something about the situation from me. He must have been delighted when he arrived and found you at my house.' She brightened. 'Here come Anthony and Dominic. I must tell you, I am almost as astonished by your news that they are half-brothers as I was when I saw Mr Pierce standing in the front hall.'

'I suppose the connection explains some of the friction between them.' She watched Anthony and Dominic come toward them across the park. 'I hope they have been able to put aside their differences now that the truth is out in the open.'

Priscilla tightened her grip on her parasol. 'Emeline,' she said with a certain studied casualness, 'do you think Mr Hood will like my new gown and headdress?'

'Priscilla, you look spectacular. Mr Hood will no doubt fall down and worship at your altar, just as Pierce predicted.'

Priscilla made a little face. 'I would rather he showed me how to use his microscope.'

Anthony and Dominic were almost upon them. Emeline realized that they were both moving with long, purposeful strides, not the casual saunter that was the hallmark of fashionable gentlemen. She was even more startled by their attire. They were certainly not dressed for an afternoon promenade in the park. Their boots lacked the gloss of a recent polish, and their comfortably cut coats reminded her of the sort of fashions favored by Mr March. Even their cravats appeared to have been donned in haste. Neither man had bothered to tie an intricate or stylish knot.

'Something is amiss,' Emeline announced.

Anthony and Dominic came to a halt in front of them.

'What the devil are you two doing here?' Anthony demanded without so much as a polite inclination of his head. His hat was tilted low over his eyes, giving him a sinister air. 'Are you both mad?'

'I beg your pardon?' Emeline was incensed at the uncivil greeting. 'If you will recall, the four of us made arrangements to meet here today.'

'That was before we learned that you two spent the afternoon with a murderer,' Dominic growled. His hat was also slanted across his brow at a menacing angle.

'You know of my appointment with Mr Pierce?' Priscilla asked.

'Tobias and Mrs Lake discovered a note of it when they searched his lodgings.' Anthony glanced from Priscilla to Emeline and back again. 'Are you both all right?'

'Yes, of course we're all right,' Emeline said evenly. 'What is more to the point, we believe we quieted any suspicions Mr Pierce might have had by letting him know that the investigation was not going well.'

Priscilla frowned. 'Why are you both dressed so oddly?'

'Mr March did not allow us much time to prepare for a social call,' Dominic said rather dryly. 'He was most insistent that we find you two immediately and see you safely back to Number Seven Claremont Lane. Mrs Lake wishes to speak with you both immediately. Then we are to escort you directly home, Miss Priscilla.'

'Tobias does not want either of you out and about on your own now that Pierce has taken an interest in you,' Anthony added.

'For pity's sake,' Emeline grumbled. 'We are both quite safe, I assure you. Pierce will have no more use for us now that he's got the information he wanted.'

'Yes, well, that is precisely the point, isn't it?' Anthony shot back.

There was a rather sharp edge on his words, Emeline thought. But before she could muster a crisp retort, he took her arm very firmly and hauled her toward the gate.

'I hardly think that we are in any danger,' Priscilla said quickly.

'The man is a murderer.' Dominic took her elbow. 'In any event, Tony and I do not have time to waste promenading through the park today. We have work to do.'

'What sort of work?' Emeline demanded, skipping a little to keep up with Anthony's long strides.

'We are to keep Pierce under observation from sunset to sunrise,' Anthony said. 'We have some preparations to make, so we must get you two home.'

She had had enough of this, Emeline thought. 'Kindly do not treat us as though we are a pair of silly little girls who cannot be trusted out on our own. I would remind you that Priscilla and I dealt with a murderer today. We are not incompetent.'

'Quite right,' Priscilla said just as forcefully.

Anthony turned his head to scowl at Emeline. The rays of the late-afternoon sun angled beneath the canted brim of his hat, giving her an unshadowed view of his features for the first time.

'Your *eye*.' She came to an abrupt halt, forcing him to stop too. 'And your lip. You've been hurt. What on earth happened to you, Tony?'

Priscilla stopped just as suddenly and swung around to peer very closely at Dominic's slightly averted features. 'There is a dark bruise on your jaw, sir. Dear heaven, did the murderer attack you last night? How did it happen? Why weren't we told?'

'Damnation.' Dominic grimaced, winced, and then touched his jaw. 'I assure you, it was not Pierce who was responsible for this.'

'Certainly not.' Anthony reddened. 'Devil take it, the man's a *hairdresser*.'

'And also a professional murderer, if Mr March and Aunt Lavinia are correct in their conclusions,' Emeline pointed out. 'But if it was not Mr Pierce who did this to you two, who was it?'

Anthony exchanged an unreadable glance with Dominic. Then he shrugged.

'It was quite dark in the street outside Pierce's lodgings last night,' he said. 'I accidentally collided with the edge of a stone doorway.'

'I see,' Emeline said. 'Doorways can be extremely hazardous.'

Priscilla gave Dominic a searching look. 'And you, sir? Did you suffer a similar misfortune?'

'Stumbled on the step,' Dominic muttered. 'Struck the railing.'

Twenty-Eight

Shortly before midnight that evening, Anthony opened the sack of pies he had purchased just before nightfall and took out one of the two remaining meat pies. He offered the sack to Dominic, who lounged against the opposite wall of the narrow alley.

Dominic helped himself to the last pie.

'Tomorrow night I will purchase a larger number,' Anthony promised around a mouthful of leaden pastry.

'It is our own fault that we ran out so quickly,' Dominic reminded him. 'In hindsight, we probably should not have given half of our supply to that pair of urchins who chose to spend the night in the doorway of the button-and-ribbon shop.'

Anthony thought about the two youngsters they had met earlier that evening. The boys had been no more than eight or nine years of age, cheerfully brash and impudent and imbued with a streetwise knowledge that would have better suited men of twenty. They had also looked very hungry. Neither he nor Dominic had been able to resist giving them some of their pies. The pair had been delighted and had sped off with their treasures to settle into their doorway at the far end of the street.

'On second thought, maybe I can persuade Whitby to make us a batch,' Anthony said. 'I'll also ask him for some more of that cold salmon and chicken he provided for us this afternoon.'

'An excellent notion. Tell him to double the amount this time in case those two youngsters are in that doorway again tomorrow night.' Dominic munched his pie. 'But it may not be necessary. From the sound of it, this business probably won't continue much longer. March seems very sure that Pierce will make a move soon. He says the hairdresser is not only arrogant, he is consumed with a need to prove that he is as good as the last Memento-Mori Man.'

Time passed. Out in the street, the slant of moonlight shifted slowly. Aside from the odd carriage or cart, nothing moved. The light in Pierce's window had gone out half an hour ago. He appeared to have retired to his bed.

'Did it strike you that there was something different about Emeline and Priscilla this afternoon?' Anthony stretched his arms high overhead to relieve the stiffness.

'Different?' Dominic pondered the question for a moment. 'I hadn't thought about it. Why do you ask?'

'I don't know. Just seemed that they were both in particularly fine looks today.'

'They are always in fine looks.'

'Very true.'

There was another lengthy silence.

'I think Priscilla is attracted to you,' Anthony offered after a while.

'She is attracted to the contents of my laboratory, not to me.' Dominic sounded glum.

'Don't be so certain of that. The two of you do have a great deal in common.'

'Huh.'

'You find her pretty. It was never Emeline who interested you, admit it. The only reason you flirted with her was to get at me.'

Dominic shrugged. The movement of his shoulders was barely visible in the shadows. 'You're in love with Miss Emeline, are you not?'

'Yes. Her aunt wants us to wait to announce our engagement, but Emeline and I have other plans. First I have to convince Tobias to marry Mrs Lake and move into Number Seven Claremont Lane.'

'So that you and Miss Emeline can take over his house?' Dominic sounded intrigued. 'A very clever notion. Do you think he will agree?'

'I'm having some difficulty convincing him of the wisdom of my plan, but I have every hope of success.' Something flickered at the mouth of the alley across the street. 'Did you see that?'

'What?'

'I think there's someone standing in the entrance to the alley that leads to the rear of Pierce's lodgings.'

The figure moved, slipping cautiously out of the deep pool of darkness into the moonlight.

Dominic straightened swiftly. 'Yes, I see him. Make that her. It's a woman in a cloak.'

'I'll wager it's Pierce in his female attire,' Anthony whispered.

'You're right.' Dominic kept his voice equally low and soft. 'Don't move. We must not let him see us.'

The cloaked figure drifted swiftly down the street. Pierce did not carry a lantern, apparently content to rely on the bright moon. There was an eerie lack of sound about his movements.

'Like a ghost in the night,' Dominic whispered.

The old bawd took another long swallow of gin and wiped her mouth with the back of her hand. She squinted at Tobias across the planked table and cackled wetly.

'They called me Mother Maud in those days,' she said. 'Made a nice living selling the babes and young ones, I did. Ye'd be surprised how much of a market there is for a healthy little boy or girl. All types of folk, high and low, came to buy my wares.'

The woman gave him a cold chill in his vitals, but Tobias did not allow his revulsion to show in his expression. The tavern, tucked away in the bowels of one of the worst neighborhoods in the city, was a dark, smoky hell. It made the Gryphon look like an exclusive gentleman's club.

Mother Maud stopped talking and waited expectantly.

He put a few more coins on the table. Next to them he placed the memento-mori ring that he had found in Fullerton's bedchamber at Beaumont Castle. The little gold coffin glinted evilly in the candle-light.

'Smiling Jack told me there's a rumor that several years ago you sold two small boys to a man who wore a ring similar to this.' He opened the coffin.

Mother Maud stared at the tiny death's-head for a long time. Then she switched her attention to the little pile of coins. Her uneasiness was plain to read in her face.

He added another coin to the heap.

'Aye.' Mother Maud drank some more gin, as though to steady her nerve. 'I did some business with a man who wore a death's-head ring.'

'Tell me about the business.'

'He was different from my usual clients,' Maud said at last.

'In what way?'

'Most of 'em what purchased the children set 'em to work. They trained the boys to pick pockets or steal or beg or climb the chimneys. The girls went into the brothels or were put out on the streets to earn their keep.' She raised one bony shoulder and let it drop. 'There were some who purchased the little ones for reasons that I did not want to know.'

If some of the children had been used in ways that gave even Mother Maud a few qualms, Tobias thought, he'd rather not know about them either. But he had to get the truth tonight.

'The man who wore the ring,' he said. 'Why do you think that he wanted to obtain two young boys?'

Maud took another swig of gin and set down the bottle. Her rheumy eyes glinted malevolently. 'He said he was a man of business but he had no sons to take over the firm. He told me that he wanted to take on some apprentices. Teach 'em his trade.' She squinted. 'But if all that was true, he could have got what he wanted from a proper orphanage, eh?'

'Instead, he came to you.'

'Aye, that he did. He paid Mother Maud handsomely, he did. And I gave him value for his money, I did. Two healthy lads in prime condition. Both smart as whips. Brothers, they were. One was about eight years of age. The other was four or five, I think.'

'What happened to their parents?'

'The mother died in a brothel. Both boys were on the street when I found 'em. The older one was looking after the younger. Picking pockets. Stealing what they could from the drunken gentlemen who take their pleasures in our part of the city.'

'What of the father?'

'Who knows?'

Tobias glanced at the ring. 'What do you think became of the two boys you sold to this man?'

'Well, now, I never asked and that's a fact.' Maud snorted. 'That's why my clients came to me in the first place, y'see. On account of they knew I wouldn't ask any awkward questions.'

'Did you ever hear any gossip concerning the nature of the trade this man planned to teach the two boys?'

'Aye.' Maud brooded on the ring. 'There was talk now and again over the years about the man who wore a gold death's-head. Some said that if ye paid him enough, he'd get rid of anyone ye wanted, even a rich man or a fine lady. But only if he agreed that they deserved it.'

'Do they say what became of this man who was in the business of dealing death?'

Maud raised her gin bottle. 'Heard he'd retired. Left the business to his apprentices.'

Anthony stood with Dominic in the night-shrouded park across the street from Number 20 Treadhall Square. The town house they were watching was an elegantly designed three-story affair, one of several in a row. Each had a front area enclosed with a waist-high iron fence and a gate.

They had followed Pierce, according to Tobias's instructions, and made no move to stop him, keeping a considerable distance behind him. The activity of the busy streets had covered their footsteps.

But a few seconds ago they had arrived in the square just in time to see their quarry vault lightly over the railing that guarded the front area of one of the town houses. Pierce disappeared down the flight of steps that led to the kitchen entrance located below the street level.

'If you ask me, there's only one reason why he went down there dressed in that cloak,' Dominic said. 'And it wasn't because he's been summoned at one o'clock in the morning to dress a lady's hair.'

'I know.' The reality of what was happening before their eyes sent a chill through Anthony.

'Hell's teeth, what are we supposed to do now?' Dominic whispered. 'The only thing we can do is pound on the front door and try to raise the household.'

'They'll likely think we've gone mad, ranting and raving about a murderer inside their home.'

'Have you got a better plan?'

'No.'

'We'd best make haste, in that case.' Anthony started forward. 'I doubt that it will take Pierce long to complete his business. The man is a *professional*, if you will recall.'

Together they raced across the street and went up the steps of the silent town house. Anthony seized the heavy brass door knocker and banged it loudly six or seven times.

'That should rouse a maid or a footman,' Dominic muttered.

But to Anthony's amazement, no one came to the door to demand an explanation for the late-night disturbance.

'Try again,' Dominic said. 'Harder, for God's sake.'

Anthony pounded the knocker a few more times. Still no

response. He took a step back and looked up at the darkened windows of the upper floors. 'Perhaps whoever lives here gave his servants the night off.'

'This is a large house. I cannot believe that every single member of the staff would be given the same night off. There must be someone inside.'

'We've got to do something quickly,' Anthony said. 'Maybe we should smash a window'

'And get taken up on charges of housebreaking? I don't think that is such a terrific plan. Wait, I've got an idea.'

Dominic let his small pack slide off his shoulder and lowered it to the ground. Untying the cord that secured the opening, he reached inside and drew out what appeared to be two sticks.

'What have you got there?' Anthony asked.

'A couple of tubes containing my new explosive formula.'

'*Explosive formula*?' Anthony hastily stepped back a couple of paces. 'Hold on, here. What the devil are you doing?'

'I admit the mixture is still in need of refinement, but in small amounts like this it creates a very handsome display of fireworks. I brought the tubes with me tonight because it occurred to me that they might come in handy if we needed a distraction or a weapon of some sort in the event the hairdresser noticed us and tried something violent.'

'That was very farsighted of you.' Anthony watched Dominic strike a light. 'Damnation, man, have a care with those things.'

'I'm using both of them because we need a disturbance that will arouse the entire street as well as anyone inside this house.' Dominic lit two strings attached to the sticks. 'This should do the trick.'

He hurled the sputtering tubes far out onto the pavement. There was a short, tense moment during which the sticks sputtered and sparked.

Then, with a crack and an ear-shattering roar, the explosive-filled casings erupted.

Lightning danced in the street.

Bright strips of fire sparkled and flashed. The fireworks sounded like a dozen pistols fired at once, over and over again. The noise boomed off the walls of the town houses and echoed on the stones of the pavement. 'Very impressive,' Anthony shouted above the din.

'I'm trying to develop more variety in the colors of the display,' Dominic yelled back. 'At the moment I'm limited to red, white, and greens.'

A window on the upper floor of a neighboring town house opened with a bang. A man in a nightcap leaned out.

'Fire,' he screamed. 'There's fire in the street. Summon the watch.'

Several more windows slammed open. Other heads appeared. The shout of *fire* went up across the square. A woman shrieked. Doors were flung wide. One of them was the door of Number 20.

'What's this?' A woman with a head covered in sparse gray curls and a cap stood in the entrance, clutching a faded dressing gown around her thin body. She peered blearily at Dominic and Anthony.

'What's going on here?' she demanded.

'There's a murderer inside the house,' Anthony shouted.

'What's that you say?' She cupped her hand to her ear. 'Speak up, young man.'

'A *murderer.*' Anthony pushed past her into the front hall. 'He's come to kill someone.'

'Stand aside,' Dominic ordered, following Anthony into the hall. 'We must stop him.'

'Now, see here, what d'ye think yer doing?' Alarmed, the woman fell back. '*Help! Help!* There's housebreakers here.'

Anthony decided to change tactics. 'The *fire,*' he shouted directly into her ear. 'We've got to get everyone out of the house.'

Her eyes widened in horror. 'Fire, you say?'

'Is there anyone else here?' Dominic yelled.

'The master. Upstairs in his bed.' The woman glanced uncertainly up at the ceiling. 'He can't walk. He'll be trapped up there.'

'We'll bring him down,' Anthony promised.

He ran for the stairs, Dominic hard on his heels. They took the steps two at a time and emerged onto a darkened landing.

Anthony saw the flare of candlelight emanating from the door of a bedchamber at the end of a long hall. A cloaked figure appeared in the entrance of the room, silhouetted by the glare behind him.

'There he is,' he yelled at Dominic.

They charged forward. The intruder left the doorway and fled in the opposite direction. When he reached the end of the hall, he whirled to face them, the wings of his cloak flaring wide.

'Watch out,' Dominic said. 'He might have a pistol.'

They slowed warily. But the intruder did not pull out a weapon. Instead, he yanked open another door and disappeared down the back stairs.

'Bloody hell.' Anthony launched himself forward again. 'He's getting away.'

'Tony, the bedchamber,' Dominic shouted. 'He set it ablaze.'

Anthony became aware of the fact that the glow of light from the doorway of the bedchamber was too intense for a candle flame. He slammed to a halt, spinning around to stare into the room. Dominic was already inside, using a blanket to beat at the flames that leaped at the end of a massive four-poster bed.

A thin man in a nightcap cowered against the pillows, arms flailing helplessly. 'Save me, save me! She tried to smother me. Tried to murder me in my own bed.'

Anthony seized a heavy quilt. Dominic grabbed the other end. They flung it over the bedding in an attempt to smother the flames.

The killer ran through the streets, barely able to think clearly enough to follow the map in his mind. When he could not run any farther, he ducked into an alley to catch his breath. He yanked off the blond wig and the cloak and dropped both on the paving stones.

Chest heaving, he stood for a moment, trying to collect his senses and his nerve. Bloody hell, but that had been close. Much too close this time. His heart was pounding, and he knew it was not just because of the mad dash to safety. He could no longer deny the fear. It surged through him, clouding his brain and making him want to vomit. *Was this how it was for you, Zachary? Did you ever know this frantic, gut-twisting sensation?*

He still could not fathom the fact that he had been so nearly caught in the act. Where had those two come from to loose that shower of fire in the street and hound him through the house, chasing him away before he could complete his business?

But he knew the answer. Miss Emeline and Miss Priscilla had lied through their pretty teeth. March and his companion had not only made significant progress in their investigations, they had identified him as a suspect.

March had set that pair to watch him tonight. They had followed him, hoping to catch him in the act.

The game was finished. March had won.

He glanced back at the little heap of clothing and the blond wig.

That was all the evidence that existed to connect him to this night's botched business. He would leave them here. Even if someone found the items, they could not be linked to him.

Nevertheless, he dared not take any more chances. March had friends in high places.

He moved cautiously out of the alley. When he was sure that there was no one about, he broke into a run again. He had a good head start. It would take those two some time to deal with the fire and make their report to March. He needed only a few minutes, he reminded himself. He had been well-trained in his craft. He was prepared for any contingency, even failure.

He would vanish for a while, he promised himself. Perhaps he would go to Paris for a year or two. Or mayhap Italy. When he returned the next time, he would come back as a gentleman. No one would recognize him, let alone connect him to the murders he had committed this summer.

The thought steadied his nerves as he fled through the moonlit night.

A short time later Anthony stood beside Dominic and peered glumly into the darkness of the back stairs. He slammed the palm of his hand against the wall.

'Damnation. We almost had him.'

'He set that fire to distract us when he realized we were about to awaken the household with the fireworks.' Dominic shoved his fingers through his hair. 'He gave himself plenty of time to get away.'

'Well, one thing is for certain. He knows now that he's been found out. He'll no doubt have disappeared into the stews or bolted for some safe place where he thinks he can hide.'

'I don't suppose there's any point going back to his lodgings,' Anthony muttered. 'He won't be fool enough to hang around now.'

'I do not look forward to informing March that we flushed out our quarry and then lost him.'

'Neither do I.' Anthony closed his fist around the ring he had discovered on the bedside table. 'But it is not as though we had a great deal of choice in the matter. That damned hairdresser was willing to burn down this entire house and everyone inside in order to make good his escape.'

'Come.' Dominic turned away from the staircase. 'We've got to find March. I hope he has returned from his latest visit to the stews.'

Anthony swung around and followed him swiftly down the hall.

*

The killer entered his lodgings through the back door, the same way he had left a short while ago. He stood there in the deep shadows, breathing so hard that the air rasped in his lungs. The rage and fear were still pouring through him. He wanted to smash something.

'Damn him, damn him, damn him,' he chanted into the darkness.

He could not dawdle, he reminded himself. He had to move swiftly. There would be time enough for vengeance against March later. Time enough to prove that the man could be beaten.

He went into the bedchamber and shifted aside the picture on the wall. Placing the flat of his hand on a section of the wood, he pressed gently. The panel slid open on a soundless whisper of well-oiled hinges.

He opened the safe and took out the pistol, the letter, the remaining memento-mori rings, and the jewelry and money that his clients had given him in exchange for his services.

His next stop was the wardrobe. He would take only one change of clothing. He hated to leave the rest of his fine garments behind, but he could not afford to be encumbered with luggage. The tenets of his training were strict on that point. When flight was necessary, one fled with as little as possible.

He opened the door of the wardrobe and found himself looking into the face of his killer.

Before he could even react to the shock, the murderer put the pistol to his temple and pulled the trigger.

Twenty-Nine

Tobias held the lantern up so that the glare illuminated the back door of the hairdresser's lodgings. Anthony and Dominic stood slightly behind him, watching tensely as he tried the knob.

'Unlocked.' Tobias handed the lantern to Dominic and took out his pistol. 'I doubt if he is still here, but I do not want either of you to take chances. Stay behind me.'

'He will be miles away by now,' Anthony grumbled. 'We almost had him, Tobias.'

'If he had not had the wit to set that fire, we would have caught him,' Dominic agreed.

'You did the right thing,' Tobias said. 'You had no choice but to deal with the blaze. Do not blame yourselves for Pierce's escape. If you had not interfered, Sir Rupert would be dead by now. The old cook as well, I suspect.'

He opened the door so suddenly that it banged against the wall. The lantern light slanted across the empty kitchen.

He moved warily through the small room. Anthony and Dominic followed.

'Give me the lantern,' Tobias said quietly.

Anthony handed it to him. He set it on the floor and used the toe of his boot to push it out into the narrow hall. No shadows flickered on the wall. There was no movement in the small parlor.

Tobias leaned around the corner. From here he had a clear view of the sitting room. Satisfied that it was empty, he stepped out into the hall, picked up the lantern, and, hugging the wall, went swiftly toward the door of the darkened bedchamber.

The scent of fresh death hit him before he saw the body on the floor.

'The hairdresser is still here,' he said flatly.

Dominic and Anthony came to stand beside him. They stared at the horrific scene.

'His head.' Dominic sounded odd. 'His head. There's so much blood and . . . and other stuff.'

'God have mercy,' Anthony whispered.

It occurred to Tobias that this was the first time either of the younger men had encountered violent death.

'Stay here, both of you,' he ordered.

He went cautiously into the room so as to avoid damaging any useful evidence. But there were no bloody footprints, no bits of fabric torn in a scuffle. No signs at all that anyone other than Pierce had been here tonight.

The hairdresser lay sprawled facedown in a dark pool of congealing liquid, lifeless fingers loosely wrapped around the handle of the pistol.

'He must have known that it was over.' Anthony swallowed audibly. 'He realized that we were hard on his heels and that it was only a matter of time before we saw him hang. So he elected to cheat the gallows.'

'He took his own life.' Dominic wiped his brow with the back of his hand. 'The gentleman's way out.'

Tobias looked down at the dead man. 'Just like his brother.'

Shortly before daybreak, Lavinia went with Tobias to give the news to Aspasia. She came downstairs at once when her sleepy housekeeper informed her that she had callers. She had obviously still been in bed, but Lavinia noted that she somehow managed to appear very fashionable in a dark satin dressing gown, soft kid slippers, and a little lace cap.

'Pierce shot himself?' Aspasia sank down onto the sofa. 'Dear heaven. Just like Zachary.'

'After Anthony and Dominic nearly caught him in the act of committing murder tonight, he must have realized that it was finished,' Tobias said.

Lavinia watched him move to stand in front of the darkened hearth. She sensed the tension in him. He had been like this, restless and brooding, when she opened the door to him a short while ago. She had given him a large glass of the brandy he had provided for himself, but it did nothing to soothe his spirits. He told her the tale of the night's events. She had elected to accompany him when he said that he was going to take the news to Aspasia.

'I don't understand,' Aspasia said, clutching the edges of the dressing gown at her throat. She looked bewildered. 'From what you tell me, he had a head start. Why would he not simply flee the country?'

'I cannot pretend to know his mind,' Tobias said. 'But from the beginning, this entire affair has been about imitating his brother. Perhaps when he realized that he had been found out, he decided to leave this world the same way Zachary did.'

'By his own hand.' Aspasia closed her eyes briefly. 'It is all so dreadful.'

'Tobias talked to an old woman in the stews tonight who once sold babes and children,' Lavinia said gently. 'Several years ago she provided two young boys to a man who told her that he had no sons of his own and wanted apprentices to take over his business.'

'I think her client was the original Memento-Mori Man,' Tobias said, never taking his eyes off the cold hearth. 'It appears that his apprentices did, indeed, try to carry on in his footsteps.'

'And now both are dead,' Lavinia said quietly.

The battered hackney carriage that had conveyed them to Aspasia's address was waiting for them in the street when they left a short time later. Tobias handed Lavinia up into the cab and then got in and took the seat across from her. In the weak glow of the interior lamp, his face was stark and grim.

'I know how this case has plagued you.' She grasped the handhold to steady herself as the aging vehicle jerked into motion. 'But it is over now.'

'Yes.' He looked out the window into the night.

She sensed the darkness in him and knew that he was in danger of sinking down into his own private little corner of hell.

'You will no doubt feel more yourself in the morning,' she assured him.

'No doubt.'

She searched her brain for some other means of breaking through the ice in which he had encased himself. When she came up with nothing helpful, she decided to take the forthright approach.

'Very well, sir, out with it. You are in a very odd mood for a man who has just concluded a successful inquiry into a case of murder. What is wrong?'

For a moment she did not think that he would respond. But eventually he turned his head to look at her.

'Pierce was not much older than Anthony and Dominic,' he said without inflection.

Quite suddenly she understood.

'And not much older than Sweet Ned either.' She reached across the small space and took his big hands in hers. 'Tobias, you cannot save them all. You do what you can and that is all that you can do. It is enough. It *must* be enough. If you do not accept that truth, you will succumb to a sense of despair that will make it impossible for you to save anyone.'

His fingers clamped fiercely around hers. The storms in his eyes threatened to sweep her down into the depths. He did not speak, but after a while he pulled her into his arms.

They held each other until the hackney came to a halt at her front door.

Tobias got out, handed her down, and walked with her up the steps. She opened her reticule and found her key.

'There is something else,' he said, watching her fit the key into the lock.

She looked up quickly. 'What is it?'

'This affair is not yet finished.'

'But Pierce is dead by his own hand. What else is there to discover?'

'The identity of the Memento-Mori Man.'

'But, Tobias, you said yourself, it is likely that he is no longer alive and, if he is, he will be quite elderly. Why do you feel you must find him?'

'I want to know who was responsible for turning two young boys into professional murderers.'

Thirty

Lavinia saw the lamp in the shop window the following afternoon. It was a lovely piece designed to imitate an antiquity in the Roman style. The delicately carved relief depicted the story of Alexander cutting the Gordian knot.

It was perfect.

Without a moment's hesitation, she entered the shop.

'Wedgwood,' the shopkeeper informed her. 'Lovely, is it not? Just the thing for a gentleman's study.'

She held the lamp in the palm of her hand for a moment, enjoying the feel of it and imagining what it would look like sitting on Tobias's desk.

'Yes, it will do nicely,' she said.

A few minutes later she was back outside on the street, the lamp safely swathed in several layers of protective paper tied up with a string. She put the package into the basket she carried on her arm, nestling it among the ripe peaches she had purchased on a whim from a fruit seller on the corner. If nothing else, the fruit would make a pleasant change of pace from currants.

She paused in the shop doorway to raise her parasol.

At the end of the street Aspasia Gray, dressed in a stunning walking gown and fine kid half boots, alighted from a dashing little carriage. She walked toward the door of a dressmaker's shop.

Lavinia watched her disappear through the doorway.

On impulse, she decided to take a different route back to Claremont Lane.

This was probably not the most brilliant notion that she'd had in her brief career as a private-inquiry agent, she thought a short time later when she found herself in the park across the street from

Aspasia's town house. But now that the notion had come to her, she found she could not put it aside. Her intuition was in full bloom, filling her with a sense of great urgency.

It was not only Tobias who was obsessed with the sense that this case had not yet ended, she realized. She had awakened with a similar certainty this morning.

There was only one other person in the small park. An elderly man dozed on a wrought-iron bench, his gloved hands folded on the head of the walking stick propped between his knees.

He opened his eyes when she went past and regarded her with politely veiled masculine appreciation. She suspected that he had been something of a charmer in his younger days.

'There is nothing lovelier than a redheaded woman in a park on a summer afternoon,' he said in a low, raspy voice. 'Good day to you, madam.'

She paused and smiled. 'Good day to you, sir. I did not mean to awaken you from your nap.'

He moved one hand in a surprisingly graceful gesture. 'I have no objection to being awakened. My dreams are those of an old man and therefore not of great import.'

'Rubbish. Everyone's dreams are important.' Impulsively, she reached into her basket, selected a peach, and held it out to him. 'Would you like one of these? I could not resist them. They looked so plump and juicy.'

'How kind of you.' He took the peach from her gloved fingers and regarded it with a small, private smile. 'I will enjoy this very much.'

'You're welcome. And do not ever tell yourself that your dreams are not important.'

'Even if they are the dreams of my younger days and came to naught?'

She contemplated that for a moment. 'It is surely a wonderful thing when one's dreams are realized. But in truth, that does not happen very often, does it?'

'No, it does not.'

'Perhaps it is for the best. Not all dreams are good. Some are no doubt best left unfulfilled, and others are probably never meant to be given shape and substance.'

'I will not quarrel with that, my dear,' he murmured. 'But allow me to tell you that, from the perspective of my years, some dreams are worth the risk required to make them real.'

'I believe you.' She hesitated. 'Perhaps what really matters in the end is that we took some action to make our finest dreams come true. Even if we fail, we will have the satisfaction of knowing that it was not because we lacked for strength of will and determination.'

'Ah, a philosopher after my own heart.' He smiled. 'I could not agree with you more, my dear. It would be a sad thing, indeed, to look back at the end of one's life and know that one had lacked the resolve to take a few risks, eh?'

She found herself transfixed by his vivid blue eyes. 'Something tells me, sir, that if your dreams failed, it was not because you lacked resolve.'

'And something tells me, my dear, that we are alike in that regard.' He took a small penknife out of his pocket and started to peel the peach. 'I am glad that you still have many years left in which to shape your dreams. My doctor has informed me that I only have about six months. A bad heart, I'm told.'

She frowned. 'Bah, pay no attention to the doctors. They are wrong more often than not when it comes to predicting that sort of thing. None of us knows how much time is allotted to us.'

'True enough.' He took a bite of the peach, eyes narrowed with a pleasure that was almost sensual.

'There is an herbalist in Wren Street named Mrs Morgan,' she said. 'My mother always claimed that she was far more skilled than any doctor. I suggest that you seek her out and tell her about your symptoms. She may be able to prescribe a tonic that will help you.'

'Thank you for the advice. I shall follow it.' He ate another bite of peach. 'Come here to enjoy the sun, did you?'

'Well, no, not exactly.' She glanced at the door of Aspasia's town house. 'I am going to call on someone who lives here in the square.'

He followed her gaze, squinting a little. 'Would that be Number Seventeen you're looking at?'

'It would.'

He returned his attention to the peach. 'The lady who lives there has gone out for the afternoon. Saw her depart in her carriage a short time ago.'

'Really?' Lavinia murmured smoothly. 'How unfortunate. It appears I have missed her. Well, then, I'll just leave my card with her housekeeper.'

'Housekeeper's not home either.' He took another loving bite of the peach. 'I saw an urchin go to the door. He must have given her a message, because a short time later she took off in a great hurry.'

'Indeed.'

She had planned to talk her way into the house by persuading the housekeeper that she had important news for Aspasia and would await her return. *No need to put me in the drawing room. The library or Mrs Gray's study will do nicely*. She had hoped to have an opportunity to look around a bit when the housekeeper inevitably retreated to the kitchen to make tea. If nothing else, a visitor could always make the excuse that she needed to use the necessary.

Admittedly, the plan had been somewhat vague and she really had no idea whatsoever of what it was she hoped to discover. But she felt compelled to learn more about Aspasia Gray.

'There is no one at home.' The old man raised his bushy brows. 'It would appear that you'll have to come back another time.'

'Evidently.' She stepped back. 'Well, I must be off. Do not forget the herbalist in Wren Street.'

'I won't.' He pocketed the knife. 'I shall not forget our little discussion of dreams either.'

'Neither will I. Good day, sir.' She gave him another smile and walked away.

She crossed the street and went to the corner. There she paused to glance back over her shoulder. The old man had finished the peach and returned to his nap. His chin was tipped forward onto his chest.

She darted into the narrow alley that led behind the town houses and counted garden gates until she reached the one that serviced Number 17.

The gate was latched from the other side, and the top of the stone wall was several inches above her head. She required something to stand on if she hoped to get over it.

She glanced around and saw an old ladder that had doubtless been left behind by a gardener. It was the work of only a moment to angle it against the stone wall of Number 17. She climbed quickly to the top. When she looked down she saw a conveniently placed bench.

Hiking up her skirts, she got first one leg and then the other over the top of the wall. She lowered herself to the bench.

All was silent and still at the back of Number 17. She made her way to the kitchen door and opened her reticule to remove her new lock picks.

She was chagrined that the business of picking the lock took her far longer than it would have taken Tobias. But in the end, she heard the satisfying *clink* that told her she had been successful.

She stopped breathing for a few seconds, opened the door, and stepped stealthily into the back hall. A cramped staircase designed for the use of the servants was to her left. The lure was irresistible.

Intuition told her that if Aspasia Gray had any secrets, they would be hidden upstairs in her most private chambers.

Tobias sat down at his desk and slowly opened the journal of accounts that had belonged to the murdered wig-maker. He did not know what he hoped to discover this time that he had not found the first time he went through Swaine's transactions, but he was certain he had missed something important.

Last night he had told Lavinia that he wanted to find out who schooled Zachary Elland and Pierce in the art of murder. But later, alone in his bed, he had dreamed about wigs, the journal of accounts, and the memory of Pierce handing a small business card to Lavinia.

When he awoke shortly before dawn he knew that the case was not yet concluded. There was another murderer, one who would soon kill again.

Emeline stood in the lobby of the Institute with Priscilla and watched Anthony and Dominic come up the steps.

Each was once again dressed in the first stare of fashion, and there did not appear to be any signs of hostility between them. Nevertheless, she could see at once that something was wrong. Both men moved in a somber and deliberate manner.

'I vow, they look as if they have been asked to dig some graves,' Priscilla said.

Emeline recalled what Lavinia had told her about how Anthony and Dominic were with Mr March when the hairdresser's body was found. 'The scene in Mr Pierce's bedchamber must have been quite ghastly last night.'

Priscilla swallowed. 'I can certainly understand that it might not have left either of them in a mood for a science lecture today. I am not feeling particularly enthusiastic myself. It is quite troubling to imagine Mr Pierce lying there on the floor in a puddle of blood, is it not? He was so young and handsome and talented.'

'Indeed, and if it is difficult for us, one can only imagine how it must have been for Anthony and Dominic. I know that they have both lost people they loved in the past, but I heard Tobias tell Aunt Lavinia that neither of them had ever before witnessed such a violent and bloody end.'

'I suggest we forgo the lecture and find a shop where we can purchase some lemonade and talk quietly,' Priscilla said.

'Excellent notion.'

The entry in the wig-maker's journal was so succinct as to be maddening.

One wig of medium-length yellow hair

The price and the date of sale were neatly noted, but there was no clue to the identity of the person who had made the purchase. Tobias contemplated the date for a long moment. There was no getting around the fact that it had been sold two days *after* the Beaumont house party. The murderer could not have worn it at the castle.

There had to be an earlier sale of a blond wig. There was no other reason for the wig-maker to have been murdered. Perhaps Swaine had forgotten to note the color in one of the transactions. Rather than search for the records of blond or yellow wigs, maybe he would do well to examine each entry individually and see if he had missed something of significance, Tobias thought.

Fashionable ladies used a variety of fanciful names to describe the colors of their gowns, he reminded himself. He'd heard Lavinia and Emeline toss around words and phrases such as *Russian flame*, *aurora*, and *pomona* when talking about the latest hues and shades. Perhaps the wig-maker had applied some word other than yellow or blond to describe a pale-haired wig.

Emeline caught Priscilla's eye across the small table and nodded slightly. Priscilla responded with a knowing look. Forgoing the lecture had been the correct decision.

Anthony and Dominic had been willing enough to agree to the change in plans and had accompanied them to the little shop where they all purchased glasses of lemonade and some small cakes. But both men remained subdued. Conversation had been stilted at best, until Emeline came straight out and asked for a complete description of what had occurred the previous night.

'I think we have the right to know,' she said gently. 'After all, Priscilla and I were both involved in the investigation.'

It was as though a dam had been breached. Anthony and Dominic started to talk, taking turns to relate the entire tale from beginning to end. Eventually they reached the conclusion.

'There was so much blood.' Anthony wrapped his fingers very tightly around the glass. 'It was impossible to credit how much of it there was.'

Dominic stared into his own lemonade. 'Mr March turned him over to examine the wound. I vow, I could not have done such a thing myself.'

'Mr March has encountered violent death on several occasions,' Emeline pointed out. 'I expect that he has learned how to fortify himself against the sight.'

'And the smell,' Anthony muttered.

Priscilla clasped her hands in her lap. 'I cannot imagine putting a pistol to one's own head and pulling the trigger.'

Dominic said nothing. He continued to ponder his glass of lemonade.

'The pistol was still there in his hand when we found him,' Anthony said. He looked down at his own fingers clutching the lemonade glass.

They all followed his gaze. No one said a word for a few seconds; they just gazed morbidly at his right hand.

A prickle of dread crept through Emeline. She did not take her eyes off Anthony's fingers.

'Which hand?' she whispered.

Anthony looked up with a quizzical expression. 'I beg your pardon?'

'You are holding that glass in your right hand.' She swallowed. 'Was that how you found Mr Pierce last night? With the pistol clutched in his right hand?'

'Yes,' Anthony said.

Priscilla went very still. 'You're quite certain that it was his right hand?'

'Flung out to the side beside his head.' Dominic demonstrated by holding up his own right hand. 'Like this.'

Emeline looked at Priscilla and saw evidence of the same shocked comprehension that was sweeping through her.

'Oh, dear,' Priscilla said. 'Something is very wrong here.'

Tobias ran his finger once again along the list of transactions that Swaine had made the day of the house party at Beaumont Castle. Again he stopped cold midway down the page.

He studied the wig-maker's brief notation concerning one particular sale as intently as though it had been written down in a secret code. He knew how Alexander must have felt when he finally gave up trying to untie the Gordian knot and took a sword to the problem.

'Yes.' He closed the journal of accounts and got to his feet. A great sense of impending doom descended on him. 'Of course.'

He heard footsteps pounding in the hall just as he reached for his coat. Anthony had not run through the house like that since he was a youngster. There was someone else with him. Dominic, no doubt. Those two were rapidly becoming inseparable.

The door of the study burst open. Anthony and Dominic rushed into the room looking like two tubes of fireworks ready to explode.

'Tobias, he was left-handed,' Anthony shouted.

'Emeline and Priscilla are sure of it.' Dominic slammed to a halt. 'They spent an entire afternoon with him when he curled their hair, and they remember very clearly that Mr Pierce was left-handed.'

'Thank you, gentlemen.' Tobias opened the desk and took out his pistol. 'Your information conforms with my own memory. I recall that when he handed Mrs Lake his business card, Pierce used his left hand. No, the hairdresser did not commit suicide. He was murdered, just as Zachary Elland was murdered three years ago.'

'Where are you going?'

'To continue my investigation.' He came around the edge of the desk and strode toward the door. 'This matter is far from finished. I need your assistance once again.'

'Of course,' Anthony said.

'What do you want us to do?' Dominic asked.

The shock of the sobering events of last night was wearing off rapidly, Tobias thought. Perhaps both of them were, indeed, cut out for this line of work.

'Where are Miss Emeline and Miss Priscilla?'

'We left them in the lemonade shop.'

'Go back and collect them immediately. Escort them to Mrs Lake's house.' Tobias walked swiftly along the hall. 'Stay there with them, and do not let any of the ladies out of your sight until I come to tell you that they are safe.'

Whitby, a stoic expression on his face, already had the front door open. Tobias went through it and down the steps to the street.

'What is it?' Dominic was hard on his heels. 'Do you have reason to believe that they may be in danger?'

'Yes,' Tobias said. 'Mrs Lake most of all.'

The old man looked up at the woman who had stopped in front of his bench.

'There is nothing lovelier than the sight of a beautiful woman in the park on a sunny day,' he murmured.

'I doubt that you have been capable of doing anything more than look at a woman in several decades, old man,' she said coldly.

He shrugged. 'I still have a few dreams.'

'They are no doubt as tired and faded as you are.'

'You may be right. My doctor tells me that I have only six months. A bad heart, you see.'

Aspasia Gray reached into her reticule and removed a pistol. 'In that case, I'm sure you will not mind doing a lady one last favor before you cock up your toes.'

Lavinia pulled open the last drawer in the back of the large wardrobe and saw the blond wig. Satisfaction blazed through her.

'I knew it had to be here somewhere.'

The wig alone hardly constituted proof of murder, she reminded herself. She needed more evidence, preferably something that would link Aspasia to the events of the past. But the false hair was most certainly a start. She could not wait to tell Tobias.

At that moment she heard the muffled sound of the front door opening downstairs.

Her palms tingled. For a second or two she could not move or breathe.

With an effort, she broke through the paralyzing fear. She jerked back out of the wardrobe and turned quickly toward the door. Whoever had just come into the house had entered through the front hall. If she moved quietly, she could retreat the same way she had come, down the back stairs.

She crossed the carpet and paused at the doorway to listen.

'I am well-aware that you are up there, Lavinia,' Aspasia called from the foot of the master staircase. 'Come out at once or I will lodge a bullet in the old man's head. That should take care of his faded dreams once and for all, don't you agree?'

A queasy, weightless feeling seized Lavinia. Aspasia had taken the old man hostage.

'I knew from the start of this affair that you would likely make things difficult,' Aspasia said. 'You never cared much for me, did you? That is why I set a pair of street boys to keep an eye on you today, even though the affair of the Memento-Mori Man was supposedly over. When they saw you leave the shop and start toward my house, they came to tell me.'

She sounded closer now. Lavinia heard heavy, muffled footsteps and realized that Aspasia was forcing the old man up the stairs.

She took off her silver pendant. Holding the end of the chain in one hand, she stepped out into the hall and went slowly forward to stand overlooking the railing.

When she looked down, her fears were confirmed. Aspasia and the old man were halfway up the staircase. She had a pistol leveled at his temple.

The old man was breathing heavily. The air rasped in his lungs. He grasped the railing in one hand and clung to his walking stick with the other.

He paused and looked up at Lavinia. 'Forgive me, my dear,' he managed between labored gasps.

'Let him go, Aspasia.' Lavinia moved her hand slightly, letting the silver Minerva pendant catch the light streaming in through the high windows that illuminated the stairwell. 'He cannot hurt you.'

Aspasia was amused. 'Of course he cannot hurt me. But he is useful at the moment. I have learned a great deal about you in recent days, you see. You have much in common with Tobias. You both have a noble streak. Neither of you would allow another to die in your place while you fled to safety.'

'I am not fleeing, Aspasia.' Lavinia let the pendant dangle with what she hoped appeared to be a supremely casual lack of concern, as though she did not even recall holding it in her hand. But she made certain that it glinted and glittered in the sun. 'See? I am standing right here. You can let him go.'

'Not yet.' Aspasia frowned at the pendant and then shook her head once, as though the sight of the gently swinging silver confused her. She prodded the old man with the pistol. 'Not until we are closer. Pistols are so very unreliable at this distance, you see.'

'You would know, wouldn't you?' Lavinia asked. 'Indeed, you are an expert. How many people have you murdered, Aspasia?'

'Counting the deaths that Zachary and I plotted together?' Aspasia laughed lightly. 'Thirteen in all.'

'An unlucky number,' the old man wheezed.

'Quiet, you fool.' Aspasia pushed the nose of the pistol against the side of his head. 'Or I will pull the trigger now.'

'No.' Lavinia leaned out over the railing and swung the pendant steadily. 'Aspasia, look at me. Listen to me. He has nothing to do with this matter. You can let him go.'

'My advice is to run.' The old man halted once more on the stairs, clutching the banister for support, and drew another ragged breath. 'She's got only the one pistol, I believe. In the time it takes her to reload after she shoots me, you will be able to escape.'

'I warned you to be quiet, old man.' Aspasia raised the pistol and made to strike him with the handle.

'You shot the hairdresser last night, didn't you?' Lavinia asked quickly, hoping to distract her.

'Yes.' Aspasia lowered the hand holding the pistol, frowning intently at the glittering pendant. 'I had no choice. He was blackmailing me. I was to leave the first of what he no doubt intended to be many payments in a small lane off Bond Street. As if I were one of his *clients*, if you can imagine.'

Lavinia saw a shadow shift in the hall below the staircase. Her first thought was that it was a trick of the light. Nevertheless, her spirits lifted a little.

It was suddenly vital to keep Aspasia talking.

'Why was Mr Pierce blackmailing you?' she asked. The pendant continued to sway in a gentle arc. 'What did he know about you?'

Aspasia gave her a dazzling smile. 'You mean you haven't reasoned it out yet? You disappoint me, Mrs Lake. I not only became Zachary's lover, I also became his partner.'

Lavinia was stunned. 'His *partner*?'

'Why do you find that so odd? You and Mr March are partners, are you not? Unfortunately, Zachary kept some of his secrets to the end. Evidently he took the precaution of writing a letter. In it he confided the nature of my connection to some of his business affairs. For some reason that I do not understand, the letter must have disappeared for a time. But it somehow found its way into someone's hands quite recently.'

'Why did Elland make you his partner?'

Aspasia smiled coldly. 'Because he loved me and because he recognized a kindred spirit.'

'Tobias was right in that regard.'

'Do you know, Zachary rather enjoyed his role as the daring spy. I think he actually considered himself something of a hero. But unfortunately, that sort of thing rarely pays well. In fact, it did not pay at all. So Zachary continued to ply his trade while he worked for Crown and Country.'

'You assisted him?'

'He enjoyed teaching me his craft, and I discovered that I loved the thrill of the business. There is no drug or elixir quite like the rush of intense excitement that comes with the kill. There is such a feeling of *power*. You cannot even imagine the sensation unless you experience it yourself.'

'But if you loved him and you were partners, why in heaven's name did you kill him?' Lavinia demanded.

'Zachary began to revel far too much in the games he played with March. In his mind, they were two consummate chess players engaged in the ultimate match. But I could see that March was closing in rapidly. I insisted we get rid of him. Zachary and I quarreled over the matter. He would not listen to me. He was so sure that he could continue to outfox his pursuer. He had a strange obsession with March. I think he wanted to prove to himself that he was the superior hunter.'

'But you knew that it was only a matter of time before Tobias had him taken up on charges of murder, didn't you?'

'Yes. I also knew that when that happened, the truth about my connection to some of the deaths would come out. I thought about trying to kill Tobias myself, but in the end I decided that it would be simpler and ever so much safer to get rid of Zachary.'

'When it was finished, you moved to Paris.'

'I thought it best to leave England for a time.' Aspasia smiled. 'I wanted to give Tobias a chance to forget any nagging questions that might lead him to me. Then, about two months ago, I returned to London to resume my life.'

'And your career as a murderess as well?'

'For me, it is a sport, not a profession,' Aspasia said. 'I went hunting on several occasions in Paris and had planned to continue the pastime here in London. I find my little adventures a very effective tonic for ennui. But the morning of Beaumont's house party, I received the first blackmail note and that bloody ring.'

Understanding struck Lavinia quite forcefully. 'You did not know who the blackmailer was, though, did you? So you employed Tobias to find him for you.'

'We each have our talents. I am expert at making the kill, but I admit I have no particular skill for the investigation business.'

'What happened last night?' Lavinia asked.

'After you identified Pierce as the killer, I set some street boys to watch his lodgings for me. The same urchins who followed you today, as a matter of fact. In any event, when Pierce left to carry out his commission, they came to tell me. I went directly to his rooms to search for Zachary's letter.'

'But you did not find it.'

'No. I found a safe in the floor, but it was empty. I decided to wait for Pierce. I intended to try to force him to tell me the location of the letter. I hid in the wardrobe. When he arrived, I could hear him breathing hard and I knew at once that something had happened. I watched through the crack in the door and saw him unlock a second hidden safe. That was all I needed. When he opened the door of the wardrobe, I shot him, took the letter, and left.'

The old man was slumped heavily against the banister, still struggling to breathe. The shadows in the hall shifted again. Lavinia saw Tobias emerge and move toward the foot of the staircase. He held a pistol in his hand.

'You made a couple of mistakes along the way, Aspasia,' he said.

'*Tobias*.' Aspasia turned slightly, eyes widening in shock. 'How did you—'

What happened next occurred in the wink of an eye. The old man straightened with the speed of a striking viper. He lashed out with the walking stick in a short, brutal arc that caught Aspasia at the back of her head with a sickening thud.

She toppled forward in a curiously slowed motion. The pistol in her hand exploded harmlessly, filling the hall with thunder, smoke, and the smell of burning gunpowder.

She fell headfirst down the staircase, thumping horribly against each step. Tobias had to put his back to the wall to avoid being struck by her.

Lavinia was so transfixed by the sight of Aspasia's hurtling body that she did not even notice the old man climbing swiftly up the staircase until he reached the landing and paused beside her.

'You, Mrs Lake, are the stuff of dreams.' He smiled. 'If I were even thirty years younger, I assure you that this matter would end in an entirely different fashion.'

She stared at him, speechless.

The old man glanced back at Tobias, who was coming up the staircase, pistol in hand.

'Or perhaps not,' the old man said dryly. 'Your Mr March is worthy of you. Indeed, I only wish that I'd had the opportunity to take him on as an apprentice years ago. He would have made a fine heir to my business.' He tipped his hat. 'Good day to you, madam. I trust you will remember our discussion of dreams from time to time.'

He went quickly past her, opened the door that led to the back stairs, and disappeared.

To Lavinia's surprise and enormous relief, Tobias did not give chase. When he reached the top of the stairs, he halted beside her and slowly lowered the pistol.

Together they stood gazing down the hallway at the place where the old man had vanished.

'Are you all right?' he asked quietly.

'Yes.' She pulled herself together. 'Aspasia?'

'Dead. I suspect her neck was broken before she took that tumble down those stairs.'

Lavinia swallowed heavily, thinking about the speed and power of the blow that had felled Aspasia.

'Tobias, surely that was not who I think it was,' she whispered. Tobias reached past her to pick up a tiny object sitting on the railing behind her. He held the little ring between thumb and forefinger. A grinning death's-head worked in gold caught the light.

'I think we may congratulate ourselves, my love,' he said quietly. 'I believe that we have both just encountered the legendary Memento-Mori Man and lived to tell the tale.'

Thirty-One

They gathered in Joan's elegant yellow, green, and gilt drawing room. Tobias and Vale lounged against the walls near the windows. Lavinia sat on the sofa across from their hostess.

'My condolences on the loss of your client,' Vale said to Tobias. 'I assume that under the circumstances, you will be unable to collect your fee.'

Tobias's face was set in grim lines. 'Unfortunately, that is indeed the situation. We shall miss our fee, but at least I am not also missing a partner.'

Lavinia pretended not to hear the remark. Since the events of yesterday afternoon, Tobias had not overlooked any opportunity to make pointed comments about her close brush with disaster.

'There are one or two things that I do not yet fully comprehend.' Joan handed a cup of tea to Lavinia. 'Tell me more about the wigs.'

'We will never know where Pierce got the blond wig he used in the course of the murder at Beaumont Castle,' Lavinia said. 'I warned Tobias at the outset that it might be difficult to track down that particular purchase. Personally, I'm inclined to think that Pierce acquired it in Paris. He mentioned to Emeline and Priscilla that he had studied his hairdressing art there. All we know is that he did use one. And Aspasia knew that also because we told her. Upon returning to London, she concluded immediately that I was a nuisance she could do without. She purchased a blond wig of her own and went into the stews to hire a footpad to frighten me off the case.'

'She made certain that Sweet Ned noticed her hair, hoping that if he was caught, we would conclude that it was the Memento-Mori Man who had employed him,' Tobias said.

'What of the events at Swaine's wig shop?' Vale asked.

'I finally managed to make sense of things yesterday when I went through the wig-maker's journal of accounts a second time,' Tobias said. 'I was searching for an earlier purchase of a yellow-haired wig, assuming that the killer must have bought his before leaving for Beaumont Castle. But I came across two other transactions that were extremely interesting. One for a blond wig purchased two days after the murder.'

'And the other?' Joan prompted.

'A black-haired wig purchased the day of the house party,' Tobias said softly. 'The wig-maker had noted it in his records as a *black wig in the Egyptian style*.'

'Tobias realized that Aspasia had been in the shop on at least one prior occasion,' Lavinia said.

Vale's brows rose. 'That was enough to make you suspect that she was a murderess?'

'The fact that she had purchased her Cleopatra wig from the one and only wig-maker who died under mysterious circumstances in the course of this investigation struck me as something other than a mere coincidence, yes.'

Vale smiled. 'When you put it like that, I can certainly see your point.'

'The sale of a blond wig two days later suddenly took on a new significance,' Tobias said. 'As did the fact that a summons from Aspasia was what had lured Lavinia to the cemetery. I also somewhat belatedly recalled that Pierce was left-handed. Anthony and Dominic Hood confirmed that memory. Given that the pistol with which Pierce had supposedly shot himself was found in his right hand, I was strongly inclined toward the conclusion that there was another killer hanging about.'

'Tobias reasoned that Aspasia was the one person involved in this affair who not only had strong links to what happened three years ago but who also knew we had concluded that the hairdresser was the new Memento-Mori Man.'

'When I added those details to one other odd fact, the pieces of the puzzle slipped into place,' Tobias said.

Vale looked interested. 'What was that fact?'

'I never understood fully why the killer had sent that first death's-head ring to Aspasia. I comprehended well enough that he might wish to challenge me. He seemed obsessed with emulating Elland, and I thought it possible that he blamed me for the fact that

Zachary had been driven to take his own life. But why would he bother to taunt Aspasia? She claimed that it was because she had once been Elland's lover. Granted, one cannot expect sound reasoning from a killer, but somehow that did not seem to make great sense to me.'

'Indeed.' Vale studied him. 'He was clearly fixed on you as his opponent. Why would he concern himself with his brother's lover unless there was some profit in it?'

'He did have a reason for sending that ring to her,' Lavinia said. 'It was his way of assuring her that he knew her secrets when he informed her he had a certain letter that he planned to use to blackmail her.'

'Very well,' Joan said. 'I can see why you rushed to Aspasia's address yesterday afternoon, Tobias.' She looked at Lavinia. 'But what on earth made you decide to search her house yesterday?'

'An excellent question.' Tobias gave Lavinia a dark look. 'You may be assured that I asked it myself.'

'Not that he paid any attention to the answer,' Lavinia said briskly. 'I vow, he would not leave the matter alone last night. It was most annoying. He carried straight on through a cold supper that I was attempting to enjoy. Eventually I was obliged to ask him quite forcefully to leave the house and come back when he was in a better mood.'

'Well?' Vale prompted. 'What is the answer? Why did you go to search Aspasia's town house?'

There was a short silence. Lavinia could feel all eyes on her. She took a sip of tea and put down her cup.

'Impulse,' she said.

Tobias looked even more grim.

'I saw Aspasia in Oxford Street yesterday,' she continued. 'When she alighted from her carriage I noticed her half boots and I thought of something that Sweet Ned had said when I asked him to describe the attire of the woman who had employed him. Among other things, he mentioned that she wore a pair of low kid boots.'

'Expensive and very fashionable.' Joan's expression brightened with understanding. 'Of course. Ned told you that the woman was dressed in an old gown and you reasoned that the killer's boots should have matched the poor quality of the rest of the clothes.'

'Not exactly. What struck me was that a male killer who wore an old, unfashionable gown to hide his gender would likely not invest in a pair of very expensive kid half boots. Indeed, when I saw the murderer in Beaumont Castle that night, he was wearing plain, sturdy leather shoes. Just the sort one would expect a housemaid to possess.'

'The sort of footwear that a man could run in, should the need arise,' Tobias added drily.

'Very clever of you,' Joan said.

'Then I noticed that Aspasia's hair was dressed in a profusion of curls and ringlets,' Lavinia continued. 'It reminded me that Sweet Ned had also mentioned that his employer's blond wig had been done in a very simple style with a knot at the back. It suddenly made sense that someone who was not an expert hairdresser would select just such a plain design for a wig meant to be a disguise.'

'Very well,' Joan said. 'That explains the impulse to stop by her house on your way home. After all, Aspasia seemed to be safely occupied in shopping.'

Lavinia made a face. 'Unfortunately, she had set a pair of street lads to watch me. When they saw me head toward the street where she lived, they ran back and warned her that I was on my way to her address. She always made sure her little spies knew where to find her. She quickly followed me on foot. She saw me talk to the old man in the park and then she saw me disappear down the alley behind Number Seventeen.'

Tobias folded his arms. 'At that point, Aspasia, too, acted on impulse. She realized that if Lavinia was sneaking into her house it meant that she herself was now a suspect. She understood at once that she had to get rid of Lavinia and leave the country immediately.'

'So she seized the nearest hostage and tried to use him to take me captive,' Lavinia said. 'But instead of an aged, infirm old man, she chose a retired professional killer.'

'What was the Memento-Mori Man doing in the park in front of her house?' Joan asked.

'Obviously he was waiting for her to return home.' Tobias reached into his pocket and removed the death's-head ring he had found at the top of the staircase in Aspasia's town house. 'I believe that he went there to kill her. He was no doubt the one who had the message delivered to the housekeeper inducing her to leave the house for the afternoon.'

'He was waiting for his quarry,' Vale said. 'But Lavinia showed up first.'

Tobias eyed Lavinia. 'She no doubt complicated matters for him but he seemed quite tolerant about the change in his plans. His ability to adjust his strategy on the spur of the moment was no doubt one of the reasons for his professional success years ago.'

'Where do you think he is now?' Joan asked.

'On his way back to his cottage by the sea, no doubt,' Lavinia said quietly. 'I suspect that he only came out of retirement to avenge the deaths of his apprentices.'

'At least that is what he would have us believe,' Tobias growled. 'Personally, I would not put any credence in anything he told you, Lavinia.'

She looked at him. 'He was an old man, Tobias. And unarmed, except for his walking stick. You could have chased after him and shot him dead yesterday. Why did you let him go?'

Tobias clasped his hands behind his back and gazed out the window into the park. 'I think he allowed himself to be taken hostage because he knew you were in that house and Aspasia intended to murder you. His goal was to protect you. By dispatching her when he did, he may well have saved your life. I owed him something for that.'

There was a short silence while they all contemplated the admission.

After a while, Lavinia cleared her throat. 'There was one other reason why I gave in to impulse yesterday and went to Aspasia's house.'

They all waited.

'I was looking for any excuse to connect her to the murders,' Lavinia said. 'I never did like that woman.'

The envelope was on the step in front of Number 7 when Tobias arrived for breakfast the next morning. A prickle of awareness tingled between his shoulders when he stooped to pick it up.

He straightened swiftly and turned, searching the street. The only person about other than himself was an elderly gardener industriously clipping a hedge at the corner. The man's face was shielded by a broad-brimmed hat. If he noticed Tobias's scrutiny, he gave no sign.

Tobias watched him for a while before he examined the design imprinted in the blob of black wax that sealed the letter. He smiled to himself. When he looked up again, the gardener had disappeared.

He opened the door and stepped inside the front hall.

'There you are, Mr March.' Mrs Chilton came toward him, wiping her hands on her apron. 'I thought I heard someone on the step. You're just in time for breakfast.'

'I know. A stunning surprise, is it not?'

She rolled her eyes and waved him off toward the breakfast room. He went down the hall, envelope in hand, and found Lavinia and Emeline at the table in the sunny little chamber.

'Good morning, sir,' Emeline said cheerfully. 'What have you got there?'

'A letter that I found just now on your front step.'

Lavinia lowered her newspaper and eyed the envelope curiously. 'On the step, you say? I wonder who left it there?'

'Why don't you open it and solve the mystery.' Tobias took a chair and handed the package to her.

She glanced at it with absent curiosity and then uttered a tiny yelp when she saw the death's-head imprinted in the black wax.

'The Memento-Mori Man must have left it,' she told Emeline while she unfolded the letter. 'I wonder what on earth he—' She broke off when a bank draft fell onto the table. 'Goodness. *A thousand pounds.*'

'Read the letter,' Emeline said, brimming with excitement. 'Hurry, please, I cannot stand the suspense.'

Tobias poured coffee for himself. 'Something tells me we have just been paid our fee for the case of the Memento-Mori Man.'

Lavinia studied the elegant handwriting and read the letter aloud.

My Dear Mrs Lake and Mr March:

I trust the enclosed draft will cover the fees and expenses for your services in this recent affair. I apologize for the inconvenience and the danger to you both.

I am aware that you likely have some lingering questions. I shall attempt to answer them. It is the least I can do under the circumstances.

You no doubt wonder why I did not take action against Aspasia Gray three years ago. The sad fact is that I never suspected her of murder. Indeed, I accepted the verdict of suicide in part because I knew that it had satisfied you, Mr March. I was inclined to trust your judgment in the matter.

But there were two other reasons why I was willing to accept that Zachary had put the pistol to his own head. The first was that I knew him very well, having raised him from the age of eight, and I was aware that he possessed the sort of romantical, melodramatic temperament that is sometimes associated with those who take their own lives.

The second reason I accepted it – and I pray you will forgive me, Mrs Lake – was that at the time it simply never occurred to me that a lady would take up the profession in which I had trained my apprentices, let alone manage to take one of them by surprise. I knew nothing of Mrs Gray's partnership with Zachary, of course.

A year ago another of my apprentices prepared to take up the career for which he had been trained. He had grown to adulthood idolizing his brother, and he wanted nothing more than to prove that he was as bold and daring and professional as Zachary.

Shortly after he arrived in London, he went to Zachary's old lodgings and found a letter in the hidden wall safe. In the course of their apprenticeship, I impressed upon all of my boys the importance of maintaining two safes. Anyone who conducts a search is likely to be satisfied with the discovery of a single secret hiding place.

'One of my many mistakes three years ago.' Tobias slathered currant jam on a slice of toast. 'I found the first safe because Aspasia had made certain that I would do so. But obviously even she did not know about the second safe.'

In his letter to Pierce, Zachary made it clear that he had taken Aspasia Gray not only as his lover but also as his partner. It was evident that he was passionately in love with her, but his training ran deep. As a precaution against her betrayal, he implicated her in the letter. He no doubt intended to send it if he ever had cause to become suspicious of her. But he delayed too long and the letter was never mailed.

When Pierce found the letter in the second safe, he saw only the financial opportunities. When Mrs Gray returned to

London he made plans to blackmail her.

He also sent a note to me, informing me of his discovery. Unfortunately, I was traveling at the time and therefore was not at home when the letter arrived. When I finally received it, I understood the danger and made arrangements to come to London at once. But as you know, I was too late to save Pierce.

I arrived at his lodgings shortly after you and your young friends went in through the back door and found the body, Mr March. I watched you from across the street when you came out, and I knew at once that my worst fears had been confirmed.

With two apprentices dead after a connection to Mrs Gray, I no longer had any doubts about the identity of their killer. I went to see her yesterday afternoon and you know the rest.

I regret to say that neither Zachary nor Pierce proved to be well-suited to the business. Zachary developed an unfortunate taste for the darker passions aroused in the course of the hunt and lost sight of the importance of selecting only quarry that deserved to be hunted.

For his part, Pierce was interested primarily in the financial aspects of the business and, while I am happy to say that his early selections were more in keeping with the firm's goals, I fear it was only a matter of time before he, too, lost sight of the higher purpose for which he had been trained. But regardless of the outcome, both young men had been my apprentices and I had a duty to avenge them. It is done.

There is nothing left to be said. I shall fade back into my retirement and trouble you no more.

Oh, one more thing: Mrs Lake, I stopped at the herbalist's shop in Wren Street as you suggested and was given a very fine tonic. I have every expectation of outliving my doctor. Perhaps I still have time for a few more dreams.

Yours truly,
M.

'Well.' Lavinia refolded the letter very slowly. 'I trust that is the last we will hear of the Memento-Mori Man. He didn't tie up all the loose ends, though, did he? We will never be able to prove that Lady Ferring and her friends Mrs Stockard and Lady Huxford were among Pierce's clients, but I cannot say I am entirely sorry about that. One cannot help but admire their fortitude and determination to achieve justice in their own way when it was denied to them by the world, can one?'

'The names of Pierce's clients are not the only lingering questions the Memento-Mori Man failed to answer, so far as I am concerned,' Tobias said around a mouthful of scrambled eggs. 'I've still got two more.'

Emeline looked at him. 'What are they, sir?'

'First, I'd give a great deal to know whether or not he actually is retired or if that was just a tale he told us to discourage us from searching for him.'

Emeline shuddered. 'We can only hope that he is no longer actively plying his trade.'

Lavinia frowned at Tobias. 'What is your other question?'

Tobias swallowed the eggs and reached for his coffee. 'We know he obtained two apprentices from Mother Maud, but who is to say that he did not take on others? I would very much like to know how many apprentices he trained in all.'

Thirty-Two

Three days later they walked through the large park to the remote, overgrown area where Tobias had long ago established his private retreat. They spread a blanket on the grass in front of the old Gothic ruin and unpacked the picnic lunch Mrs Chilton had prepared. Sunlight slanted, warm and dappled, through the leaves of the trees.

Tobias examined the array of small savory pies, pickled vegetables, cold chicken, hard-cooked eggs, cheeses, and breads as he opened the bottle of claret. 'Mrs Chilton has outdone herself.'

'She always does where you are concerned.' Lavinia reached into the basket and removed the package wrapped in paper and string and handed it to him. 'This is for you. To celebrate the conclusion of the Memento-Mori Man affair.'

He looked at the package with a decidedly bemused expression. It occurred to her that, although he had given her several gifts, this was the first one she had presented to him.

'Thank you,' he said.

He took the package from her hand and opened it with such exquisite care that she suddenly wished she had found something far grander and more expensive to give to him.

But when he got rid of the paper and string and held the lamp in his hands, the pleasure she saw in his eyes told her that she had made the right choice.

He examined the intricately worked relief. 'Alexander cutting the Gordian knot.'

'I thought of you immediately when I saw it in the shop window'

He lowered the lamp and looked at her. 'I shall treasure this, my sweet.'

'I'm glad you like it.'

He poured claret into two glasses and handed one to her. She cut two slices of one of the pies and arranged them on the plates together with some pickled vegetables, chicken, and eggs.

They ate and talked for a time. When the meal was finished, Tobias leaned back on his elbows and drew up one knee. He looked at her.

'It would seem that love is in the very air these days,' he said a little too smoothly. 'Anthony has made it clear that he and Emeline will soon announce their engagement.'

'It was inevitable. They are made for each other.'

Tobias cleared his throat. 'It is also very apparent that Dominic and Priscilla are enthralled with each other.'

'Indeed,' she murmured. 'Priscilla's mama is quite pleased. Dominic has charmed her.'

'Yes, well, I have it on good authority that marriage involves great risks for a woman.'

'Mmm.'

He hesitated. 'Is that how you see it?'

She stilled in the act of replacing an empty plate in the picnic basket. For some reason it was suddenly very difficult to order her thoughts. Her pulse started to race madly.

'It involves risks for a man as well,' she said cautiously.

'Perhaps, but not quite the same sorts of risks.'

'No, I suppose not.'

There was a short silence.

Tobias cleared his throat. 'I have been given the impression lately that our current arrangement may not set the best example for Emeline and Anthony.'

'If they choose to disapprove, that is their problem, not ours.'

'Well, that is certainly one way of looking at the matter.' Tobias drummed his fingers on the blanket. 'Anthony mentioned the other day that if you and I shared Number Seven Claremont Lane, he and Emeline could move into my house.'

'Tobias, if you are hinting that we should get married merely for the convenience of Anthony and Emeline, I must tell you—'

'No.' His jaw tightened and his eyes heated. 'I am suggesting that we get married for my sake. I had intended to wait until the ship in which I have an investment returns, but I cannot put this off any longer.'

She stared at him, feeling trapped and breathless. She had spent the past few weeks wondering what she would do if he asked her, and now the moment was upon her.

She licked her dry lips and swallowed. 'Oh.'

'I do not have a great deal to offer you, but I am not entirely destitute. In addition to the house that I own, I have some other, smaller investments that I have made over the years. The private-inquiry business seems to be getting somewhat more reliable of late, possibly because I now have you for a partner. I cannot give you diamonds and private carriages, but we will not starve nor will you lack for a roof over your head.'

'I see.'

'I love you, Lavinia.' He sat up slowly and reached for her hand. 'I have come to dread going home to my lonely bed. I want to spend my nights with you. I want to sit by the fire with you on cold winter evenings and read by the light of my new lamp. When I am unable to sleep at three in the morning because I cannot stop thinking about a case, I want to be able to wake you so that we can talk about it.'

'Tobias.'

'I am asking you to take the risk of marrying me, my love. I swear, I will do everything in my power to ensure that you never regret it.'

She twined her fingers tightly with his. 'Tobias, you misunderstand. I think everyone misunderstands. Yes, marriage is a risk for a woman, but I do not fear marriage to you. Rather, I am afraid that you are the one who would regret such a close and unbreakable alliance.'

'How can you even suggest that?'

'I am so very different from your beloved Ann. From all accounts she was an angel, good and kind and sweet-tempered. I cannot possibly take her place.'

His hands enclosed hers. 'Heed me well. I loved Ann, but she has been gone a long time. I have changed in the years without her. If she had lived we would no doubt have changed together, but that was not to be. I am now a different man in some ways. I seek a different kind of love. I am hoping with all my heart that you can say the same after all these years without your beloved poet husband.'

Joy flowed through her, pure and clean and certain as the sun that warmed them.

'Yes. Oh, yes, my love.' She leaned forward and kissed him on the mouth. 'And, yes, life has changed me also. Tobias, I must tell you that until I met you, I never dared to dream that love could be this rich and deep and wonderful.'

He smiled and slowly, deliberately, pulled her into his arms. She was intensely aware of the strength in his hands and the certainty in his eyes. The summer day was as perfect and clear and dazzling as an exotic gem lit by fire.

'Does this mean that my offer is accepted?' he asked, lowering his mouth to hers.

'With all my heart.'

In the instant before he kissed her, she had a fleeting memory of her conversation with the old man on the park bench.

Some dreams are worth the risk required to make them real.